# The Topkapi Secret

# The Topkapi Secret

Terry Kelhawk

*A Novel*

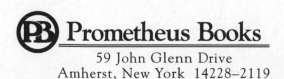

Prometheus Books
59 John Glenn Drive
Amherst, New York 14228–2119

Published 2010 by Prometheus Books



Inquiries should be addressed to
Prometheus Books
59 John Glenn Drive
Amherst, New York 14228–2119
VOICE: 716–691–0133
FAX: 716–691–0137
WWW.PROMETHEUSBOOKS.COM

14 13 12 11 10 5 4 3 2 1

Library of Congress Cataloging-in-Publication Data

Kelhawk, Terry, 1955–
Topkapi secret / by Terry Kelhawk.
p. cm.
ISBN 978–1–61614–213–1 (cloth)
1. Koran—Manuscripts—Fiction. 2. Islam—Fiction. I. Title.

PS3611.E38T65 2010
813'.6—dc22

2010020539

Printed in the United States of America

*If we reject the Prophet's companions,*
*question their integrity,*
*and doubt their reliability,*
*we will be left with no base to believe the Koran,*
*as well as the Sunnah of the Prophet,*
*and all of our beliefs in Islam will be*
*nothing more than a fairy tale.*

—Dr. Ahman Abdullah Salamah,
*Shia and Sunni Perspective on Islam*,
Jeddah, Saudi Arabia, 1991

# INTRODUCTION

You are about to undertake a journey of mystery and discovery. The contemporary characters who will accompany you are fictional, but the manuscript evidence, historical figures, and settings are in accordance with respected sources. The character of Emily Eliot was invented for the plot. References for sources and glossaries of foreign words can be found at the end of this book, as well as on the Web site http://www.terrykelhawk.com.

May you enjoy discovering the hidden truths that could change the world in *The Topkapi Secret*.

—Terry Kelhawk

# PART ONE

Chapter 1

# MARRAKECH, MOROCCO
## March 31, 2006

"I can't see!" Angela cried out.

Angela Hall had never been in a sandstorm. Like most people, she relegated such phenomena to the Sahara Desert. She could not even imagine a sandstorm in Marrakech. So she was caught by surprise when the bright blue Moroccan skies clouded with sand.

Angela's contact lenses were grinding the sand into her eyes, and it hurt. Sand was everywhere. It was seeping into the folds of her clothing and chafing her skin. *True dermabrasion.* Her face had never felt anything like this before.

Breathing was difficult. Against her will, her eyelids kept pressing down against the onslaught of the sand. Angela reached for Fatima's arm, feeling frustrated, dependent; however, she had no choice but to rely on another. At that moment Fatima stepped into the street to flag a taxi. Angela grabbed at air. Blinking, she stumbled and nearly fell.

Once the taxi came into view, Fatima could see that it was occupied. It sped by, heedless of their plight.

Taxis disappear like mirages when a sandstorm hits Marrakech. The lucky and the experienced grab one quickly or get off the streets. Fatima was experienced. But neither woman was lucky that day. By the time the sand had come, they were poorly situated for taxi grabbing.

A few minutes earlier, before the storm hit, they had ambled peacefully along, discussing the gardens of Marrakech.

"Menara's nice, but I prefer La Majorelle," Angela had said. "It has a lush, secluded feeling, with its paths winding through palms and bougainvilleas."

"But Menara's grander," replied Fatima. "It reminds me of a small Taj Mahal, the way the pavilion reflects in the water."

"And the way the sultans tossed their concubines into it every morning?" Angela asked, referring to the notorious practice of the sultans of Marrakech. "Did you ever wonder if they could swim?"

Fatima, a defender of women's rights, ignored this, saying, "I prefer it today, with families picnicking under olive trees, and happy children playing."

Like most Arabs, Fatima struggled in distinguishing her *p* and *b* sounds in English. But her accent was mellifluous, for she was of the educated Moroccan elite who speak French better than Arabic.

Fatima nudged Angela's elbow and challenged her in return. "And besides, who knows what mischief La Majorelle has seen—it's been owned by artists!"

"Good point. But La Majorelle definitely wins for color—cobalt blue walls and pots—like the color of the Moroccan sky," Angela said, palm up in demonstration.

Fatima looked up. "At this moment, the sky looks more gray than blue."

When they had arrived at Menara Park, the weather had been fine. The skies were still clear when they left, so Angela and Fatima proceeded on foot to the open-air marketplace of Jemaa al-Fna.

But the weather rapidly changed.

"For some reason I will feel safer when we are inside the ramparts of the city," Fatima said. She knew what could happen when the clouds and wind met in this way.

Sand started kicking up around them. Within a few minutes, it went from nuisance to menace.

They had gone two-thirds of the way along the avenue and were approaching the twelfth-century walls—the oldest in Morocco.

A second taxi passed, but when they flagged it down, someone else pushed in first.

*Sand brings out the grit in people.*

"It's OK," Fatima spoke over the wind, directly into Angela's ear. Then she pulled her hijab over her nose and mouth. "Just hold on to me. We're getting close to the wall. We can go through it at Bab el-jedid. That is near La Mamounia, and there are always taxis at that hotel. If not, we can go inside for tea and wait."

Angela could see little through her tearing eyes, just a blur where her feet used to be. Any encouragement was welcome.

They had visited the gardens of La Mamounia yesterday. That legendary spot now loomed as paradise itself: Arabic art deco architecture; Winston Churchill painting in the gardens. She wasn't sure which sounded better—a taxi to her room in fifteen minutes or tea in paradise immediately.

Unfortunately, she was not to have either. At least not in the time or context of her choosing.

She bent over and clung to Fatima's *jelaba* as if she were a little child.

## Chapter 2

# TOPKAPI PALACE MUSEUM

## Istanbul, Turkey
## March 31, 2006

How can the blood of the same murdered man be on documents in two cities thousands of miles apart? This was a question Mohammed Atareek had asked himself hundreds of times. Today, he hoped to find the answer.

Mohammed walked into the First Courtyard of Topkapi Palace Museum. Bearing the *tugra*, or monogram, of Mahmut II, the gate testified that this was the home of the sultans of Turkey. From within these walls, they had ruled a large portion of the world for four hundred years.

"We will see if the Turks are as cooperative as the Uzbekis," he thought.

Last year Nasir had acquired microfilm of the Samarkand Codex, an early Koranic manuscript, from Tashkent, Uzbekistan. From it, Mohammed and Nasir had made photocopies to study. Getting access to a similar manuscript, the Topkapi Codex, was not proving to be so easy.

"The Uzbekis may be cooperative," Mohammed thought, "but where do they get the nerve to tell UNESCO they have Uthman's codex, stained with his death blood? Especially with Topkapi making the identical claim! If Topkapi Palace pushes for recognition of its own bloody document as a 'World Treasure,' what will UNESCO say? Will it favor one over the other or will it simply say, 'first come, first believed'?"

He smiled. A sense of humor protected against anticipated disappointments.

Mohammed was in the first of the four courtyards of Topkapi Palace. It was a leafy and shady place. Its giant sycamore trees were pruned up high, giving the feel of a tropical canopy.

Within this courtyard lay an architectural anomaly next to the sixth-century Haghia Eirene church. The structure—which was neither Roman, nor Byzantine, nor Ottoman in appearance—was passed daily by thousands of people without notice. At first glance it resembled a Victorian bungalow of the sort that proliferated first in India, then in California. But it was larger than a home. Its gothic arched windows and pitched roof resembled a mission church—an impression reinforced by the palm trees framing the four irregular gray steps, which Mohammed now climbed.

Once inside, he stopped at the secretary's reception desk.

"*Merhaba*," he said, then switched quickly from the Turkish greeting to the common second language of English. "I'm Mohammed Atareek. I have appointment with the director."

As Mohammed expected, he had to wait. And wait.

Four days earlier, Mohammed had also been in this office. He met the director regarding an application to study the Topkapi Codex he had sent two months prior. The director professed recognition of his request but said the board needed a few more days.

*Mere formality and a sham.*

Mohammed knew it, and the director knew it—and he knew the director knew it, and the director knew that Mohammed knew it. But that was how things ran. Formalities were not to be neglected—especially not in a place with such a long history of formalities as Topkapi Palace.

So he waited again today.

He began to think that the director had left through a back door, when the secretary called him into Ergun Türbe's office.

"Come in, come in, it is nice to see you again, Mr. Atareek," Türbe said in a warm way that seemed to Mohammed more Arabic than Turkish. He offered Mohammed apple tea in a glass cup with a gold rim and handle.

Impatient to get started, Mohammed took a sip of the sweet drink before it had cooled and struggled not to spit it out. He swallowed hard, ignoring the burn. After exhaling a mouthful of steam, Mohammed put the cup down, tried to look dignified, and spoke.

"Honorable director, I like your tea and big hello. Tell me, this means we will be working together, right? That would be very, very nice," Mohammed said with enthusiasm, and rolling his *r*'s. "I am loving Turkish food and hope to stay!"

"Certainly that sounds agreeable," the director said. "We are honored by the attention from yourself and Dr. Nasir Atareek. It was a difficult decision, but the board has decided not to allow any further study on the codex at least for the next several years."

"Further study?" Mohammed leaned forward and placed an elbow on the director's desk. "You mean it has already been studied? I haven't been able to find any published research on the codex. Please tell me where. I would love, very, very much love to read it!"

The two men locked eyes for a quiet moment. Their faces sustained pleasant expressions, but under the façade was an arm wrestle of the wills.

Mohammed lost. But then, there was more than individual will involved.

The director sat back in his chair. "We feel that there is no need for more examination. After all, the manuscript has been with us since the time of Uthman. What more is there to learn?"

"*If* it has been with us from the time of Uthman," Mohammed echoed, surprised at the unguarded words that left his mouth.

"What do you mean? Caliph Uthman was reading it when he died. We even have his death blood on it."

"Ha-ha!" Mohammed laughed and slapped his thigh. Such pretense was funny to him. What was the point in being diplomatic, now that he had lost his case? He wanted to go further and say, "Tell that to the Uzbekis!" but he held back.

The director was surprised by this outburst. He had never met anyone with the "*fahalawy*" type of Arab personality that Mohammed displayed so well—overconfident, witty, ingratiating, and alternately sensitive and insensitive.

Mohammed composed himself. "May I ask your professional opinion?"

"Of course," said the director, wary.

"What do you think of the Samarkand Codex?"

"Yes, I know the Samarkand Codex. It is most likely one of the official copies authorized by Caliph Uthman, but hardly his personal copy. That honor lies with the Topkapi Codex."

*Oh, that we knew, director, oh, that we knew.*

Mohammed's words belied his sarcastic thoughts. "The Topkapi Codex is indeed wonderful. Perhaps you would be very, very nice and let us study a copy of the codex or review your findings?"

"At the present time, they are in preparation for publication and, sadly, not available."

*Cool liar.*

Mohammed smiled and picked up the apple tea. There was no longer any point in talking.

## Chapter 3

# CENTRAL PARIS
## March 31, 2006

Arguably the best view of Paris belongs to the Arabs. The Institut du Monde Arabe is located on the banks of the Seine, along the Quai de la Tournelle. Its modern, bluish glass exterior is adorned by an intricate lacelike pattern in an arabesque style. From the upper floors and roof, the institute overlooks the river and the two most famous islands within this artery of Paris: Île Saint-Louis and Île de la Cité. From here, one can watch the tourist boats laze up and down the river as they pass the historic townhouses on the Île Saint-Louis.

It is said that the Gauls first settled Paris on the Île de la Cité in the third century BC. Now, the island houses the jewel of the city—Notre Dame Cathedral. The "flying buttresses," which have enabled this medieval masterpiece to stand for nearly a millennium, are best viewed from the rear side of the cathedral. It is this rear—to some the most beautiful aspect—which is finely viewed from the Institut du Monde Arabe.

A little park lies in the shadow of the buttresses, softening their cold stone with a touch of nature. Red flowers grow. But here, man is master over nature: geometry prevails over plants, as well as over stone. Topiary cones point upward, and planched trees form elevated hedges, looking like green loaves poised on sticks. Beyond the garden, a stone wall keeps the river at bay.

Two men walked together within this garden. One of them had an office in the institute, and the other was a visitor to France.

"How soon do you think your findings will be ready for publication?" The inquiry was made by an immaculately dressed man in a language that passing tourists did not think was French.

"Please, sit," said Professeur Ibrahim Berger, pausing at a bench along the gravel path. The gray-haired professor was also well dressed. "I'm afraid, Monsieur Aswad, that I do not quite understand the purpose of your visit to Paris. I agreed to see you out of courtesy, but I am not sure what I can tell you that would not be equally clear through our usual channels."

"Yes, yes, certainly." Monsieur Aswad smiled almost too broadly. A hint of gold shone from a tooth on the right side of his mouth. "The chief has been receiving regular communication from you, but as you know, the chief is a man of great foresight and consideration. He has decided that this point of the operation is critical, and he is sending me to confirm findings before their publication."

"Humph." That was all Ibrahim could say at the moment. He crossed his leg and held his knee. He looked away, staring blankly at a couple walking beneath the buttresses.

Yes, the chief was a man of foresight.

*But he was also a man of caution.* Sending a heretofore unmentioned party to examine their clandestine activities did not sound like the chief.

*I, too, must be cautious.*

Someone had dropped a crumb onto the decomposed granite trail next to Ibrahim's bench. From a nearby branch, a bird hopped down to snack on it. Then the bird arched its neck and gazed up at Ibrahim, unafraid.

*This is a godsend.*

Ibrahim bent over and spoke to the bird, as if it were his pet. He pretended to be the world's greatest animal lover. Yet all the while his mind was busy, thinking and weighing thoughts. Aswad's credentials looked good, but...

*I have always doubted face value. Why should I stop now?*

He must find a way to stall Aswad until he could contact the chief in person.

Ibrahim was thinking fast, but it seemed much too slowly. There must be something he could say to Aswad. Something noncommittal that would sound cooperative.

Surely the chief would understand the delay. Even commend him for his diligence. He might scold him lightheartedly for being a doubter. That was the worst that could happen. *Right?*

It was getting late in the day for sightseeing. The tourists were leaving. Shadows were falling, but the cathedral was not yet lit up.

Aswad was also uncertain. The professor was being inscrutably quiet. Should he venture another question?

He wagered that patience and discretion would get him what he wanted in the end. He was particularly good at patience and discretion.

Chapter 4

# TOPKAPI PALACE

## Istanbul, Turkey

## March 31, 2006

No.

*The answer had to be no,* thought Mohammed. Nasir had predicted it, and Mohammed himself had suspected it would be so.

But he had to try.

Mohammed walked out of the mission-like office building into the first courtyard. He paused. He was not prepared to say good-bye forever to Topkapi Palace and all that it contained.

On a path directly across from him stood a guard, rigid, in front of twin white booths. The concentrated, immobilized posture that is the pride of the Turkish military unnerved Mohammed for some reason. To the left of the guard was a lawn overlooking the water of the Golden Horn and the shore beyond. Mohammed shifted his gaze there and kept walking.

*Once more, before I leave Istanbul I will see the Topkapi Codex.*

He turned left, toward the twin towers of the Gate of Salutations. He passed through it and the sunny second courtyard, with its conical cypress trees and inconspicuous harem entrance. He went through the third gate, the colorful Gate of Felicity. He walked around the Sultan's Audience Pavilion, descended its platform, and entered the third courtyard. His destination lay in the rear left corner of the third courtyard.

*The Sacred Relics Chamber.*

Mohammed stepped into this series of rooms, which had been the private chambers of the sultans until Murad III moved into the harem. The suite had an atrium, a reception chamber, and a throne room.

A tour group in front of Mohammed was blocking his access.

The guide was speaking, "The architecture is fifteenth century. Notice the dome. Iznik tiles line the walls, including some from the sixteenth century, when Turkish tile-making was at its best. You can see their pure white ground. This room, the atrium of the Sacred Relics

Chamber, houses items of interest to people of the three monotheistic faiths: Moses' staff, Joseph's turban, and King David's sword—the one he used to decapitate the giant Goliath, whom he had shot with a rock from a sling."

The group pushed around the case to see David's sword, making guttural sounds at the thought of Goliath's headless body.

Mohammed tried to get around the side of the group. He accidentally stepped on the corner of a woman's long skirt, apologized, and backed up. Then he got a better look at the guide and stopped, having never seen such a creature before—a young woman with spiky short black hair, tight gray clothes, and purple shadow encircling her eyes. She should have looked grim, but she didn't.

"To the right of this suite lies the treasury, full of rare and priceless jewels. But it is the contents of the Sacred Relics Chamber itself that are considered the most valuable of the palace. It is the greatest such collection in the world." The guide had a surprisingly impish smile, which she shared with Mohammed. Mohammed smiled back.

"Islam began in Saudi Arabia. It was there that the Prophet Mohammed called people away from polytheism to the worship of one God, Allah, and there the Islamic Empire began. So how could so many jewels and relics be concentrated in a few rooms in this European foothold of Turkey?"

*The winner takes it all.* Mohammed Atareek had an answer, but he stayed silent.

The gothic pixie continued her memorized speech in excellent English. "When the rule of the Ottoman Empire extended from Asia to North Africa and Europe, the sultans acquired the treasures of the world—starting with Sultan Selim I, known as 'the Grim.' Over the years, other things arrived, even from the Kaaba in Mecca, Islam's holiest shrine."

*You mean they stole them.* At least, that was how Mohammed Atareek saw it. Selim I had no moral scruples about taking the relics from the Egyptian caliph himself, the legal head of Islam.

"The throne room has the holiest treasures: the Mantle of the Prophet and the Standard of the Prophet. After the Prophet Mohammed died, these treasures were kept by his successors, the caliphs, who were both religious and military leaders. Come and see," the guide invited her group to follow. She was neither dramatic nor dry.

She spoke as if all of this were of no great importance but simply for the diversion of visitors such as themselves.

The pixie guide began pointing to relics behind the closed glass security door of the throne room. "This is called the throne room, but actually it was once the sultan's bedchamber. Can you see this large open silver shrine? To me, it looks like a canopy bed. And do you see a golden box on the golden throne inside the silver shrine? It contains the mantle worn by the Prophet Mohammed. The caliphs believed the Prophet's mantle had power because he had worn it, so they also wore it when they fought. It was even worn nearly a thousand years after the Prophet Mohammed's death, when Mehmed III fought the Hapsburgs in 1596."

Mohammed wanted to get in closer, but he would have to wait.

"Next to the mantle is a silver casket containing the Standard of the Prophet. This is the flag or the banner under which he won his battles. It, too, was used for centuries after his death. And in front of the shrine you can see the swords of the Prophet Mohammed."

Mohammed took one last look at the pixie guide as she led the group out of the chamber and then turned his attention to the room behind the glass door.

Chapter 5

# TOPKAPI PALACE
## Istanbul, Turkey
## March 31, 2006

Mohammed Atareek stared through the glass door at the most holy relics of the Sacred Relics Chamber. In the background he could hear the continuous, mournful tones of the chanters; holy men who sang passages of the Koran for this holy room. Now they were chanting the *Fatiha.*

*Bismallah Ir-rachman Ir-raheen.*
*In the name of God, the merciful, the compassionate.*
*Praise be to Allah, Lord of the Worlds,*
*The Beneficent, the Merciful.*
*Owner of the Day of Judgment.*
*Thee alone we worship; Thee alone we ask for help.*
*Show us the straight path.*
*The path of those whom Thou hast favored;*
*Not the path of those who earn Thine anger nor of those who go astray.*

It seemed an appropriate tribute. For there, at the foot of all the ancient relics the guide had pointed out, lay the unmentioned Topkapi Codex, one of the earliest Korans and claimed to be *the* Koran that Caliph Uthman was reading when he died. *The one with his blood.*

This important relic of the faith and the mystery surrounding it had been an ongoing obsession of Mohammed Atareek. He stared at the two pages open for display, his mind swimming with questions. Which Koran had Uthman been reading—and which was stained with his blood? The Topkapi Codex, as the Turks claimed, or the Samarkand Codex, as the Uzbekis claimed? Perhaps neither. Perhaps Uthman's Koran was destroyed by his assailants or lost over time. Perhaps the whole story was nothing more than a legend fabricated by the Sunnis to smear the Shiites. Such partisan hadiths, or traditions, had been known to exist.

This was a personal quest. Mohammed hadn't used grant funds to come to Istanbul. He had paid for the flight from Beirut himself. He had reasoned that if he were allowed to study the Topkapi Codex, he would discover secrets that had been hidden for centuries. If he were denied access to it, or to copies of it, he would have firsthand proof that Topkapi Museum was at least unnecessarily restrictive, and possibly permanently obstructive to research on the codex.

This was the proof he would now carry back to Beirut.

Every day while awaiting the board's decision, Mohammed Atareek had visited this room. He stared at and coveted access to the Topkapi Codex. Then he had gone next door to the manuscript room, where he examined other displayed manuscripts from the museum's collections. Mohammed studied carefully and took notes, while tourists were herded through.

To tourists, all the ancient manuscripts looked alike. They were just old paper. Every day he had watched them gaze into the throne room without even seeing the Topkapi Codex. If they did look at it, they saw no more than a page from an illuminated hymnal, the kind that sells for fifty bucks on the Internet.

He doubted many visitors even knew what a codex was or understood its significance as the world's first "book" with turnable pages. Before that, writings were rolled up on a scroll or carved onto something cumbersome, like stone or clay.

Now to Mohammed, each page of a manuscript sang a different song. That song was its story.

The story that mattered to him was not the one written in the words on its pages. The words of the Koran were purportedly those of God as revealed to the Prophet Mohammed. That was a different story. The story that interested the Prophet's namesake, the researcher Mohammed, was not in the words themselves but in the story spoken by the medium that carried those words.

The vellum, or paper, on which the letters were written had a message. So did the type and color of the ink. The thickness of its application. The style of the writing. The angle of the letters. Their size. Their variation from page to page. The binding. The complexity of the decoration.

To him, each of these features spoke more than the message itself. They told the truth. They told the book's age, where it was made, how many scribes worked on it, and through these messages, the very history of Islam.

The glass of the door steamed up under his nose. He felt the hot moisture reflect back onto his face.

*So close and yet so far away.*

Mohammed was tall enough to be able to look down on the codex. But it wasn't good enough. How he wanted to examine it intimately. To see every millimeter of it. He longed to touch and smell it as a lover craves his beloved.

The script of the codex fascinated him. Its letters were written in an early form called Kufic script, or, more accurately, *al-Khatt al Kufi*. This was one of the earliest forms of writing used in Korans, and the only one named after a city—Kufa, in Iraq. Its overall effect was very precise, with angular letters extended in horizontal lines punctuated by perpendicular forks. The spread of the letters gave the codex its landscape shape. There were no ornamental scrolls. Originally there were no dots or dashes. That sort of detail came much later.

Yet sometimes he imagined the strokes were stick figures: like skaters fallen on the ice, their blades pointing upward. How he wished those figures would stand up and speak.

*Someone needs to expose what is in the Topkapi Codex.*

Apparently that someone would not be him. Overwhelming frustration came upon Mohammed.

Surely the Topkapi Codex had been studied before. The director had said as much. Why were they trying to keep him from looking at it? If they had studied it, then why the secrecy?

An answer, a conjecture, came into Mohammed's mind.

*Yes, it* must *be as I have thought.*

## Chapter 6

# NORTH AFRICAN AIRSPACE
## April 3, 2006

Sometimes you don't care what your seatmates think of you.

Angela grunted as the overweight man in the aisle seat jabbed her. Didn't he realize that there was such a thing as a zone of neutrality? In this case, it was the armrest. It was provided by the airlines as a tacit reminder that each passenger had purchased only a limited amount of space.

Someone else was to have sat in the seat next to her.

*If it hadn't been for the sandstorm, she'd be with me now, and everything would be different.*

On most return trips from conferences, Angela reviewed the syllabi, noting what stood out, and thinking about how she could use it.

This time, when she picked up the conference binder, it fell open to Fatima's lecture—the one she was never able to present. How could Angela concentrate?

Until then she had done a good job of just sitting and forgetting. As the plane lifted off from Morocco, she had let her worries fall, as if they were grains of sand trickling off the wings to join the desert somewhere below. She even dozed a little.

In that semi-sleep of the seatbound passenger, she could visualize the sands of North Africa as she flew above them.

A sandstorm can alter forever the landscape of sandy regions, but who would have thought it could bring its mutating force into the city as well?

The meal came as a welcome distraction—you have to think about how you can eat in so limited a space.

Then the woman in the window seat, glad that Angela was awake, began talking about her vacation in Morocco. It was predictable and boring. But when her tale came to the cobras at Jemaa al-Fna marketplace in Marrakech, it struck a raw nerve in Angela. She promptly closed her eyes and turned her head, careless of how rude she appeared.

In her mind, Angela saw the sand again. How could she forget it?

And the faces. Especially Fatima's mother's face. Although it was the first time they had met, she could read grief in the eyes—puffy and red—and in the wrinkled forehead. Angela felt as if she somehow held her responsible for what had happened. But how could she foresee it?

She shook her head on the headrest. With her eyes still closed, she had flashback feelings. They were only *feelings* because Angela hadn't *seen* what had happened.

But she would never forget how she had felt—that combination of sensations would forever be held within her body. The feeling of the sand. The feeling of standing helplessly on the curb if but for a moment, when Fatima had said, "Stand here. There's another taxi pulling up beside us. Let go of me so I can run for it—I'll be right back to lead you."

But she never came back.

Angela had heard the wind. She blinked another tear. She coughed. She smelled the putrid grease of *khalia* from a street vendor's cart. Then she heard a donkey's bray. She could feel motion. She opened her eyes as wide as she could but could see only blurs.

Here her flashback became visionary, because she could see in her mind what she had not seen in person.

In her rush to get a taxi for Angela, Fatima had stepped off the curb in front of a parked donkey cart. Usually such donkeys were well behaved, but the sandstorm had made this one jittery. As Fatima bolted in front of him, the sleeve of her ochre-colored *jelaba* brushed across the donkey's nose.

The donkey could take no more on that sand-swept day. He brayed and started, and in doing so jolted into the street.

Instead of flagging down the taxi, Fatima was pushed under it by a rampaging donkey.

Angela remembered the sounds—the taxi's horn, the screech of brakes. The squeal of the cart wheels as they rolled… and Fatima's muffled scream.

And the colors. Colors she had never seen. The orange *jelaba.* The white donkey with green ribbons. And the blue cart. Cobalt blue—the color of the Moroccan sky.

# Chapter 7

# SAN FRANCISCO
## April 4, 2006

Angela was a day late. Delayed by the trip to Fez for Fatima's funeral, she had missed the first day back to class after spring break.

Tuesday morning at 1:30 a.m., Angela pulled into the driveway of her Pacific Heights home. The garage, as in most of these hilltop homes, was beneath street level. She was blessed to be on the view side of the street. That meant a steep driveway, but it provided the inimitable Pacific Heights view.

Here, you could sit at home, surrounded by sybaritic luxury, and look directly over the San Francisco Bay at Alcatraz Island and Marin County. You could imagine yourself a ruler, isolated in a palace at the top of the world, like Theseus overlooking the harbor of ancient Athens. In the daylight, you felt as if you were flying. On windy days, spinnakers would cover the water like party flags. But now it was dark and the water was invisible. Tiny lights twinkled in the distance, beyond the bay.

In the back wall of the garage was a small elevator. Considering the size of Angela's suitcase, they could both fit in the elevator only if one rode the other. She decided to walk, and sent the case up alone.

Simple stairs took her into the kitchen, where she had a drink of water. She walked into the beige marble foyer, paused beneath the grand split staircase, and listened for her husband.

There was silence. She did not call out. Talking with John was never easy, and now she was tired after a twenty-hour trip home from Morocco.

Falling asleep, Angela heard a sound that made her heart jump. Was John home?

# Chapter 8
# BEIRUT, LEBANON
## April 4, 2006

A fleck of paper flickered in the afternoon light. It was a strangely pretty thing, like a miniature butterfly, but it shouldn't have been flying. The fleck was a corner from an ancient page. Mohammed hadn't been sleeping well since he returned from Istanbul; he dozed and let a valuable book drop.

*I need a walk.*

Mohammed went for a cup of Arabic coffee at one of the many cafes on the Corniche, the promenade on Beirut's seafront. Following this, he walked to the beach. With salty sea breeze in his nostrils and caffeine in his veins, he felt revived.

On the beach next to him was a couple trying to trail a kite. On another part of the beach, a man was whispering into a woman's ear.

*Is he lying?*

Since Mohammed had lied, it was natural to assume other men did. He remembered lying to several women at the same time, hoping they would all keep secrets. He still loved the chase, but what he chased was different now. Replaced in the way steak replaces baby food.

*Would these couples be in love if they knew everything about each other?*

His friend Omar had kept a secret. Omar left his wife in Lebanon to study in America. There, he married again and got a green card. When Omar came back for a visit to his family, he told Mohammed about his scheme with number two and laughed. Mohammed laughed too. It seemed a good trick then.

But now he wondered. As far as Mohammed knew, neither of Omar's wives ever discovered he was double-dipping. Were both marriages legal? Were the children in America legitimate?

That was a *private secret*, affecting a handful of people. But what about *public secrets*? Secrets that could change people's way of life. Perhaps even change an entire society.

*Can such a secret be a human rights violation?*

He left the beach and stepped back onto the Corniche, walking through the crowds without seeing anyone. Except for Ahmed. Ahmed was standing on the corner behind Mohammed when he turned around. He seemed to be showing up everywhere lately.

*I'll confront him.*

Mohammed walked right up to Ahmed with a big smile and said, "*Ya*, Ahmed! Great to see you. How's it going? Hey, I have an idea. Why don't you go back to Yemen and find yourself a wife, so you can walk the Corniche with someone besides me!"

## Chapter 9

# UNIVERSITY OF CALIFORNIA, BERKELEY

## Department of Women's Studies

## 10 a.m., April 4, 2006

"Let's face it, English literature is dead."

Doc Molly was never one to mince words. Other people might be reluctant to tell a professor her field was a "has been," but Doc Molly called them as she saw them. It was this intrepid attitude that had made her a hero in Vietnam. Just how many lives she had saved was an item of speculation—the thing campus legends are made of.

After the war Molly took on another fight. In her view, women were not getting a fair shake in this world, and her bulldog determination was set to change that. She started studying Women's Studies when there wasn't much to study, got a PhD, and stirred up a few faculties before coming to Berkeley. Now she wanted to retire.

"I'll tell ya, kid," she said, knocking ashes off a cigarette, "I'm getting ready to pull out of this pompous manhole. Check out some deserts and jungles—call it a final sabbatical if you wish or just a lifelong vacation. But before I go, I wanna be sure that this department is still goin' strong." She waved a finger at Angela as if she were presaging some sort of crime. "I don't wanna have to come back here for any search and rescue operations. My back's not up to it anymore! Ha!"

Angela, often at a loss for how to respond to Doc Molly, said, "I do wish you the best of retirement. But I can't see what that has to do with English literature. Are you thinking of studying again?"

"You are funny! No, kiddo, I've had enough of both study and action. This is it: have you looked around this campus lately? Not many white folks left, are there? Same goes for all the UC campuses. And California as a whole. We're in the minority everywhere. That's OK by me, I'm used to standing out, but it should worry you a bit, I think."

"Oh? Why?"

"Why, Angela! What do Asians and Mexicans care about Shakespeare and Dickens and Austin?"

"But the greatest thoughts of..."

"Think reality, not ideals! Think women! More than half of the university students in America are women. Now here is a field that just keeps on growing! No danger of job senescence there."

Angela was quiet.

"You may know that Fatima was being groomed as my replacement. Poor thing checked out too soon for that... not that I blame you for it." Doc Molly extended an arm and looked Angela in the eye in a way that implied that if she had been there herself, she could have prevented Fatima's death. "But there we have it. She's gone. And all our other lecturers are guests from other departments."

This was true. Angela was one herself.

"I'm gonna go out on a limb and ask you if you'd like to be vice chair of the department next fall. I'll groom you up, and in a year or two I'll head off. Then you'll be a full professor! Whaddya think?"

Angela was surprised. "Well, as you point out, I am a Doctor of English Literature. I'm not qualified to head your department."

"I'll let you in on a little secret: in some ways you are more qualified than either Fatima or I would ever be."

Doc Molly leaned back in her chair, stretched her arm over the top, and crossed her husky legs in a masculine manner. "Look at me. I'm good at groundbreaking, but finishing touches aren't my strong suit. Either I brush people the wrong way, or they're too distracted by my sexual identity to make headway with the issues."

Doc Molly's sexual orientation was another item of campus conjecture. She had been living with the same woman for thirty years. Her appearance and manner seemed almost stereotypical. She had never said she was lesbian, yet she was hardly the kind of woman who would balk at coming out of the closet.

Listening to her now, Angela understood. *Nothing would hurt this woman's baby.*

"And Fatima, she was not without disadvantages. You, on the other hand, would be a poster child for this department—tough but feminine looking, well spoken, and well connected."

"I see," Angela responded. It was clear what Doc Molly foresaw. The department would flourish under someone people felt comfortable with. Someone "American." And someone who was wealthy and had lots of rich friends.

"As for the qualifications," Doc Molly went on, "I don't see a big problem there. Women authors are your expertise, right?"

"My doctoral thesis was on early women travel writers."

"And a lot of them were pioneers in women's rights, weren't they?"

"Yes, I suppose so."

"And you just accompanied Fatima to a weeklong conference on women's issues."

"That's right."

"And you have already been guest lecturing in Fatima's intro course?"

"Yes."

"Then that brings me to my two-point deal: help me by finishing Fatima's introductory course this term, and..."

"And..." Angela asked, waiting to hear the cost of a professorship.

"...do research overseas this summer on a women's rights issue. Then write up some sort of magnum opus, or just write a report and we'll call it a magnum opus, and come to work with me in the fall as vice chair of the Department of Women's Studies. I'll retire a year later, and you'll be queen, kid!"

## Chapter 10

# UC BERKELEY
## Introductory Course
## Department of Women's Studies
## 3 p.m. April 4, 2006

If it were true that Celts migrated from Galatia to Ireland two millennia ago, Dr. Selim Soglu probably descended from those who stayed behind.

At the head of the lecture hall stood a man of moderate build with light brown eyes, wavy black hair swept back, and surprisingly pale skin. His English was clear and sophisticated, with only a slight accent—as if he had memorized his lecture on "Women in Ancient Western Religions" or perhaps read it. It sounds dull. But he wasn't.

The classroom contained about 150 students, only about 10 of whom were men. From the back row, Angela sat and observed.

"Nowhere can we better see the importance of women in Middle Eastern religions than in my home country of Turkey. For example, this picture shows a nine-thousand-year-old mother goddess statue in the Archaeological Museum at Ankara. She is from a cult that existed for thousands of years throughout the Mediterranean." His PowerPoint lecture was illustrated with numerous examples of grotesque feminine votive statues with exaggerated breasts and bellies.

"Here you see a similar goddess, the Palestinian goddess Asherah from 700 BC. The fertility religion spread deep into Europe, as exemplified by this statue of the Venus of Willendorf.

"In establishing a society, what do people first think of? Survival. Fertility of the earth and its people meant survival. In fact, the meaning of the word *Anatolia* is 'land of good mothers,' reflecting the fertility of this part of Turkey. Since a woman brings forth children, she is in a true sense a 'creator.' For primitive peoples, it was a short jump from 'a creator' to 'The Creator.' So the most important god, if not the only God, was the mother of the earth. If she were happy, she would send rain for crops, and would make women fat and fertile."

Selim paused for effect, shrugged, and raised his hands over bent elbows. "Whether they were fat first or fertile first, we don't know. But the men liked it.... Turkish men are different now, I assure you." He smiled and looked down, as if covering something.

The girls laughed.

*They think he's cute.*

Then he broke the spell. "They say Americans are getting fatter, so maybe in a few years we will know which comes first, fat or fertile?"

Only one person laughed—a geeky guy. Everyone looked at him and he shrank.

Without a break Selim went on. "Worship of the fertility goddesses involved offerings of food and secret rituals.

"Can you think of any fertility rituals we might have now?" he asked. He flashed up a picture of a couple having sex, followed by a picture of a test tube. "Ooh, looks expensive," Selim said, and projected up a picture of a film star pirate with his foot on an open chest full of gold.

*He knows how to keep their attention.*

"What about infertility rituals?" he asked. A photo of birth control pills went up. Selim cupped his hand around his mouth and whispered as if telling a secret. "I hear you can get these cheap in the student center...." He waved at them and resumed a normal voice, "...but then you already know that."

Next Selim showed a series of architectural ruins and statues. "Now we transition into a second religious tradition with strong female characters: the Greco-Roman.

"The temple of Artemis in Ephesus was one of the wonders of the ancient world. Its huge statue was believed to have fallen from heaven. Little is left now except a column and a turtle pond; but from smaller copies we know that her front," he paused and asked the audience, demonstrating an area on the slide with his laser pen, "what do you call this in English?"

The students yelled out all kinds of answers from the obscene to the simple.

"Ah, yes, her... front was covered with rows of ovoid structures that resemble eggs. Some people say they are numerous... breasts, but to most of us the shapes look like Greek 'egg and dart' molding."

Angela recognized the molding from the living room of her 1904 Palladian-style home.

"So we see how the fertility cult merged into the Greco-Roman system, as it did in other cities that honored the goddesses Demeter, Hera, and Gaia.

"From ancient Greek plays, although they were written by men, we know some details of women's secret societies. For example, in his tragedy *The Bacchae*, the playwright Euripides tells us about the Maenads, women who tore a man apart in a religious frenzy." A photo showed a Roman stucco relief of the Bacchae.

"Aristophanes wrote a comedy about a society called *The Thesmophoriazusae.* Two men wanted to know what happened in Demeter's cult, but the penalty for men intruding on the cult was death. So they dressed like women, what I think you call 'drag' in America." He showed a photo from *Beach Blanket Babylon*, the perennial favorite San Francisco stage show, with two men wearing table-sized hats—one supporting the Golden Gate Bridge and another the Eiffel Tower. The students laughed in surprise at this local anachronism.

He then discussed the enigmatic frescoes on the walls of the *Villa of the Mysteries* in Pompeii and ended with the emergence of women in Christianity.

"The third important female presence in Middle Eastern religion is represented by the Virgin Mary. Ephesus is sometimes called the City of Two Holy Women because the Virgin Mary moved here with Saint John. Her simple home was designed in the shape of a cross. In Ephesus she began to attain the honor that brought the impression to Arabia that she was the third member of the Trinity. In fact, the Koran tells us in sura five that besides Allah, Christians worship Mary and Jesus as gods."

Selim ignored a background rumble from the students. "In conclusion, for thousands of years, while women struggled for significance in society, they most readily attained it in religion. At first this was in relationships with men through fertility cults. Eventually they became independent of men, living in monastic communities where they could study and develop careers apart from men and family responsibilities. I believe more on the monastic tradition will be covered in your lectures on Women in the Middle Ages."

He looked at his audience and raised his hands, palms up, one at a time. "Perhaps you Berkeley women will discover a way to combine the pleasure of the fertility phase with the intellect of the monastic?" He paused and winked at his audience. "Be sure to let me know."

Loud applause broke out. The class had forgiven him for implying that they were fat.

*He likes to play with an audience.*

A hand went up. "Doesn't Mary Magdalene come into early religion?"

Selim answered, "Let's think logically. If there were a god and she were his representative, no one could stop her, could they? And if there's not a god—what difference does it make?"

As the class ended, a group of students surrounded Selim and asked questions about women in religion. Angela could see a tattoo peeking out from under a tight pink camisole on the back of a student with streaks in her hair. She was holding a paperback book, saying, "If you can't trust a bestseller, what can you trust?"

# Chapter 11

# UC BERKELEY
## Department of Women's Studies
## 4:10 p.m., April 4, 2006

The students were leaving. Selim looked up as Angela approached.

"Angela!" he held out an arm and wrapped it around her for more than a brief moment. "I heard about what happened in Morocco. So tragic. How are you doing?"

"It was hard. I was there. It was so strange."

She didn't want to talk about it and changed the subject. "Here's something new: Doc Molly just asked me to take over this class." She forced a little smile. "Which is why I am here spying on you."

"I was hoping it was for another reason—like maybe you missed me?"

Angela ignored this. "And Doc Molly offered me the vice chair of her department if I would do some research this summer."

"Aaaahh! Fate would have it so. What have I told you? You will come to Turkey with me." He spoke slowly and smoothly, with as much enthusiasm as his aristocratic nature would allow.

"But I am married, remember?"

He bent over and whispered confidentially, "He's all wrong for you. I have told you this before. You are much too gracious to admit it, but you know it's true." He stood up and continued reasoning, "And it is only for the summer. So, either you are sensible and leave him permanently or you keep up the pretense of a happy marriage and say he understands. Either way you will join me this summer in Turkey."

"Frankly, I just heard about it. I haven't even thought about what I'll do."

"You don't need to, *angel*, just trust me. It will be on—what do you call it—automobile? No—autopilot. I will arrange everything for you. Istanbul is my town. You will have your own house—no, two—one in town and one on the Bosporus."

He could see she was trying to speak, but he kept talking. "You will have me as your personal guide to sites all over Turkey. No one could be better. You know my doctorate is in Turkish Culture."

Selim raised a finger as if remembering something important. "Oh, yes, the cultural stuff. I remember, you love opera. I will take you to the Istanbul International Music Festival. We will see Mozart's *Abduction from the Seraglio* in the original seraglio! They perform it there every summer, Angela, and only in Istanbul—"

At the mention of this opera she had to stop him. "Selim, I am touched by your generous offer," Angela said, hand on heart, "but I think tomorrow morning you will realize you can hardly keep to it—"

"Certainly I can!"

"—and as you may recall, I said Doc Molly wanted me to go somewhere to research women's issues, not to have a grand vacation!"

"Oh, oh, I was going to explain to you before you put your pretty hand over your beautiful heart." He looked at her bosom in a way that made Angela even more uncomfortable than his hug had. "Istanbul is the perfect place for such research. Turkish women have been leaders in women's rights. I will set you up at Istanbul University, where they have a Women's Research Center."

Angela looked doubtful and shook her head. "I don't speak Turkish."

"It is not a problem. They have books in English. Just say '*arkadaş*' and they will do *anything* for you."

"Look. I'm not disagreeing with you. But I haven't even thought about this yet. I need to do some research on... where I should do research. That is, if I decide to take up Doc Molly's offer."

"You will. You will see how wise Doc Molly is and accept her offer. I will send you some links to online sources." He paused and looked pleadingly into her eyes in a way the coeds would have found irresistible; but Angela was not a coed. "All I am asking is for the sake of international relations... for the sake of world peace..."

Angela looked straight at him. "World peace?"

"*Tamam.* OK, for my sake."

"That sounds more like it."

"Please review the links and tell me what you think."

"All right." She gazed at him steadily. "For the sake of... *world peace.*"

## Chapter 12

# BEIRUT, LEBANON

## April 5, 2006

"Ibrahim Berger. That was the name of my greatest friend," said Nasir. "His wife, Elena, called me today. They say he threw himself into the Seine."

The balcony door opened. Nihla brought out strong Arabic coffee, two espresso cups, and two pieces of baklava.

"Thank you, daughter," said Nasir Atareek.

Mohammed waited for Nihla to retreat. "Why did he do it?" he asked.

"His wife was surprised. She said there was trouble at the institute, but that was nothing new. There was always trouble at the institute."

"There is always trouble everywhere," Mohammed added.

"That's what bothers me."

"It bothers me too, but forget about it! What can we do? We have ideas, but the world doesn't listen to us beautiful Palestinians!"

"Mohammed, hush! This is no time for humor."

It was a hot, dusty afternoon. Nasir was sweating. Fumes rose from a bus below to where they were sitting on the balcony of their apartment. The combination of afternoon sun, exhaust, sweat, and overly sweet coffee was nauseating to Mohammed. He found it difficult to focus when he was nauseated.

"Really, I am sorry about your friend. It is hard to lose someone you were close to."

"It's not just that. What bothers me is that trouble was nothing new to Ibrahim, and from the sounds of it, he was in less trouble than ever."

"What about his health? Maybe he had cancer."

"Elena says his health was excellent. No, what worries me is who he was and what he was doing."

"What was he doing?"

"I don't know," Nasir raised his voice and hand, "but I'm wondering if he was *one of us*."

Mohammed was interested now. He and Nasir had often wondered who was "one of us."

"What makes you think that?" he asked.

"Nothing specific. Nothing recent. There was little recent about our relationship. Remember, we both got our doctorates at al-Azhar. That's where we met."

Mohammed knew well that Nasir went to al-Azhar in Cairo, Egypt. It was the largest Islamic university in the world, and to many, the most prestigious. Although Nasir seldom spoke of it, Mohammed also knew in detail the story of Nasir's years there, his rise to fame, then his loss of professorship and banishment to Lebanon. By the time Nasir was comfortable speaking about it, he was chosen to be "one of us" and had to reestablish a low profile. But he was never certain it was low enough.

"Tell me about him," Mohammed asked.

"Ibrahim's story was much like mine. We studied together. We shared everything—from our deep secrets to our questions about academics and life. Our questions began simply as a study exercise. We would quiz each other to see who was brighter."

"So you were competitive in those ancient days," Mohammed said.

"We would think up questions that became more and more difficult until they were too difficult to answer. We would go behind each other's backs looking for answers. Sometimes we would ask the older students, but they were more clueless than us. So we would ask professors."

"And did you sneaky boys find answers?"

"We found that professors didn't like certain questions. And we didn't want to risk our grades. So when we couldn't find an answer, we would fake a hadith about it, and claim it was very rare, but with an impeccable *isnad*."

"How did you pull that off?"

"We didn't! We knew we were lying to each other, but that became the fun of it."

"Ooooh, so you did have fun when you were in school. Wait until I tell your students what a liar you were!"

"Mohammed, seriously. We did not lie to the teachers or students. We both knew it was a joke, because we quoted our own collection of hadiths."

"What was the name of the collection?"

"I will never forget it." Nasir looked off with a distant look and fond smile seldom seen on him. "*Sahih al-Hoot*."

Mohammed started laughing hysterically. Coffee sprayed out of his mouth. He put his hand to it, jumped up, and rushed over to the planter by the edge of the balcony where he shook off his hands.

"Ha-ha! *The true stories of the whale!* No wonder they threw you out!" Mohammed kept laughing. He was especially susceptible to a joke when he was tired of sitting.

Zahara Atareek, known as ImmMohammed according to the Arabic custom of naming parents after their firstborn, opened the sliding glass door to the balcony. She walked out holding a letter. "A nice surprise came in the mail today. You got a letter from your old friend Ibrahim Berger."

Nasir and Mohammed looked at each other. The color drained from their faces.

"Is something wrong?" ImmMohammed asked.

Nasir turned to her with a sober look. "Elena called me today with news. Ibrahim died last week."

## Chapter 13

# SAN FRANCISCO
## 8:30 p.m., April 4, 2006

Angela stayed late at the university reviewing Fatima's curriculum for the course Doc Molly had asked her to direct. Whether or not she accepted the offer of a permanent position, it seemed only right to help with this class, in memory of her friend Fatima. She could have brought the material home to review, but it seemed easier to do it on site, and frankly, she was happy for an excuse to be late.

The schedule and syllabus were well organized. It was not the first year Fatima had taught the class. There would be several guest lecturers from other departments, and the lectures Fatima planned to give had good notes and references. It would be work, but Angela had a little extra time this term and found it easy to give lectures. She would tell Doc Molly in the morning.

When she got home, a light was on in the living room salon, and she entered to see if John was there. The room glowed in its pale shades of gold and yellow. Compound classical moldings decorated the fifteen-foot-high walls—and some of them did resemble the ovoid shapes on the goddess Artemis.

In the center of the room was a round inlaid fruitwood table. Prominently displayed on it was a box in yellow paper, tied with a shiny gold bow. Angela walked over and picked it up.

The tag read:

*To the Woman Who Has Everything—*
*What You Always Wanted*

The handwriting was John's. The package must be hers. Certainly, the dedication looked sweet, but Angela knew John.

She opened the box.

She heard footsteps down the curved staircase and around the corner into the salon.

# Chapter 14

## BEIRUT, LEBANON

### April 5, Beirut Time; April 4, San Francisco Time

Very carefully and slowly, as one might remove a Koran from its case, Nasir extracted Elena's letter. He looked away, beyond the balcony. Then he unfolded it and read it to himself.

"Hey, heaven forgive you," Mohammed said. "Tell me what it says!"

Nasir never looked up. Eyes transfixed on the paper, he read softly and deliberately:

*My Dear Nasir,*

*In recent years we have not communicated, but I recall our youth together, and believe that our souls still share much.*

*Yesterday a man calling himself "Aswad" made an appointment to speak with me about my current research. Actually, I doubt his name and think he is interested in Sahih al-Hoot. I thought you should know in case you get a similar request, so you will not be as inadequately prepared as I am.*

*I love my wife and children, and have always sought the truth.*

*May Allah have mercy on our souls.*

*Your friend, Ibrahim Berger*

"Well, that's one mystery solved," said Mohammed.

"What?" asked Nasir, who saw more mysteries now than before reading the letter.

"Ibrahim *was* 'one of us'!"

# Chapter 15

# SAN FRANCISCO
## 9 p.m., April 4, 2006

When John entered the salon, he found Angela seated and in tears, with the opened box and its contents on her lap. Inside she had found the deed to a house in the Berkeley Hills, an obituary of a Southern magnate and his wife, and a last will and testament.

"So the feminist bitch has finally returned home. What? Is there no one left to fuck at the university?" John's face was red.

Considering what she had just read, the false accusations seemed irrelevant. Angela looked up at John, face shining with tears, and said haltingly, "Honey Jean is dead. Your parents. A plane crash. You must already know. I'm so sorry."

"Yeah, they're dead. You'll be glad to know you were remembered in Mom's will. She left you a house," he said in a childish, sassy tone, "with a few goddamn million dollars 'for renovation and upkeep.' What a joke!"

"I never asked for anything from her. I just loved her. You know that," she pleaded.

"Yeah, you loved her all right. You loved her right away from me, you deceiving bitch! She gave you everything you wanted, including her heart. And me, do you know what she left me? Oh, I get my share of the estate, all right—but only after I do a turn in the mental hospital and some damn shrink signs me off! What kind of parents are those? I'm glad they're dead. They can go to hell, I don't care."

Angela rose up. This way of talking was abhorrent to her, but nothing new. How could she not sympathize with him when his parents had just died? She gently reached out for his shoulder, but he beat her hand away.

"You don't mean that. You know they loved you," Angela said.

"I know they loved you!"

"Honey Jean loved everyone."

"She should have kept her love a little closer to home. You too."

"When did the plane crash?" Angela asked.

"A few days before you left on your damn trip."

"What? And you didn't tell me? You let me go away and miss the funeral?" She sat down and started crying again. "Honey Jean, I'm so sorry, I'm so sorry."

"Well, that's what you get for your damn gallivanting. You just wanted to go do your thing, and I let you go do it. But now you are free. You can gallivant as much as you want. Just sign the papers and be done."

"What papers? We don't sign, do we?"

"I mean, sign the goddamn divorce papers. Here, look!" He grabbed the box from her. Under the will were divorce papers, very complete and in accordance with their prenuptial agreement.

"Please, you can't mean it. You're just upset over your parents' death. No one should ever make such an important decision at a time like this!"

"What? That's beautiful! Is the society girl afraid divorce will take a little glimmer off her image?"

"It's not that, you know it. I don't care about image."

"No. It was for the money that you stayed married to me."

Angela wanted to say, "No, it was for the money that you stayed with me!" But she didn't. And she couldn't tell him now that the main reason she stayed with him was for Honey Jean, so she said nothing.

"Just sign and get out of here." John threw the divorce papers at her and left the room. He poured a Campari from the bar near the kitchen and took the elevator up to his computer room. There he locked the door and put on heavy metal music.

Angela refused to think about what he was doing up there. She sat back down and put her head in her hands.

"Honey Jean is dead." The thought kept passing through her mind, but she couldn't believe it. Honey Jean and Tom-Tom Hall were buried. She saw Fatima's burial, but missed her in-laws' funeral.

More than in-laws. Honey Jean was Angela's mentor and second mother. Tomas Hall was a good man who lived to work and as a result was fabulously wealthy; but to Angela, Honey Jean was the real star.

What Angela knew of society, of style, and of charity she had learned from Honey Jean. Coming from the lower-middle class, the notion that someone could be rich as well as kind surprised Angela.

Once, early in their relationship, Angela had gone with Honey Jean to visit an Atlanta inner-city charity. Honey Jean held and played with the children, heedless of her Carolina Herrera suit.

On the way home Angela said sincerely, "Honey Jean, you are a good woman. I am glad to have you for a mother-in-law."

"Why, thank you, sugar," Honey Jean answered, "but don't you go on like that, calling me good. Sweetie, if I were good, I'd be out there in Papua New Guinea in a sarong, teaching tribal people to read."

She paused, then added, "Actually, I did think of tryin' it once—but my fashion consultant forbade it. 'Honey Jean,' he said, 'y'all just don't have the legs for a sarong!'"

Both laughed.

"So I gave it up and started trying to brighten the corner where I am. 'Make the world a better place, or y'all just takin' up space.' That's what I say. Don't you agree, sugar?"

"Honey Jean," Angela remarked, "for once I can't agree with you."

"Why's that, sugar?"

"There's nothing wrong with your legs!"

Honey Jean was from the upper crust of Charleston, and Angela from a factory family of Dearborn, Michigan, but that didn't get in the way of their relationship—perhaps it even helped.

Nature had given Honey Jean two sons, the elder of whom was called Duke Thomas. "Duke" was not an official name, but it had been used by everyone since the boy's birth to distinguish the firstborn from his father, the "king." Duke Thomas had married Cornelia, a young woman from historic Madison, Georgia. Cornelia was society, and very much involved with the committee to "save the town that General Sherman refused to burn" on his infamous Civil War March to the Sea. But she was spoiled and frankly mean-spirited, although Honey Jean would never put it that way. Cornelia had a large family and no time for the Halls of Atlanta.

Honey Jean was pleased when her younger son, John, married Angela. She was the daughter Honey Jean had always wanted, and she loved her like her own child. And there were no parents to get in the way.

Angela was in awe of Hall Hill, the family's expansive Buckhead estate. She loved belonging to a family again—a good family. Honey Jean's love and lessons opened her to a world she had never known. Within a decade Angela had become much like her teacher.

There was always something big happening—studies at the university, social events at Hall Hill, shopping excursions to New York, snow skiing in Aspen, water skiing in the Bahamas, vacations in Europe. Thus it took Angela years to recognize the gradual change in her husband.

But by her first year of graduate school, it was obvious that something was wrong. Angela and Honey Jean talked about it. Finally, they came up with a plan: in a year, when Angela finished her master's degree at Emory, she and John would move to San Francisco, where John would manage Hall Enterprises' Western Division. It would be hard to break up the family, but they hoped getting John away from his parents would bring him out of his shell.

When the couple first settled in San Francisco John was still doing well on the face of things. The city welcomed them, and he liked that. Honey Jean and Tom-Tom bought them a house just blocks from the Getty and the Spreckles mansions; and with the help of San Francisco's top designers, Honey Jean and Angela made it one of the most fashionable homes in the area.

The couple made their debut at the "Series A" San Francisco Opera Gala in September, where they were an instant hit. Honey Jean's training had paid off for Angela, and John pulled it together. Everyone was optimistic about this new life.

As the years went on, and it became clear that John was struggling more and more with depression. Honey Jean saw how Angela suffered too. She encouraged her, but one option was never suggested. Divorce.

She never told her directly not to divorce John, but at strategic times she had said, "John is Southern Baptist, and of course we don't believe in divorce." Angela chose not to point out that John didn't seem to know he was Southern Baptist. Maybe it was because of the strange, almost guilty look Honey Jean would get at those times.

John knew that his parents disapproved of divorce, and he knew that they loved Angela. So, no matter how he blamed his wife for his unhappiness, as depressed people do, he did not divorce her. To face off with Angela and the lawyers and his parents would take more strength than a depressed person had. And who knew? Duke Thomas and his wife might walk away with the entire fortune.

As John's depression grew worse, he tapered off all social activities—first his own, then theirs as a couple. Now he tried to stop Angela from going outside the house whenever possible. He was jealous of every word she spoke to anyone, male or female.

Her fall welcome party was the last "ordeal"—John's term for parties—Angela ever planned to have at their Pacific Heights showplace. Angela would miss such events, but it wasn't worth the trouble.

Over the years John started doing more and more work from home, rarely bothering to dress and go down the hill into San Francisco's financial district. For his home office, he had chosen the style of a Victorian gentleman: in shades of dark red and brown. And when the blinds were closed, they were so very, very dark.

## Chapter 16

# UC BERKELEY
## April 5, 2006

Angela felt like she had lived years since seeing Selim the day before. She didn't want to talk about John. But after what had happened last night, she was actually considering going to Turkey this summer.

Selim was right: Turkey was a center of women's rights reform. Ataturk, the Father of Modern Turkey, believed that women should have equal rights with men in every respect. He ended polygamy and started coeducation. In the 1934 election—the first in which women could vote—eighteen women had been elected to parliament.

Now there were two universities in Istanbul with Women's Studies Departments or research centers: Istanbul University and Marmara University. In addition, the Women's Library in Istanbul, established in 1991, was the first and only center that compiled documents on and by women in many languages.

But Angela still had a few questions to ask Selim, especially about the living arrangements. He had become a friend only last term. Angela was in the habit of giving a faculty party every fall, to which she invited new and visiting faculty. Selim had come to her last party, and ever since then, he had expressed very warm feelings toward her. Too warm.

He had come for a year to Berkeley's Center for Middle Eastern Studies' Ustaad Program, which featured visiting scholars from moderate Islamic backgrounds. Because he had entered the program late, Selim had to work from an office in Wheeler Hall, which housed the English Department . . . and Angela. That made avoiding him problematic.

Selim's wife had just died. Most people cling to family during grief, but Selim ran away. This puzzled Angela.

She exited her office to the left and walked down the putty-colored hall with its series of doors. As she approached Selim's, the last one, she heard noises, like he was trying to move the desk against a wall or the door, but it was stuck.

Angela twisted the knob and said, "Selim, do you need help?"

Just as she twisted the knob, the pressure on the other side of the door caused it to pop open. Out fell the girl with streaked hair, tattoo to the floor, and beneath Selim, whose starched white shirt was open and black pants unzipped. The two appeared to be stuck together. Selim looked at Angela, red-faced and mortified.

"Oh, I guess not." Angela said coolly and walked away as if nothing had happened.

## Chapter 17

# BERKELEY, CALIFORNIA

## April 6, 2006

*Selim seems to be spreading a little more than Turkish culture.*

UC Berkeley's Center for Middle Eastern Studies (CMES) is one of the most recognized in America. Its visiting professorship programs include the Sultan Program in Arab Studies, which teaches a deeper understanding of the Arab world (funded by the Sultan bin Abdulaziz al-Saud Foundation) and the al-Falah Program, designed to promote understanding of Islam in the West, in exchange for bringing Western technology to Saudi Arabia.

This term, CMES was hosting a film series called *Istanbul: Melancholy and the City.* Selim's expertise in this area made his presence in Berkeley especially desirable.

Selim knocked on Angela's office door, wondering what he should say. "I . . . ah . . ." he stammered.

"Never had sex with a tattooed girl before?" Angela's tone was matter-of-fact.

"No. I mean . . . I am such a fool. I suppose this means you will not be coming to Turkey with me this summer?"

"On the contrary. A fool you may be and most probably are. But 'The Incident of the Tattooed Girl,' shall we say," Angela said, "actually encourages me to go to Turkey this summer."

Selim looked at her, perplexed. "What you saw makes you want to go to Turkey?"

"Yes," she smiled. "I feel totally at ease now. Before I was nervous that perhaps, forgive me, you loved me a little. Now that I know you don't, I'm cool with going to Turkey."

"Oh," Selim replied sheepishly.

"Some things are still unsettled," she said, hoping he wouldn't press her for details, "but I am starting to think I might need a few Turkish words. What was that 'magic word' you told me about? *Succotash*?"

"*Arkadaş*. It means 'my friend.'"

"Thank you so much, *arkadash*."

# Chapter 18

## BEIRUT, LEBANON
## April 7, 2006

"Mohammed, what's happening? You've scarcely been out of your room for two days," Nasir called, banging on his door.

He tried to be tolerant of what he considered Mohammed's erratic lifestyle. He and ImmMohammed preferred that Mohammed be married with a family, but it was good to have him near, especially with the amount of work they had to do. It also gave Nasir insight into Mohammed's activities. Living together, it was difficult not to sense that Mohammed was chasing something.

"Oh, come in, come in! *Mumtaz!* I am finding wonderful things!" Mohammed was his hospitable self and relieved to have a break.

"What, Mohammed, can be so interesting that you are late for ImmMohammed's cooking?"

"Only the best, the very best!"

"Her cooking or your project?"

"Both, of course! Soon I will eat and be very, very happy. I have been a goat sniffing through the flock of sheep to find who else is 'one of us.'"

"Oh, so that's it, is it? Mohammed, I have told you before the pointlessness of such a quest. It doesn't matter who else is doing what! What matters is that we do our part to the best of our abilities."

"*Habeebee*," he said, using a term of endearment, "as you know, I have always disagreed with you on this. But because you have less hair than me, I have respected your wish."

Nasir was insistent. "And we should keep it that way!"

"If Ibrahim were still alive, we could, but not now."

"You didn't even know Ibrahim. Why this sudden desire to avenge his death?"

"I don't give a damn about Ibrahim's death; I'm worried about ours! Think! Poke your big Palestinian nose out of your ivory tower and take a sniff at what's going on!"

Nasir was surprised at Mohammed's tone. Often Mohammed had

pushed his humor to the limit, but he had never been openly disrespectful.

Mohammed continued. "We know that Ibrahim's death wasn't natural. In fact, the letter he sent you makes it highly doubtful that it was even suicide. He was worried that what he had been working on was of interest to someone he didn't trust. If that person—'Aswad'—or whoever he really is, found out what Ibrahim was working on and killed him for it, don't you think he will come looking for the rest of us? Who knows, maybe he has already found us."

Mohammed paused. Nasir sat quietly, looking down.

*It's true.*

Nasir couldn't deny it anymore. The risk of the work they had been doing the last several years had gone from hypothetical to real. Mohammed was clever. Maybe he had a good idea of what they should do.

Verbally, Nasir neither agreed nor denied the proposition, but Mohammed could see he had made his point.

"What should we do?" Nasir inquired.

"I don't know. So far I only have one idea. Research. It sounds straightforward, but the more I look into it, the more complicated it gets. I am trying to find everyone in the world who is expert in Arabic or Islam or ancient manuscripts. I started checking the rosters of the professional organizations we belong to. Now I am checking all the universities with departments of Islam or Middle Eastern Studies. After I assemble the lists of names, I need to research each professor to see what he or she published. From there, we will need to read between the lines to determine who are likely candidates to be 'one of us.'"

"*We* will need to read between the lines?"

"*Habeebee*, it would be so much faster with your help. You already know a lot of these monkeys and could say which are very likely and very unlikely."

"Really?" Nasir seemed genuinely surprised.

"*Mit akid!* You could jump-start the whole project. For example, make a list with all the experts you know who were like Ibrahim."

"That should be a short list." Nasir sounded doubtful.

"Short list is good. Look," he scrolled through a file he was making on his computer, "I have about five thousand names here. Can you imagine how long it will take to investigate all of these guys?"

"Could I look at that list? I mean, could you make me a printout?"

"Sure. Why? Have you got an idea?"

"I was just thinking I could scan over it and see if anyone jogged my memory."

"*Habeebee*," Mohammed laughed at his success of enlisting this reluctant recruit, "you're a natural!"

# Chapter 19

# UC BERKELEY

## April 7, 2006

Office hours are posted on a bulletin board next to each UC Berkeley instructor's office door. During these times, students are welcome to make appointments or to stop by to discuss class work.

The proportions of the fourth floor of Wheeler Hall are not as generous as the lower three. In fact, the ceiling is so low that there are cutouts to make room for the window wells in the small offices. Most of each office's walls are banked by books, and Dr. Angela Hall's was no exception.

Angela was in her office between classes, looking out at the glimpse of green. She was slipping into unhappy thoughts, which were becoming more and more unavoidable, when there was a knock on her door.

"Dr. Hall?" asked a pretty blue-eyed student. She was distinguished by a black hijab, and was, as Dr. Hall rightly guessed, an American convert to Islam.

"Yes," answered Angela, with a smile that hid any trace of sorrow.

"Hello, my name is Maryam," the young woman said, using her new Muslim name. "I am so sorry about what happened to Dr. Kareem," she said, in reference to Fatima.

"Please come in and have a seat."

"Thank you. I am here on behalf of the Muslim Students Fellowship. Our annual 'Know Islam Week' is next week."

"Yes, I saw the posters."

"Dr. Kareem was going to be a member of our panel for the 'Women in Islam' presentation on Thursday. Now that she is . . . gone, it leaves us with a hole for a faculty voice."

"Dr. Kareem left many holes."

"Well, the thing is, I understand you are a Muslim, and I am wondering if you would consider taking her place on the panel?"

Once again Angela was being asked to fill Fatima's shoes. This time it was really a stretch. She had never even been to an MSF meeting; how could she help? She stumbled for an answer.

"Ah . . . well, yes, I am a Muslim, but I am certainly no expert." As if by way of excuse and explanation she added, "I've read the Koran, of course, but I understand it takes years of study to be able to speak sensibly on Islam. Fatima—Dr. Kareem—was well studied on such things, but I am not. I am sorry to let you down, but there it is."

"No, that's perfect! We're not looking for an expert. We have a woman from the Islamic Propagation and Public Relations Network coming for our expert opinion. What we want from you is just the ordinary professional Muslim woman's voice. Absolutely any experience you have had would be valid."

*Any experience?* Angela thought, but what she said was, "Oh."

"For example, you were raised Muslim, right?"

"Yes," answered Angela, surprised that her private life was common knowledge. Apparently Doc Molly wasn't the only source for campus gossip.

"You would be asked questions like: Did your parents encourage your education? What obstacles did you face? How do you practice your religion? Why do you choose not to cover your hair? Does being a Muslim woman keep you from fulfillment?"

To Angela it sounded like prying. She was used to appearing in the society pages, but this was different somehow. Maybe because religion hits deeper than the color of your hair.

"Yes, I could answer those questions," she replied, "but I am very busy this term. I'm taking over Dr. Kareem's classes."

"The meeting is at 7 p.m. and will require absolutely no preparation. Just show up and be your wonderful self!"

*Do I have "poster child" stamped on my forehead?*

It wasn't the first or last time Angela rewarded compliments.

## Chapter 20

# BEIRUT, LEBANON
## April 10, 2006

"Mohammed, here's your list. The ones I've checked in blue ink I know, or know of. I only recognize a couple hundred of them."

"Wow! Really, that's so great! Because if Dr. Nasir Atareek doesn't know them, they are nobody!"

"The red checks are by names of those who I think are possibly of our frame of mind. I mean, they might be a little open-minded, either because I have spoken with them or I know of their teaching or research. I can get that for you, but I didn't think you needed it now."

"OK. That can be later," said Mohammed.

"The ones with question marks I'm not sure about. They don't have extreme reputations and have spent some time in the West."

"Which means either they are open-minded or they are openly deceptive and potentially dangerous."

"You could be right."

"It looks like there are about fifty red checks. Let me start Googling them. That way we can see what they have been up to recently."

"And me? Am I done? Can I get back to the manuscripts and let you carry on here?"

"Sorry, *habeebee.* Step two. Could you take another look at the list?"

"What for this time? I'm certain I've checked all I know."

"Aaaahh," said Mohammed, lifting his chin and then clicking his tongue. "The great Dr. Atareek has checked off those he suspects might be 'one of us.' Now he needs to look at those he thinks might be 'one of them.'"

## Chapter 21

# UC BERKELEY
## April 12, 2006

Dr. Angela Hall and Dr. Selim Soglu crossed Bancroft Street after curry at Juli's Café, where she had agreed to discuss the trip to Turkey. John was wrong about her and Selim, at least as far as Angela was concerned, but she wasn't going to stop living because of his complaints. That's a mistake her mother had made. In a mismatched marriage to Pete O'Connor, Angela's mother, Malaak, had stayed at home, watching her husband drink himself into an early grave. After he died, she went back to school and became qualified to be an Arabic-English industrial translator. She had found a way to support the family and use her brain, but twenty years too late.

Angela and Selim crossed Sproul Plaza. It was a typical day on the plaza in the life of Berkeley. The sun was out, and so were the students. They were sprawled on the lawns and sitting on the benches, fences, and wall of the fountain. Tables for many campus action groups were set in a row under the trees.

The noise was at din level. The Mexican and East Indian student groups were in large booths opposite each other, both blasting out ethnic music. An aged hippie war protester was walking with posters and a megaphone, and seemed to be ranting against the war in Iraq.

The next table on the right was the MSF *da'wa*, or outreach table. There were posters and flyers up for "Know Islam Week." Tonight's topic was "The Miracle of the Koran." A Pakistani student dressed in white handed them a flyer.

Angela said to Selim, "Maybe I should go to this. I'm on the panel tomorrow night, and I should probably have an idea of how these go."

"I'm going to both. Part of my research here has been to see how Islam in America is different than in the Middle East. Angela, it will be a pleasure to watch you."

"Watch me squirm, you mean!"

As they walked away, toward Sather Gate, Angela could hear a strident voice in the distance. "Your book has been changed. The Koran has never been changed! It is exactly the same as it has been since . . ."

# Chapter 22

# EASTERN HOLLAND
## April 16, 2006

An athletic man in a biking suit, about thirty-five years old, rode a bike on trails through the bulb fields between Noordwijk and Keukenhof Garden. Most of the riders on this sunny Sunday afternoon were out to enjoy the weather and the scenery; tulip season was at its peak.

Maarten was in training. He had started biking again as a break—to work off the fatigue of studying manuscripts, and also to get out of a house full of crying triplets. He was developing a regular riding routine. On alternate days he would take routes northeast and southeast. Saturdays he would also swim at the university.

Sundays he would start at his home in Leiden, circle the De Valk Windmill, and get on the bike trail out of town toward Lisse. At Lisse he would lock up his bike at Castle Keukenhof, walk across the street, and enter Keukenhof Garden, where he would jog around the nine miles of paths, keeping clear of tourists as much as possible. Then he would rest by his bike, have an energy snack and a drink, and ride home. On days when he was feeling especially energetic, he would ride from Keukenhof into the fields toward Noordwijk. That is what he did today.

By the time he arrived home he would be well rested, and hopefully the triplets were on their way to bed.

On Sunday, April 16, Aimee put the children to bed by herself and went to bed alone. She fell asleep hoping to hear her husband return at any minute. But Maarten did not return.

# Chapter 23
# BEIRUT, LEBANON
## April 17, 2006

Nasir walked down the hall of his home toward the connecting door of the apartment next door, which he used as a laboratory.

"*Ya*, Nasir! I think I've found something. Come here!"

"Certainly you have, Mohammed. Whether or not it is significant, let me decide." This was about as close to humor as Nasir could get.

"Do you remember a 'Maarten Hoog'? He's one of the names checked off in red on your list."

"Maarten Hoog, Maarten Hoog. Yes, I think he was one of the kids presenting a convention I went to in Morocco about ten years ago." Nasir bent over the computer screen to examine the photograph. "Yes, that's who I remember. Why?"

Mohammed pointed at an article. "It says here that he was associated with the University of Leiden—and get this, he was an expert in ancient manuscripts. They have a blurb on him because apparently he was one of Holland's hopefuls for the Tour de France this summer. He had competed regularly a decade ago but stopped when he got a position at the university and married. It says he took the semester off from the university to train and to help his wife with their triplets! Ha!"

"Does that leave much time for manuscripts?"

Mohammed laughed. "Heaven forgive you, what do you mean insulting the dead that way? Of course he studied manuscripts. Triplets would give any real man all the time in the world—he'd be out of that house forever possible!"

"Mohammed, what do you mean, 'the dead'?"

"He died while biking yesterday. They say there was no suspicion of foul play," said Mohammed.

"Oh…" Nasir sensed more was coming.

"Do you need me for a few days?"

"Now, Mohammed…"

"Yes, I'm going now. I think I will get some money since I'm flying out in the morning. I'm very, very glad you agree that the Dutch police are tooootally incompetent if they think there is no foul play!"

“Actually, Mohammed, we are behind with the manuscripts, due to these extracurricular projects you take on. If you would just focus, we’d be done much sooner. The chief is waiting for our input for the first publication.”

Mohammed turned and looked at him with a huge smile. “It won’t matter how far behind we are when we are dead!”

“Sooner or later, your poking around will draw attention to us and then we’re bound to get killed! Just keep a low profile; it’s best for everyone. We can ask the chief what’s up.”

Mohammed stood up. He couldn’t resist patting the top of Nasir’s head. “Don’t worry, *habeebee*,” he said, “your little Mohammed has plenty of ways to escape.”

“It’s not the ways to escape that worry me. It’s the ways to kill.”

Chapter 24

# AMSTERDAM, HOLLAND
## April 18, 2006

Mohammed landed at Schiphol International Airport in the early afternoon, rented a car, and drove west twelve miles to Haarlem. But he didn't stop to eat by its canals or visit the Dutch master paintings in the Frans Hals Museum. He turned south on N208, the Bollenstreek Route, toward Lisse and Leiden.

Holland had put out its red carpet for Mohammed. "Bollenstreek Route" means the "Bulb District Route." He passed through field after brightly striped field of yellow, pink, and red tulips.

It was Tuesday, so the weekend crowds had thinned out a little, but the occasional car was decked with flower garlands from roadside stalls.

*Dutch people are sooo silly about flowers!*

Mohammed did not know where to go, but he had a good idea of how to find what he was looking for. Because of its history and picture-book preservation, Leiden is a tourist town. There would be lots of English speakers.

He parked and started walking around the fabled and gabled town of three-story brick buildings. Near the university were several cafés of the type frequented by students. A few strategic questions, and he was driving out of town, knowing where Maarten lived and where his funeral would be held.

Maarten lived on a farm, not far outside Leiden. There was a long gravel driveway up to the tidy brick farmhouse. It, too, was gabled, and had traditional tablecloth-lace curtains in the windows. A few trees flanked the house, but otherwise the lawn was mostly flat, giving way to fields and low-lying crops. Not far to the left was a canal of some sort. Way to the back, nearly out of sight, were colorful streaks of spring bulbs, like those that had lined Mohammed's route to Leiden.

Several cars were parked in the driveway. Mohammed drove up, having no idea what he would do or say, but feeling confident. He went to the front door and rang the bell. He could hear much commotion within: the screeching voices of children playing and the low din of many adult voices.

A stocky middle-aged matron answered the door. She was by no imaginable means Maarten Hoog's wife, yet she had an air of authority about her as she spoke. What followed was a flood of Dutch words, none of which he could understand. She stopped speaking, left hand on her waist and right hand extended, as if expecting to receive something. For a moment Mohammed considered handing her a bribe, but when he looked in the matron's scowling eyes he thought better of it. What she had said was, "Oh, hello, young man. I'm sorry, but Mrs. Hoog is not up to receiving any of Dr. Hoog's students today. You are welcome to attend the funeral tomorrow. I will tell her of your call. You may give me the sympathy card."

Mohammed simply shook his head, at which the matron, probably Mrs. Hoog's mother, withdrew her hand and closed the door.

This was not the interaction Mohammed had hoped for. One thing was clear: he had been dismissed and could not speak with Aimee Hoog herself—not with her bodyguard around!

*It's time for Plan B.*

# Chapter 25

# LEIDEN, HOLLAND
## April 19, 2006

Mohammed sat alone in the back of a Dutch Reformed Church. Music was playing. He did not know what he would learn from the funeral, but he was certain it would be of value. Shortly before the service began, a broad-faced but pleasant-looking young woman sat beside him.

"Are you one of the family?" she asked in Dutch.

Mohammed was not sure what she said, but he deduced from where she sat that she was not family either.

In English he said, "I'm a foreign student," which he thought should cover everything, being both true and untrue at the same time.

"Strange about the break-in yesterday," she replied in English, "being where Dr. Hoog's office had been. And just a few days after his death."

The expression dropped off of Mohammed's face.

*How do you leave a funeral without being noticed?*

He grabbed his face and faked a whimpering sound, as if suddenly overtaken by grief at the mention of death. Mortified, the girl apologized profusely as he got up to leave.

Once outside, his red face burst into laughter as he raced to the car. He had to get to Maarten's house, and fast!

Mohammed's car screeched around tight corners and through narrow streets, over and along canals. At one point, he had to back up because he went the wrong way. The car jolted into an outdoor cheese display. Cheeses flew.

Mohammed wanted to stop and check the map, but the angry grocer was throwing a fit. He hit the gas, skidding on good Gouda as he left.

He found the way out of town toward Hoog's farmhouse. When he drove up the driveway, it was as he had hoped: empty. What better time to guarantee no one's home than during the funeral of its master? Good! He must work fast, for the competition would be here soon.

He parked to the side of the driveway. If anyone saw the car, hopefully they would think it belonged to one of the relatives. Mohammed had an idea. The house itself was not the kind of place one would leave valuables, not with three toddlers. Something stirred in his mind, something he had barely noticed the day before. Mohammed directed his gaze to the distance, down the driveway, beyond the house.

*Martin's bike shed.*

The shed had a rickety old door with a padlock. Since Mohammed had picked more locks than he cared to admit, the lock easily gave way. The shed was clean, as if it were used regularly. There was a professional speed bike on a wall rack. At the back of the shed was another door. Mohammed lifted the lever slowly and peeked inside. What he saw made him smile.

There, on the other side of the shack's wall, Hoog had added an office. It was simple, with a broad, flat desk beneath wide windows.

*No wonder Maarten chose this spot for his study.*

The windows looked out to a covered porch and a lawn slightly sloping to a canal tributary in the distance. To the left was a large canal. The view was restful.

Besides being a world away from Maarten's family, the study's windows threw natural light onto his research materials. Specialized lighting apparatuses were mounted over the desk. On the desk were a customized stage, adaptable to hold anything from a paper fragment to an entire codex; a camera on a stand; a microscope; a microfilm reader; and, of course, a computer. All of these items were similar to those in Mohammed and Nasir's lab. He felt right at home.

Mohammed could imagine Maarten here, poring over manuscripts like he himself did. But where were the manuscripts? Was he even working on them his sabbatical? Had they been stolen from the school after all? Mohammed had guessed three things. First, there had to be manuscripts. Maarten must have been killed for something. Second, the manuscripts would be at the farm somewhere, since Maarten was on sabbatical.

Mohammed turned around to see a metal storage cabinet behind him. His heart beat with the excitement of anticipation. He put his hand on the leverlike handle and pushed down. It was unlocked.

*Poor Maarten, so trusting.*

He could hardly believe his eyes, for on a shelf were two manuscript boxes nearly identical to ones he and Nasir had. Called "drop-open" boxes, they had detachable covers made of acid-free boards, tied together by linen tapes. The top cover had a window through which the researchers could peek at the manuscript inside.

Mohammed picked up the first box. He glanced at the label, which was in both Arabic and English: *Dar al-Makhtutat* followed by the words "Holy Koran" and a series of letters and numbers. Before he could untie one of the tapes, he stopped. Through the open doors he could hear someone coming down the gravel. His third bet was also correct.

The murderer had reached the same conclusions he did.

## Chapter 26

# LEIDEN, HOLLAND
## April 19, 2006

Mohammed thought so fast that he was almost not thinking at all. He must have subconsciously planned an escape because at the sound of the gravel crunching, he sprang into action, dashing back into the storage room. With his height and strength, he easily tore the bike off its support and rolled it into the lab. Then Mohammed reached back, locked the door between the office and the shed, and threw a chair against it. He rested the bike against the desk just long enough to put the two drop-open boxes into its basket. With uncanny quiet, he opened the porch door, mounted the bike, and rode out onto the back lawn.

Maarten had been a little shorter than Mohammed, but the bike's excellent design made up for the difference. Mohammed rode straight, staying in the cover of the shed and out of the line of sight for as long as possible.

There was no way to head back to the driveway or the road without being seen. He would have to ride through the fields. Holland was a biking nation with an outstanding network of bike trails; he was aware of this but had no idea of where to catch one. His current options of escape were only two: the canal to the left or over the small wooden bridge straight ahead.

Not being in a boat, and not wanting to wade with the manuscripts, he chose to ride over the bridge. It was about the length of his bicycle and covered a small branch of the canal.

Mohammed was pedaling as fast as he could when something dawned on him: that kind of bridge was needed for only one thing—cattle. The bridge had an ingenious trough at the far end sized to catch cattle's hooves so that—what with the canals and the bridge—only a fence was needed by the road for the animals to be effectively corralled. As this awareness grew, a horned creature came into view from near the large canal.

*A bull!*

Apparently the bull saw Mohammed as a threat to his territory, for his front hoof was scratching the turf in front of him.

*Where now?*

Not back, not with the murderer there. Not the canal, he had already decided that. What was in the distance, separating this field from the next? Another bridge, he hoped. He pedaled faster, which, because he was riding in grass, was not very fast at all. The bull was still eyeing him, not yet committed to a fight.

Mohammed would try to keep a low profile until he could find a way out. But how do you keep a low profile when you are a large man on a large bicycle plowing slowly through grass?

Two cows had lifted their heads to look at the distraction. One of them actually took a step in Mohammed's direction.

That was it. The bull turned. He had reached his limit of tolerance. Mohammed was a threat that must be extinguished.

The bull again scratched the turf with his foreleg, then thrust his immense weight into motion and started running. Mohammed was convinced he felt the earth rumble beneath his tires, so he looked left and saw the bull running toward him, the gap between them narrowing.

He fought the urge to get off the bike and run. He kept going in faith that if he could make it to the end of the field, there would be another cattle-proof bridge. And if there wasn't? Well, he'd "cross that bridge when he came to it."

The bull was a stone's throw away.

*Yes, there is a bridge ahead!*

It must be cattle-proof, for there were succulent-looking crops on the other side. But could he get there fast enough? He thought he could hear the bull's breathing. He definitely heard it calling him.

Mohammed turned to look at the bull.

*Bad move.*

It was just a few yards from him. This unsettled Mohammed, and his wheels slid in the mud. He could not recover himself in time. The bike fell sideways, unseating Mohammed. A corner of the top manuscript box hit the mud.

Mohammed pushed the box back into the basket, getting mud on the second box as well. But irreplaceable manuscripts lose significance when your irreplaceable life is at stake.

There was no time to remount the bike. But, good news: the mud was at the base of the bridge. Mohammed held the bike by the handlebars and ran across the bridge as quickly as he could. He thought he could feel hot bull breathe on his buttocks, but it was just warmth from the friction of vigorous riding.

He passed over the hoof trough and turned his head. The race had been extremely close. If it hadn't been for the trough, the bull would be goring him now. As it was, the bull was standing with his two forelegs on the bridge; apparently as far as bull discretion would allow him to go. Mohammed could smell his anger.

Then the oddest thing happened. Mohammed detected a change of expression on the face of the bull. It was almost as if he were smiling. He raised his head and snorted, throwing mucus into the air as if saying, "Well, Arab boy, I gave you a run for your money, didn't I? So who's cool now?"

Relief, coupled with the bull's comical look, overcame Mohammed, and he exploded into laughter.

"Mister Bull," he said in Arabic, throwing a hand into the air and then settling it on his hip, "you are sooo cool. But you exhausted yourself for nothing. Of all the women I have ever had, not one has been a cow!"

## Chapter 27

# LEIDEN, HOLLAND
## April 19, 2006

Man and bull faced each other like soldiers over a trench in World War I after a truce had been announced. The two opposing forces dipped their heads and went their ways: the man riding between crop rows to the north, and the bull strutting to his harem in the south, proud that he had ridded his world of a rival.

Mohammed smiled. His pulse tapered toward normal. The sun was shining, and he was heading for a field of tulips. It was turning out to be a lovely afternoon. He had what he wanted. True, the boxes were a little muddy, but inside, the manuscripts were safe. Soon he would find a trail. He'd return to Maarten's house and pick up his car. Apparently the murderer had not noticed that he had gotten there first.

Mohammed passed into the field of tulips.

The feeling you get walking down your street is very different than that of driving it. Likewise, riding a bike between closely planted rows of flowers, as Mohammed was, you experience tulips in an entirely different way. And not just tulips—daffodils, narcissi, hyacinths, and irises. The combination of fragrances, colors, and rough ground was almost disorienting.

Mohammed was not disoriented; however, his sense of relief at his narrow escape and the beauty of the flowers may have taken the edge off his caution. He didn't notice the car pacing him on the road to the right.

Then came the moment the driver of the car was waiting for. His quarry had found a bike trail that ran through the fields.

Mohammed's legs and rattled back were relieved. Now he could make faster progress.

But the trail also connected with the road. The car turned onto the bike trail. The trail was not built for automobile traffic, but the car was tiny and barely roadworthy to begin with. It was the kind of vehicle that a student might drive, if he were lucky enough to have one. The car's wheel carriage was narrow. Most of the time, the driver could keep both wheels on the trail, and all of the time, at least one.

Mohammed was thirsty. A couple biking by directed him to a restored windmill. It had a rest area with a few chairs and a snack bar, but they were not sure if it was open.

"It will be open for me. All the world loves crazy Palestinians! Thank you sooo much, my Dutch friends," he said, waving broadly.

The car was closing the gap.

Mohammed heard a surprising sound and turned around.

*A car on the bike trail.*

He was not immediately alarmed. Perhaps it was a maintenance crew. But, strangely, the car was going so fast that it was actually damaging the trail more than maintaining it.

The car drew close. Mohammed could see a black-haired man driving it. Something about his appearance alerted Mohammed to get off the trail.

*Back into the fields!*

Mohammed veered into the flowers again. This time he was not quite so careful to keep between the rows and rode over some of Holland's national heritage.

But that destruction paled in comparison to what would come. The small car was feeling empowered. If the bike could take on the tulips, it could too! Down over the raised trail and into the flower field it flopped, getting stuck momentarily in the transition.

The two were about evenly matched. It was tough biking in the troughs, but a small car with a low carriage and two-wheel drive was disadvantaged too.

High effort, low progress. At some stages, it looked as if the chase had been filmed in slow motion.

A group of American tourists on a biking tour watched with interest.

One yelled out, "Hey, what's going on out there?"

The group stopped entirely.

"Whoa, they sure do cultivate funny here in the 'Old Country'!" another said, and everyone laughed.

"Hey, director, is that usual for this time of year?"

The tour director, a former biking champ, said, "Honestly, I've never seen anything like it before in my life!"

A lawyer in the group who had grown up in Holland said gruffly, "Let's call the police. This is sheer recklessness!"

Mohammed's bike would get caught in a rut and slow down. The car would draw closer. Then the car would get caught in the same rut, made bigger by the bike. As the car struggled, it would swerve, plucking up tulips. In the wake of the race was a shambles of tossed flowers.

Unless the car got permanently stuck, Mohammed knew he would never be able to beat it as long as he was on the bike. Sooner or later the car would overpower him. An idea formulated in his mind. He didn't know how his strength would pair against the driver, but he outmatched nine out of ten men, probably more.

The windmill was coming into sight. He must plow on until he got within running distance of it.

When he was about thirty yards away he heard a grinding sound. The car was stuck. Probably it had eaten a few too many flowers.

Mohammed seized the opportunity. He reached back and grabbed the boxes, dropping the bike into the path of the car. Then he ran up to the windmill.

The window of the refreshment stand was out of view of the windmill door. He opened the door and ran inside.

His pursuer saw him. Mohammed knew the man would follow him.

The door opened inward. He stood behind it, peeking through the crack. As the pursuer approached, Mohammed slammed the door in his face, knocking him onto the planks.

This gave Mohammed a minute to get upstairs and check it out. There was not much available to work with.

*A rope.*

There were no clean options.

Mohammed worked silently. He stood on the top floor of the windmill and faked a worried look. It wasn't totally fake, but he wasn't as worried as he looked, either.

All went as he had hoped. When his pursuer reached the top of the stairs, fixed on Mohammed's face, he didn't even notice the old trick: a rope around the stair posts, which tripped him quite effectively.

He fell forward. There was a thud, but the creaking windmill drowned out the sound.

Quickly, Mohammed tied his pursuer's hands behind his back and began coiling the rope around his body.

The captive started hollering. Mohammed hoped the squeaking of the mill had covered it, but he couldn't take any chances. He didn't want to have to explain his life's story to the Dutch police.

Mohammed wrapped the rope around his captive's neck to stop him from talking. As Mohammed was trying to think of what to do with him, the man flinched. His feet kicked through the rickety old railing.

The resulting destruction appeared to fill him with hope. He kept kicking, trying to get at Mohammed.

Mohammed did not know how to stop him or how to get him downstairs. While he was looking around for something else, the man kicked one time too many.

Like a fish sliding off the deck of a boat into the sea, the black-haired man slid through the gap in the stair rail. He was suspended by the rope wrapped around the top railing where Mohammed had tripped him. It was still tight. The rope around his body was tight too, and not slipping—at least not fast enough to let him die by falling instead of by suffocation.

Mohammed looked at him and said the Arabic equivalent of "Oh, dear, you do present a dilemma. Either I heartlessly let you hang there in this pathetic way and come to your natural end, or I assist you and endanger myself and the free world in the process."

The man made a choking sound.

"OK, maybe not the free world. Just the truth. And I've staked my life on truth."

He started walking down the stairs. When he came face to face with the man he said, "What did you stake yours on?"

The dying man moved his lips and blinked slowly.

Mohammed exhaled and walked solemnly downstairs. He did not wait for the flailing to stop.

On the ground floor, a butter churn was on display. He opened the lid. As he had predicted, the pursuer was too interested in catching him to stop and make a search. A small mouse ran out of the churn. He picked up the two manuscript boxes. One of the linen tapes had already been partly chewed through.

He walked out of the windmill and tied a fragment of rope around the door handle. Then he picked up the bike and rode away—this time on a trail.

Another couple passed him on their way toward the windmill.

Keeping his face from their direct view, Mohammed waved and called out in English, "It's dead up there. The windmill's closed!"

# Chapter 28

# BEIRUT, LEBANON
## April 24, 2006

"Mohammed, if this is the way experts treat manuscripts, what hope is there for civilization?" Nasir inquired, exasperated.

Mohammed looked at the muddy manuscript boxes.

"I know you weren't feeling well when you came home last night, but before we start to look at these, you simply must tell me what happened," Nasir insisted.

Mohammed was ready for him. "I'm afraid we were right about Maarten's death. It was not an accident."

"Do you have proof? Did the police say that, or did you hear a confession?"

"No."

"Then your fears amount to nothing!" Nasir said.

"Are these boxes nothing?"

"These boxes are a disgrace! Couldn't you possibly have been more careful with them? Or are you going to tell me they were muddy when you found them? I simply won't believe that. No researcher would keep manuscripts in boxes like these. The risk is simply too great that the dirt..." He ran his finger along the edge, "...mud, it looks like, would contaminate the contents."

"You're right. I should have cleaned the boxes before I showed them to you!" He knew this would annoy Nasir.

"Then you certainly would have contaminated the manuscripts! Now explain this."

"It's quite simple, really. I got them from Maarten Hoog's house."

*So far, so true.*

He thought it best to summarize as close to the truth as possible.

"I went to the funeral. I met someone there who told me the manuscripts were at Maarten's house. I met Maarten's mother-in-law at the house. She thought I was a student and I got the manuscripts. Simple!"

Not wanting to upset Nasir with the full truth of what had happened, Mohammed had to manufacture some details. He considered it *taqeeya*—lying for the cause.

The goal was to give Nasir the impression that the situation was serious. This would justify Mohammed's possession of the manuscripts and would keep Nasir interested in helping him discover who was after the researchers—and was willing to kill them.

"And the mud?"

"I'm afraid the boxes fell in the mud as I was leaving the farm."

"You dropped them?"

"Certainly not!"

"And how do you know Maarten was murdered?"

"His office at the university was broken into."

"But the manuscripts were not there?" asked Nasir.

"*Alhamdulillah*, no! They were waiting for us at Maarten's home."

"And what about the would-be thief... or murderer?"

"He was caught."

"What took you so long to get back here if the funeral was on Wednesday?"

"Haven't you ever heard? Amsterdam is a very exciting city!" Mohammed made a sly expression. It had the right affect.

"Mohammed! I thought you said you had given up that kind of life?"

"Who said I haven't? Ha-ha, I've caught you! Heaven forgive what a filthy mind you have!" Mohammed conveniently flew into a laughing fit, nodding his head and pointing at Nasir.

*Success!*

# Chapter 29

# LEIDEN, HOLLAND

## April 19, 2006, Revisited

True, Amsterdam was exciting, but Mohammed had not returned there. Having already had plenty of excitement in the tulip fields, he stayed put in the Vermeer-worthy town of Leiden.

Immediately after the incident at the windmill, Mohammed felt fine, as is so often the case after a traumatic event. The adrenalin gave him a feeling of luck, and the manuscripts in his basket a sense of accomplishment. He could go home from this quest successful.

But those good sensations vanished the second he heard his hotel room door shut behind him. The last door he had shut was on a human life. Could it really be that he had walked away and let a man die?

He washed his face and went back out. He hoped walking around town would distract him from these thoughts.

Dusk was arriving. Watching the water flow by should have been cathartic, but it wasn't. Earlier in the day the canal had been active with water traffic. Now it was dead.

*Dead.*

Mohammed passed a few restaurants, but he wasn't hungry. The memory of a face with bulging eyes turning purple suffocates an appetite. He went back to the hotel.

*They say the first kill is the hardest.*

This unsettling thought kept rattling through his brain. Of all his bad deeds, most of which he regretted, he had never killed anyone.

*The first kill?* He hoped there would be no more.

Thursday he didn't leave the hotel room.

Friday morning he awoke with the realization that he needed to get out of town.

"I am sooo stupid! Riding around telling people I am Palestinian. I may as well give them my address. If the police don't find me, perhaps 'one of them' will."

But before he left, he needed to finish his local research.

First, he needed to hide the manuscript boxes. He got an idea. He wrapped them tightly in a plastic laundry bag and placed them in the bidet. Then he took a hand towel and moistened it. After his morning bowel movement, he did a final wipe with the hand towel—enough to leave a light brown stain. Then he arranged the towel over the bidet in a way that totally covered the boxes beneath but looked oh, so casual.

"That's good! Even if you find them, Mister Thief, this will make you unclean, like a 'filthy infidel' and unworthy to touch them. Ha!" He rubbed his hands together and smiled, encouraging himself with the confidence in his voice.

To complete the look, he threw the damp bath towel on the floor.

As he left the room, he hung the "Do not disturb" sign on the door—it would do no good if the maid came and removed the towels.

*The rest is fate.*

He was reluctant to go downstairs for the complimentary breakfast, but he would be seen as soon as he stepped outside anyway. Besides, he was hungry.

He was full of hopes that closely resembled dreads. He hoped there would be no suspicion. He hoped the people on the trails had been too distant to see him clearly. He hoped the refreshment stand worker saw no more than the tail of his bike.

He hoped he was in the clear. The only person who might be able to connect him with the Hoog house was the matron at the door. He hoped she thought he was a student, that she would say so if the police asked about an Arab visitor. And he hoped his rental car was not noticed at the house the day of the funeral. And that the girl at the church would not remember him.

While he ate a breakfast of boiled egg with meat and cheese sliced so thin you could see through them, he hoped and also thought. He thought of what was ahead of him: what he needed to find out, and how he might accomplish it.

*Whom did I kill?*

This seemed an obvious starting place. From the age and appearance of the victim, he was probably one of Maarten's graduate students. He could ask around campus, or he could try to find photographs in some campus publication.

He drove to the University of Leiden, the oldest in Holland and one of the most prestigious. It had strong programs in Middle Eastern Studies, especially Arabic and Turkish. Someone there had to speak

Arabic, or English. In spite of his experience with deception, there was no way he could fake it in Dutch.

*I need to get a list of the students in Maarten's department.*

The university administration office seemed like the best place to find such a list. A young woman working there looked Lebanese to him—both Arab and European at the same time. He decided it was worth a try.

He walked up to the desk and politely greeted her in Dutch. She looked up at him. Then he switched to Arabic, still using the same tone of voice, "Excuse me, but by any chance are you Lebanese?"

She was surprised. "*Awa.* Yes, I am."

Mohammed immediately and subconsciously clicked into his "tease 'til you take" approach, which worked at least ninety percent of the time with both men and women. Especially women.

"Ha-ha!" he said a few decibels louder than an instant before. Yara nearly jumped out of her seat.

"I knew it, I knew it! Oooww, little sister, you can't fool your big Lebanese brother! I can tell from across the room when I see a Lebanese face." Mohammed bent forward a little and lowered his voice. "We Lebanese are the most beautiful people in the world. Isn't it true? Just look around this room. Who else here is as beautiful as us?"

Yara opened her mouth but said nothing. It wasn't really a question.

"What beautiful part of our beautiful country do you come from?"

"Arnoun."

"Ah, yes, I know it. Just below Beaufort Castle." He suddenly feigned shock and put his hand on his heart. "But sister, now I have found you out," he shook a finger at her, "that means you are Hezbollah. I will have to report you." He looked around, "Where's the dean's office?"

"He's not in today."

"That's it! I have to move to this country. If you don't want to work, you just stay home."

"He's away at a conference. You are so crazy!"

"Sister, think. What would you say if you were the dean and you wanted a day off?"

She was getting brave enough to answer back. "If I told you that, you would broadcast it and I would never be able to use it. So, if you don't mind, I'll just keep it to myself."

"Ooooh, you are tricky! Tell me little, how long have you been bringing sunshine to this cloudy nation?"

"My parents moved here when I was small."

"Ahhh, but your Arabic is so good! And your accent! We know the Lebanese accent is the best, the best! The most bee-uuutiful of the Arab world. It is so smooth." He put his chin up and patted his throat. "Just as smoooooth as . . . my camel's rear end!"

She laughed and put her hand to her mouth. Arabs were always raving about the Lebanese accent—perhaps it was the years of French occupation—but she had never heard it described quite this way before.

"Oh, that reminds me, I hear my camel calling," he said, "I'll be right back as soon as I tighten his muzzle."

Mohammed walked out of the office.

The administration office had several desks and counters scattered around. Everyone looked at Yara quizzically. Not knowing how to explain him, she said, "He's my cousin," which in a way could be said of any Lebanese who visited her, so she didn't feel too guilty about it. And it seemed like the only explanation that would make sense.

Mohammed wanted to do some little nice thing for Yara. He could only find a bar of Dutch chocolate at the nearby student store. It was simple, but it should serve.

Mohammed reentered. He extended the chocolate bar to her and said, "My camel sends you this. He is sorry he cannot come in to give it to you himself, but he is smoking a water pipe with a professor's horse right now and doesn't want to offend him."

There is an Arab cultural line between being very friendly and openly flirty. Mohammed knew how to walk it well. Being flirty would have implied that he thought Yara had loose morals. Being very friendly was brotherly; although it often had the same effect.

He proceeded to tease her about her workmates, the condition of her desk, and then the color of her blouse. He laughed a lot and got her laughing too. He made it seem as if life were good, and to be enjoyed. Which in fact, at that moment it was.

"Really, sister, I'm serious. You are the nicest person I have met here in Holland. I think I will come to graduate school here. But just to be sure, I would like to ask a few questions of some of the students in the Department of Middle Eastern Studies. That would be wonderful!"

At the last, he rested his hand on his chin so she could be sure to see his face, even if she did the modest Arab thing and looked away. Then the coup de grâce: he ended with a smile that extended to the corner of his eyes.

It worked. Yara gave Mohammed a course list and lists of the graduate and undergraduate students in Maarten Hoog's department.

Mohammed walked around campus, following through on his claim to interview students. Since he did not want to spend weeks at this, he had a plan to narrow the list.

He would stand outside the Department of Middle Eastern Studies asking for specific men with Middle Eastern names. He would talk to the ones he could find, and see if any were missing. Then he would investigate as many details of that person's life as he could find.

By noon he had crossed several men off his list. *Still alive.*

He had suspected that the man he had killed was not an Arab, based on his appearance. Turkish was his guess. During the grand exodus for lunch, he found a Turkish-looking student and used the few Turkish words he had learned during his trip to Istanbul. They were enough to make a connection.

"Hey, *arkadash*!" he called to him. "Do you know Mehmet Kasap?"

The student looked shocked. He spoke in Turkish, then repeated in English. "Haven't you heard, *arkadash*, they found him dead yesterday. Killed himself in the old windmill."

*Fools! How can you hang yourself with your hands tied behind your back?*

Then the student said something enigmatic. "He must have failed."

"Failed at what? A class? The term isn't over yet, is it?" asked Mohammed.

"Sorry," the student said, starting to leave, "I have to go. *Jumma'* prayers today, you know."

"Where?" Mohammed asked. "I would like to go."

"*Tamam*, but I'm going to the one in Dutch. You would probably want to go to the one with the Arabic *khutbah*. Oh, that's where Mehmet went. It meets *orada*," he pointed. "Over there."

"*Tesekkur ederhim*," Mohammed said, thanking him.

After the Friday prayer service, Mohammed stayed and spoke to a few students as well as the imam who had given the *khutbah*, or message. Then he drove by Mehmet's apartment. A police car was parked outside, so he kept moving on.

*I need to check out of my hotel now.*

What he found out at *Jumma'* prayers provoked even more questions. He wanted to stay in Holland and ask them, but if he did, he might have to stay a very, very long time.

No suspicious words were said as he checked out. But in his room the picture had changed.

*Someone has been here.*

The room was in disorder. Not torn apart, but everything had been moved, as if it had been checked and replaced. He ran into the bathroom and pulled the towel out of the bidet.

*They didn't find them!*

The ancient Korans were safe.

That morning he had packed his clothes before he left, as a precaution. They had been rumpled through but were still in his suitcase. He put the manuscripts in the special case he had brought for them and left.

He dared not pass the desk again, which was wise. The desk clerk was in the process of making a call to report that he had returned. He quietly found his way out the back, through the kitchen.

If they were looking for him, he might not even be able to fly out of Holland.

*Germany, here I come!*

Chapter 30

# CLAREMONT DISTRICT

## Berkeley Hills, California

## 5 p.m., May 14, 2006

Most of the Emily Eliot house was shaded by large conifers, but one of the porches caught at least some afternoon sun every day of the year. Angela was seated in this spot on Sunday afternoon, finishing the handout on "Women Adventurers and Travel Writers" for her final lecture in Fatima's course. It covered her favorite women, including Freya Stark, Gertrude Bell, Lady Mary Whitley Montague, Beryl Markham, Maude Parrish, Amelia Edwards, Lilias Trotter, and, of course, Emily Eliot, whose house she now inhabited.

Angela selected anecdotes from her book to introduce this remarkable group of women. People liked stories of iconoclasts and reckless adventurers.

Angela had intended to keep her doctoral research, titled "How Women Adventurers and Travel Writers Impacted the Society of Their Day," to the academic community. But as she progressively shared her research with Honey Jean, she, too, became fascinated with these women.

This group of writers had been largely overlooked. Men focused on *Men.* The academic community and the East sniffed at them as "Orientalist," meaning pompous Westerners. Nevertheless they were a subject whose time had come. These were women that *Women* could be proud of and live vicariously through. They had done the daring deeds that men do, like explore the Nile, spy for England, and trek through deserts; they had done things men could not do, like investigate harem life firsthand; and they had done things that no one should do, like run off alone to the Klondike on their wedding day.

With Honey Jean's encouragement—and financial backing—Angela tweaked the thrust of her research from analytical to biographical, sensationalized a few bits, and voila! Besides a thesis, she had a great book, titled *Skirts on Camels.*

Now Angela inhabited the Arts and Crafts bungalow of one of her heroines. You couldn't say the house was perfect, because no house is, but she was certain Emily—and Honey Jean—would approve of how the renovation was updating it yet preserving the architectural components Emily had brought from around the world. Angela's favorite, a small parlor, had eighteenth-century French boiserie in grayish green, with gilt trim.

In truth, Angela did prefer her Palladian Pacific Heights home, but living there was no longer an option. John had made her move, although probate was still open.

Even though there were large windows in Emily's house, the dark wood inside and the tall conifers outside made it rather gloomy. Angela preferred light, but during this period in her life, there was something appealing about having a dark hole to crawl into. The first few times she visited the house, this consoled her. It made her feel like she deserved to curl up and cry.

But by the time the contractors had come, she recognized this tendency and fought against it. She purposely had the plastered walls painted warm colors, and thinned out the trees in order to let in more light and view.

Now, seated on her porch on a warm spring afternoon, she had an odd sensation. She used to sit in her salon in San Francisco looking over at Berkeley. Here she sat in Berkeley looking at San Francisco.

*Is John sitting there now?*

She set down the handout and picked up the letter sitting on the table beside it.

## Chapter 31

# BEIRUT, LEBANON
## May 15, 2006
## (May 14, PST, USA)

N*asir is in denial.*

He refused to talk about the problem Mohammed considered urgent: Who was killing manuscript researchers? Nasir seemed unbelievably able to believe the unbelievable—that the deaths of Maarten Hoog and even his good friend Ibrahim were natural. He was content that they had Maarten's manuscripts.

Three weeks had passed since Mohammed had returned from Amsterdam. He and Nasir were double busy, studying not only their own manuscripts but now those of Maarten too.

Each manuscript study entailed detailed photos and microscopic examination to view any possible writing underneath the current text, since in centuries past it was not unusual to recycle velum in the way Renaissance artists repainted canvas. Then there was analysis of writing style to determine the age and location of origin, as well as cataloging of the passages and pages present to determine whether the loose pages were likely from that or from another Koran. The size, cover, and order of the chapters, or suras, as they are called, were also important.

Whenever his mind was not needed to focus on the work at hand, and sometimes even when it was, Mohammed found himself coming back to the problem of "them," and the deaths of fellow researchers, which to him were unrecognized murders. He loved to bounce ideas off people and was frustrated to have no one to talk to about this urgent situation. He started thinking he should have told Nasir the truth about how he had gotten Maarten's manuscripts.

But before he had resolved much, his thoughts would pop back to his manuscripts, or politics in Palestine, or his property there, or questions regarding Islamic Law, or his favorite quest of all—how to access the Topkapi Codex. The result of this wandering attention was the resolution of no single issue. However, little by little, invisible progress was being made on several fronts.

*What had happened to the manuscripts Ibrahim was working on?*

Mohammed had wanted to call Elena immediately after they got her letter, to ask her if Ibrahim were studying any manuscripts when he died, and if she knew where they were. But Nasir said such a questioning would be unforgivable during her time of grief. Mohammed deferred to his elder, and didn't call.

He didn't regret that. If anything, he should have gone in person. Now the urgency was greater, but the trail would be cold.

As Mohammed saw it, if Ibrahim's manuscripts were still around, then his death could be suicide. If there were no manuscripts in his possession when he died, there were two possibilities: one—he never had any and killed himself; or two—he had had them, but they were stolen in conjunction with his murder.

He was also working on approaches to find "them." Every day he would Google the lists of experts Nasir had thought might be "us" and might be "them."

First he narrowed the list. Some had died. Some he could find no information on, and others had ostensibly left the field—although any of these could still be in the game, just low-profile players like themselves. Once he finished going through the list, he started over again to update their activities.

But while researching on the Internet he stumbled onto something. *Paltalk.*

There were hundreds of "chat rooms" in Arabic on Paltalk, which hosted ongoing live verbal discussions on a variety of topics. Many were religious channels where Muslims debated "infidels." On others, Muslims debated among themselves the points of law and practice of the way of the Prophet. One could speak anonymously, so there was tremendous openness.

The chat rooms with the most promise, he thought, would be those discussing the promotion, protection, and preservation of the purity of the faith.

Mohammed loved to listen to the strident proclamations, and he was often tempted to get himself a "handle," or invented name, and tell them what he knew. But now was not the time. He was still trying to learn who could possibly want to kill academics—innocent researchers like Ibrahim, Maarten, Nasir, and himself.

Mohammed found it satisfying flipping back and forth between several rooms until he found one discussing a potentially fruitful topic. At times he would hear about related blogs and Web sites and check them out too. He began to spend most of his free time monitoring Paltalk.

*OK, boys, this is a siege.*

It was a game of waiting and watching. Sooner or later someone would give something away, and Mohammed would be there to hear it.

## Chapter 32

# CLAREMONT DISTRICT

## Berkeley Hills, California

## 5:30 p.m., May 14, 2006

*Dearest Angela,*

*I am not able to come to you in person, but want to share with you one last time.*

*Surprise! I bought you a house! Why?*

*First, because I want to surprise and thank you. After reading your book,* Skirts on Camels, *I developed a deep appreciation for those women. Emily Eliot helped me find courage. Do you remember when she was traveling from Damascus to Palmyra, and was kidnapped by a notorious sheik? That was when she learned "True courage is not the absence of fear, but staring it in the face and walking straight into it." That proverb has been as good as a therapist to me. Living married to Tom-Tom I've needed to apply it many times!*

Angela paused in reading. She remembered Honey Jean's fear of flying, and could imagine the last time she had applied it.

*I asked my agents to keep an eye out for any house on the market in northern California that had been owned by a literary figure. It took two years, but imagine my delight when Emily Eliot's house itself came up for sale!*

*The second reason is because I think one day you may need a place of your own. I hope not, but you may.*

*My father died before I entered college. He suffered from depression, and finally took his own life. This was such a scandal in Charleston society that my mother moved our family to Atlanta. Good came of this, of course, because there I attended Emory University and met Tom, and you. But it may be from my father that our John gets his tendencies. For years I couldn't admit this.*

*Never be afraid to seek the truth, like I was. As Emily said, "Ignorance is perilous: it keeps us powerless."*

*I know you tried to please John. You married young: it may have kept you from developing into who you really are. When you are free, you will have a chance to find out.*

*May this house surround you with love. And may it remind you that Emily used to say, "I'm not dead yet!" and begin another adventure. When you get the chance Angela—embrace it!*

*Love forever, Honey Jean Hall*

A few birds started squabbling high above. A family squabble, no doubt.

*Family. I don't have one anymore.*

Her husband didn't want her. She had no children. Honey Jean was family, but she was dead. Her parents were dead.

But... as the letter said, *she* wasn't dead.

And actually, she *did* have family of her own. She wasn't close to them, but they were family.

*Yes! I will go to Dearborn and visit them. Right after the term ends this week.*

She felt a warm spot on her chest, but she wasn't sure if it was the thought or the patch of sun coming through the trees.

Just then she heard a loud whistle.

Doc Molly was stomping up the front steps. Apparently she had been a closet fan of the skirted women who rode camels and was excited to see one of their houses.

When she got close enough to be heard by bellowing, the Doc announced in a booming voice, "Hey, kid, you sure do look purdy sitting there. It reminds me, *'There is nothing like a combination of liveliness and loveliness for landing a place in the sun!'* Remember which one of your traveling ladies wrote that one?"

Angela smiled and called back, "Maude Parrish, of course! Doc Molly, welcome to Emily Eliot's house. I'm house-sitting for her the next few decades, but I'm sure she won't mind a visitor!"

## Chapter 33

# PARIS, FRANCE
## May 19, 2006

"Yes, of course I remember your family. Nasir was my husband's dearest companion for many years. He often spoke of their times together at al-Azhar," Elena Berger replied. She spoke decent Arabic, with a low pitch and a combination of French and Algerian accents.

Elena's father had been a high-ranking officer in Algeria before its independence. She returned to France to attend university, and, more comfortable with colonial culture than Parisian, she and Ibrahim became friends. They remained friends during the time he was studying at al-Azhar, and when he returned to France, disillusioned with Algeria and Egypt, they were married. They had raised two children, lived in a townhouse on Île Saint-Louis, and been very happy.

*She sounds very sad.*

Mohammed was very careful to moderate the tone of his voice and pose his questions well. "Aunt Elena," he said, using the common Arabic term of respect, "I know this is probably not the best time for me to call, but I have a few questions for you about Uncle Ibrahim. Would you mind?"

"Not at all. I love to talk about him. It brings him back."

"I know what you mean. Auntie, I am wondering if you know of any special projects he was working on before he died?"

"He was always working on a special project. I suppose I can tell you now, what difference would it make? For the last few years I believe he was working on some old Korans."

"Wow, wow, wow," Mohammed said under his breath.

"What, *habeebee*?"

"What was he studying them for?"

"I don't know any details. He wasn't supposed to talk about it, and I didn't press him. We respected each other."

Madame Berger fidgeted with a few expensive bibelots on the Louis XV table beside her. The beautiful flat seemed so empty now. So purposeless. Like her life.

Mohammed took a long shot. "By any chance, Auntie, do you still have the manuscripts?"

"Oh. I'm sorry, Mohammed. He never brought them here. My self-control only goes so far. Sooner or later I would have looked at them if he had—I read just enough Arabic to get me into trouble. I believe he kept them in his office at the Institut du Monde Arabe. You could ask them there. They did send me a box of things after he died, but there were no manuscripts in it. Only a few personal effects. His photos, desk set, things like that."

"I see. I suppose I could call the institute. Who would you suggest I speak to there?"

"Mohammed Ahmer is the general director. He would probably know what happened to the contents of his office. May I ask, *habeebee*, why you are interested in Ibrahim's work?"

"Auntie, have you ever heard of Sahih al-Hoot?"

The woman unexpectedly started laughing. "Oh, so that's it? He was back to work on al-Hoot? Some big fish never die."

## Chapter 34

# UC BERKELEY
## May 19, 2006

Angela had a few minutes before she gave a final in her Victorian Novel class. There were only ten students in this upper-division class, which made her think that Doc Molly might be right about the future of English literature.

During the break she checked her cell phone messages and returned a call from Doc Molly. Fatima's landlord had finally sent the police to the university to find out what had happened to her. Would Angela please call Morocco, ask what to do with her stuff, and get rent money for the last two months?

Angela still had Fatima's mother's number.

The Kareem house was in the garden district of Fez. As she called, she remembered the last time she had walked through the gate in the imposing outer wall and along the paved walkway of the front garden to the open door. Inside she was overcome by the conflicting emotions of awe and grief. The rooms were white and glistening, like a wedding cake, with tier upon tier of intricately carved plaster arches and domes, lit high with small windows. But on the marble floors below, the women hovered over a hidden white form, too mangled for viewing, and cried.

Fatima's mother answered her call, but she directed Angela to call Fatima's older brother Hamzeh, at his office at the university where he taught.

"Fatima's things? We don't want them here. Sell whatever you need to pay off her debts, and do what you want with the rest—keep it or throw it out," he said in a tone that seemed to add "for all we care."

His attitude reminded Angela of when they had met, the day of the funeral. He had arrived shortly after she did. Angela was standing near Fatima's mother when Hamzeh entered, kissed his mother, and said, "So, Fatima's dead?" in a cold voice, as if he had expected it.

And Angela had thought it strange that there was no Muslim religious ceremony, no *Salat al-Janaza* for Fatima. The men of the family simply took her body to the burial site. Angela went with the mother and other women who had read Koranic verses over the grave.

Now, Hamzeh impatiently agreed to fax Angela notarized papers giving permission to dispense with Fatima's possessions.

## Chapter 35

# DEARBORN, MICHIGAN

## May 28, 2006

*Aunt Mona is a nag.*

This unhappy realization came to Angela Sunday afternoon. The passing years and her eagerness to find family had dimmed this detail. Mona was a complainer, she knew, and a gossip—that practically went without saying—and often entertaining. But the nagging was hard to take. Poor Uncle Mohammed was usually the brunt of it.

She had always loved her uncle, Mohammed Sharif, and his peaceful manner. When she was a child he would speak to her as if she were a real person, not at all the way that grown-ups usually speak to a child. Whether it were a little girl showing him a butterfly or an imam discussing the Koran, each received the same attention. It was said that when the Prophet Mohammed looked at a person, it was as if that person was the only person in the world. In this way, Uncle Mohammed was just like his Prophet.

As far as Aunt Mona was concerned, he could do nothing right. An adult herself now, Angela could see that he was too unearthly for Aunt Mona's practical and rigid world. This might be why Uncle Mohammed would spend much of the day at the park at the end of the street or at the Islamic Center of North America—America's largest mosque and new showplace—to pray and have religious dialogues.

Their house was one of the tidy, gabled brick dwellings on one of the shaded parallel streets north of Ford Road and south of Warren Avenue. Angela's childhood home, now inhabited by her brother, was just a few blocks away on a similar street with similar houses. Her childhood friends had lived nearby. Her grandfather lived next door to Aunt Mona.

Angela had the vantage of both an insider and an outsider at the same time. Having lived and visited many places, Angela could see just how unique her hometown neighborhood was. It looked like many other such neighborhoods in America, but with one major difference. Nearly every house was inhabited by Arabs. In fact, until she went to Fordson High School she did not even have non-Arab friends.

Now, as on most evenings during the few weeks between cold and hot weather, the family was seated on the front porch. Her aunt's house originally had a small porch, but it had been extended years ago so the whole family could sit outside at the same time.

And their house wasn't the only one. Many of the houses in the neighborhood had extended porches.

Angela looked around at the most peculiar scene: rows of houses looking like something from Grimm's Fairy Tales, populated by groups of Arabs on the porches, drinking Arabic coffee they were warming over portable burners. Many were dressed in total discord with the style of their houses—women in hijab scarves, men with Western shirts, but some with tight hats or in white robes. Angela's writer's mind couldn't help inventing a little scenario.

*It's as if a genie has whisked them all from Damascus and planted them in a European village without their even noticing it. They simply keep talking and drinking coffee!*

"Here he comes now," Aunt Mona complained as Uncle Mohammed approached. "Where have you been? Your family comes all the way from California to see you and you just take off and leave. Angela is so hurt!"

Angela was mortified. Mohammed looked knowingly at her, and she was relieved.

"Were you talking to your buddies in the park all afternoon? I hope you found a few Shiites and told them a thing or two about *muta'a* marriage!"

Aunt Mona turned to Angela. "Can you believe it, dear, temporary marriage has found its way to Dearborn! Most of my friends are Lebanese, and you know I am not one to be judgmental, but when you get too many of those Shiites together, no good comes of it. Isn't that right, Mohammed?"

She did not expect an answer. Uncle Mohammed sat down and slowly poured coffee from the copper-clad beaker into a small porcelain cup, the size of a shot glass.

"Things have really changed here since you were a child. So many immigrants! First the Iraqis and now the Yemenis! Oh, my dear, the poor Yemenis, hardly Arab at all, they are. So poor. And ignorant! You would not believe it. Most of them can scarcely sign their names. Their women are treated as little more than dogs. Isn't that right, Mohammed?"

"Really, Auntie?" Angela was surprised. She had learned in school that Henry Ford liked Arabs, and started hiring them to work at the first Ford plants. Soon, more and more Lebanese started coming, then other Arabs, until Dearborn, Michigan, home of the Ford Motor company, had the highest concentration of Arabs in America. There had been few Yemenis when she lived there. It was mostly Lebanese with some Palestinians, like themselves, who were culturally similar to Lebanese, and a sprinkling of other Arabs.

Uncle Mohammed looked at Angela without speaking.

"Yemen is so near Africa, you know. They have picked up some very backward African traits, I can tell you. I know we should respect veiled women, but when they are all covered in black, and what with their blood being mixed with *abd*, you can hardly even see the tiny bit of black flesh around their eyes."

The word "*abd*" took Angela aback, until she remembered that Arabs use the word for "slave" to describe black races.

Aunt Mona continued: "How can we make friends with women like that? Some of the men have more than one wife. When a girl hits puberty, boom! That's it. They pull her out of school and make her sit home until they can find a husband for her. And they have no idea of how to keep house. Most of them even have to be trained in how to turn on a water spigot! Their yards are such a mess; I hate to even go into their part of town. It is a good thing they have their own mosque."

Angela had a very sober expression on her face. Aunt Mona was talking very fast, and Angela, a little rusty in conversational Arabic, had to concentrate hard to catch it all. And she was trying to process what of this monologue could be true, and what was exaggeration.

"Uncle Mohammed," she asked, "What do you think?"

She knew uncle would be kind, but honest.

"Well," he answered slowly, "we were just discussing at the mosque yesterday how to help the new Yemeni immigrants."

*Very good answer.* But Angela was still not sure what to make of the sociology here. It seemed that now that there were more and different groups of Arabs here, the sense of *ummah*, of community, was strained.

Uncle Mohammed got up to leave. "Excuse me, please. Mosquitoes."

Angela looked around at this primarily Lebanese neighborhood. Everyone looked so content. She looked next door at her grandfather's house.

*Except there.*

A twinge of guilt overcame Angela.

"Auntie, have you seen much of my Grandfather O'Connor?"

"He doesn't come out much, *alhamdulillah*," she looked up to heaven and then back at Angela, "forgive me child, but we keep our separate ways. From what I can tell he is pretty much the same."

Just then a dusty old Mustang drove up. Angela recognized the head inside long before its owner came out and showed his red hair. It was duller now than his childhood carrot top, but sure enough it was her brother "Re-Pete"—Peter O'Connor Jr., her father's look-alike son.

Chapter 36

# DEARBORN, MICHIGAN

## May 28, 2006

Re-Pete walked up beside the porch but did not set foot on the Sharif property.

"Well, if it isn't the millionaire bride, home to do charity with the factory folk." His voice had a mocking tone. "What happened? Prince Charming dump you?"

Angela struggled not to grimace. He had been drinking and made a wild guess, but it came too close to the truth.

"Hello, Re-Pete. Nice to see you again. Come up and share some coffee with Aunt Mona and me."

"No, thanks. I didn't come here for A-rab coffee. I'll be in visiting grand-daddy if you want me."

Aunt Mona folded her arms and looked at Angela with a sour expression. "*Ya Allah!* Except for the brown eyes he's Pete all over again."

"I really should go next door and say hello to grandfather before it gets too late."

"My niece is a brave woman," Aunt Mona said with the sweetest smile of her entire visit.

Half an hour later Angela came back.

Aunt Mona put a hand on Angela's shoulder, as if consoling her. "How did it go?"

Angela shook her head; it was not what she had hoped for. "He didn't seem to recognize me. He's gotten senile."

"Gotten?" Aunt Mona chuckled. "Always was, if you ask me!"

"He was going on and on about 'that damned A-rab prophet who lives next door. Thinks he's Jesus or something, but he's a dirty pedophile. I saw him with a string of little girls. Someone ought to put him on his camel and send him back to A-rabia!'"

Angela gave a gruntlike laugh. "It would be funny if it weren't so sad . . . and mean. Do you have any idea what he's talking about?"

"I suppose the intolerant old grouch is slandering my husband, whom all the world knows is a saint," she said, acknowledging Uncle Mohammed's goodness. "But the pedophile part, where could he get that? Oh!" She giggled. "He must mean my granddaughters! You know how nice your uncle is to children. It seems he thought my little girls were his wives! Oh, ho, ho! I have to tell this to your uncle!"

"Grandpa must have mixed up Mohammeds past and present."

"I'm sorry, and I know he's your grandfather, but how he and Re-Pete and your dead father can be your flesh and blood, I can't imagine!"

"Auntie, I don't mind telling you that my parents' marriage has always been a mystery to me. They were totally mismatched. Mom was serious and intelligent. Dad was good times and liquor."

"That's the way I remember it, dear, and I can see the best of them both in you."

"Not the liquor, I hope?"

"No. I think we know who inherited that part."

As she said this, Re-Pete emerged from the house. He was carrying a shotgun.

*So that's why Re-Pete was visiting grandfather. Scavenging.*

"Not much point in staying around to talk to that old geezer," he said to her as he walked toward the Mustang. He shut the trunk on the gun. "See you around, sis. Next decade, maybe."

They watched him pull away.

"Tell me, Angela, can you remember anything good about Re-Pete?"

"Not much. He and Dad were for each other. Mom and I kept pretty much to ourselves. That was a good thing, I guess, because that's how I learned Arabic."

Aunt Mona redirected her nagging. "Angela, forget about the O'Connors. They didn't deserve Malaak, and they don't deserve you either. And why you want to spend the summer in Turkey makes no sense to me. Go to your own people. Go to Palestine. You have a cousin getting married there in July. And you haven't been there since you were what, ten?"

*Don't I always have a cousin in Palestine getting married?*

"And if you have so much time, go to see my sister Zahara in Lebanon. She looks much like your mother did. Or go to Egypt, or to any Arab country—we will find connections for you there from our friends in Dearborn. Go where the food is good and you can speak the language. Your Arabic is OK, dear, but you are out of practice."

"If Dad caught me speaking it he would start one of his anti-A-rab tirades, and Re-Pete would join in. I still can't believe how Father could curse the 'damned Arabs' for getting all the best jobs at Ford and taking over the neighborhood, right in front of Mom. She was so brave, but it hurt her. Tell me, Auntie, how could she marry him?"

Aunt Mona looked at her tenderly, incredulous. "You honestly don't know? Malaak never told you?"

"All I know is that she was living here with you, which is another mystery—why would a nice Muslim family send their girl to live with her sister in America when she was only fifteen years old?—and she met and married the boy next door. I know you wouldn't have set it up. How did it happen?"

Aunt Mona put her hand to her mouth and rubbed her lips. "Well, I suppose there's no harm in your knowing. Oh, dear, how shall I put it. Your mother and I were close. I was five years older, and when your uncle moved us to America, we missed each other very much for those two years.

"Then Uncle Ayman got up to his old tricks again," she continued. "When your mother told me about the situation, I was furious. I spoke to your Uncle Mohammed, and he called your grandfather and insisted that Malaak come to America to be with us. Here she would be safe."

"What are you talking about, 'safe'?"

"Because she was pregnant, of course!"

Angela's jaw dropped. She had never been so shocked in her life. All this time, and she had never known.

"Not Re-Pete!" she said.

Aunt Mona laughed. "No, not Re-Pete. No one doubts who Re-Pete's father is!"

"Do I have a sister?" Angela asked, hopeful.

Aunt Mona pushed at the air with her hands. "Hold on, now, dear. Your mother had a miscarriage as soon as she came to America. But I'm sorry to say she couldn't get over it. I kept telling her it wasn't her fault, that I knew about Ayman, but she felt dirty somehow. She used to tell me that she would never marry."

"Was she angry?"

"Sometimes she was. But many times she would just sit and cry on my shoulder. I remember one Saturday, she had cried all the morning, and in the afternoon she walked down the street to visit a friend. When she came home she stopped in the front yard to talk to your dad. Later she said to me, 'Mona, maybe I will marry.' But she said it joylessly."

"So why did she marry Dad?"

"She was beautiful! The most beautiful girl in Fordson High. Your father wanted her."

"Of course I can understand that. But why did *she* marry *him*?"

"I've asked myself that over and over. He was an amateur musician. Always out playing at parties and drinking. I knew he would be no good for her. She could have had any young man in this town. Many came to our house asking your Uncle Mohammed what he could do for them. He presented them to your mother, and she refused them all—even young men I had heard her praise."

"Wow."

"Do you know what I think? She didn't feel good enough for the kind of young man that she would want."

"Beauty doesn't mean anything if you feel ugly on the inside."

"And she didn't want to be a burden to your uncle and me. She married the boy next door because he was a dirty American, and he didn't deserve anything better than what Uncle Ayman had made of her."

"What a strange sort of martyrdom. Poor Mom needed post-traumatic counseling, but people didn't get it in those days."

Aunt Mona folded her hands and wore an expression of disgust. "And Uncle Ayman needed castration!"

## Chapter 37

# BEIRUT, LEBANON
## May 31, 2006

Mohammed flopped into a chair on the balcony where the family was having breakfast.

Nihla exclaimed, "Mohammed, you're a wreck!"

ImmMohammed flattened down his hair as she walked by with a jar of apricot jam. "Oh, my boy," she chuckled, "just look at you."

He wore the same shirt as yesterday and had dark circles under his eyes and a two-day beard. Obviously, he had been up most of the night.

"Paltalk?" asked Nasir.

"Coffee," answered Mohammed.

Mohammed sat unaccountably quiet throughout the meal. He even let Nihla pass off a few remarks without rising to the occasion, which surprised everyone, including himself. But he was exhausted, and his mind was elsewhere. For the past few days, he had been on the trail of a fresh lead.

When the women had taken everything but the coffee away, Mohammed opened up.

He fingered the coffee cup and spoke slowly. "I know who 'they' are," he said in a quiet voice that was both casual and confidential at the same time.

Nasir said nothing. He looked Mohammed in the face and waited.

"Ibrahim and Maarten were murdered. Ibrahim's manuscripts were stolen. I know who murdered Maarten. I have no idea who murdered Ibrahim, but I know the name of the group that is behind it all."

"And so?" Nasir sounded disinterested.

"So we have to stop them."

"There I disagree with you. No one is bothering us. We have heard nothing from the chief. Let's just keep on doing our work."

Mohammed was annoyed and too tired to argue with him. "Fine," he said. Then he rose from the table and went to bed.

# Chapter 38

# ISTANBUL, TURKEY
## June 1, 2006

There was no one to meet Angela at the airport. She knew Selim would be in Ankara on family business, but he had supposedly arranged something. Angela waited an hour, which she considered respectful. More than this she considered stupid, so she used a survival skill she had learned from Honey Jean, and had a taxi take her to the best hotel in the Sultanahmet district.

The cold reception continued. Although the drive to the hotel was beautiful, with views of the sea and old city walls, the taxi driver was curt. At the hotel it was no better.

*Is it the American passport, or are my traveling clothes rumpled?*

The bed looked tempting to Angela; she hadn't slept in over a day. But she knew well the best prevention for jet lag was to keep moving until dark. She took her guidebook and walked out. From her hotel it was a short walk down the hill to the historic center.

First, the Hippodrome. The tour book assured her that it was as significant as the Roman Coliseum. Important events had occurred there since AD 330, when Istanbul, then called Constantinople, was inaugurated as the capital of the Roman Empire. The Hippodrome could seat one hundred thousand people for sporting events. Once, after a chariot race, a revolt had broken out that ended up with thirty thousand people trapped and massacred inside.

*These people take sports seriously.*

All that was left was the oval outline that served as the perimeter for a park.

Angela walked through the beautifully landscaped public parks that connected the Hippodrome with the Blue Mosque and Hagia Sofia Church. She kept pulling out her camera to shoot yet another angle of the domed and turreted buildings. She loved the way the fountains threw droplets high into the air, as if a lace veil interposed itself between the buildings and the lens.

Families and tourists walked by cooling fountains and bought roasted corn from street vendors with red carts. Compared to Morocco, where she had been a few months before, far fewer women wore hijabs; about twenty percent, it seemed. Many of these had bright floral designs. Abayas, nightgown-like outer garments, were not common, but some women wore long vests or khaki overcoats, even in the ninety-degree heat.

*Most of the covered women are either heavy-set, old, or Arab tourists,* Angela observed. *The younger ones dress Western, although more modestly on the whole.* She smiled at a devious thought. *Perhaps when you're no longer beautiful, you may as well become religious.*

She ambled around the cobblestone streets beyond Hagia Sofia and found herself at Topkapi Palace. She would be studying there soon, but she wanted to peek at the palace today.

Angela had read that the Topkapi Palace Treasury held the second-greatest collection of jewels in the world, with the originals—not copies—always on display.

She saw the Topkapi Dagger, jewel encrusted and gold, with the world's largest emerald. But what struck her more than the emerald was the dainty enamel basket of flowers. *A feminine touch on the scabbard of death.*

And she saw what was probably the best "Dumpster-diving" find ever: the Spoonmaker's Diamond. According to legend, this eighty-six-carat diamond, one of the world's largest, was discovered in an Istanbul rubbish dump by a spoon maker in the seventeenth century. It was brought to France and eventually sold by Napoleon's mother to ransom her famous son.

The collection lived up to the magnificence of its renown. There were crowns, golden thrones, and jewelry pieces large enough to be seen from the top balcony of the San Francisco Opera House. But to Angela, the lighting and drab black background of the displays were substandard. And most unforgivable was the dusty state of the jewels.

*They should auction a little piece and buy a vacuum cleaner!*

The palace was mostly one story. The exterior was stone, but from a distance it looked like the gray-white stucco she saw on cheap buildings in California. And the "ranch house" style of a series of porticoed rooms arranged around grassy courtyards left her with a distinct impression of an American elementary school.

Later, she found a better vista from the hotel's roof terrace: a 360-degree view over the architectural wonders of the city.

*Ah, now that's more like it!*

At dusk, she was making some notes on what she had seen and jotting down ideas for her research when the unexpected show began. The weather was perfect. The sky was mellowing to pink when the first call to sundown prayer was heard. One by one, the muezzins of mosques all over the city started their calls, until Angela was surrounded by calls to prayer.

Angela recognized the words of the chantlike call, for they were in the sacred language of Arabic. The same call was heard here in Turkey as in every Muslim community around the world. It was part of what bound the *ummah* together.

*Allahu akbar, Allahu akbar*
*I bear witness that there is no god except Allah*
*I bear witness that Mohammed is the messenger of God*
*Come to prayer*
*Come to prosperity*
*Allahu akbar, Allahu akbar*
*There is no god except Allah*

She stood up and walked around the perimeter, looking at each mosque in turn, now floodlit, and each silhouetted by a different color of sky.

The calls overlapped, like a ten-part version of "Row, Row, Row Your Boat." It was polychromatic in sound the way the sky, with its shades of pink, peach, yellow, and blue, was polychromatic in color.

*Pacific Heights, you've found your match.*

She sat back down. The feeling of being surrounded by beauty and holiness at the same time was one of the most moving sensations in the world.

*Tomorrow I will buy a Koran.*

"Where have you been?" The voice on the phone was angry.

"Excuse me, who is this?" Angela asked.

"You won't be able to pronounce my name. Just call me Arzu. I went to pick you up at the airport. I waited there for two hours, walking around and around. I was standing there with a sign with your name on it. Weren't you looking at all? You were supposed to look for the sign."

"In fact I did look, but I couldn't find you."

"That's not possible. There was only one place you could have come out, and I was standing there with the sign. What are you trying to do? Don't you realize how this makes me look?"

"I'm afraid I don't understand. I haven't complained. I just didn't see you. What possible motive could I have to miss my ride?"

"Americans!" Arzu answered.

"What?"

"Just meet me in the lobby in half an hour."

"Certainly I will meet you. Tomorrow morning at ten o'clock."

## Chapter 39

# BEIRUT, LEBANON
## June 1, 2006

Mohammed had been quiet for two days. Today was Thursday, and he had worked in the lab all day. Wednesday he had slept most of the day, worked in the lab a little in the late afternoon, spent a few hours on the Internet, and gone to bed.

Zahara Atareek could sense that Mohammed needed some cheering, so she made *minsaf*, a favorite Palestinian dish from his childhood. Then she urged her husband to find out what was wrong with him. Nasir felt guilty, knowing it was him, but said nothing.

After dinner he went to see Mohammed, who was in his room listening to Paltalk.

"Heeey, come hear this, *tfaddal*," he said, in his usual inviting voice.

"Mohammed, I'm sorry. I really am very interested in what you have discovered."

"Forget about it. I was tired."

Mohammed turned down the volume on Paltalk and continued as if no time at all had passed since he began this conversation. "I admit I am puzzled by the silence of the chief. Perhaps it's too risky for him to tell us."

"Too risky?"

"Ah, you're right, maybe it's not that. Maybe he can't because he's being held prisoner in Beaufort Castle!" Mohammed joked, referring to the Crusader castle captured by Saladin.

Ordinarily this flip would annoy Nasir, but tonight he was glad to be back on speaking terms with Mohammed.

"Let's start at the beginning. First Ibrahim dies. We don't know who killed him."

"We don't even know he was killed," Nasir cut in but stopped himself and raised his hand. "Sorry, sorry. Go on."

Mohammed continued. "I called Elena. She said Ibrahim was working on manuscripts when he died. He kept them at the institute."

"Let's call. See if they still have them."

"They don't. The director of the Institut du Monde Arabe says they were picked up by an Arab man calling himself 'Jabbar' something. He told them he was from the research group in charge of the manuscripts Ibrahim was working on, and showed them some sort of paperwork."

"Do you think he worked for the chief?"

"There's more. His secretary apparently overheard him speaking to me because an unusual thing happened."

"What?"

"She walked into his room and interrupted to say that Ibrahim had received a call from an Arab man the day he died, and she saw the two of them together when she was on her way to the metro. She did not think of it as being important at the time, but as far as she could see from a distance, the man resembled 'Jabbar,' but he called himself something like the dam in Egypt."

"Aswad," said Nasir.

"And Elena is sure she doesn't have the manuscripts?

"She's sure."

"Next, Maarten. He was killed by a grad student named Mehmet Kasap."

"Turkish?"

"Immigrated to Holland from Eastern Turkey with his family as a boy."

"How did you find that out?"

"He started chasing me after I got the manuscripts and he had a leeetle accident."

"A dead-end?"

"Ha-ha! You are funny today," Mohammed said. "I did a little research on him. The most interesting facts I found at the Friday *khutbah.* The imam praised Mehmet, an Arabic scholar who was leaving Holland to continue his studies elsewhere. Mehmet had been disgusted working with infidels. They were unworthy to handle the Koran. He was so pure in heart, the imam said, that he suffered every time his teacher touched an old manuscript. It was not a coincidence that the two of them died in the same week. It was sad that Mehmet would not continue with his studies, but he would be in paradise now, having served in jihad. The imam then exhorted all those in the room to take Mehmet as their example in the fight against the infidels and Western aggression."

"Ah, so they preach like that in Holland too," said Nasir, being used to this in the Middle East. "Tell me more about the imam. How old was he and what was his name?"

"Exactly!" Mohammed exclaimed. Nasir was slow, but also a truth seeker. When Mohammed had sufficient proof, Nasir would admit his mistake. That time was now.

"He's between your age and mine. He went by Abu Alim, which sounded like a made-up name to me, and I didn't see him on your list. When I got home I researched all I could find on him in Arabic and English. Not much was written, there may be more in Dutch, but that won't help us. I kept listening on Paltalk. Remember, no one uses their real name, but he had a distinctive high-pitched voice with an Egyptian accent, so I thought I might recognize it. About a week ago, I heard him on a jihadist room."

"What was he saying?"

"The same sort of thing, encouraging the faithful to promote the faith and keep it unpolluted by infidels, and he let a Dutch word slip."

"Do you think he is leading some kind of group?"

"I don't know who is leading it, but he referred us to a Web site, which in turn referred us to a blog on which someone wrote, 'If you really care about the integrity of the Koran, and are willing to die, or kill, for it, consider joining the Mus-haf Brotherhood.'"

Nasir tightened his lips and nodded his head slightly. He knew *mus-haf* referred to early Koranic manuscripts. "There's a Mus-haf Brotherhood? They've been killing Koranic researchers? It's a bit of a stretch, but it could fit. What do you think we should do about it, Mohammed?"

"I think we need to tell Jamal al-Hajji as soon as possible."

# Chapter 40

# ISTANBUL, TURKEY
## June 2, 2006

*Eastlake Style is what we'd call it in San Francisco,* Angela thought, but didn't dare tell Arzu, or "Our Zoo," as she thought of her.

Arzu was driving her through the streets surrounding Topkapi Palace on their way to the house Selim was renting to her. The area had many preserved Ottoman-style houses. They were angular, two- or three-story townhouses with closed-in balconies that overhung the street. From these, the women of the house could observe the activities on the street while still secluded.

The façades were clapboard, either varnished wood or painted cheerful colors. The bright white fringelike wooden trims both accentuated their boxy appearance and softened it at the same time.

Despite the Victorian flavor, the cobblestones leading to the door of Angela's townhouse were a clue that this was not San Francisco. Arzu quickly showed her the house and left—which suited Angela fine.

On the inside, the townhouse reminded her of a Swiss chalet, yet it was distinctly Turkish. Some of the walls were paneled, and the bathroom was Turkish tile. The floors were wood. Ottoman-style furnishings were used throughout—carved chairs and tables, upholstered benches attached to the walls, window seats, and Turkish carpets.

Selim would meet her here tomorrow morning and officially show her around Istanbul. Angela was feeling the twin hands of jet lag and overwork pushing down her shoulders, so she was glad for a day to rest.

The kitchen was thoughtfully stocked with simple foods, which are the best for jet lag. She opened the windows and let the warm breeze freshen the air. Fully clad, she still felt like an odalisque as she relaxed on the built-in sofa, drinking tea and reading.

On the floor in a corner was a suitcase of study materials she had brought with her. Angela reached in and selected one of her favorite books: *The Turkish Embassy Letters* by Lady Mary Wortley Montagu.

Lady Mary's wit always made her laugh, and her descriptions of eighteenth-century harem life were tantalizing. As the wife of the English ambassador, she was one of the few outsiders allowed into Ottoman harems—visits that were anticipated as much by the bored wives and concubines as by herself. And she brought Turkish fashion and the smallpox vaccine back to England.

Until the late afternoon, Angela was on the sofa with Lady Mary, slumbering off and on, ensconced amid mountains of cushions. Unhappy thoughts of her life back home were gone.

Then she felt very awake and went walking. There were many little offices and shops in other Victorian buildings nearby. Turkish pottery, although brightly colored like her own collection of majolica pottery, was like none she had seen before. It was very lively and also textured. At first the colors were too garish for her, but she heard them challenge, *Be bold! Take hold of a new life!*

So she bought several pieces to make a "majolica room" of her back hall in Berkeley.

And she held to her promise. In one of the little bookshops, she bought a Koran.

# Chapter 41

# ISTANBUL, TURKEY
## June 3, 2006

"Welcome to the cage."

Selim dramatically invited Angela into a room of Topkapi Palace.

"Is this the part of the harem where they kept the disobedient concubines?" she responded. "It certainly has more exquisite tiles than our prisons in America."

"Perfect! You fell into my trap."

"Am I to be the next inmate in this prison? Hmm, not too bad. Just bring me my research materials and a box of chocolates, and I will stay here until I have written enough to satisfy both you and Doc Molly!"

"Not that kind of trap. Although I'm delighted to think of you as a disobedient concubine. I was testing you, to see how much you know about the harem, or *heramlik*, as we call it in Turkish."

"I could have spared you the trouble. All I know is where the entrance is. Otherwise, I've only read comments from women travel writers, and theirs was an outsider's view."

"Theirs was not a view 'from the cage.'"

"OK, Selim, so what was . . . is this cage?"

"The room you are standing in is where the royal princes were kept as prisoners, totally shut off from the outside world."

"That sounds cruel. Like the tower of London."

"Actually, 'the cage' was a mercy. Before that it was the law that the new sultan had to kill his brothers. The most notorious example is Mehmet the First. He had all nineteen of his young brothers circumcised to get them ready for heaven, then strangulated. The oldest was probably eleven."

Angela whispered quietly, "'This is the English, not the Turkish court, not Amurath an Amurath succeeds, but Harry Harry.'"

"What did you say?"

"Shakespeare. A line from *Henry IV*. He knew Turkish history—and human nature. But Selim, that kind of injustice doesn't sound like Islamic law."

"It wasn't, it was the Ottoman law. The idea was to prevent brothers from fighting each other to become sultan, which is always a risk in monarchies. Something they did worked, because they had the longest-lived dynasty in the Muslim world."

"In spite of killing their own princes?" Angela paused. "The world rejoices when a son is born. Those mothers must have cried."

"In the seventeenth century the sultans were starting to loathe fratricide too. They had an idea," Selim continued. "If they could keep a close eye on their brothers, they would not need to kill them. So the princes were locked in these beautiful matched rooms, with no outside contact except for mute eunuchs and barren concubines."

"Hear no evil, produce no evil."

"Exactly. The only formal education they received was from the Palace School *before* they came here, and many came as small boys."

Angela laughed. "No wonder the sultans had a reputation for running wild in the harem. It looks like that's the only training they had!"

"You laugh, but there is a lot of truth in what you say. Before they began shutting them up, the princes used to participate in military campaigns and administering the provinces. They trained to be true leaders and good sultans, like Selim the First and Süleyman the Magnificent. Afterward, when they came to power, they were uneducated and inexperienced."

"When you have lived in a cage long enough, you don't want to come out."

"Sultan Selim the Third tried to make reforms but fell into disfavor with the Janissaries, and he ended up killed by the chief eunuch."

"Oh, I've heard of the Janissaries. Lady Mary said despite the sultan's great pomp and wealth, he lived in fear of the Janissaries—his own guard."

"What else did she say?"

"That the only truly free people in the empire were the women."

"Based on?"

"The fact that the clothing they wore outside the house totally covered them, making them anonymous, so they could go anywhere and do anything! Do you think she was right?" Angela asked.

"Don't women always do just what they want?"

"Not where I come from."

"So that's why you're here. To write about how women can get what they want?"

"I don't know what I'm going to write about. I need to learn more first. It will probably be something about how women's rights developed in Turkey, and what the world can learn from it."

"Just write about yourself," Selim said.

"What?"

"You already have what women want."

They had walked into the Pavilion of Sultan Murad III, within the harem. Considered one of the most beautiful rooms in the palace, it had been built by Sinan, Turkey's famous sixteenth-century architect. Intricate floral and arabesque patterns of blue, coral, and gold covered the walls and ceilings. And there were two huge carved gilt canopy beds.

Angela laughed. "I'm not sure what you mean, but if you refer to spending a night here," she said, pointing out the beds, "that's not what I want."

"Too bad. As Minister of Culture, I could get you one."

Angela continued. "Most women don't want to be beautifully dressed in a harem. We just want a chance… to show what we are made of."

"I'm looking," Selim said.

She could see that he did not understand. "No," she laughed. "I mean we just want to be treated equally with men."

"And be killed like the nineteen sons of the sultan who built this room?"

"Wow. So this was his room. How sad. All that work for nothing."

"What work?"

"What those two beds went through to make twenty sons!"

## Chapter 42

# ISTANBUL, TURKEY

## June 4, 2006

"Selim, I want take to advantage of you."

They were finishing lunch in the Kebab House, which had earned a reputation for having the best kebabs in Istanbul. Angela only liked tender meat, and theirs qualified.

From their seats on the upstairs patio they overlooked the Spice Bazaar, the Süleymaniye Mosque, the Yeni Cami Mosque, and the Galata Bridge.

"I don't know what that means, Angela, but I like the sound of it." He smiled hopefully.

"I mean, what's the point of having the Minister of Culture for your friend if you're too proud to learn anything from him?"

"I can teach you. I will dedicate my life to it."

"I won't be here that long—unless someone breaks into your cage tonight, circumcises and kills you."

"Uhh. If you promise to prevent that, I will take you to Istanbul University, Marmara University, and Istanbul's Women's Library. And of course, you can ask me anything you like."

"That's exactly what I want. A combination of both. I could read books—but then I also want someone to bounce ideas off of, someone who knows how things work in Turkey, and the history here. Otherwise I could spend a lot of time reinventing the wheel or coming up with utter nonsense."

"Yes," he rubbed his chin, "I can see your point. There are already too many people spreading nonsense about Turkey. We're trying to get into the European Union, you know."

"Well, I can't promise I'll get you in. . . ."

"I will settle for getting into your bedroom."

The time had come to say something. Angela could not face a summer of sexual harassment.

"Selim. You are very nice. I like being with you and learning from you—and you are helping me a lot, more than I could hope. But please remember, I am married."

"Were married," he reminded her, raising a finger.

"But..." she paused, thinking of how to say this nicely, not wanting to insult her tutor "... as I said, I want to study a harem, not be part of one."

"I am not married...."

She had to make it clear.

"Selim, frankly, I'm not attracted to men with sultanic appetites."

"I'm not... oh, you mean..."

"The tattoo. That's right. Don't feel badly about it. I'm not judging you. It's just that even if I were over John, I'm not attracted to men who are attracted to... *women*... I mean all women in general."

"Please let me explain about the tattooed girl," Selim softly pleaded.

Angela took a deep breath and let it out. "Go ahead."

"I was not trying to seduce her. She came to my office and stood right next to me and..."

"And?"

"It's been a long time since I saw my wife."

"I am sorry about your wife. All I am saying is that I am glad we are colleagues and friends, and I would really like your help—as long as we are just friends, you know, *arkadash*."

"No problem, *arkadaş*," Selim said in his sophisticated, matter-of-fact way. "You study, and then you bounce me. And if you do a good job, I'll reward."

"I don't think that's quite what I said," Angela laughed.

"Now for your first reward."

"Reward?"

The Bosporus cruise is a scenic ride up the sea through the riverlike channel that separates two continents and connects the Sea of Marmara with the Black Sea.

Being a peaceful day, the water was smooth, and the buildings on the banks shone in the sun. Angela's head kept turning from side to side, wanting to see whatever she wasn't.

She had been to many places since she married John, so most new places reminded her of old places. The Bosporus cruise reminded

Angela of the Rhine cruise, especially where rocky crags were surmounted by castles looking from Europe to Asia, or Asia to Europe. But there was none of the oompah-pah music that the Rhine boats played.

Reminiscent of the villas along Lake Como, the banks were lined by modern homes, and eighteenth- and nineteenth-century villas, called *yalıs*, and Victorian palaces where the royalty moved when they tired of Topkapi.

But Turkey was definitely unique. One country, two continents. Its significance first struck Angela on this boat, Selim's yacht.

"Selim," she said loudly enough to counter the noise of the boat, "I am like Turkey, like the Bosporus—one part East, one part West."

In Yeniköy the boat turned around and took them a few miles back toward Istanbul. They would go to the Black Sea another day. Selim had something else in mind now. The yacht docked in front of a series of three beautiful *yalıs* that appeared to be attached to each other.

Their wooden exteriors were painted similarly to the townhouse Angela was renting. But they were much larger and more elegant. The two flanking *yalıs* looked nearly identical and were painted white, with white wooden shuttered balconies on the upper floors.

The middle *yalı* was coral colored, with arched windows and pilasters that were edged in white. A black iron balcony extended from the second level, and the top level was recessed in the front, creating an open terrace between the walls of the two flanking *yalıs.*

"These *yalıs* look like they had the same architect," Angela observed.

"That's because they were once all part of an old Russian mansion that my father split into three parts. This one is mine," Selim pointed to the white one on the right, "and that one is my brother's," he pointed to the white one on the left.

"And whose is the middle?"

Selim looked at her directly. "It's your reward."

"Oh, Selim, it's beautiful, but I have the townhouse, remember?"

"That's your study. This will be your home." He paused. "And you're not renting either. Just consider it Turkish hospitality!"

Angela didn't know what to do. Money was not the point.

*If I refuse, will it be an insult? If I agree, what will I owe Selim?*

## Chapter 43

# ISTANBUL, TURKEY
## June 4, 2006

"Which is more beautiful—Istanbul from the roof of your hotel, from the balcony of your *yalı*, or from the deck of this boat?"

"Teacher, if you keep asking unanswerable questions, I'll never pass," Angela answered.

"That's the idea," stated Selim.

Angela didn't want trouble, so she had at least temporarily agreed with Selim's housing plan. Now they were on a sunset cruise, and Selim was quizzing Angela on the topography of Istanbul—the seas, the headlands, the bridges, and the mosques silhouetted against the sky.

"Istanbul has a strategic location like San Francisco," Angela observed. "Land surrounding sea, I mean."

After dark they ate a delicious Turkish meal. On alternate days the cook traveled between Selim's *yalı* and his sister's estate on the Asian side of the Bosporus Bridge in the exclusive *Yedi Tepe*, or Seven Hills district.

"Tomorrow, when we fly out of here, you will see a view like you never imagined. San Francisco will be humbled," Selim boasted. "I will have my pilot circle the Cessna around each mosque and monument."

"Your pilot?" Angela asked.

"Yes. Remember, I said I would show you Turkey. Tomorrow we fly over the Aegean islands to the coast of Asia."

Angela's heart stopped for a moment. She thought of Honey Jean and Tom-Tom's last flight over the Bahamas. It must have shown on her face, for Selim caught something.

"Is anything wrong?'

"Oh, nothing." Angela forced a smile.

## ISTANBUL TO KUŞADASI
## June 5

It was a beautiful day for flying. In order to show off Istanbul, the pilot made a few steep curves that Angela doubted would be legal in America. Leaving the city that straddled two continents behind them, Angela saw Asiatic Turkey beyond the Bosporus.

The Turkish islands looked to her like Greek islands in summer: brown and green, with rocky coastlines and deep blue/gray water. They were nothing like the Bahamas.

Angela struggled to keep her mind on the view and off Honey Jean.

As they approached their destination, Selim's pilot circled the ruins of ancient Ephesus. Angela could see there were two sites: the first city, where only a single erect pillar remained from one of the wonders of the ancient world—the Temple of Diana; and the less ancient but more impressive ruins of the second city.

The elevated beige marble lobby of their luxury hotel in Kuşadasi overlooked the sea with large open windows. Like all hotels in the area, it had only a small beach. In the surf they found a green wine bottle with a Turkish love letter inside.

"I can't translate it," Selim said.

"It's too difficult for the Minister of Culture?" Angela asked.

"It just wouldn't be right."

They resealed it and tossed it back into the Aegean.

## KUŞADASI, TURKEY
## June 6

At breakfast Selim delivered another surprise: Angela was to tour Ephesus alone. He had been called to Ankara on urgent business and would need to spend a few days there; but he had arranged the best guide possible, second only to himself. The plane, a Sovereign, would come back tonight and fly her to Istanbul in the morning.

He gave a very reasonable explanation. "Someone has brought in a few broken pieces of marble to the national office. Apparently they were dug up with recent groundwork around the Southeast Anatolian Project. They need me to take a look at them to see if an excavation might be necessary, which would slow down the entire dam project."

"Wow, you're on call. I'm impressed! Being married to the Minister of Culture must be like being married to a doctor," Angela said before thinking.

"Would you..." Selim stopped himself midsentence.

## Chapter 44

# ISTANBUL, TURKEY
## June 8, 2006

*When Selim isn't flirting, I'm quite comfortable with him. He's almost like a brother.*

Besides possessing well-groomed sophistication, Selim and Angela were both triple-elite: they had social status, financial status, and academic status. Few others on any continent shared this combination. They didn't have to excuse their wealth or hide who they were from each other, as they sometimes did around those who were prone to jealousy or greed.

Angela determined to spend the first three weeks studying women of Turkish history, especially of the Ottoman era, and then move to the modern reforms that came with the Turkish Republic and Ataturk. She would spend the day reading in her townhouse or studying at the universities and libraries. And she would visit relevant places around Istanbul.

In the evening, she would return to the *yalı* to enjoy the cool evening breezes off the Bosporus. Usually she would meet with Selim for discussions over dinner, but occasionally during the day, as well. Some days he would be out of town. He didn't always say where he was going, and Angela didn't feel comfortable asking. Those days she would entertain herself or go out with new friends from the universities.

Selim brought interest to her studies by pulling out anecdotes from Turkish history or by stimulating her with a question to research for their next meeting. This gave the work a focus and brought the characters to life. And it kept her from feeling alone.

One day while at lunch in her townhouse, Selim and Angela were discussing the early sultans.

"Have you heard the stories of Sultan Ibrahim on the Marble Terrace?"

"No. Where is that?"

"You haven't seen the Marble Terrace? What about Süleyman's Pool or the Bagdad and Revan pavilions, which are on it?"

"I'm surprised I could have missed a porch big enough for all that, but I don't recall it."

"Come, I will show you."

And since her townhouse was down the street from Topkapi, they went straightaway.

"It's someplace you could overlook," Selim explained as they walked. "If the narrow passages from the third court were blocked for some reason, you would have to go through the garden in the fourth courtyard. It's directly behind the Sacred Relics Chamber. Do you know where that is?"

"Oh, yes, I remember. Not far from the jewels. But I haven't gone there. Frankly, relics seem bogus to me. And why would Muslims have relics anyway? We worship only Allah."

"They are souvenirs of Mohammed. My ancestor—I mean, namesake—Selim the First picked them up while he was conquering Egypt. I don't think they're worshipped, but people are encouraged by them. This way," he motioned. "We'll have to go through the garden. Do you see how green and simple this garden is?"

"Restful."

"It wasn't always like this. This used to be the flower garden of the palace. The sultans filled it with the most beautiful and the rarest flowers in the world. Then they would have private festivals here."

"You mean orgies?"

"Ah, they were splendid affairs. Besides the plantings, they would set up wooden walls covered with flowers and canaries in cages. It was so natural looking, you couldn't tell inside from outside. During the tulip craze everything was covered in tulips. At night there were lamps lighting the walls, with glass reflecting bulbs. And the whole palace was lit up as well."

"And let me guess," Angela laughed, "the sultan would sit up somewhere on a platform, watching his concubines run around. Then he would grab one and ravish her in the bushes."

"Actually he took her up to the platform."

"And ravished her in plain sight?"

"No, never! The chief eunuch pulled the curtain first!" Selim pretended indignance. "You insult Turkey's national character when you suggest such a thing. Did you know there's a law against that?"

"Where was the honor of Turkey when one of the sultans gathered naked virgins around him in the palace garden—I guess that would be here—and chased them naked himself, neighing like a stallion?"

"Now that was Sultan Ibrahim. Not much of Turkish honor in him. He was executed for his debaucheries." He paused and then lifted a finger. "Aha. So that's what you taught at the University of California before I came—to judge a nation by its worst."

"Oh. Now you insult the American character. But we don't have a law against it. There's not enough prison space for that."

## Chapter 45

# MARBLE PORCH, TOPKAPI PALACE
## Istanbul, Turkey
## June 8, 2006

Upon entering the Marble Porch, the presence of place overcame their conversation.

Angela said, "Wow! I can't believe I missed this!"

"The architecture here is the best in the palace," Selim said, referring to the Revan and Bagdad pavilions, "the supreme work of Turkish style. Although they are replicas of two that Murad the Fourth saw during campaigns in Persia."

"Now this is what I imagined a Turkish palace would be like! It's the perfect setting. Like a painting by Gérôme. In my mind, I can see naked concubines splashing in the pool and fountain, or seated there, richly dressed, lounging on carpets and cushions, listening to lutes."

"You imagination is so good, I can almost see them too!"

"I'm sorry to tell you, Selim, but before I saw this I agreed with Lady Mary that Topkapi architecture was not impressive."

The two pavilions surrounding Süleyman the Magnificent's Pool resembled each other in interior decoration and in shape, both being octagonal with overhanging roofs, but they differed in size and prospect.

"The Bagdad Pavilion," Selim explained, "is the larger one with the sea and city view. The Revan Pavilion is smaller and has the pool view."

"What's behind the colonnade over there, to the right?" Angela asked, pointing out an area to the right of the Revan Pavilion.

"That's what connects the Revan Pavilion to the Sacred Relics Chamber. Remember, the Sacred Relics Chamber was once the sultan's private quarters. There was a little passageway so they could easily get to the pool."

"Of course, like we have in California—master bedrooms with glass doors onto the pool patio."

Ornately carved and latticed marble edged the Revan colonnade and Süleyman's Pool. Within the pool was a three-tiered square fountain.

"This pool, or *havuz*, is all that is left of the water gardens of the palace," Selim said. "Sultan Ibrahim used to sit here in this little bronze gazebo overlooking the pool. It's called the *Iftar* Kiosk because the sultans used to break their fast here at sundown during the month of Ramadan. When he turned around, he could also see the waterways, and the terraced gardens leading to them."

"Great place for watching the sun go up and down," Angela said.

"He would also get comfortable and watch puppet shows or comedies on the terrace or his concubines singing and dancing, swimming and lounging."

Angela thought about Ramadan's prohibition from sexual relations as well as food during daylight hours.

*He was probably thinking of breaking more than one kind of fast.*

"Sometimes Sultan Ibrahim would get up and throw everybody into the water."

"Sounds like a California poolside party."

"But once, Ibrahim tied up his entire harem in sacks, about three hundred of them, and threw them into the Bosporus," he turned around and pointed to the sea, "just off there."

"Why on earth would he do that?"

"For the fun of choosing a new harem."

Angela looked out across the Golden Horn, sickened by what those women faced for the whim of a man who supposedly loved them.

"And we call America a throwaway society," she said.

"But let's not focus on the bad players. This was originally the porch of Süleyman the Magnificent. Süleyman used to lounge in this very spot with his one and only wife, Roxelana, the passion of his life."

"Roxelana," Angela rolled the name off her tongue. "That sounds like a Las Vegas showgirl. Was she a concubine?"

"Originally, yes. We don't know much about her, but there are legends. Here in the seraglio she was given the name Roxelana for one of three reasons, depending on the story you believe: either because she was from the Russian Ukraine, because she was from Ruthen in Poland, or because she had red hair."

"I like the red hair version. My father was a redhead, and so is my brother."

"Were they? When the sun hits on your hair at a certain angle, you are too."

Selim stopped. "Oh, my god, she probably looked like you." For a moment, Selim's eyes scared Angela because of their detached expression.

"You're not going to give me any reincarnation crap," she said indelicately, to startle him.

"Excuse me for being rude." He waved a hand in front of his head. "It's just never occurred to me before that you resemble Roxelana."

"Why should that matter?"

"I've always been fascinated by her, and the mystery that surrounds her."

He quoted something in Turkish.

"Was that gibberish anything I should know?"

"Süleyman's poetry. I'm not sure how it would sound in English."

"I love poetry. I've never been able to write it, but I can appreciate it."

"I'll try translating it. Roughly it goes,

*Throne of my lonely niche,*
*Light of my bedchamber,*
*Your eyes of mischief,*
*Intoxicate me with your love.*
*My very own queen, my everything,*
*My beloved, my bright moon,*
*My intimate companion, my one and all,*
*Sovereign of all beauties, my sultan.*

"Turkish poetry being new to me, I'm not sure how good a poet he was," Angela commented, "but he sounds like a tremendous lover. You realize, of course, if we knew the truth about Roxelana you'd probably be disappointed. Maybe she was just another sex toy...."

"Some said she was the devil and cast a charm on him. Why else, they said, would he disband the entire harem?"

"Scandalously unnatural!"

"But Süleyman only saw the good in Roxelana. To him she was beautiful, intelligent, and great fun. His name for her was *Hurrem*, which means 'the laughing one.' She became the first legal wife a sultan ever had."

"What, Turks don't marry?"

"Remember the antidefamation law...."

"Anything more about Roxy and Suley—oops, is that defamation?"

"I'm glad you're not European, or we wouldn't have a chance at the EU!"

"Your law, your problem. Back to the dark side of..."

"Roxy? I'll let you discover that for yourself. Study the 'Sultanate of Women.'"

# Chapter 46

## BEIRUT, LEBANON
## June 10, 2006

"Thank you, gentlemen, for your patience. I haven't been feeling well, and this is the first day that I could get out."

"Well, Jamal, we would be happy to meet at your house, especially since you've been ill," Nasir said.

"Frankly, Nasir, I am glad for the opportunity to get out. I've been in and out of bed for weeks, so it's nice to see a little life again."

Jamal al-Hajji was a self-professed infidel of the worst kind. He had traveled the route of Nasir and Ibrahim two decades earlier, and ended up becoming what imams warned would happen to anyone who questioned Islam—he became an atheist. He was an apostate under a death fatwa.

Al-Hajji now lived out his last days in semi-hiding in Beirut, under an assumed name, like an old Nazi in Brazil. He was sound in his academics and still retained a historical interest in the development of Islam, so he had been invited to work on the same project as Nasir and Mohammed.

Although in his eighties, al-Hajji's mind was sharp. He remembered not only the multitudinous volumes of Islamic learning, which he taught at the Islamic University al-Madinah al-Munawwarah in Saudi Arabia, but he continued on with clever insights into the new manuscripts. It was he who noticed the difference in ink composition between AD 640 and 655.

Nihla brought in some coffee and sweets. She almost departed without saying anything, but al-Hajji smiled at her and asked how she was.

She answered, "I'm glad to see you are well today, Mr. al-Hajji. Did you come alone? I don't see Ahmed with you."

"He left me at the door. I sent him to buy some fresh fish." Al-Hajji was a gourmand, when his health was on target. Since he had ceased to believe in the afterlife, he made it a point to enjoy everyday life. Today he felt good.

Nihla looked disappointed about Ahmed, al-Hajji's live-in assistant.

Mohammed noticed and grimaced a little. "Give him my greeting," she said and left the room.

"I think I know why you have asked me here," Jamal al-Hajji said.

"We were wondering what you have heard from 'the chief.'"

"You mean Lord Fenburton, of course."

"We refrain from using his name," Nasir said indignantly, "just as he requested."

"Yes, I know, I only say that here, among us. I wonder if 'the chief' ever found out that we discovered each other's identities?" Jamal asked.

He referred to a time, several years earlier, when the project was new. He and Nasir had accidentally met and recognized each other while looking for the same equipment at the same time. It had been too much of a coincidence, and although they were under strict instructions to maintain secrecy, it became evident that the academic geniuses of al-Azhar and al-Madinah al-Munawwarah had at last joined together on one of the Islamic world's greatest projects.

Nasir stated, "We never talk about that. We simply get our manuscripts, study them, and return them. We do as we are told."

"The same with me, Nasir. The odd thing is that I haven't received my next set of manuscripts. They are overdue by more than a month. I returned my last set, according to protocol, but I have heard not a word since."

Nasir shook his head. "Strange."

"At first I didn't think anything of it. I was sick a lot—my diabetes is getting worse. I thought it was because I was sick that they weren't sent, but of course that wasn't it because I didn't tell him about my illness. Then I was so sick I didn't care. I just struggled to get well. But about a week ago I started getting better. I placed inquiries through all our usual channels, with no result."

"But he must still be alive," Mohammed added, "because I've been Googling him every day and nothing shows up in the obituaries."

"I have had an ominous feeling for some time," Jamal chose his words carefully, "but nothing that I care to speak."

There was a moment of silence while each man reviewed his own suspicions.

Nasir solicited Jamal's advice. As the senior member present, his word would be the most regarded. He would be the *mukhtar*, the elder. "We, too, have been placing inquiries in the usual channels with no results. We are at a loss as to what is happening and how we should proceed. Jamal, what would you suggest?"

Jamal al-Hajji spoke pleasantly, as if what he said was the logical choice between fresh chicken and old fish. "Then I suggest we try all the unusual channels."

## Chapter 47

# ISTANBUL, TURKEY
## June 13, 2006

There is a pricey restaurant in Istanbul, down by the waterside, where the fish is purported to be the freshest in town. When you arrive, you survey artistically arranged catches of the day. From these you make a dinner selection and have it cooked to your preference.

Selim brought Angela there before dark so they could clearly see what they chose.

"I have a surprise for you tonight," Selim said.

As they walked to their table they passed steaming pots into which customers had put their lobsters.

"Are Turkish baths really that steamy?" Angela asked.

"More. Have you seriously never been to a Turkish bath? And you a friend of the Minister of Culture?"

"Is that so shocking?"

"It's a huge oversight. You are here to study Turkish culture and history. Without an understanding of the bath, its significance, and its influence on everyday life, you will never understand Turks," Selim told her. "Angela, you must do research on this and report to me. Agreed?"

"This doesn't sound like a women's rights issue to me. Back home, baths had nothing to do with the women's movement."

"Turkey is not America."

"*Alhamdulillah!*" said a voice behind her.

"Oh, here's your surprise," Selim said.

Angela turned around and, knowing Selim's flair, expected to see some delight—perhaps an ice sculpture.

The surprise was as cold as ice, and as welcome as four-day-old fish.

Angela forced a smile. "Hello, Our Zoo."

Arzu was wearing full-length dark clothing with a black hijab surrounding her face. It did not frame a smile. She said, "Hello, Ang…"

"Angela," Selim finished. "I know you two have already met and are probably glad to see each other again and do some girl talk…."

*Is he crazy?*

"... but I ask you to consider the poor man in your midst."

Angela looked at Selim. She had seen his expression before.

"Angela, you've been studying harems and I thought you might like to talk to my sister. She's an expert in them." He gave her a wink out of the eye Arzu couldn't see. He had set the stage. Now he would watch the action.

"Not from personal experience," Arzu clarified. "I did research in harems at university."

After they had ordered *mezes* and several seafood dishes, Arzu started her lecture in a defensive tone.

"The purpose of the royal harem was not to serve as a brothel. It was to provide the sultan with an heir, and to serve as educational institution and finishing school for the wives of future officers of the empire."

"I'm glad they weren't hung up on virginity, like so much of the Middle East," Angela said, wide-eyed. Selim suppressed a smile.

*He's enjoying this. Fiend.*

Arzu spent about half an hour telling Angela things she already knew about harems, like that the word *harem* really implied "sacred or protected." A harem was a social institution in which women, including wives, female relatives, concubines, and children were kept safe from the dangerous outside world. With such a vast population as the royal harem had, there were rules and protocols to be followed.

She reviewed the complex hierarchy inside the royal harem. Concubines had different levels, each with its duties. These ranged from servant to harem managers to near-wife status of *kadin* and *haseki*, or "favorite."

*She omitted the fact that wives were vanishingly rare.*

The most powerful woman was usually the queen mother, called the *Valide Sultan.* "Since it was difficult to ensure a consistent sultana," Arzu explained.

*Because wives were expendable.*

"Besides women, there were children, including boys up to age eleven," Arzu continued, "and eunuchs. The eunuchs also had a hierarchy, each having different duties and honors involved with serving and protecting the women."

*She's leaving out details about the eunuchs.*

It seemed that Arzu considered eunuchs to exist only as appendages to the harem, as if they themselves were irrelevant. Yet Angela had found them to be one of the most fascinating aspects of the harem.

"Isn't it interesting how one abusive system leads to another?" Angela said, trying to appear objective.

"What do you mean?" asked Arzu.

"For example, slavery enabled polygamy, which required eunuchs to maintain it."

Angela knew it was not just the bodies and souls of enslaved women who suffered in the harem, but also of men. At the height of the harem, under Murad III, there were about 1,200 women and 1,600 eunuchs who were nearly equally black and white, but the latter group was never let near the women. The physical and psychological suffering eunuchs endured through castration and its aftermath was intense.

Angela decided to kick a little dust and said, "Since castration was not part of Islam, how do you explain the major role it played in the harem system?"

"Yes, it was a tradition held over from the ancient world." Arzu was only slightly put off by this question. "The Ottomans merely employed those who were already made eunuchs. There is no Islamic law against that."

Angela said, "But some castrations were actually performed within the palace walls."

## Chapter 48

# ISTANBUL, TURKEY
## June 13, 2006

A few days before, as part of her harem studies, Angela had read the graphic and horrific descriptions of castration procedures. She could not help but visualize men suffering them in anguish: their testicles and/or penis cut off or twisted into oblivion, then cauterized with boiling oil. Many times they did not survive, and tragically, if they did, they were often doomed to a life of sexual desire without sexual ability.

"Who suffered more in the seraglio," Angela asked Arzu, "the hundreds of women kept to indulge one man or the eunuchs who served them?"

Arzu's mouth dropped open.

"I know there is good and bad in every culture," Angela went on, "but why do all the books on harems say the West misunderstands them, then go on to give numerous examples of precisely what the West finds repulsive? Perhaps, from its own perspective, the West does understand harems and just doesn't like them. Isn't that OK, since modern Turkey doesn't like them either?"

Plainly, Arzu disagreed. She did not directly answer but took another tack.

"You mustn't think that all harem women were victims. Consider the one-hundred-fifty-year period known as the 'Sultanate of Women.' This proved that although women never directly ruled the empire, they could influence men and international relations, as well as rise to authority within the harem."

Arzu narrated the events of the Sultanate of Women, starting with Roxelana, followed by Nurbanu and Safiye, who exerted power over husband and son. Both women were in correspondence with queens of Europe, influencing Turkey's relations with France, Venice, and England.

"Interesting, isn't it," Angela interrupted, "that these powerful women all started out as, and frankly remained, slaves."

"I suppose you could call it a *form* of slavery…"

"I certainly *would.* And what is more amazing to me is that for hundreds of years the rulers of one of the world's greatest empires were the products of forced sexual relations between a master and his slave. In America we'd call that rape."

Arzu grew impatient. "You Americans simply don't understand what it was like here in the old world. Some of the harem girls voluntarily went there."

"We understand. We went to war to stop slavery in America a hundred years before it stopped in the Middle East and Africa . . . if it truly has stopped. . . ."

"No. I repeat, you Americans simply don't understand. I was hoping you would be different, but I can see I am wasting my time." She arose to leave. "Thank you, Selim, for the fish, it was most excellent. Excuse me, I must leave now."

As they watched her dark form retreat, Selim said, "You really are naughty, you know."

"Are you angry with me? Defamation and all that? I love Turkey! But your sister, Selim, is the patron saint of patronizing. She has no objectivity—and worst of all, no sense of humor!" Angela paused. "You must have known what would happen if she and I got together. . . ."

"I admit," he bowed his head, "I've been wanting to see something like this for a long time! Turkish women are the preservers of religion and tradition, but sometimes my sister goes too far."

"So far as revenge?" Angela queried.

## Chapter 49

# ISTANBUL, TURKEY
## June 22, 2006

"I have a surprise, which I hope will make up for Arzu," said Selim. "Tonight, I'll take us to the International Istanbul Music and Dance Festival's production of *Abduction from the Seraglio.* Guess where we'll see it?"

"In Topkapi Palace, the seraglio, of course, where the sopranos will be rescued from the *cruel* Turks by tenors singing beautifully in German!"

"If that is how you see it, I change my mind."

"You can't. That was the promise you made in San Francisco. In fact," Angela teased, "Mozart was the main reason I agreed to come to Turkey."

"And I used to think you were smart." He held up the tickets as if to tear them. "My Turkish honor demands I destroy these and take you to a Turkish play. Did you know that Istanbul residents typically go to live theater more than other Europeans?"

Angela snatched the tickets out of Selim's hands. "I'll take your word for it. Let's go to Mozart instead. But don't expect me to forgive you for Arzu unless the production is better than *Aida* in Rome's Baths of Caracalla!"

"It won't be the first time the Turks have defeated the Romans."

"Or," said Angela, thinking of this opera written when Mozart was young and in love, "the first time the Austrians have defeated the Turks."

After they had returned to the *yalıs* and said good-night, Selim pulled out his cell phone and hit return. A call had come in during the opera when his phone was on silent.

"*Merhaba*, Mustafa," he said. "Sorry I missed your call. I was out on business."

"What do you mean 'business'?" There was an edge to the voice on the other end. "Running all over Istanbul with the American infidel?"

"She's not an infidel!"

"So it's true, you admit what you've been doing."

"I'm doing nothing wrong. It's my job to 'run all over Istanbul,' and I can take whomever I want with me. In fact, it looks better if I'm not alone."

"You need to come to Ankara."

"I was just there last week."

"You need to come again. I don't think you quite have the concept of what we're up against. You could ruin everything."

"I think you are taking this far too seriously. It's nothing! There is no problem at all."

"Just like there was no problem when you joined the *Mevlevi* in Konya, and then the Alivi? And then that affair with your wife—that was a real killer!"

"Leave my wife out of it!"

"OK, but only if you cooperate."

"What do you want, Mustafa?"

"Meet me in Ankara tomorrow. I think you need to renew the vision. And another thing. Get rid of the American infidel, whatever it takes, or I'll do it for you."

# Chapter 50

# ISTANBUL, TURKEY

## June 23, 2006

The next morning, Angela read while lounging on her sofa in the soft sunlight. Images of the seraglio and the music of Mozart were dancing in her head.

She wore a loose gold and rust colored caftanlike dress with brocade trim she had bought from a shop around the corner. She liked to wear it while reading because it was cool, comfortable, and costly all at once.

Today she was reading about Turkish baths, when the phone rang. It was Selim. He was in Ankara.

*I wonder why he didn't tell me last night?*

On their way to the opera he had reminded her to read about the baths, and that he would discuss them with her—she thought he had said today. Maybe she was mistaken.

As it turns out, she was glad. There were many lurid details she was happy to learn about but would rather not discuss with Selim.

The baths were "hot" in more ways than one. Who wrote what about who did what in the Ottoman baths was fuel for the counter-Orientalist argument that the West willfully misunderstood the East.

The *hamam*, or Turkish bath, was a word she recognized, since it also meant "bath" in Arabic. In the art museums of Europe she had seen paintings of women in Turkish baths. Even then they seemed to her to be an excuse for painting naked women, not a social statement. To get an accurate picture, she read accounts of all the Western writers she could find, as well as translated Turkish sources.

*Selim is right. A lifestyle, even an entire culture, was largely centered on the ritual of the baths.*

Angela found that the roots extended back to the Roman baths. There were numerous public baths in every Turkish town. Topkapi harem at one time had about thirty; some were private and some communal. They were heated by a combination of pipes under the floors and fountains of steamy water on the walls. The sexes bathed separately.

Not all the accounts of Turkish baths could be true, or at least not concurrently. One group, which included Lady Mary, asserted that nudity was the norm. Others recounted that at least gauze was worn, which was the current custom.

The earliest accounts told of naked women lounging in steamy rooms, inspecting each other closely for signs that another treatment with the arsenic-ridden depilatory called "rusma" was becoming necessary. The women bathed each other and at times enjoyed it so much that they became lovers.

Although communal nudity may not have been the routine, it was indisputable that, to the Ottomans, two of the greatest sins were hair and lack of cleanliness.

A whistle blew. Angela looked up to see steam rising from her kettle. She got up and made mint tea.

*How do I sort out these contradictory accounts?*

Eventually she pieced together that the process involved three rooms:

The *outer hall* was where you would arrange your cushions and tapestries then disrobe in the semi-privacy.

In the *tepid room*, you would be groomed and massaged. Soap abounded, and the marble floors became perilously slippery. One sultan slipped to his death.

Then you would steam yourself in the third, the *hottest room.* Intense heat and steam in this room produced an ethereal scene, which in some people induced an opiumlike state of unreality. You could see little. You got into nearly boiling water. You felt that you might not survive. Then you heard voices and saw undressed women—real or imagined—running and laughing or singing Turkish songs.

Surrender took over and plunged you into deep relaxation.

Moving slowly, you returned to the tepid room, rinsed off in the central fountain, perfumed, and dressed. Back in the outer hall again, you lounged indefinitely on your own tapestry sofa, lightly clad, drinking coffee and eating delicacies.

Angela paused with her chin in her hand to visualize the scene.

*So sensual. And yet the baths helped liberate women!*

Islamic law encouraged men to keep their wives at home. But bathing gave women a sanctioned chance to get out.

The custom did little for the elite, who had private baths in their homes, but for the middle-class women it was a breath of independence. To pray, one had to be clean. To be deeply clean, one had to go to the baths. So bathing became a religious duty even the most reluctant husband could not refuse his wife.

Women took full advantage of the opportunity and spent many hours there several times a week in freedom away from home. As soon as they suspected body hair might be on its way, off they would go.

An Ottoman woman who went less than once a week was considered "devoid of delicacy and dirty." So she put a man's honor at stake. Not to mention the delights of his bedchamber.

And once outside the house, robed and anonymous, the women had liberty and could go wherever they wanted.

The bath ritual was a quixotic mix of sex and religion that reminded Angela of old Hollywood films. Who can argue with both God and nature at the same time?

## Chapter 51

# ISTANBUL, TURKEY
## June 27, 2006

"Have you read Pierre Loti?"

"As it happens," Angela answered Selim, "I am reading him now."

"Perfect for our lunch today."

Selim took her to the Pierre Loti Café, up the Golden Horn, on the hill above the Eyüp Sultan Mosque. Loti's former haunt was full of Turkish tiles and brass, ninetheenth-century furniture, and waiters in period dress.

"It's touristy here," Selim said, "but I thought you might like it anyway. You've never read him before?"

"No," answered Angela, "I know he's popular in Europe and Turkey, but he's not in America—too flowery and introspective, not to mention risqué for a century ago. But yes, this place does have atmosphere. I can almost see Azyade, lounging in the corner."

The corner table did have a woman lounging at it—an attractive woman who came in after them and who seemed to be eyeing them in spite of her posed nonchalance. She was, however, more fully covered than Azyade would have been when she seduced the French sailor in Loti's semiautobiographical novel.

Selim looked nervously at the corner and took a deep breath. He shouldn't have brought Angela here. He really would have to be more discreet.

"So you are reading *Azyade*?" he asked.

"No, *Disenchanted*. I guess you know it's about the women of the Ottoman period. So sad how they were married young—usually to an old stranger—and would exchange one locked harem for another."

Selim said, "Sounds like you've been reading my grandmother's life. Yes, that was common until harems and polygamy were legally abolished."

"I hear *Disenchanted* was the *Uncle Tom's Cabin* of Turkish women."

"Uncle Tom? I never heard of him. Did he come to Turkey?"

Angela laughed. "*Uncle Tom's Cabin* is the book on slavery that helped start the American Civil War."

"Are you suggesting Turkish women were slaves?

"You sound like Our Zoo! That's not what I said, or Loti either."

"What did he say?"

Angela paused.

The lines from Djenan's farewell letter in *Disenchanted* went through her head:

*Tell them, André, that our lives are smothered in sand, are one long death . . .*
*Sleep, sleep on, poor souls. Never discover that you have wings . . .*
*Be their advocate in a world where men and women think . . .*

"I've gotten myself into a corner," Angela thought. "What shall I say?"

She didn't want to offend Selim. Why was she arguing women's rights with him? To satisfy Doc Molly? To honor Fatima?

Angela punted. "I know what your sister would say. She would quote,

"*The key to paradise is at the feet of the mothers.*"

"You are right! She probably would. That's a good hadith."

"But all it means is that mothers have to be guardians of Islam, like your sister, because Islam is the way to paradise." Angela continued gently, "The hadith doesn't protect their rights. *Disenchanted* exposed this. In that way, it was revolutionary."

Angela looked pensively at the woman in the corner.

## Chapter 52

# BEIRUT, LEBANON
## June 29, 2006

"La, la, la! You simply cannot go, Mohammed!"

"I have to go. We're not making any progress this way," Mohammed replied.

"You harassed Elena, and what did you learn? Nothing."

"That's not true. I learned that the manuscripts had been taken. That was important."

"You mean you didn't find any manuscripts. If you go to England you will not make it back for the wedding. You know how difficult it is to travel to Palestine from Lebanon. It will take us days to get there!" Nasir was not only negative; he was angry.

*Family should come first.*

"This is the thing," said Mohammed, his hands pushing the air, palms down. "First an Arab man visited the Institut du Monde Arabe, saying he was part of the independent project that Ibrahim was on. He took the manuscripts *after* Ibrahim was killed. Then Maarten was killed, and then communication with Fenburton stops, and we all go crazy trying to figure it out.

"Now we know why," Mohammed continued. "Someone has to go to England and sort out what happened and figure out the status of our project. We can't just sit around forever, waiting for the Mus-haf Brotherhood to catch us. Jamal is too old and sick to go. I don't know Bilal well. You are his mother's cousin. You go to the wedding. If I can, I will join you."

"And if you can't? How can I explain that?"

"Tell them that I'm saving our lives."

## Chapter 53

# ISTANBUL, TURKEY
## June 30, 2006

Angela and Selim were having dinner on the terrace of his *yalı*, overlooking the Bosporus. Tonight was a celebration. Angela had finished her study of Ottoman women and was ready to move on to the modern era.

On the table were heavy silver candelabras of the kind used at Dolmabahçe Palace, mountains of flowers, gold-rimmed china, and an antique damask cloth. Flanking the table were candelabras and cascades of flowers. A live string quartet played in the background. Selim was making it special.

The candles and their reflections were flickering in the breeze, the drapes were peeking in and out of the French doors, and Angela's loose auburn curls seemed alive.

"I see the old Angela has come back," Selim commented.

At UC Berkeley, Angela had usually dressed professionally and even more so, often wearing society suits. But while she was researching in Istanbul, she went casual.

"I love it!" she had told Selim at her townhouse one day. "No one here knows me—and Turks expect Californians to dress somewhere between casual and crazy—so I am free. I feel incognito, like Audrey Hepburn in *Roman Holiday*!"

Tonight she had slipped back into her old image—a classic dinner dress and expensive jewelry.

Selim, in contrast, dressed more professionally in Istanbul than in Berkeley because this was his territory. But the dark pants and vest he wore tonight were not professional; they were both formal and approachable at the same time. Or maybe it was the open neck of his white shirt.

The temperature was perfect as they sat at the table, sated with food and soothed by the fragrance of flowers.

"Aunt Mona was wrong."

"What?"

"Aunt Mona said I shouldn't come to Turkey for two reasons:

because I don't speak the language—well, she was right about that—and because the food is no good. That's where she was wrong. My compliments to your cook. I love Turkish food. It's colorful. And the sauces and soups are excellent. They are flavorful without being too spicy."

"That's because Turkish food is not just Turkish. Do you remember what you told me about the sultans?"

"That rather than masters of empire, they were slaves to vice?"

"Right. And what were their vices?"

"Lechery, greed, and gluttony. Oh, I see what you mean."

"In their gluttony, the sultans pushed their chefs to discover more and more delicacies from around the empire."

"So you are showing me how good came from evil?"

Selim almost said something, and then changed his mind. "What did you study today?"

"The lives of ordinary women during the Ottoman period. There's not a lot to read. Most of what is recorded on Ottoman women is about the harems of the sultans and their officials. Court records and official documents seem about all we have for the poor. From these we know that women were selling their own textiles in Bursa, and that some widows managed their farms, that sort of thing."

They had a brief discussion, during which Selim again pleased Angela with his open-minded interest.

"Now that you have finished this study, how do you compare Ottoman women with those of 'the West' from the same period?"

"Choose your poison."

Selim was a little surprised at this response, but he played along. "Alcohol, please. Would you care for some champagne?"

"*Haram!* What would Arzu say?" Angela teased.

"Will I never escape my sister?"

"Maybe not, but if I were you, I'd keep trying. What I meant is that both systems were unfair but in different ways. For example, Islamic law, based on the Koran, states that women should inherit half as much as men. This law is still in effect and upsets women nowadays, but in the days of Mohammed and the Ottomans, it was really protective of women. Ottoman women had more control over their finances. Their dowries remained under their control as a buffer in case their husbands divorced them. As a result, wealthy women could sponsor building projects."

"True," agreed Selim. "Like the bridge the Valide Sultan built in

1845, to connect the old town with the diplomatic center. Now I will be literary—in Peyami Safa's classic Turkish novel *Fatih-Harbiye*, to cross that bridge was to pass from one civilization to another."

"That's what's so fascinating about Turkey—the uneasy beauty of mixed civilizations."

"We hope to take the best from both," said Selim.

"But watch for the two-edged swords. In the past in the West, the lack of a religious law allowed women to be denied an inheritance. On the other hand, this same lack *allows* women to inherit equally, as they do in the West now, but cannot under Islam."

"So if I want to be rich, I should marry a Western woman?"

"Only if she's from a rich family." Angela smiled. "But more important than money, at least to me, was the ability to go out and mingle with men. One sultan even made a law restricting how many times a week women could leave the house! In the Ottoman Empire, women were allowed out mainly to go to the baths because it was a religious duty. But in the West, women could go out in public at will and freely mix with men."

"But think of it, Angela." Selim held out his hands. "They missed out on Turkish baths."

Selim moved on. "I've heard music coming from your *yalı* at night. Have you been dancing?"

"That's how I get my exercise. I use the buffet cabinet for a ballet bar."

"Would you care to dance?" he asked.

Angela said nothing; she had been set up, and there was no way out. When Selim came over to pull back her chair, she stood and turned around. Her hair flashed red in the torchlight.

"Ah, Roxelana," he said. "If you were dressed like a concubine, I would believe you were her, reincarnated."

Angela blushed. The early Ottoman concubines wore short tight jackets that swept under the breasts, leaving them totally exposed, like ancient Cretan maidens. Later they were covered with the thinnest transparent silk, which was even more seductive.

*I hope Selim's not thinking about* that.

But Angela caught Selim looking at her breasts. Then he flushed, and they both laughed.

Selim assumed a perfect dance position and took Angela into his arms.

Just then, as if on cue, a soft soprano voice in the background started singing the love theme from the Saint-Saëns opera *Samson and Delilah.* The lights of Asia twinkling across the Bosporus blended into the stars overhead.

*How did he know that's my favorite aria?*

Selim whispered into Angela's ear, "I meant if you were dressed like a *sultana*—in layers of silk brocade, embroideries, a feathered turban, and a coat laden with jewels. Things like my great-great-grandfather Süleyman would have given to Roxelana."

Angela looked up at Selim in surprise and stopped dancing.

"Does that mean what I think it means? You *are* a prince?"

"My family had been living scattered over Europe from the end of the Ottoman Empire until the exile order was rescinded fourteen years ago. Then we moved back to Turkey."

The aria ended. The singer stopped.

*Why is he telling me this now?*

Angela walked back to her seat.

Selim looked confused but followed her.

"Tell me about it," Angela said, as if it were a problem that needed to be resolved.

For the next hour Selim told her of the wanderings and trials of his family. Since their return to Turkey, they had managed to reclaim much of their property and although no longer "royal," they were favored by the people and were much in the public eye. Some of the family even had political ambitions.

Selim was obviously disappointed with Angela's response to his revelation.

Angela smiled, as if she were making the best of a bad situation. "That must be why we're watched whenever we are in public. Drat! I thought it was my glamour."

"I wouldn't totally discount that..." Selim said.

Angela took a deep breath. "Well, I need to finish some reading tonight."

Selim came around to her chair and helped her up. She smiled as if nothing had happened.

She kissed him on the cheek and left. He watched her leave, carrying the moonlight on her shoulder.

Half an hour later Angela was reading, basked in warm light and cream-colored satin sheets. A sound startled her, and she looked up, surprised to see Selim standing at the far end of her room, shirt open halfway and carrying a single red rose.

*Uh-oh.*

Angela put down her book. "Did you get lost on your way to the bathroom, little boy?" she said in attempt to lighten the situation.

"I realize you are leaving for Palestine tomorrow and I forgot to say good-bye. I'll be leaving too."

"Indeed? Whither wander thou?"

"To Cypress, to be with my boys, who are with their grandparents for the summer."

"Good-bye. I'll see you in two weeks." She smiled as if it were the most natural thing in the world to have an uninvited suitor in her bedroom.

He approached her bed, walking with a smile and manner that made Angela admit to herself, *God, he is handsome.*

He held the rose just above her hand and said, "You could be my Roxelana."

"Could I?" Angela paused. Was she asking him or herself?

"For romance, Selim, there's no one better than you. But there are a few things keeping us apart. Good-night. I hope you can find your way back in the dark," she said. She held the rose in her left hand, and smiling, turned off the lamp.

Angela turned her head on the pillow and closed her eyes, pleased that she had resisted romance with a prince.

Selim was a friend. She did not want a lover. In fact, she had never seen a convincing love relationship and doubted such a thing existed. Just deceptive romance and quivering under the sheets.

And when she was tempted to believe in love, she remembered two faces: John's on an angry tirade, and Selim's with the tattooed girl.

*Ah, what a liberating thing it was to see others at their worst.*

## Chapter 54

# ISTANBUL, TURKEY

## Early morning, July 1, 2006

*A noise.*

Angela felt trapped. She wanted nothing more than to get out of the *yalı* quickly. Selim would not actually rape her, she was sure, but he might barge in again with roses and Turkish history.

*That Roxelana bit is beyond romantic; it's creepy.*

She got up. But it was three in the morning. There would be no ferries from Yeniköy to Istanbul now, she didn't have a car, and Selim's driver would be asleep. She didn't even speak enough Turkish to call a taxi.

*I'll just get dressed and doze in that chair until morning.*

By the time Angela got dressed, she wasn't sleepy. So she went online to read about Palestine and found an article on the beginning of the Second Intifada:

> *In the days before July 2000, there had been an air of hope lingering from the 1993 Oslo Accords—hope that the agreement which had softened the hostilities of the First Intifada could expand into lasting peace. But Palestinian president Arafat and Israeli prime minister Barak could not attach themselves or their peoples strongly enough. They had conflicting and greater attachments to the outcropping of land known as "the Temple Mount" to the Israelis, and "Haram al-Sharif"—the Noble Sanctuary of al-Aqsa Mosque to the Arabs.*
>
> *Besides this, there were reports of archaeological travesties being allowed by al-Waqf, the Palestinian entity in charge of supervising the Temple Mount. During the creation of a handicapped entrance and additional restrooms, portions of columns from early Israeli history were cleared away and thrown down the hillside into the Kidron Valley. Muslim remnants were respected. There was no scientific documentation of placement and context of the destroyed artifacts. History was lost.*
>
> *After July 2000, Arafat had his Tanzeem militia on standby.*
>
> *Then, on September 28, 2000, Israel's Ariel Sharon, leader of Israel's right-wing Likud Party, visited the Temple Mount. Speculation endures as to his motive. Was it simply to show homage? Could it be to inspect the mistreat-*

*ment of artifacts? Or was it the direct "in your face" sort of challenge that the Palestinians took it to be?*

*The result: the Second Intifada, or "uprising," of the Palestinian people. Young men went into the streets, demonstrating their objections by throwing rocks at the powerful Israeli war machine. In a world that loves winners, but is inspired by the courage of the weak against the strong, these boys looked like heroes—until you heard the hate slogans they sang and recited.*

*But not all young men have such a limited arsenal.*

*The Gaza Strip is the most densely populated spot on the planet. Joblessness and hopelessness abound and bring with them, as they always do, discontent and violence.*

*Between January and November 1, 2001, 52 Palestinian suicide bombers killed 250 civilians, and injured 2,000 more. Those who die carrying the bombs are martyrs, they say, who will take 70 relatives with them to paradise. Those civilians who die with them, according to their teachings, will enter paradise with the bomber, themselves a sort of martyr to unnatural death. Not to mention political gains.*

*Security became heightened throughout Israel and the occupied territories of Palestine. Previously crossing a checkpoint was a relatively simple matter. You would drive your own car up to a booth manned jointly by Israeli and Palestinian soldiers, working together. You would show your papers, and by and large pass unhindered.*

*With the Second Intifada, checkpoints became like international border crossings. Except that now they were manned only by Israelis: two or three guards in the booth, and two snipers above in towers or on roofs.*

*If you happen to be in Palestine during an Intifada, forget taking your own car from Palestine into Israel, and even to most places in Palestine. Take a taxi to the checkpoint. The soldiers will check your paperwork and compare your name against those on the "black list" of wanted individuals. Then you take a long walk down an armed corridor in the open air; for example, the one outside Ramallah being about a ten-minute walk. On the other side of the corridor, if you want to travel to Jerusalem, you must take a specially approved taxi with yellow license plates.*

*Beware: there are three ways you can get killed at a checkpoint:*

1) *You may inadvertently be caught in the cross-fire between the Israeli army and the Palestinian Tanzeem Militia,*
2) *The guards may get suspicious of someone and shoot preemptively. For example, you may be shot in the confusion when one soldier tells you to "go" and another says "stop." In that situation, anything you do is wrong.*
3) *A suicide bomber may target the Israeli guards at the checkpoint.*

*It is never safe to cross a checkpoint during an Intifada. But then, how much life can one surrender to caution and still call it* life?

From what Angela read, the situation was not a great deal better now. She felt tense.

*Another noise. Outside.*

Angela reached for the nearest weapon she could find—a spiked-heeled shoe, and crept out on the balcony.

The seas were rough. Below, a boat knocked against the dock, reproducing the worrisome sound. She looked up again. There was no one on the balcony either, but to the east, in the far distance, the glow of early dawn was backlighting the Asian side of the Bosporus.

*The sky is shedding roses. . . . I carry the vision with me into the next world.*

That's what Loti's heroine Djenan said as she left Istanbul, and life.

No, Angela would not come back to this *yalı*.

## Chapter 55

# COTSWOLDS, ENGLAND
## July 1, 2006

Unsung Masterpieces of the Eighteenth Century *opens today at the Ashmolean Museum in Oxford. While Reynolds, Gainsborough, and Richard Wilson have become British cultural icons, the current exhibition features works by their lesser-known contemporaries.*

*Lady Elizabeth Fenburton is a contributor and one of the organizers of the exhibit. Speaking from Fenridge, the ancestral family estate she explained, "The eighteenth century had such a wealth of excellent painters that many went unrecognized. The idea for the exhibition came from a painting by Tilly Kettle, which found its way back home to Fenridge, after two hundred and twenty years. Because of competition in England, Mr. Kettle went to India, where one of our families sat for him there. The painting traveled from India to America, where it was found at auction a few years ago."*

*Although the exhibition was delayed two weeks due to Lord Fenburton's accident and subsequent coma last April, Lady Fenburton has inspired the museum staff with her resilience and enthusiasm. Works by Maria Cosway and English sitters of Vigée Lebrun will also be featured.*

Mohammed looked at the newspaper article again. After months of daily scrutinizing the Internet, this was all he could find. But it was enough to convince Nasir that he needed to go to England in person.

Today was not a visiting day for Fenridge, but the gates to the stately house were open, so he drove down the gravel to the roundabout in front of the house and parked.

He saw a gardener in a wide-brimmed straw hat at the right side of the house, deadheading flowers.

"Excuse me, ma'am," Mohammed asked respectfully. He had never been in England before, but knew it was formal. "Would you know if the family might be home today? I'm looking for Lady Fenburton."

The figure stood up and put a garden-gloved right hand to her forehead. She looked at Mohammed with surprise. Although her clothes were casual, she was not what Mohammed had expected. She was mid-twenties, with mousy hair, pale skin, full pale pink lips, and widely set gray eyes with no makeup.

"That would be Mum. She's probably in the library; it's her favorite spot in the morning." She looked over the tall Arab man in front of her.

*He's not a tourist. I wonder what he wants.*

"I'm sorry, but I'm not sure Mum will receive you without a reference. Perhaps if you tell me who you are and what you want, I might be able to assist you. I'm Olivia, her daughter."

Mohammed paused a minute to size up the situation. The girl was serious, not flirting. Nevertheless, he knew the kind. Palestine was rich in opportunities to know girls superficially and enjoy them deeply. That was the kind of relationship he had looked for, and always found, when he lived there.

The girls of one's own village, of course, had to be kept virgins. One's family honor was at stake. But there were ways for a man to enjoy women. In the resort areas, for example, the Dead Sea and Red Sea, one could find secular Arab girls who enjoyed a good time as much as he did, or who were prostitutes.

And there were tourist girls. Many who came with fathers for pilgrimage came with him for pleasure. He had known a lot of girls like this mousy one in the hat, whose passion blossomed into full ardor under the Middle Eastern sun.

Many a morning he had awoken not knowing the name of the girl beside him but knowing her religion and region by a glance at her body. Those with olive skin and shaved pubic hair were Middle Eastern Muslims, and those with white breasts and pink nipples were Christian tourists.

But it was his first time in England, and he wasn't sure how seducing her would benefit or harm his plan. He smiled at himself, feeling very mature at being able to put the goal first.

Olivia misunderstood and smiled back.

"Thank you, Olivia. I am Mike. I was working with your father on a project and wanted to talk to your mother about it."

"Ooooh." Olivia spoke pages of meaning with this less than one word. She looked more deliberately at Mohammed, as if it were just registering that he was Arabic and as if that meant something to her. "Where are you from?"

Mohammed decided it would be best to answer this one truthfully. "Palestine."

"Excellent!" Olivia turned. "Follow me. I'll take you to Mum, but I don't think it will help. She knows nothing about manuscripts. Mum's eighteenth century—paintings and porcelain. Dad was manuscripts. I'm flowers and pots; in fact, that's what they call me: 'Old Pots.' We each have our field."

They walked around the right side of the house, passing by the floral borders. Olivia spoke rapidly, "I mean, not a flower field, except me. That is, we each have our own area of interest. It's rather by way of being a family tradition, begun by my great-great-grandfather. Except DW."

"DW? What's a DW?"

Olivia laughed. "It's a *who*, not a what! My younger brother, Dexter Worthington. He goes by DW. Everyone who knows him says it stands for 'Decadent Wastrel.'"

"What's that?"

"Oh, I'm sorry. I forgot those are rather big English words. 'Decadent Wastrel' means . . . ahhh . . . that he doesn't have a hobby. That's a family tradition too—every generation has its decadent wastrel."

They had passed through the formal gardens to the back of the house. The house was constructed of mellow Cotswold stone.

*Like the stone of my house in Lebanon.*

They went up the back terrace steps toward the open French doors of the library.

Lady Fenburton had angular features, with fair skin and hair that was a mixture of yellow, white, and gray. She was seated on a dark leather sofa reviewing files in a room of dark paneling broken up by shelves of books with gold tooling.

"Mother, I'd like to introduce you to Mike, an associate of father's."

"Lady Fenburton, thank you for seeing me. Would it be possible, I wonder, to see Lord Fenburton as well?"

"Certainly not!" she said in a tone more indignant than angry. "His lordship is in no condition to see anyone. He is still in hospital, in very guarded condition."

"I realize this is difficult, Madame, but I appreciate your indulgence. Do you know anything about the manuscripts your husband was working on, or anyone he may have been working with?"

"The impertinence," she said, almost to herself. "My husband's affairs were quite his own."

"Excuse me, Mother," Olivia interrupted, "but wasn't there some provision Father made? I seem to remember he said something we were to do if anyone came here asking about his research."

"Yes, you are right," Lady Fenburton reluctantly admitted. She walked over to the drawer of a Georgian desk and pulled out a card. "Here you go, young man. If you call on our solicitor, he may be able to assist you."

"Thank you, Madame," Mohammed said. He had never met anyone as imperious as her, and felt ill prepared to extract information from her. But he had to try.

"May I ask one more *leettle* question? Did anyone visit him asking about his work, perhaps an Arab, before his accident? I know this is an imposition, but lives may depend on it."

"I have no such recollection. That will be quite all, thank you," she said by way of dismissal. "Olivia, please show the man out."

As they walked down the terrace steps, "Pots" walked off to the left, the opposite of the way they had come. Behind the hedge to the far left was the entrance to a maze of high yew hedges. "Follow me," she said.

## Chapter 56

# COTSWOLDS, ENGLAND
## July 1, 2006

Pots entered the maze without looking back. Mohammed didn't know what to do, so he followed her. He had never been in a maze before and was getting disoriented.

"The layout of the garden is old, by Capability Brown, but the maze is not at all ancient, it's Russell Page, only about fifty years old," she said. Her words and actions seemed inscrutable to Mohammed.

When they got to the center of the maze there was a small gazebo, barely large enough to hold the bench they sat on.

"This is my secret spot. Where I come when I want to be alone."

Mohammed wondered what was coming next. Women had done this sort of thing to be alone with him before. But he was not comfortable at making love on demand and in the open air of a strange setting.

"You say you are from Palestine. Have you ever been to Jericho?" Pots asked.

"Yes, of course," Mohammed answered, wondering where this was leading.

"That's wonderful! I've inherited my great-grandfather's pots from his expedition to Jericho. Studying and recording them is my life's work."

After fifteen minutes discussing Jericho and her collection, she extracted something he was reluctant to give.

"Will you take me to Jericho someday? I really want to go, and Mum would never take me. I want to see where these marvelous lozenge-pattern potteries were found!"

"Of course, Pots," he said, as if the prospect delighted him. "It will be wonderful! And you must show me your pots collection sometime." Mohammed had no interest in archaeology, but he definitely had an interest in this family.

"Thank you so much!" Pots smiled like a girl he had given carnal pleasure to. "You have no idea what this means to me. And since you are so nice, I believe that you must be good. Not like the other man."

"What other man?" Mohammed asked.

"The one who came here a few days before Father's accident. I'm surprised Mother did not recall it."

*I'm not surprised at all.*

"I overheard her tell him that Father was not home, that he was at Oxford, the university, you know, where he lectures. He said," she imitated a low Arabic voice, "'No problem. I will wait for him in his study.'"

"And?"

"She said, 'You will do nothing of the sort,' and sent him packing."

Mohammed laughed. "Lady Fenburton, I hand it to you. At least you did one thing right."

Mohammed continued, "Did you recognize him or get his name?"

"No, and I only saw him from the side. All I can say is that he looked like an Arab and had a gold tooth. And there is one more thing you might want to know. If the solicitor is of no help, you might want to talk to DW."

"Could I see him now?"

"Oh, I suppose you don't know. DW disappeared after father's accident. He had begun working with father on the manuscript project and actually seemed interested. Everyone was so hopeful for him. Before that, you see, he was constantly playing Internet games, DOTA, and World of Warcraft. He scarcely came out to eat. Just biscuits and tea in his room. Seldom read for university. We were very worried."

"Of course," Mohammed said in a sympathetic-sounding voice that melted female hearts.

"But last semester he took the place of Father's assistant, who died in a skiing accident. DW was finally interested in something. He pretended to be disinterested to the parents, but we were close. I know he cared about the project."

"So he was a researcher, like me?" Mohammed paused. "Why are you telling me this?"

"Because," Pots answered, "you say there is danger, and I believe you. You seem honest. And I know where DW is."

## Chapter 57

# LONDON, ENGLAND
## July 3, 2003

Once inside, Mohammed could see that this was nothing like his own lawyer's office. The first thing he noticed was a clicking sound at the door behind him. For a split second he had the unreasonable feeling that he was trapped.

He turned around. A small red sign had appeared above the door handle and read, "Occupied with Current Client. Please wait."

This gave him a modicum of comfort, as he assumed the sign was visible from both entrance and exit sides of the door.

"Whitten, Harley, and Doggerel" was the name of a law firm on the business card the less than affable Lady Fenburton had given to Mohammed. The iron railing and glossy black door outside looked no different than others on this street, renowned for its legal prowess and astronomical fees.

All the surfaces inside seemed redoubtably glossy—like the black granite floors and the stainless steel reception console. The walls were also covered with stainless steel, buffed into repetitive whirling circles. Behind the stainless steel surface was hidden steel armor, protecting everything as if the entire office complex were a bank vault.

The reception console was unoccupied, but the counter had a button embedded in it. Below the button it said, "Press here for service."

Mohammed pressed.

Then a slight hum followed as a screen elevated from behind the console. It featured a very pale female face with blonde hair pulled straight back, projected against an electric blue background. She looked not quite human.

The face said, "Please wait while your fingerprint is being processed."

A hidden stereo system then played classical music. Mohammed paced the floor for about three minutes, under the watchful eye of the pale face. The way she blinked every few minutes added to her unnatural and unnerving appearance.

*Why can't they just hire a cute secretary like everybody else?*

"Thank you," the head said. "You may enter, Mr. Atareek."

*How does that head know my name?*

The molded steel door disengaged from its arched lintel and opened, revealing the true thickness of the door and walls.

Mohammed rechecked the card in his hand. It did say "solicitors," not "bank." He walked in to the next room, observing the wall as he passed. The vault door closed behind him.

Here he met an actual secretary sitting behind a wood desk in a paneled room.

*That's more like it.*

She was not as pretty as the artificial one, but she was less unsettling. Mohammed smiled broadly at her, more from relief than from his desire to establish a relationship, but Evelyn blushed a little and smiled back.

"Good day, Mr. Atareek," she spoke in clipped English which accentuated the *t* and *k* in his name. Please have a seat. Mr. Whitten will see you shortly."

In contrast to the high-high-tech entry, Mr. Whitten's office was traditional British legal at its best. Mohammed felt warmer in it, especially when the secretary brought in tea.

"In short, there's not a lot to it, Mr. Atareek. Lord Fenburton simply instructed us to give a letter to anyone whose fingerprints he had programmed into our system. You do recall giving him your fingerprints, I assume?"

Mohammed nodded. "Yes." He had had no idea that this was what they were to be used for. Since Fenburton had arranged for them to get British passports as a safety net for rapid emigration if necessary, he assumed they were being taken for the government's sake.

"You will receive one letter addressed to both you and Dr. Atareek. I am instructed to tell you that I have no knowledge of the other people in your group. Only Lord Fenburton knows, and the fact that you are here confirms that he is unable to reveal those names."

"Excuse me," said Mohammed, "but the computer must know who is on the list. Would it be possible to get printout? It would be very helpful to me and may save lives."

"I have been instructed that it may just as easily *destroy* lives," Whitten answered dryly. "The computer does not know your names. When one of you enters the firm and gives your fingerprint, it is sent through the Internet to an ultrasecure, fingerprint storage system out of the country. They electronically identify it and match it with one on file in the system. The match triggers a response appropriate to the person of the fingerprint and the firm it originated from. 'Whitten, Harley, and Doggerel' has record of neither the names nor the fingerprints of people in your group."

Mohammed said, "That, Mr. Whitten, is too bad." Then he had an idea. "Do you know how many letters there are?"

Whitten looked indignant. *These Arabs are utterly void of decorum.* "That's not something I am at liberty to reveal."

"Oh," Mohammed said.

"I am also to underscore that there is a degree of urgency involved, and that you should take his instructions seriously."

*Obviously.*

"The last instruction is that you are to read the letter on the premises before you leave, so that you are aware of the contents in the event," Whitten paused, seeking the appropriate legal words for "of its violent removal." He ended up saying, in less than his legal best, "something happens to . . . it when you leave the firm."

"If that 'something' happens to me as well as the letter, it will not much matter if I have read it or not, will it?"

Mr. Whitten gave a tolerant smile. "That is all I have for you, Mr. Atareek," he said dismissively.

"Hey, Mr. Whitten, where's my letter?"

"Evelyn will get it for you."

Back in the waiting room he was met by the secretary, who escorted him into a side room. Once again he heard a click when the door shut, and a little red sign popped up.

The room had an appearance like the steel entry. A black cushioned chair and a stainless table were its only furnishings.

*Looks like a suffocation chamber.*

When Mohammed sat down, he could see a square on the wall opposite him. His act of sitting seemed to trigger the square, which was a panel within the stainless steel wall. It opened to reveal a niche.

Mohammed stood up and reached into the niche to retrieve a letter. It was addressed to *Dr. Nasir Atareek and Mr. Mohammed Atareek.*

## Chapter 58

# LONDON, ENGLAND
## July 3, 2003

Mohammed sat down and opened the envelope. The letter from Lord Fenburton read:

*Esteemed Colleague—*

*The fact that you are reading this missive signifies that I am dead or incapacitated. Rest assured, it will not be suicide: it is impossible to entertain the idea of dispatching oneself when such important information as we have is about to be released to a planet unnecessarily at war over a lie. Reaction to our revelation may initially increase the disorder, but we join in the hope that peace will ultimately ensue.*

*My goal with this letter is to see to it that the project continues without me.*

*You were selected for this project because of your superior research abilities; and as far as could be determined by me, your view of politics and religion were favorable to it. In other words, I did not believe you were murderers or terrorists.*

*At the time of writing this, I cannot exclude the possibility that my assailant may have been one of you. We must therefore proceed with the assumption that one of you may be a traitor. For this reason, I am not releasing to you who the other team members are: I am protecting them from you and you from them.*

*How, then, can we continue with the project? I have given the matter a great deal of consideration, and have settled on the following plan:*

*To review: the Yemeni Department for Antiquities has only permitted us to study twelve manuscripts at a time. You received two manuscripts in each shipment, to study according to our specified protocol. Each set was sent to you from a different location, and returned to a different location, to prevent determination of where they were processed. Your findings were sent to me and securely stored until we had reached a point suitable for publication. Then I would write the summary data, giving you each credit as coauthors.*

*The protocol will now change. You will receive no more manuscripts. I am suggesting that you publish your own data independently of me and the group. This is a change from our goal of publishing all the data at once—but that is no longer an option.*

*Your independent publication will accomplish three things: First, it will ensure that the world has access to your data, should anything happen to you.*

*Second, it will convince those acting as my agents that you are not a traitor. Third, it will ensure that you are committed to this project regardless of the risk.*

*I have arranged another agency to act as my agent in this last part of the scenario, but you will have no way of knowing who this is. They have been instructed to scrutinize the* Middle East Manuscript Review, *the journal to which you are to send your paper for publication. If they find the detail to be up to their expectations, you will be considered safe. They will then endow the first publishing author with information that will enable him to find the accumulated previous research and the names of the others within our study group.*

*As you may infer, the situation is urgent, and whether you are loyal or traitor, your life is in jeopardy.*

*Your brother for truth and peace,*
*Lord Algernon Fenburton*

## July 4

"Mohammed, you will miss Bilal's wedding. This is exactly what I told you would happen!" Nasir yelled into the telephone.

"I know I will miss Bilal's wedding, but this way he can miss our funeral!" Mohammed yelled back. "I need to make one more stop before I go to Palestine. You go to the wedding. Then I insist you leave Palestine immediately and go directly to the hill house. When I get back, I will stop by Beirut, pack up the lab, and meet you there," Mohammed calmed himself. "If we don't hide, the Mus-haf Brotherhood will kill us *all.*"

# PART TWO

## Chapter 59

# RAMALLAH, PALESTINE
## July 7, 2006

Angela Hall had been in Palestine for five days.

A journey into or out of Palestine is always tiring, but she quickly recharged and was having a great visit. Her Arabic was getting slick. She had seen all around Ramallah, visited beautiful terraced farms, and met what seemed like half the population of the city—and those were just her relatives!

About town in San Francisco, Angela rarely saw anyone she knew, much less a relative. But here, she started to treat everyone like a relative. This saved time and embarrassment. If they weren't related, they wouldn't notice because Palestine is light-years ahead of San Francisco in friendliness. However, if she acted this way when she got back in San Francisco, people would think she had gone psychotic. She was encouraged by Freya Stark's first virtue for travelers: *Admit standards that are not one's own.*

The wedding of her distant cousin Bilal had been the highlight of her visit so far. She had enjoyed the preparations and the celebration, but it didn't feel like a wedding. With the women segregated from the men and dancing wildly together, she kept flashing back to Selim's lecture on secret women's societies. The only male presence they could expect was a brief appearance by the groom. She hoped he wouldn't get lynched by the Bacchae.

*Cooking and gossip.*

These were the mainstay of Angela's visit. Next to seeing relatives, Angela was in Palestine to learn how to cook—or at least the aunts thought so.

They were shocked that she had never learned Middle Eastern cooking. She did not care to explain that her father had hated it, as did her husband, and they had had a cook three days a week in Pacific Heights.

Rather, she said with a flip of her hand, "We have a cook!" which made it seem as though she could not cook, although she could.

"Cooking is not one of my hobbies," she would announce to her guests. After that, they were easily pleased.

*Why should I learn now? My marriage is over. How do you make* minsaf *for one? Minsaf,* the traditional dish of lamb, simmered with dried yogurt cheese and served over rice with yogurt sauce, is made for a hungry group to grab at with their hands, not for lonely professors reading term papers.

*Perhaps I could have a party and serve Middle Eastern food.*

In her former life, when she entertained in her San Francisco showplace home, she had parties catered. Whatever the night's theme, she would have the ultimate caterer in that field. The year they had a pre-opera party for *Turandot,* she had the "Chinese restaurant of the year" cater. For *La Traviata,* she reproduced Paris in a way, said the society column, that rivaled scene I of the opera.

Those were routine events for their social set. For fund-raisers she went all out. The Inner City Shakespeare Fund, promoting both culture and the poor, was a favorite charity. For it, she staged scenes from *Hamlet* throughout the house. Most of the guests and all the workers dressed in Renaissance attire. People said they had "felt the Bard" like never before. It was well worth the thousand-dollar-a-ticket price... as of course were the children of the charity.

And since Angela was trained to be poised, no one guessed at the real drama that went on behind the scenes.

But her world had changed. Now, when she returned to California it would not be as the social star, the "Series A" jet-setter of San Francisco. She would be single—and she didn't know how to live single.

*If the aunties discovered my divorce, I know what they would say: "How can a man be happy when his wife doesn't cook Middle Eastern food?"*

Today the dears were feeling fulfilled: they had taught Angela how to make *maktube,* the classic "upside down" meal of Palestine. She was to line the bowl with seasoned lamb or chicken, layer cauliflower, fill the center with rice, invert, and voila! A beautiful mound of food.

It might be good to have a few Middle Eastern recipes on hand. But was this to be all she would take away from her visit?

## Chapter 60

# RAMALLAH, PALESTINE
## July 8, 2006

*I used to like being a woman.*

What should she do? Angela craved something beyond cooking and gossip. She could imagine the shock on Aunt Rana's face if she so much as asked if she could sit with the men when they discussed politics. Or if she could see some of the sights. This must be how the princes in the cage felt—knowing there was a wonderful yet forbidden world just beyond the wall.

*Perhaps if I were a man . . .*

Her aunts and uncles assumed, and rightly so, that she would want to meet *all* the family. They did not even think to ask her if she would like to see *some* of "the Holy Land." Her plan had been to do both. Ramallah was nice, perhaps the most prosperous town in Palestine, but hardly one of the historic sites or scenic marvels.

Angela's relatives were Westernized Muslims. Some of the women wore hijab, the traditional head scarf, in public, but not all. The men and women in her family would sit in the same room, but the men grouped separately and discussed politics; the women, home life. Farm areas were more traditional. The women there covered more and left home less, and men and women lived more segregated.

But at least the farm girls in her family were educated. In some Palestinian villages—for example, those around the conservative Muslim stronghold of Hebron—many girls were kept out of school and illiterate. Observations and discoveries such as these helped keep her visit interesting.

Angela had visited a family olive grove today. The rolling hills, stone fences, and sun filtering through the gray-green leaves seemed so peaceful. But she had seen disturbing things too. There was a refugee camp nearby, and her mind kept going back to images of its many children: poor and dirty. Playing soccer in the dusty street. Were these children hungry? Were they being educated? Did the girls have a chance of learning? Could anything be done to help them?

She had helped many poor children in America. There, she knew what to do. And she had sponsor-children in Africa and the Caribbean.

*What can I do for the needy children of my own people?*

Angela may have lost her celebrity in San Francisco society, but such was not the case with her teenaged girl cousins in Palestine. She welcomed their questions about life in California. Not having had sisters or daughters, it was a nice; but tonight, she was distracted.

"Is it true that in California women wear bikinis to work?"

Angela was trying to think of a diplomatic way to break free and ask the adults about local charities for the needy children when everything changed.

"*Alhamdulillah! Ya, Mohammed!*" Aunt Rana jumped up, screaming and jiggling her corpulence with what Angela at first took to be a religious exclamation.

The next thing she knew, the girls at her table and everyone else was jumping and screaming and running to the door. She was not sure what had happened, but with the intense commotion, even by Palestinian standards, it must surely be that the Intifada had ended, or that Mohammed Abbas had arrived.

*Wrong Mohammed.* Mohammed Atareek had arrived.

Angela remained seated. Not knowing the new arrival, it was unnecessary and even unfitting for her to lose repose over his entrance. This being Arabia, any guest's arrival was hailed with pleasure, whether heartfelt or not. But here was more than the usual reception she had seen over and over the last few days. Through gaps in the crowd she caught a glimpse of *who* it was but could not perceive *why*.

The hugs and kisses he gave were as big and looked as genuine as the ones he received. The unknown man was a favorite of young and old alike.

"Uncle Mohammed, Uncle Mohammed!" the children called. He was tall. As he grabbed the small children and threw them up into the air, catching them over his head, they squealed with delight. Then he pulled out prettily wrapped packages of sweets for them.

"Thank you, Uncle Mohammed! Thank you!" they chorused as they sat down to divide the goodies up.

To the old he was equally attentive. He greeted each of the elders with respect, inquiring after their health or a child of theirs who had moved away. The middle-aged men were queried about their business;

the mothers were complimented on their cooking feats of former years, and teased into promising more.

You could hear his loud laugh and exaggerated stock phrases all over the house. Before she saw no more than a raised arm and a flash of his dark head, she could tell that he exuded Palestinian warmth and hospitality in the extreme.

Apart from Angela, who was out of sight at the table, Mohammed greeted everyone personally and, as was customary when there was a large group, sat down with the men. Politics are always in fashion in Palestine, and this topic dominated the men's conversation. The growing popularity of Hamas, and the uneasy workings between Hamas and Fattah, were discussed. Individual leaders were named. None of them were trusted fully. As the old Arabic proverb goes,

*With my cousin against the foreigner,*
*with my brother against my cousin.*

Hamas had a firmly engrained reputation for terror, which would hamper Palestine's negations with the West and Israel. The PLO was less terrorist now than it had been in the years of its formative youth, but it had become corrupt. So the conversation went. It was a choice of lesser evils, as it always was.

"In Palestine we vote, we have freedom," said Cousin Ismael. "We choose our crooks!"

All the men laughed, except Uncle Hanbal. Poor Uncle Hanbal seemed too filled of the difficulties of the Palestinian life and character to admit any of the pleasures of it.

The girls drifted back to Angela. She set aside her questions about the charity for now, since there was no opportunity to ask. Instead she was bombarded with more girlish questions.

"No, dears," she belatedly answered the question about bikinis. "There are too many fat Americans. It's bad enough seeing them in bathing suits on the beaches, let alone in the offices!"

She knew the girls would like this. They did, and started laughing. Then one alluded to a very fat girl they knew. "Can you imagine how Rabab would look, walking around an office in high heels and a bikini?"

Angela laughed with them, although not deeply. They were rolling, quite literally, some with their arms and heads on the table and others holding their sides, as they went on and on in detail.

*Too much of Palestinian humor is ridicule-based—making fun of people, or tricking them to make them look a fool.*

Angela saw it as an outgrowth of their "shame and honor" culture, but it was not the sort of humor she was used to. Hers was based on wordplay or making light of everyday situations. It was difficult to transition to what she considered lower humor, but she was trying to "admit standards not one's own."

The girls laughed so loudly that everyone in the house heard them and looked. Mohammed also looked, and for the first time he saw Angela. His expression registered surprise, then something else. Yet he was deep in conversation and, although curious, was not able or inclined to explore her presence.

Mohammed had more than fun in mind with his visit tonight. He easily guided his conversation with the men into the economic results of the political situation. Things were bleak, the men reported. The Intifada was making it difficult to impossible for construction workers to get into Israeli territory, where the jobs were.

Angela overheard them talking and thought, What an irony: this interdependent love-hate relationship where Israelis depend on Palestinian labor and Palestinians depend on Israeli employment—sometimes for building the very settlements they detested!

*Like sibling rivalry.*

Angela found herself in the challenging position of being in one conversation while trying to listen to another. She was interested in everything about Palestine—and especially things like politics and economics. But it would be improper to dismiss the girls and go with the men.

The men discussed how Palestinian areas dependent on tourism, like Bethlehem, had a steep plummet of activity in everything from tours to taxis and hotels.

Farming was much more difficult because "the walls" broke up fields and blocked access to them.

"What about land prices?" Mohammed inquired casually.

Uncle Fadil answered, "It depends on who is selling and who is buying. Palestinians don't have money to buy. Israelis have the money, and are paying enormous prices—they're happy to buy whatever they've made useless to us with their cursed walls."

"Then," interrupted Uncle Mustapha, "they use the land to put their settlements on, or build highways through."

"Sometimes we don't even have a choice; the Israelis simply come to us and say, 'We want to buy your land.' This is what happened to Cousin Kaseem," said Cousin Ismael. "That land to the east of town was all he had to live on. A legacy for his family. What could he do? I'm telling you, brothers—he just sold it to the Israelis!"

At this, some of the men started jumping up, shouting, waving their fists, yelling, "*Haram! Haram!*"

Uncle Hanbal was an imam with a reputation for the extreme, like his father, Ayman. Not everyone in the family knew what Hanbal had been involved in, but those who did either respected or hated him for it.

Hanbal started screaming, "Death to Israel! Death to Kaseem! He is a traitor! May he perish and his family, *Allahu akbar!*"

"*Ya*, Hanbal," Mohammed sounded deeply concerned. "Surely you don't blame Kaseem? *Illi faat maat.* They would have taken his land either way, and he needed the money for a legacy for his children—not to mention daily food."

"Well, I have to say that I believe Kaseem was right," said Ismael. "He said he had two choices: either let the Israelis take the land and live in poverty forever but with respect; or forget respect, take the millions, and emigrate. Yesterday the deal closed. Today he left with his family for America."

There was silence. Anger against Kaseem dissipated amid thoughts of him having to start life over again in America.

"Even I don't envy him that," said Uncle Hanbal. "Life among the infidels!"

"Hush!" said Ismael. "Our cousin from America might hear us."

Which she did. But she followed Honey Jean's advice. *Consider the source.* Uncle Hanbal was simply a hothead. He had no intentions of hurting her, however much he might hate Israel and America. Mohammed looked more unsettled by Uncle Hanbal's remarks than Angela did.

Mohammed lightened up. "Did I hear you say, 'American cousin'?" he asked, standing up and looking over to Angela. He tapped Aunt Rana on the shoulder "Heaven forgive you, Auntie! Why haven't you introduced me to my cousin, the *angel*?"

Aunt Rana stood up and clapped her hands together. "Oh, my," she exclaimed. "No one introduced you to Angela? Come, come meet her! You will love her." She led him over to the table where Angela was sitting with the girls and some of the women. "Mohammed, how did you know that her name meant 'angel'?"

Mohammed answered his aunt but looking directly at Angela, "Oooooh, auntie, that is so obvious! Look." He held out his hand, gesturing to her, and put on his smile that stretched to the eyes. "*Angel* is written all over her face!"

## Chapter 61

# RAMALLAH, PALESTINE
## July 9, 2006

Amir Mueller's office was on the fifth floor of Burj Meuller, one of the nicest buildings in Ramallah.

His father, Karl, was a German cleric who came to the Holy Land on an unholy mission: assisting Hitler in getting recruits for the Axis, and he just couldn't get himself to return to the dreary Teutonic skies.

Then Karl doubled the scandal by marrying a Muslim—unacceptable on two accounts: first because the marriage did not fit with his German rank and racial purity, and second, because it did not fit his wife Maryam's faith. Muslim men can marry Christian women, but the reverse is not acceptable, since it puts a woman of faith in the power of an infidel. So Maryam's family was not happy with the marriage either.

The Muellers were thus a little more unto themselves than the average Palestinian family. But being outcasts enabled them to succeed in other ways, as constraints often do. The family's energies became more task-oriented and less people-oriented than the prevailing culture. Karl changed his profession from military to money, when there was still money to be made in Palestine.

Amir was one of the best lawyers in Ramallah—in all of Palestine, for that matter. He had the perfect combination of German industriousness and Palestinian affability, which led his practice to prosper beyond expectable bounds. He was offered more lucrative positions elsewhere, but, like his father, he would not exchange olives and sunshine—and his black-eyed woman—for all the money in Hanover.

For the past thirty years he had been Mohammed's family's lawyer.

After the greetings and over the coffee that accompanied such visits, Mohammed came to the point. "Amir, pull out the file on my land west of town."

"Do you mean your largest tract? The olive grove with the fantastic view?"

"That's the one."

"You are welcome to review it. I've updated all your files in the last two months, and I think you will find nothing amiss. Rent coming in, the best possible, considering the situation. No taxes owed. No problem."

"Amir, I want to sell it. The western grove," Mohammed said pleasantly.

"You can't be serious, Mohammed! That is your best parcel. It brings in a banner olive crop. Unless you've been losing money in the stock market or gambling—or have married four wives, I can't imagine why you would want to sell!"

"You are not expected to imagine anything, Amir! Heaven forgive you, brother! Do you think I pay these expensive fees for your imagination?" he jested. "*La!* I can do my own imagining for free!"

Following Mohammed's lead, Amir couldn't resist saying, "Well, you get what you pay for!"

"Now hush, brother," Mohammed continued, seriously. "I want you to make all the arrangements for me. No questions asked by me as to who the buyer is, no questions asked by you as to why. Agreed? Also, the transaction is to be secret. The town must not know. Do you think you can do that?"

"Oh, I know I can sell it! Tomorrow even. But are you certain? That property has been in your family since Rachel was put into her tomb!"

"Remember our deal." Mohammed waved his finger and smiled as if this were some children's game of Blink. "I don't ask who; you don't ask why."

## Chapter 62

# RAMALLAH, PALESTINE
## July 9, 2006

"Today we will make *lachm wa sabanahh*," said Aunt Rana, waving her wooden spoon with a flourish. "It is simple to cook but very nourishing and flavorful." So began Angela's daily cooking lesson. She felt like *Emeril*'s entire TV audience.

Being married to her mother's older brother, Faisal, Aunt Rana was about the age Angela's mother would be, but was nothing like her. She was loud and very round—one of the biggest women in Ramallah. Her loose skirts whorled as she bustled and banged around the kitchen with the air of a great cook, which fortunately she was acclaimed to be.

What Rana took seriously were things like the temperature of oil and the size of onion choppings. She was cheerful and delighted to have a student. But Angela was struggling inside.

*I know Aunt Rana is wonderful, and this is how she relates to people. But if all I do in Palestine is learn cooking, I'll go back to Turkey or I'll go crazy!*

Aunt Rana continued, demonstrating with the spoon. "In one pan you sauté the chopped onion, but use more olive oil so you don't brown it," she warned, her oily face shining, as if massaged with oil from the pan.

"Now, cut the lamb into cubes," she instructed, "while I make the rice pilaf."

Angela was slower with the knife than Rana, but the aunt was patient. The homey fragrance of hot olive oil and onion filled the house.

While her student was creating cubes of equal size, Rana asked, "What do you think of my nephew Mohammed?"

"Mohammed Atareek? Honestly, I don't know. I scarcely spoke to him. But I saw him kissing the babies. He seems nice... maybe a little louder and friendlier than most people...."

"That's good," said Aunt Rana, describing the meat she took from Angela and tossed into a pan. "Now we sauté the meat separately."

She looked into the pan, smiling while she watched the meat sizzle—a simple pleasure lost on Angela. "Ah, there is no one like Mohammed Atareek."

"I saw him bring candies for the children."

"Oh, yes, but I mean the gift of laughter. He looks into each person's eyes and makes them laugh."

Rana bounced easily back and forth between cooking and the spice of life.

"Notice that the spinach is washed. I will blanch it in the hot water, just for a minute, to take out the iron." Steam rose. "It is easier to digest this way."

"Then, I drain it and mix it with the meat and onion to cook. It is a good thing for you that you are married, *habeebtee.* Just before we serve it, we add the special sauce of the Middle East. Do you remember what it is?" she quizzed.

"*Tahina*?" asked Angela.

Aunt Rana put the spoon under Angela's chin and pushed up. "So this is what they teach in American schools?" she said with playful disgust.

Angela opened her mouth to say no, but then thought the explanation that there was no cooking taught in school could make things worse.

"No wonder my *habeebtee* can't cook! I mean lemon!"

"Oh, of course."

"There, you see, how easy this recipe is—so easy even an American can do it." She started laughing—like a jolly Mrs. Santa, only with a bit naughty in the nice.

"Now, let's have some mint tea while we wait for these things to simmer. *Tfaddaly, tfaddaly!* Of course, he is a saint now, compared to before the accident."

Just then there was a noise at the door.

"What accident?"

Aunt Rana arose excitedly, saying, "Oh, they're here, they're here! Put on some coffee, *habeebtee.* How time flies when women are having fun cooking!"

## Chapter 63

# RAMALLAH, PALESTINE

## July 9, 2006

It had been another evening full of food and gossip. Aunt Rana mastered the trick of praising Angela's cooking while reminding everyone that it was a simple dish, and nothing compared to her own triumphs.

By two in the morning, the other relatives returned home, and Aunt Rana and Uncle Faisal were going to bed.

"Hey, seesterr!" Mohammed called to Angela on his way to the door. "Don't go off to bed like a chicken! Sit here. Tell me, how you like Palestine?"

Angela was a little surprised to be called "sister" by him, but she was to discover that Mohammed maximized the Middle Eastern courtesy of calling women "sister." There is a little spitting sound in the middle of *akhty*, the Arabic word for "sister," which sounds angry to Westerners. As if he knew that, he always used the English word with her, either saying it plainly or emphasizing its letters, according to his mood.

Angela was tired and not feeling clever, but she sat with Mohammed in a corner near the door.

"It's wonderful. And I love having so many relatives." Angela smiled. "In San Francisco I have none."

"No relatives. I can't even imagine life like that. So you like it here? That makes big brother Mohammed happy." Mohammed sat down, straddling a chair across from her.

"I love it. I only wish I could see some of it. Aunt Rana seems to have enrolled me in her cooking class and I haven't reached the end of term yet!"

"Ha-ha!" Mohammed slapped his thigh and laughed loud enough to wake the chef herself. "You mean dear old Auntie won't take you anywhere? Don't worry, sister, what is big Palestinian brother for?" He thumped his chest. "You will see the best of Palestine—the center of the faiths."

"Really? I can hardly believe it!" Angela said in delight. "I've been feeling like a teenager on restrictions or a prince—I mean a bird—in a cage."

"And Lebanon, ahhh! You must see Lebanon too. It's the best, the best! Before the civil war in the 1970s, it was the Paris of the Middle East. And now it's nearly restored. There are villages as cute as or cuter even than Bethlehem! And we have the ceeeedars of Lebanon. Everyone in the Middle East wants the cedars, but only Lebanon has them!"

"I thought you were a loyal Palestinian. Please explain to me what you are doing up in Lebanon?"

"Actually, I went up there for my education," he started to explain. He sounded very matter-of-fact about it. "In Palestine, education is a problem, sister. I left school when I was fourteen years old. Can you believe it?"

"Maybe I can."

He continued, ignoring this. "One year, I think it was the year after the First Intifada started, I went to school only seventeen days in the entire year!"

"You rascal!" Angela scolded in English.

"What's 'rascal'?"

"Someone who is not doing as they should... but it's not as bad as a 'scoundrel,' so don't get angry. It's not like I reminded you that hell is your destiny...."

"Hey, OK!" He hit her gently with the map. "Remember who your host is! Do you want to have a good time and see the sights? Or do you only want to see the ovens of Palestine?"

"I'm burned out on that."

"But seriously, sister," he continued, "you got it wrong if you think I didn't go to school because I was a, what did you say, 'rat skull'? Not for that, sister. It was because the Intifada disrupted everything in Palestine! I only went to school for seventeen days because that is all it was open. There was always some reason school was closed down. For example, everyone would strike on sixth and ninth days of the month—because like that is the day First Intifada started."

"So what did you do?"

"When school was closed, we didn't know what to do. I swam a lot, got really strong." Mohammed flexed his biceps. "Sometimes I would go out and throw rocks with my friends. We Palestinians, we are the best, the best rock throwers in the world! We are also verrry good with slingshots. No bird was safe around my house!" He laughed in delight at his mischievous youth. "If it was a tasty one, my mother would cook it. Sometimes I would kill a dozen leeetle birds."

"Miscreant!"

"'Miss Crete'? Sister, why do you keep calling me names I don't know?"

"Because I am an English professor, and I love words. And you, my cousin, give me a chance to use many adjectives. The more I learn about you, the more words beg to be let out. It doesn't matter if you understand them. They are happy just to be spoken."

"You have learned tooo much from books! Now you need to learn from your big Palestinian brrotherr."

"What? How to kill birds? That's hardly a skill I need in San Francisco!"

"You surprise me, sister. How can you think of going back to America now that you have seen Middle East? You are crazy, *majnoona*!"

"I'd be crazy to stay here. You said the educational system is bad. Where would I teach?"

"You said you were rich! Why do you need to teach? Forget about it. Just move here and learn to cook."

"I suppose that's your only concept of acceptable activity for women?"

"Of course not! Someone has to feed babies."

"If I moved here, would I ever get out of the house, or would you keep me in it—for my own safety?"

"Seesteerr, don't be fool," he said in English, and then switched into Arabic. "In October we let the women out. We need everyone's help for the olive harvest! Ha-ha!" He laughed loudly and shook his head.

Angela sensed that this was whole fun, but half earnest too.

"That does *not* convince me to move here. It's a good thing you're a farmer and not in sales!"

"Ah, you wound me. Every Arab wants to make a good deal. OK, let me change the deal a little. Education is good in Lebanon. I told you I am studying—"

"You told me you left school at age fourteen. How does that fit with good education?"

"Be nice, leeetle sister, or I will ignore you! Then who will show you around?"

"Not the aunties. They can't leave the house for three more months until the olive harvest!"

"Ha-ha! Oh! That's it!" He laughed and then pretended anger. "For a teacher, you should be a better learner. Now you will learn nothing!" He stopped talking and got up as if going to the door, then went into the back of the house.

Angela got up too. She picked up the map and some papers and sat back down, rightly suspecting that Mohammed could not walk away from their conversation. But she was not going to beg him to talk to her. When Mohammed returned carrying two tall glass cups of mint tea, she was flipping through travel brochures on day trips and making notes, looking very sincere.

Mohammed spoke as if nothing had happened. "What are you doing, sister?" Angela held up the brochures. "Heaven forgive you, sister. Forget about it! What do you have cousins for? If you want to see something, you go with us!"

"Or I don't go at all?"

"That's it! Now you are listening! Now I can continue."

Angela was thinking about what Cousin Dina had said about him.

*Mohammed loves to talk.*

She was tired. Let Mohammed talk.

"As I was telling you, I left school because I thought 'I'm wasting my time! I should work.' So I started working young. Mostly on the family farms. I was strong and good at work, so I became a supervisor. I had my own money at a young age, and that led to many problems, but forget about it. The point is that in many ways, I admit it, sister, I am uneducated."

"A refreshing breeze," said Angela looking around. "I feel a refreshing breeze coming from somewhere!"

"But, heeey! About the time the Second Intifada started, I decided to change. I needed more education. Frankly, I could hardly read my own language. That's when I moved to Lebanon and started studying Arabic at the American University of Beirut. Hey," he poked her gently, "that's funny. You studied English and I studied Arabic. Yet we understand each other!"

"That's doubtful. For example, I don't understand how you got into a university with such limited education."

"Oh. I studied very, very hard on my own first. Your Uncle Nasir helped me. He also helped me get into the university because he teaches there. And now I am a graduate student. This is how I came to know Lebanon, and now I see how wonderful it is. Sister, you have to come there. And you need to see your Auntie Zahara. Everyone here says she looks like your mother—I don't remember exactly how your mother looked, but I think you look a little like ImmMohammed."

"Who is ImmMohammed?"

"Sister! Don't you know that once a woman has a son, she is called by his name for the rest of her life, out of respect? *ImmMohammed* means 'mother of Mohammed.' That is what your aunt is now called. Her name Zahara doesn't matter anymore."

"No, of course not. You are right, I am learning. Woman only has her value in relation to Man. If she is married, she has significance. If she has a son, well, then, she has reached the pinnacle of her contribution to society, and that should be recognized. She receives a special name as an award. Yes, I can see how that respects—*men*!" she said.

"Ha-ha!" Mohammed laughed as if she had told a joke, surprising Angela. "I thought my job was to give you a good time and show you around. But now I see that I need to teach you our…" He looked directly at her, "…*your* culture. You think you are Arab, but you don't understand our culture at all, at all! The first lesson, sister: we do anything for our guest, and you are our guest. This is because of the Bedouins in the desert. Whoever comes to your tent, you must give him hospitality for three and a half days."

"Even enemies?"

"Of course, even if he is your enemy. You can always kill him later!"

"Love that hospitality!"

"The second lesson is gossip. When you are in the desert and someone comes to you, they are a walking newspaper—you ask about eeevrrything that is going on outside of your tent!"

"Would you mind if I looked around Palestine before I see Lebanon?"

"No problem, sister. Tomorrow we see Jerusalem. *Enti sofa ahuba kathir, kathir.* You will love it!"

## Chapter 64

# PALESTINE
# July 10, 2006

Having passed through the checkpoint, Mohammed and Angela traveled toward Jerusalem in a high-security Israeli taxi, one with the yellow license plates Angela had read about.

It was early enough that the sunlight was still angled. They would not be back until dinnertime. Aunt Rana apologized, but she would have to start cooking before Angela returned.

"*Ya, Mohammed*," Angela said in Arabic, "*Shoofa hanak medina jamila!* Over there, the city on the hill. Do you see how the light shines on it? Is it a Crusader castle or an old walled city or something?" she asked.

Mohammed seemed to ignore her question. Perhaps he couldn't see the hill town from where he was sitting.

"Sister, I hear that California is full of Mexicans now. So the government of Mexico has courage. It comes into California and makes cities just for the Mexicans to live in. And Mexico rules them."

Unused to his style, Angela bit. "Not at all! Where did you hear that nonsense? Is that the kind of junk they report on Al Jazeera now? True, there are many Mexicans in California, and some of them are there illegally, but the government of Mexico can't just come up and start taking our land and building towns for their people. That would be an act of war."

"Ha-ha! Here we have the first American who understands! *Alhamdulillah!* That town on the hill you pointed to is what is called a 'settlement.' It is land that the Israelis either took or forced Palestinians to sell them. They build a city. Then they build a protected road from there to Israel. Neither the city nor the road are open to Palestinians, in our own country!"

"Oh, my!" Angela exclaimed, in real surprise. "Now that you compare it to Mexico and California, it seems so real."

"Look over there," Mohammed pointed. "Another settlement. We will pass by several on the way to Jerusalem. The settlements are not only on the border between Palestine and Israel: there are hundreds deep in the West Bank. I will show you on the map."

"They sound more invasive than defensive."

"That's it, sister! Like a cancer spreading. Many of my friends were offered money by the Israelis for their land."

"So, do the Israelis at least pay for it?"

"This is the problem, sister: everyone knows what the Israelis want to do with it. You can't win. If you sell to the Israelis, the Palestinians consider you a traitor. Your entire family is disgraced. Many leave the country because they can't bear it."

"And if you don't sell?"

"Most of the time, the Israelis just move in anyway."

"And 'the wall' they talk about here; the one that makes the Palestinians so mad. Is that it around the town?"

"Sister, you are guessing wrong again! No, 'the wall' is not really a wall—not like the Berlin wall, which goes along the border. They can't do that, because they have built so many settlements beyond the border. So they had to build totally unconnected walls. Starting with the big cities and moving to the small towns, they surround them with walls and only one or two gates for the Palestinians to go in and out of."

"Really? That must slow down rush hour considerably!"

"Worse than that, it changes everyone's life! My family, for example: you know we have farms. They used to be a short walk from our house. We could get there in five minutes. Now we have to wait in line with the rest of the city, go out a door the wrong direction, then turn around to go back to the farm!"

"And so …"

"And so, the land becomes less valuable. It is harder for the Palestinians to work. So when the Israelis come and want to buy it, the price is cheap!"

"And the Palestinians have to emigrate. I wish Americans understood this."

"Me too, sister!" Mohammed agreed. "Your rich husband, he owns a TV station maybe?"

"No, I'm sorry. Mostly land and business."

"Then we will have to think of something else." Mohammed sounded serious.

"But look at how Palestinians respond. That's what gets them into trouble," she said. "They are so stupid! By their extreme reaction, suicide bombings, and all, they give Israelis world sympathy and an excuse to come into land. Then they cry like spoiled children."

"Now, sister," Mohammed said, unable to stay serious for too long, "don't criticize our child raising. Everyone knows Palestinian children are the best in the whoooole world!"

"You are right; no doubt our little cousins are the best noise makers in the world, just as you were the best at throwing stones!"

# Chapter 65

# JERUSALEM
## July 10, 2006

"Trust me, sister. Before I moved to Lebanon I was a tour guide. I know everything about Haram al-Sharif and the Temple Mount," said Mohammed as they walked atop one of the world's most famous hilltops.

"Such as?"

"OK, let's start easy. What's the most famous structure on the Temple Mount?"

"The Dome of the Rock. Do I pass?"

"Now think, sister. How did it get there? Was it there before Mohammed?"

"I don't think so because it looks so Islamic, but I don't really know."

"That's good. OK. Now imagine this: in AD 638, when Islam takes Jerusalem, the Temple Mount is flanked by two churches—the Church of the Holy Sepulcher on this side, and the Church on the Ascension on the other side, on the Mount of Olives, there." He pointed at the respective churches. "And what do you think was on the Temple Mount?"

"I don't know."

"Nothing was on the Temple Mount. You see, the Christians were in charge of Jerusalem. They said Jesus had prophesied the destruction of the temple, so after the Romans demolished it in AD 70, they never rebuilt here. The churches surrounding it were saying, 'You lose' to the Jews!"

"You can't be serious."

"Sounds crazy, doesn't it? Maybe it was superstition, but the Christians didn't build on it. Some even say they used it as a garbage dump."

"No!"

"So, when Caliph Umar was looking for a site to build Jerusalem's first mosque, Sophronius, the patriarch of Jerusalem, had no problem letting them build on the mount. This suited the Muslims, and even many of the Jews, since they believed Solomon's temple was being rebuilt."

Mohammed continued. "So Umar made Jerusalem a holy city, like

Mecca and Medina. In fact, the Dome of the Rock is one of the oldest surviving Islamic buildings. It was built at the end of the same century as the Prophet Mohammed lived, and it has the oldest Koranic inscriptions of anywhere."

Walking around the outside of the mosque, Angela commented, "Yes, I can see the inscriptions! I never noticed them in the photos. The mosque is so much more colorful and detailed, more beautiful in person than when you see it in pictures."

As they approached the Southern Gate, Mohammed pointed at the decorative copper inscriptions above it. "Then when Umar built this mosque, he said 'you lose!' to the Christians. Look!" He read in Arabic, "*The Unity of God and the Prophecy of Mohammed are true. The Sonship of Jesus and the Trinity are false.*"

"Wow! That's unusual for a place of worship. . . ."

"What do you mean, sister? In America, over the doors in all the churches it says, '*Jesus is God and Mohammed is not a prophet,*' right?"

Angela rolled her eyes and didn't bother to answer.

One thing intrigued Angela. At intervals throughout their visit to the Temple Mount, Mohammed pulled out a little notebook. At first she thought it was for casual notes. But it became apparent to her that he was copying something. He made no comment to her about it, which seemed odd.

*If he were sly, he would make some explanation of what he is doing.*

She knew for certain he was studying when he pulled out binoculars. He offered them to her, as if he had brought them for her to enjoy the intricately carved and painted sixty-five-foot-diameter dome.

*He had something in mind today besides just giving me a good time.*

"Seesterr, don't you agree that the blue on this mosque is the most beauutiful color in the whole world? Blue. My favorite!"

*That's an explanation?*

"Back to Aunt Rana's cooking school," Angela said as they got into the taxi.

Mohammed quizzed her. "Did you know that the Prophet Mohammed visited the mosque we saw today?"

"No, I didn't. I thought he pretty much stayed in Saudi."

"Heaven forgive you, sister! Have you forgotten the night ride of the Prophet to the al-Aqsa Mosque of Jerusalem, described in sura 17, verse 1 of the Koran?"

"No, I don't remember that. Besides, you just told me that the Temple Mount was vacant during Mohammed's life. How could he visit a mosque that was not even there until after he died?"

"Ha-ha! My point exactly! What do you know, my little sister can think!"

## Chapter 66

# PALESTINE
# July 11, 2006

It was not without a good deal of reluctance that Aunt Rana released her student from the country, and her kitchen. The family would miss her. And such a wasted opportunity for poor Angela!

Rana gave a parting admonition. "I am sure Lebanon is nice, dear, but it can't beat learning how to cook."

Angela smiled sweetly at Rana and reached for her hand.

"And I'm worried," Rana continued. "Traveling with a man, even your Cousin Mohammed—especially your Cousin Mohammed—is not without its risks."

"Like you say, Auntie, Mohammed is my cousin. In America our cousins are like brothers. And besides, I'm married."

Rana softened a little and put a hand tenderly on Angela's shoulders. "Guard your heart, dear." Aunt Rana reluctantly added a word about her daughter "Have you noticed how Basma quit coming over when Mohammed came to town?"

Now that Mohammed's business in Palestine was complete, he was anxious to return to Lebanon to see how his family was. And he had information to share with Nasir.

Getting to Lebanon from Palestine required an indirect approach through Jordan, especially because these days Hezbollah was permeating Southern Lebanon. Rumors were worse than usual along the Israeli/Palestinian/Lebanese border.

At first Mohammed regretted impulsively inviting Angela to come along to Lebanon. This complicated his plans, but he would live up to his word.

Soon, however, he grew pleased with the idea. She would provide diversion.

Mohammed continued Angela's culture quiz.

"Hey, sister, what do rich women in San Francisco do all day? Watch TV and eat chocolate? That's how they get fat like you?"

Angela raised her eyebrows.

Mohammed reminded Angela of Mercutio in *Romeo and Juliet* in that he was

*A gentleman, that loves to hear himself talk,*
*and will speak more in a minute than he will stand to in a month.*

She was glad for it—otherwise she might never see Lebanon or escape from Aunt Rana's kitchen.

"Ha-ha!" Mohammed continued. "Palestinian brother is good liar. But seriously, sister, what do you do?"

"I teach English literature at the University of California in Berkeley." Angela left out the part about Women's Studies. *Don't feed the bear.*

"You mean it's not true that you are a movie star? Little Afrah brought me a picture of you she printed off the Internet, standing with some famous people. How come I never heard of you?"

"That shows you how good Al Jazeera News is. I'm more famous than President Bush."

"Oohh, that's good, my American sister, she is good liar!" he joked.

"OK, so I'm just rich, not famous."

"And you have no children? That's not very Arab of you, sister," he scolded playfully. "But you could adopt me!"

"Actually, I have hundreds of children. I raise money for them."

"How do you 'raise money'? Out of the ground where you buried it?"

"No, out of the pockets of people and businesses."

"You thief. You are rich, and you take money from others? Just give them your money!"

"There are too many poor children even for the Hall fortune."

"Poor children where?"

"America, especially the San Francisco Bay Area."

"But American children are verry rrrich!"

"Tell that to a fatherless boy whose mother is a drug addict."

"So everywhere there are problem people. Just let them be," he flippantly waved his hand.

"But we have to *try* to make the world a better place."

Mohammed tried to cover it, but he was pleased.

## Chapter 67

# PALESTINE TO LEBANON
## July 11, 2006

When they were in line at the Palestinian-Jordanian border, Mohammed found out that Angela came to Palestine not from San Francisco but from Istanbul. He literally jumped up, clapped his hands, and said, "Sister, that is amaaazing! I want to go to Turkey. Leettle American cousin, after I show you Lebanon you will show me Turkey. *Sah?*"

He said not a word of his prior visit there or his interest in Topkapi Palace.

They had to wait at the airport in Amman for a plane to Beirut.

"Moe, it sounds to me like the aunts will not be happy until you are married. Why is that?" Angela asked.

"Sister, what is wrong with you? You know the culture. All Arabs think, 'A man needs wife.' All the time the aunties are trying to match me, and I am beeeg disappointment to them!"

"*It is a truth universally acknowledged that a single man in possession of a good fortune must be in want of a wife,*" Angela quoted to herself, knowing that he would not recognize this opening line of *Pride and Prejudice.*

"Marriage is highly honored in our culture. *Kwayyes*, OK, but they take it to the extreme. It's crazy! Sometimes that's all they can think about. Seriously, even men think that way. If a man's wife dies—boom! Just like that they have to find him another right away. "

"It's a good thing that I am not single," she said, "or between cooking lessons and matchmaking, the aunties would work themselves sick!"

"No, sister, not at all, at all! Don't worry, you would be safe."

"Why? I thought they wanted all people to be married. You mean I'm safe because I'm American?" Angela asked.

He said seriously and not maliciously, "No, because you are old and you have been married. The aunties wouldn't even think of matching you."

"Oh," a surprised Angela said meekly. She struggled to cover the embarrassment and feelings of unworthiness that his brutal honesty engendered. *How old does he think I am?*

"Men remarry, sister! They don't believe a man can manage for himself alone. Women are different. They are married once. That's it! If her husband dies or divorces her, she will take care of herself fine."

"And besides, nobody would want her," Angela said a little caustically. "They are all looking for a young, ignorant virgin who they can put their scent on and boss around!"

She looked at the people in the airport. Everyone seemed suddenly foreign. Angela took for granted that she was beautiful, but that was in America, not in the Middle East, where many girls are married at fifteen.

*By thirty, you're probably seen as granny material.*

Back in America she would have dozens of suitors when her divorce was finalized. And they wouldn't only be after her money. In fact, this was a troubling prospect of her imminent divorce. She did not want to be thrust back into the competition that single people unconsciously but constantly battled. Face, figure, sex appeal, youth, personality, income, fitness, health, and intelligence were assets in a marketplace. Somehow, kindness and character seemed to sink to the bottom of the list.

Then there were the omnipresent unstated questions: Why aren't you married? Were you rejected? Do you have issues? Or did you just wait so long to find Mr. Right that *you* aren't right?

Even through the pain of marriage, when she observed her single friends, she was thankful to be out of that.

"Sister!" Mohammed turned and looked at her, genuinely surprised and unaware that his comments had offended her. "What is wrong with you?"

"You mean outside of the fact that I am old and used up? Or because I don't agree with all you are saying?"

"You don't? What? You don't think men need a wife?"

"Hey, hypocrite! You don't think so either, or I'm sure the aunties could have found you some lame, pimply-faced girl to marry by now."

"Ooooh, I get it! You don't like that I said you are old. Don't be silly, sister. Why do you care if you are old? You are married, aren't you? I won't care once I am married. Actually, I'm old too. If I don't marry soon, I will be too old for it."

"I thought you said a man has to remarry, no matter how old he is."

"*Re*marry, yes! But if a man doesn't marry by age thirty, he's a loser. He's not respected."

Angela was trying to remember how old Mohammed would be. It seemed like he was playing on the floor with cars and running around with a stick during her last visit. She scrutinized him for wrinkles and hair loss.

"So men marry for honor, not love. *Honor.* Oh, I know, I know why you're not married." She turned her emotions into a joke, but one with teeth. "All the families who know you would not shame themselves by an alliance with you! The aunties are only pretending to find you a wife, so you don't feel left out, poor baby."

"I don't need the aunties to find me a woman; although I might let them think they were helping. Really, any day I can find a dozen," he snapped his fingers, "just like that!"

"Oh, aren't you humble?"

"Humble is nothing. Proud is nothing. It is just this, sister—you know all women want to get married. It is the main thing for them. And if the man is cute and rich and funny? No problem. He can have anyone!"

"So that's what you think of women? Interchangeable. All the same. Just hopeless, desperate creatures, waiting for a man to come along. They cook and clean and give sex and get meaning in life by making a man respectable. A man can have anyone he wants. Just go to the orchard and pick a fruit. Then continue his life partying with the guys, the *shabaab.* Amazing! It is so simple, I wonder I never understood it before," she said.

"Everyone knows when a man shows his interest in a woman, she loves him back and wants to marry him. What's wrong with that? Don't you think women marry whoever gives them a good offer?"

"Maybe in the Middle East, but that's not how we see things in America."

"Rrreally," he said in English, rolling the *r* prominently. "Tell me, sister, are you rrrich?"

"Yes," she answered hesitantly, seeing where he was going.

"And were you rrrich before you were married?"

"No, but I didn't—"

"Ha-ha!" he laughed, interrupting her.

"—marry for money!"

"My little American cousin can make a deal like a real Arab! Ha-ha! You see, I told you so!" He laughed more. People looked at them and smiled, not knowing why. Even Angela laughed.

In his way, he meant it as a compliment, and she knew that. But Angela hurt for herself and all womankind.

She attacked from another angle. "You people say dating is wrong, but it keeps you from marrying someone you don't know!"

"That is not right! We know the girl very, very well before we marry. We make arrangements with the family to sit and talk for months. Then we marry."

"See, you 'make arrangements,' and *then* you talk. This means that you are engaged *before* you have a chance to know if you even want to be with her! And it's a disgrace if you don't marry the person you are courting. It's like having to get divorced before you are even married!"

"OK. If it makes you happy, I will tell you that I don't have to marry that way. I have the chance to marry many girls that I know very, very well."

Angela didn't even want to think about what "very, very, well" might mean.

"*That* certainly doesn't explain why you aren't married. Given your perspective, the only significant variable is your desire. So, why don't you *want* to marry?"

An honest answer to this question would expose who he was, and what he was doing with his life. This he could not reveal.

"Sister, it is the same as with you," he parried. "Why *are* you married?"

Angela gaped, hesitating a bit.

Mohammed jumped in with her presumed answer. "Because you want to be. Why is Mohammed single? Because he wants to be!"

## Chapter 68

# BEIRUT, LEBANON
## Wednesday, July 12, 2006

Angela awoke to a thunderous sound. Was it a bomb?

"Sister, get up! *Ma tkuny kaslana!*"

*Not a bomb. Mohammed.*

He was pounding on her door so hard that the entire room rattled. The unnaturally pleasant sound of his booming voice was not appreciated at this early hour.

"Sister, I am going to give you one day in Beirut you will never forget. You won't want to miss a minute. So *yala*, get up now, I am making eggs!"

Angela's head bolted off the pillow. "You're making eggs?" she asked herself aloud, eyes still blurry and hair tousled. "This I've got to see!"

She quickly threw on clothes and splashed her face. Loath as she was to be seen looking less than perfect, she rushed out to find that it was true. Mohammed was cooking! Yes, she got to see the rare sight of an Arab man over the stove, as he watched cubes of potatoes in a bubbling bath of olive oil.

"Wow," said Angela, "look how cute! They even make little square eggs in Lebanon!"

"Sister!" he said in a deep voice as if she had been impertinent. "What did that crazy Aunt Rana she teach you? Now this is an egg," Mohammed said, holding one up as if he were the cooking instructor, "and this is how we break it!" He made as if he would crack it on her head, and by sleight of hand slipped it to the edge of the bowl and broke it.

Mohammed scrambled eggs, then he drained the oil off the potatoes and poured the eggs over them. He sprinkled a little rosemary on top.

Angela said in amazement, "I didn't even know you were one of Aunt Rana's students. It looks like you stuck with her a little longer than I did; I didn't get to herbs!"

"I am smart Palestinian. I taught myself. When I moved to

Lebanon, I remembered this egg dish that I liked as child when my mother made it."

"ImmMohammed must be a great cook!"

Mohammed looked at her a little confused. But before he could say anything, his cell phone rang. Except for eating, Mohammed's enthusiasm was never greater than when talking on the phone with a friend he hadn't seen in weeks. After a flood of "What's happing with you, man?" or "*Shoo fi akhbar*?" in colloquial Arabic, with head shaking and loud laughter, he got off the phone and came to breakfast.

Angela had set up the terrace. While they drank coffee, Mohammed pointed out some of the sights visible from that vantage point, but they did not linger.

"Sister, you will see, I am the best, the best tour guide in Beirut!"

"I must say your touring vehicle is unique," Angela said, as she climbed into his Isuzu extended cab pickup.

"That's good!" he said, without explanation.

"Why do you need such a large vehicle for going around the city?"

"I don't use it for going around town. I walk to school from our apartment. I have it for the farm."

"The farm?"

"Haven't you wondered where your Aunt Zahara is? Heaven forgive you for forgetting her!"

For a few hours they drove, then walked around Beirut. Hezbollah had begun bombing Israel, and Beirut would soon suffer the consequences. Tomorrow it would once again be a site for charitable and nongovernmental organizations. But today, Angela enjoyed the city, unaware that she was one of the last visitors to see the splendor of restored Beirut.

Mohammed loved two things: talking and politics and was happy to educate Angela in whatever recent history of Beirut she was lacking. What she learned, in bits and pieces, amounted to this:

When billionaire Prime Minister Rafik Hariri came to office in 1992, he put 130 dollars of his own money into a company called Solidaire. His idea was to rebuild the rubble of downtown Beirut that had resulted from fifteen years of battles from 1975 to 1990. In a bold move, all the property of central Beirut was taken by Solidaire, with the property owners given shares in the company in forced exchange.

A mountain of trash was dumped into the sea to create sixty

hectares of new land for Beirut, and gleaming new buildings sprang up with state-of-the-art equipment like fiber-optic telephone lines and chilled underground water pipes. A six-lane highway connected the city with the new international airport. The potential for prosperity was even greater than it had been in 1974.

As could be imagined, not all were happy with the Solidaire scheme. Hariri paid the ultimate price.

"Here is where Hariri was killed," Mohammed pointed out as they drove by the Saint George Hotel on the Corniche. "Did you hear in America how his car was bombed?"

"Even we ignorant Americans heard about that one," she said.

Since 1990 Syria had dominated Lebanon's foreign relations. Their advent helped end the struggles of the previous fifteen years, but they were getting a little too comfortable in power for the nationalist soul of Hariri. For about five years he pursued policy to weaken Syria's grasp on the nation. Then, on February 14, 2005, he was murdered. Few in Lebanon doubted that Syria was behind the attack, which killed sixteen others. Indignation and rallies abounded, and by April of that year, Syria had withdrawn its troops.

"As I recall, neither Lebanon nor the USA were happy with Syria after that. In fact, I think we withdrew our ambassador from Damascus. Hey! The only thing our news didn't cover was how *you* escaped: I mean, since you are sooo important, you were no doubt giving advice on matters of state at the time."

After the driving tour they walked down to the American University of Beirut, where Nasir Atareek taught and where Mohammed was a graduate student. It provided one of the few green and restful spots in the bustling city, and Mohammed allowed Angela to sit for two minutes.

"Here, the whole city seems peaceful," she said, breathing deeply.

"You should see it during *Ashoura*!"

"What's that? It sounds familiar."

"Oohh, seesterr! It is such a job to teach you, I am glad you are rich, rich. You will need to pay me big! *Ashoura* is the day the Shiites remember the death of their hero, Hussein, the son of the fourth caliph, Ali. They remember the battle that killed him by marching in the streets and cutting themselves with knives."

"You are kidding me?"

"No, sister! If you don't believe me, you can look it up on the

Internet. Last February it happened, and every year in cities where there are Shiites. The city of Nabatiyé gets verrry, verrry bloody."

"But why?" she asked, still not seeing how this fit with her understanding of Islam.

"Sister! OK, you are Sunni, but you should have some understanding of your Shiite brothers. The Shiites believe in intercession. They believe that if they pray to a saint and hurt themselves to get his attention, he will intercede on their behalf to Allah. Intercession is one of the differences between Sunni and Shiite."

"But, don't we believe in intercession a little?"

"No, sister! How?"

"I heard that some Sunnis believe a martyr, even a suicide bomber, can take seventy people to paradise with him!"

"Oooooh, sister, you are getting good!"

At a nearby bookstore Angela spotted a book in English.

"*Ya, Mohammed, shoofa hada kitab!*" she said, picking it up and showing it to Mohammed.

He read the title, "*Skirts on Camels.* Sounds crazy, *majnoon* to me! Every Arab knows that camels wear saddles, not skirts! Must have been written by an American who never saw one."

"Actually, it was written by a very astute American professor of Arab descent. It is about early women authors in the Middle East, not camels. I think I'll buy it!"

"How Americans waste their money. If you want to know anything about camels, just ask me. I have my camel parked behind the apartment."

Angela looked at him for a second as if he were serious, and when he caught that look in her eye, he jumped on it, laughing and pointing, "Ha-ha! Sister, you believe anything."

"I'm just not as used to liars as you are. In fact, I think that whole *Ashoura* story is made up!"

"No, sister, I am serious about that! OK, ask your Uncle Nasir."

"If I ever get to see him..."

"I will take you to him, sister, just as soon as my camel puts on his skirt! Ha-ha!!"

They walked along the Corniche—Beirut's most famous walking strip between the ocean and the trendy shops and cafés. They stopped at a restaurant across from Pigeon Rocks for seafood. There was something of urban leisure here that reminded Angela of Santa Monica, California, or the south of France.

In the background they overheard someone saying something about Hezbollah and Israel and bombing, but such words were part of the texture of local life and did not of themselves engender unease when heard out of context.

Public bathing is not done in the beaches of Beirut, but that rule did not keep them dry. Mohammed and Angela finished off the afternoon walking along the beach, fully clothed except for their feet, laughing and splashing like kids.

It was predictable that Angela would enjoy the sunset, but this evening even macho Mohammed noticed it. Perhaps it was because the sun was setting on an era of peace for themselves as well as the city.

"Sister, it's dark!" Mohammed scolded Angela, as if it were her fault.

"So?" she asked.

"Let's get home. I have wonderful news for you!"

*Everything with Mohammed is wonderful or terrible.*

Either because he wanted her to learn more about Beirut or, as she suspected, because he was bored, Mohammed had invited four of his friends to meet them for dinner.

# Chapter 69

# BEIRUT, LEBANON
## July 12, 2006

From the radio they discovered the political and practical danger they were in, as Hezbollah entered into open conflict with Israel.

After washing off the salt and dressing in something suitable for nightlife, they returned to the Corniche. Angela wore a little black dress, and Mohammed a laced-neck black shirt he didn't seem to realize looked good on him. And neither realized they looked good together.

The friends were young and lively graduate students, but it was difficult to keep the conversation light. By chance, or choice, the four represented two for and two against Hezbollah.

Those against had family investments at stake in the "new Lebanon" and were against anything that would put them at risk. Lebanon should get over its grievances. Syria was as much a predator as Israel and was not to be trusted.

Those favoring Hezbollah felt Israel had bullied its neighbors long enough and should somehow be contained.

Political clichés and deep insights were alternately expressed.

Angela was aware that many Arabs in this part of the world don't look each other in the eye when speaking. In America she had been taught that it was considerate and success-oriented to look one straight in the eye. In return, she liked to be looked in the eye. It was a sign of courtesy and attention.

Tonight she didn't feel listened to. That was OK, because she didn't have much to say.

She struggled not to look people in the eye, and failed. So, the men perceived her as being flirtatious, unfettered by her supposed marriage. Their reciprocal flirtations she discounted as due to her own slip-ups and their Arab machismo.

The two women students were not looking Mohammed in the eye, but Angela noticed with interest how they could bat their eyes at him flirtatiously all the same.

*Is eye batting less flirtatious than direct viewing?*

Angela convinced herself that she was an objective observer.

It was a relief when the subject of politics was exhausted and they moved on to other topics. Eventually they started asking her about California, and before she knew it, she had promised them all a week skiing at her place in Lake Tahoe next winter.

Then Mohammed's cell phone rang. After his usual happy greeting, the expression on his face dropped. Everyone at the table became quiet and looked at him. He gave a weak smile.

"Hey, guys," he said, trying to make as if nothing much was happening, "I just got a call from my neighbor. It seems his..." Everyone waited in expectation for him to continue, "... cat got caught on the ledge, and he doesn't know how to get it in. I said I'd help. I've got to go."

It sounded plausible, and everyone knew Mohammed would help a neighbor in need, even if it meant risking his life.

*But they all knew it was a lie. The question was,* why?

Angela, thinking quickly, called his bluff. "That sounds interesting. I can't wait to see it!"

It seemed as if he had forgotten about Angela for a moment. Now he proposed a plan. "I'm sorry, Angela, it's not even midnight yet. You should not have to leave the fun for the sake of a cat." He turned to one of the men. "Samir, would you mind if Angela stayed with you? Drop her off at the apartment in a few hours, OK?"

"Okaaaay," he said, drawing it out a little excessively, due to the uncertainty of what was going on. But then he thought about Angela and turned to look her in the eye.

Angela got nervous and turned away. She knew what that look meant. Perhaps the evening would not be boring enough.

# Chapter 70

# BEIRUT, LEBANON
## July 12, 2006

How could he get into Jamal al-Hajji's apartment without raising any alarms? A knock at the front door would alert whoever had made Jamal nervous enough to call him so desperately half an hour ago.

Mohammed was in luck. When he arrived at al-Hajji's apartment in South Beirut, loud Arabic music was emanating from the apartment next door. It was a party. From previous visits to al-Hajji, Mohammed knew his neighbors Hala and Farha, or Sweetness and Joy as their names meant in Arabic, the two beautiful and worldly sisters who rented the apartment.

In a bold move, which Mohammed knew they would accept, he quickly opened the door and called out with raised hands that nearly touched the ceiling, "Where are my sisters? I need some sweetness and joy!"

After the briefest time socially possible, with a few jokes, loud, off-key singing, and shaking of the wrists in dance, he excused himself and went to the bathroom. He knew that next to the bathroom was a bedroom with a sliding glass door.

Quietly, he entered the bedroom.

The living room also had a sliding glass door onto the balcony. He cracked open the bedroom door and listened to hear if anyone was on the balcony. Voices and music came indirectly from the next room. He peeked around the door and saw no one.

Mohammed tiptoed onto the balcony. He climbed onto the railing and around the wall to gain access to al-Hajji's apartment, exposing himself to the brief but ominous risk of a drop of several stories.

He quietly descended to al-Hajji's balcony and immediately hid out of view. There was no one in the living room. In the next room, Jamal's bedroom, he could see a figure in bed, still.

*He's not alone.*

Mohammed saw the shadow of a man he recognized. It made him more anxious to enter and find out how Jamal was. The door to Jamal's room was closed and locked, but the door to the living room was open, letting in fresh air. That seemed to be the only access.

Mohammed attempted to move the screen door silently, but it was impossible. There was a slight squeak as metal slid against metal.

*Alhamdulillah for the party!*

He was sure no one heard him over the music.

Inside, he crept against the wall, staying out of sight as much as possible for as large a man as himself.

The music was a curse as well as a blessing. He couldn't hear the man moving in the next room. He would have to attempt a visual reconnaissance.

When he got to the hallway he could see a shadow exiting from Jamal's room and entering the bedroom next door—Ahmed's room.

As the man turned to enter the room, Mohammed got a view of his back and a flash of the side of his face. It was Ahmed. Perhaps that was not unusual, since Ahmed lived with Jamal. But Jamal had been dead serious when he called.

And now he was seriously dead.

Mohammed walked into Jamal's room and approached the still form on his bed. He reached for the wrist. There was no pulse. He felt the carotid artery. Nothing. He lifted the eyelids. No response.

He looked around. There on the bedside table lay Jamal's diabetic paraphernalia. He pushed the button on the glucose meter. It read 30 mg/dl.

Now what? Ahmed, Jamal's supposed assistant, was showing no concern that his employer lay dead with a fatally low glucose level.

Mohammed decided direct confrontation was the best approach. He walked back into the living room and crossed his arms, waiting for Ahmed.

"*Ya*, Ahmed!" he called unnecessarily loudly when Ahmed entered. "I came to visit our colleague Jamal, and he isn't looking too good to me. Have you called a doctor yet?"

Caught by surprise, Ahmed's face went blank. But he thought fast and pulled out a knife. "I don't think that will be necessary," he said, "since he's already dead."

"Oh, little brother," said Mohammed, "why are you waving that knife at me? There are no apples here. Go into the kitchen."

Ahmed lunged at Mohammed. Mohammed's large hand easily twisted the knife out of Ahmed's. It fell onto the floor, and the men followed.

Then Ahmed reached for a lamp and struck Mohammed on the

head. For a second Mohammed was dazed. Ahmed grabbed back at the knife. He got up and stood over Mohammed with it.

Ahmed jumped on top of Mohammed, but Mohammed caught him and threw him overhead in a movement that looked acrobatic.

The screen onto the balcony ripped as Ahmed landed on the floor above Mohammed's head. Ahmed's head extended through the ripped screen and onto the balcony. The remainder of his body was still in the living room. His legs were near Mohammed's head and started pummeling it.

Mohammed rolled over and pinned down Ahmed's legs. Then he crawled on top of Ahmed, walking on his knees. Ahmed flailed about but couldn't free himself.

The sliding glass door was directly in line with Ahmed's neck. On reflex, Mohammed grabbed the handle of the door. He quickly jerked it closed.

Ahmed gasped in pain as the door slammed into his neck.

With his knees Mohammed then pinned Ahmed's body against the doorpost, while his strong arms closed the door tighter and tighter on Ahmed's neck.

Eventually, Ahmed stopped moving.

"Why didn't you listen to me, brother?" said Mohammed. "I told you to go back to Yemen."

He pulled Ahmed's dead body back inside.

Mohammed needed a drink. Water. Anything. But he wanted to see what was in Ahmed's room, and he didn't want to leave fingerprints. He wiped clean everything he had touched, including the bags Ahmed had packed to leave.

He closed the sliding door onto the balcony and gave it a jerk to lock it.

*A locked room mystery.*

With any luck the bodies would not be discovered for a few days.

Then he jumped back over to the girls' balcony and into their bathroom. He washed up a few scratches. His dark shirt did not show blood, and the bump on his head was not evident yet.

Mohammed rejoined the party. If anyone had noticed something unusual, they didn't say.

To keep his cover, Mohammed stayed for a full hour and partied. It was the best acting he had ever done. Fortunately, he knew the lines well.

## Chapter 71

# BEIRUT, LEBANON
## July 13, 2006

At 4 a.m., Mohammed returned to his apartment and started opening cupboards. Angela, a light sleeper who had been half awaiting his return, put on a robe and came out. Mohammed looked rumpled, and besides being unshaven, there was just the slightest wear on his ever-ready assurance.

"Everything OK?" she asked, knowing it wasn't.

"Sister, what kind of a question is that? Everything is wonderful! It's a beautiful night in the Paris of the Middle East."

Angela kept quiet but looked doubtful.

Mohammed continued. "How would you like to see the Cedars of Lebanon? I'll make the tea, you go pack." His casual manner belied the weight of the words.

"At this hour? May I wait until morning, please? I'll do it while you are making breakfast."

He put on the kettle and pulled out two clear glass-handled cups, then spoke. "We're up. Let's go now!"

"Is it even possible at this hour? Do they offer sunrise tours?"

"Oh, sister, you are too funny! Just I am thinking that it would be sooo cool to get up there early in the morning, and that's it!" He jumped in his unique way, raising his voice. "We see the beeeuuuutiful Cedars of Lebanon!"

Angela laughed.

*He's so unpredictable and refreshing.*

She asked, "Something happened at Jamal's house, didn't it?"

"I told you eeeverrything's fine! Trust me."

"That would be foolish. OK, so be obtuse," she said, knowing he would not understand, "I'll go pack. But you'd better tell me *eeeverry-thing* when we are driving."

After Angela left, his smile faded and his face became tense. He made the tea and brought it directly to her door, wanting both to avoid further discussion and to speed up their departure. He left his tea untouched on the kitchen counter and started throwing clothes and household items into suitcases—and boxes, bags, and any other large containers he could possibly recruit for the purpose.

With the car fully loaded, Mohammed quietly, almost secretly, pulled away from the building in the early light at about 5:45 a.m.

"May I have a map?" Angela inquired. "I'd love to know where we are going."

Mohammed surveyed the streets. "It's in the side pocket," he said distractedly.

Angela took it out. "It's in Arabic. That's OK, I like a challenge," she said, folding it. "Which road will we take?"

"First we get out of Beirut. Then we go south along the coast on the Sidon Highway to Nahr ed Damour. That's where we get Route 15 into the hill country, toward Deir el-Qamar and al-Barouk. Our plantation is between them," he said in English, sounding somewhat recovered. "You will love it sooo much!"

The Beirut International Airport came into sight as they left Beirut.

They could hear planes overhead, which was not surprising. But there was a loud roaring sound that was unexpected. In fact, the car windows begin to vibrate.

"What's that?" asked Angela.

Mohammed said nothing, looking out the windows.

"Jets! They can't be serious! No! Not the airport! Get down!" he yelled to Angela.

BOOM! BOOM!

There came two momentous blasts. Angela screamed, grabbing her head.

Just as Mohammed and Angela were passing beside the airport, two Israeli fighter jets screeched over it, dropping bombs onto the runways. The reverberations made both car and road unsteady, and Mohammed's hands on the wheel struggled uncertainly for direction. The same challenges faced the other drivers, causing several near collisions and one minor one, and threw a few other cars off the road. Mohammed's ended up on the right shoulder.

"What the . . . ?" he exclaimed, adding some Arabic curse words, which seemed appropriate under the circumstances.

The roar overhead continued but seemed to change direction. Quickly he pulled back onto the road, trying to bring as much of it as possible between themselves and the airport before the planes returned.

Sure enough, the jets circled back. But this time Mohammed was prepared. His hands gripped the wheel steadily for the next two deep bass explosions.

"Wake up, Beirut!" he said wryly as the blasts resonated across the city. "I wonder how many coffee spills they're cleaning up now?"

"Seriously, what was that? Is there a base doing war games or something?"

"Those were real hits on the Beirut airport, sister. The Israeli Defense Forces don't play around."

## Chapter 72

# SIDON HIGHWAY, LEBANON
## July 13, 2006

Stunned and relatively silent, they continued driving. In a few miles, the costal tableland bore citrus groves and banana plantations. With the morning light gilding the groves, and the fruit stands closed, there was a preternatural peace—especially with Mohammed being unusually quiet.

But it didn't last long. When you are there at the moment a war begins, and you feel it, quite literally feel it shake you, it is difficult not to become political. This is a temptation Mohammed did not resist.

"Now what are you guys doing to us?" He shouted—not at Angela personally but at her. "Why do you Americans have to keep pushing yourselves into other people's business and messing up countries that you don't belong in?"

"Excuse me, Mo, but are you suggesting that America has something to do with the bombing of the airport? That's totally ridiculous! Right now we don't know what it was, but my guess is that Israel is not too happy about what's been going on the last few days and got overenthusiastic with their response. I don't think the United States Congress convened and said, 'Hmm we haven't started a war in any remote, recovering nations recently. Why don't we send the boys out for some target practice?'"

"OK. So it was Israel. Everybody knows that Israel is supported by America—its, what do you say... *Bub'bed.*"

"What?"

"*Bub'bed.* You know, toy on string?"

"Oh, in English, you mean a *puppet!*"

"Right. So you agree. Just look at the map of the Middle East: all the Arab countries. And in the middle is Israel. Everyone here knows that Israel is just a spy state for America in the middle of the Arab world!"

"Oh, aren't we Americans smart! We chose for our secret agent in the Middle East the one country all the others hate. Give me a break! You can make a lot of accusations, and they might be true, but this is off the wall."

"Sister ... I'm only telling you what everyone in the Middle East knows: the US owns Israel and at the bottom is responsible for whatever it does. This is why Saddam is seen as a hero—he stands up to the US."

"Whoa! So you're saying the US went looking for a country in the Middle East that it could use as a puppet and spy, and it found that the Jews could be bought, but not the Arabs? Well, aren't you righteous!"

A sleepless night followed by the adrenalin rush was affecting Mohammed's driving. When he talked politics in Arabic, he used animated hand gestures. And Mohammed was driving far too fast around the mountain switchbacks for Angela's comfort.

"Look," Angela continued, "you know I'm half Arab, and I love you guys. I feel part of you, and I am part of you. I hate it every time Israel violates human rights or UN resolutions. I hate it because I feel my people hurt on the other side of the world; and I hate it because my people in America will be blamed for it. There is much I am learning about the Middle East. But I think you guys need to learn more too. For example: why do you think America cares about Israel at all?"

"Because the Jews in America are very powerful, and America wants to control the Middle East." He was serious.

"That sounds like something you heard on Al Jazeera and accepted without thinking. OK, consider this: you told me you were a good swimmer and saved someone's life once. How did you feel about that person after? Would you want to see him or her die of a drug overdose? Like in the film *Lawrence of Arabia*: Lawrence nearly dies crossing the desert on foot to save the life of a boy he carries on his back. Later, when he sees the boy die, Lawrence is in agony."

She paused to catch her breath. "My American grandfather fought in the Second World War. He spent nearly three years along the front lines maintaining radio communication networks. He saw his friends killed. He was nearly killed several times himself, and has a hole in his left ear from a close shave with a bullet. He is not Jewish, or even religious. But he fought to save the Jews from Hitler. So you see, it's not the Jews that make Israel special to America; it's the price that was paid for it. When you buy something valuable, like a diamond or a house, you don't want to sell it for less than you paid, right? That's why we don't want to see Israel blown off the map. Did you ever think of that?"

Mohammed was quiet. Angela thought he had gotten her point.

Then he surprised her by laughing. "Seesterr, you have been in America too long, buying diamonds and houses from rich Jews!"

They now turned up into the Chouf Mountains. Angela checked the map. Once on track, Mohammed returned to arguing.

"Take Iraq. What does America think it is doing there? Why did you go invade it? Surely you agree that was a mistake! There were no weapons of mass destruction! You don't understand the way people think here. What does Rice know? Russia maybe, maybe Africa, but not the Middle East! How can she advise anybody? And President Bush—he probably doesn't even know Shiite from Sunni. You Americans have this crazy idea that people want your way because it is best. You can go over and force American democracy on the Middle East. Saddam Hussein was evil, I agree, everybody knows that, but he understood the situation in Iraq and managed to keep it out of civil war. Democracy is not going to work in the Middle East! What America needs to do is just find the right leader—"

"You mean 'dictator,'" she interrupted.

"—who is friendly to America, and support him in power. That's it! Then there would be peace and you could be out of trouble."

"Whoa! Look, I would not have gone into Iraq if I were president. Think of it from our perspective. What benefit did America get out of going to Iraq? Nothing for us! Just a lot of our kids killed."

"Exactly!" said Mohammed. "Yankee stay home!"

Angela continued. "But Saddam was a UN agreement violator. People forget that. For ten years inspectors were being thrown out of Iraq in violation of the UN peace treaty, which generously allowed him to remain in power if he were 'good.' Maybe he was good at keeping peace in your way, but he was stupid at keeping power."

"Ten years ago you were watching the news? Whoa, you really are old, sister!"

Angela continued. "But the most amazing thing I've heard all morning, even crazier than the bombing, is you saying that the US should plant a dictator in Iraq! You are the king of contradiction! First you say America should stay out of the Middle East and not make puppet states, and now you suggest that we do that very thing!"

"I'm just saying that Americans don't understand the Middle East, so they should not try to make it like America. If you see something good there, then OK, you can support it."

"We supported the shah in Iran, and look what happened there. All I support is Aunt Rana's cooking!"

"You see, I make my point. Americans are fools in the Middle East. They don't know anything about making peace!"

"Oh, that's rare coming from a Palestinian! You guys really put your whole selves into it: into an explosive jacket, that is, then blow yourself up in some disco or border crossing where your own people are trying to get to work!"

At that Mohammed exhaled a loud puff and looked wounded. The timing was bad. He was just passing a car on a blind curve. He barely missed hitting the oncoming car, slammed on the brakes, and pulled back into his lane, nearly tumbling them over the edge with the momentum. She had tried to play cool so far, knowing he was not one to take advice, but she hadn't had much more sleep than him and wasn't used to life in a war zone.

"What kind of maniac are you?" she burst out loudly. "Are you doing that suicide thing on me?"

As the car jerked to a stop Mohammed looked angrily at her. "What did you call me? *Never* use that word with me!"

"*Lesh La?* Why not? In America that's what we say when someone drives crazy."

He pulled back on the road, hardly slacking his pace. "It's just that it's almost the worst, worst word in Arabic."

"No wonder the East and the West can't get along. We say one thing, and you hear another."

But he drove more sensibly after that.

## Chapter 73

# CHOUF MOUNTAINS, LEBANON
## July 13, 2006

There was something about arguing with Mohammed that Angela didn't mind. Mohammed didn't mind either, but then with him it was more of a lifestyle.

Angela was suspecting it was not uncommon for Middle Eastern men to take opposing viewpoints just for the sake of conversation. To an American, the combination of guttural sounds and passionate discourse sounded as if they were cussing each other. Actually, they were sharing stimulating conversation, and possibly even learning.

Likewise with Mohammed and Angela, although the subject matter could be very heavy and the discussion animated, there were no hard feelings engendered either way. When it was over, it was simply over. Except for the stimulated condition the system was left in, it was like it had never happened.

Nevertheless, discretion was the better part of valor. Having just had the second close call on their lives that day, once the car had stabilized Angela changed to a neutral topic.

"Driving through these mountains reminds me of something I read about an English woman who moved here two hundred years ago. They say people hardly knew how to take her—some thought she was a prophet, and others, just crazy. Have you heard of Hester Stanhope?" Angela asked.

"Oohh, yes, sister, I heard about her, but not her name. I saw the ruins of her house when I was exploring this area looking for farms. Hers was over the mountains there . . ." He gestured over the mountains to the south. A little too broadly for Angela's taste, since the car swerved a bit as his arm came off the wheel. "They call her the Crazy English Princess!"

"I read that the Ottoman sultan told the Lebanese, 'Give the English Princess anything she wants.'"

"And you see, sister, how things haven't changed? Here I am, doing aaaaanything the American Princess wants. I am so nice!"

For Angela, there was no possible response but to laugh.

As they approached Deir el-Qamar, Mohammed began to play the carefree host again, a role he maintained throughout the day.

"Sister, ImmMohammed can wait breakfast for us," he said. "You are going to see the cuuuutest village in all of Lebanon—Deir el-Qamar!"

It was still early, and the shops had not yet opened, so parking was easy. He told her a little of how this was Lebanon's first capital in the early seventeenth century. They walked around the square while she admired the palace of the Chehabs and the mosque dominating the square. She commented on the beauty of the yellow stone in the morning light, the quaint buildings climbing up the hill, and the colorful flowers tumbling over the retaining walls of their terraced gardens.

"I haven't seen all the villages of Lebanon," she said, "but this one certainly is pretty!"

From some of the open windows they could hear voices and television reports talking of the impending war. Angela came out with what was foremost in her mind. "Tell me, did you know about the bombings? Is that why you tore me away at such an indecent hour this morning?"

"What, sister? Don't you think this is the best possible time to see el-Qamar? Was brother wrong?"

*He's evading the question.*

She got the feeling, not for the first time, that Mohammed was like a partly tamed animal. He seemed casual, connected, and full of fun, but if you tried to pin him down, he would sprint away.

But she was more curious than ever about what had happened when he was gone last night. Why did he come home disheveled and in such a hurry to leave?

## Chapter 74

# CHOUF MOUNTAINS, LEBANON
## July 13, 2006

Around 8 a.m., Mohammed pulled off onto a side road in the plantation hill country. Acres of olive trees passed by, like gray-green bouquets decorating the golden brown soil. Stone fences separated the farmlands. A side road to the right brought them through more groves, up to a small vineyard surrounding a stone farmhouse on the crest of a hill.

The combined effect was charming to Angela.

The stone of the house had the same mellow quality she had seen in Deir el-Qamar. There was an incomplete section of the house to the left with a standing arch that gave the appearance of an old capriccio painting of Honey Jean's. To the right was a copse of apple trees, giving way to more olives down the hill. A few Italian cypresses flanked the house, and there was one very large tree behind it. The setting reminded her of a villa John's family rented in Italy one summer—warm afternoons, lazy evenings chatting. The thought of Honey Jean in Italy brought a bittersweet smile to her face.

It was out of pace with their conversation, and Mohammed noticed. Her look expressed the way he himself felt about the farm.

*It's strange that she should feel that when she has never been here before.*

"What do you think, isn't this the cutest farm in Lebanon?"

"No doubt," she covered the enthusiasm she felt with a little sarcasm. "Just like Deir el-Qamar is the 'cutest' village in the Middle East, and you are the cleverest Palestinian!"

"Sister, you are learning!"

The house, typical of Lebanese architecture of the late nineteenth century, had two stories and was roughly rectangular. It was composed of rectangular and square stones in shades of beige, yellow, and honey. Slightly darker stone was used for the window pediments, which were both gothic and triangular styles.

*All is not poor in the Middle East.*

The few embellishments included a central two-story protrusion that provided a balcony above, as well as a covered front entry. Three gothic arches decorated both floors of the protrusion, with the upper level having a stone balustrade around the edges of the balcony.

Full-length green-shuttered windows broke up the façade and had small black iron balconies on the upper level. Angela found herself hoping that one of those magic shuttered windows would lead to her room, and that in the morning she could step outside, still in her pajamas, for a view and breath of heavy morning air before anyone was up.

They were expected. By the time they reached the door, Aunt Zahara—also known as ImmMohammed—Uncle Nasir, and an attractive young woman came running up to them excitedly, calling, "*Ahlan wa sahlan habeebtee Amerikyay! Ahlan wa sahlan! Al-bayt baytik!*"

Uncle Nasir was perhaps a little less animated but welcoming all the same. Graying and balding, he looked about sixty years old. ImmMohammed was matronly but attractive. The young woman was Nihla, who studied architecture and landscape design at the American University of Beirut, where her father, Nasir, taught.

Many kisses were shared by all. Aunt Zahara gave Angela a huge hug. She swayed back and forth, hugging her tighter and tighter, saying, "*Habeebtee, habeebtee.* How I've missed you. *Alhamdulillah!* Praise God you are here!"

Angela felt like a child being crushed by a doting old relative. Which was rather what it was. But she didn't mind. It felt good to be loved by someone.

*Someone across the world whom I barely know loves me.*

A sudden warm feeling of belonging, of being part of the good community of humankind, swept over Angela. It was a foreign feeling she could not precisely remember having had before. Except that it reminded her of having a mother. As did her aunt's appearance and perfume.

Angela excused herself to freshen up, but it wasn't just to refresh from the journey. She washed her face and then looked in the mirror. She thought, as if speaking to her reflection.

*She does look like Mother. I feel so strange.*

Her eyes filled with tears. She cried and needed to wash her face again. The sight of someone who looked like her mother in a house worthy of Honey Jean renewed her grief for the two people she loved most in the world.

# Chapter 75

# CHOUF MOUNTAINS, LEBANON
## July 13, 2006

While Angela was away, Mohammed took ImmMohammed aside and asked the Arabic equivalent of "Isn't my leetle American cousin cool and amazing?"

ImmMohammed was used to his flattering ways. "Of course, I love her. I have never forgotten her green eyes... and I know that a beautiful woman never escapes your notice," she teased.

"Of course she's beautiful, what did you expect from family? Even if far too much comes out of that American mouth."

"Ooooh," she replied, "that's good! You mean she beats you in an argument now and then?"

"I said she was amazing—not unbelievable."

Nihla interrupted. "I'll be happy to have a cousin out here. It's sooo boring. *Kathir, kathir!*"

"Strange," said ImmMohammed, "you haven't looked bored to me, the way you're glued to that cell phone. You ought to get out more and get some exercise."

"Yeah, like I said, I'll take Angela around the farm after breakfast," she said quickly, then turned to Mohammed and grabbed his arm, "Tell me, Mohammed, did you see any gardens in England? Did you take any pictures? Any of estates designed by Capability Brown?"

"Actually, yes, I..."

Just then Angela entered the room. She picked up the words "England" and "Capability Brown." She also knew of the famous landscape designer and tried to put into context what she had heard.

*When did Mohammed go to England?*

Angela thought he had left Lebanon to check on his properties in Palestine, but there must be more to it than that.

Mohammed read Angela's puzzled expression, then flashed eyes at Nihla and nudged ImmMohammed.

They must have understood his signals, because ImmMohammed came up with a quick change of subject. "Mohammed, why don't you marry?"

Angela understood. England was not a topic to be queried at this time.

ImmMohammed demonstrated with her hand. "I can introduce you to several beautiful girls right here in the countryside. Angela, dear, will you help out your old auntie? Tell Mohammed he should settle down and marry."

"Oh," said Angela, perplexed by the change of topic. "Does he have a girlfriend? I didn't know!"

"*La, la, habeebtee! Alhamdulillah!* No, dear, we don't do things that way here. But I can arrange a fiancée for him any time. Tomorrow, maybe?"

ImmMohammed's look into Mohammed's eyes and her hand on his shoulder spoke sincerely. "He is a good catch, you know. A wonderful match for any girl in Arabia." She patted him dotingly.

"Well, in America we say, 'Marry in haste; repent at leisure.' So, it seems to me if he has avoided marriage this long, there is no point in rushing it," she said, hoping she had not brought any suspicion of repentance upon herself.

"Hey, could you possibly delay marrying me to the fat neighbor girl until after breakfast? Who wants a skinny husband!"

"Mohammed, I have everything ready! Nihla, go call your father from the library."

They shared a delicious repast on the back patio. The morning sun filtered through the vines growing over the portico, a clever mixture of clematis, honeysuckle, climbing roses, and grapes, each planted around a different pillar. The grapes were of two varieties, red and green. Some of the green had ripened, and Mohammed made a show of reaching up on tiptoe and plucking a few fresh bunches, proudly displaying both his produce and his healthy physique.

They dined on typical breakfast staples: *khubis*, flat pitalike bread, some of which was topped with *zaa'tar*, a mixture of cumin, oregano, and sumac; which made a pizzalike pastry called *mankoushi*. *Lebany*, fresh cheese made from yogurt allowed to drain overnight in cheesecloth, was also served, along with *tahina* and a sweet syrupy dip made from grapes. And there was *fuul*, traditional breakfast bean with olive oil, cumin, and lemon.

The meal took unnecessarily long because they simply enjoyed being together in the freshness of the day. Angela told them stories about California, avoiding mention of John whenever possible, and ImmMohammed was more than glad to share stories of their lives and many friends.

"What is that large tree that partly shades the patio?" Angela asked.

Nihla answered with surprise, "Why, cousin. That's one of the famous Cedars of Lebanon!"

"Oh," answered Angela. "How wonderful that you have one! I thought the cedars grew only in a few special groves."

"Mohammed," Nihla called to him sarcastically but lightly, "I thought you said this woman was smart!"

"Hey, they are mostly in groves!" he said in Angela's defense. "You know that. I bet smart cousin even knows the name of one grove."

"*Cedars of the Lord*?" Angela asked.

"Yes! Ha-ha, Nihla, I told you!" Mohammed cheered with exaggerated zeal, as if she were winning a game show. "OK, Nihla, your turn. Tell little cousin about the groves around here."

She acquiesced, as everyone seemed to do to Mohammed. "Let's send her to Tannourine!"

Mohammed agreed readily and loudly, clapping his hands and stomping a foot in delight. Aunt and uncle joined in.

Angela didn't get it. She was in that uncomfortable position of knowing she was the butt of a joke and not knowing how to respond. She just sat there with a neutral smile, awaiting the enlightenment she was sure would follow.

Mohammed closed his mouth and tried to control his excessive laughter. He did not want to offend Angela. "Oh, sister, Nihla, you are too cruel! Where is your love for our little American cousin?"

"May I ask where little cousin is being sent?" Angela ventured. "I am suspecting it is not someplace warm and friendly?"

"Pfff!" They all stifled explosive laughs. Mohammed patted the air with his left hand, as if to stifle the noise. "*Kwayyes, kwayyes.* OK. *Habeebtee* Angela, I am sorry to tell you that your cousin wants to send you to the grove where the militia planted land mines during the Lebanese Civil War. Now no one can go there... if they want to come out alive!" And at this, all but Angela broke out laughing again.

"OK, I'm sorry," said Nihla. "There are two other groves around Barouk, not far from here. They are part of a nature reserve of about five hundred square kilometers."

"Sounds beautiful," said Angela. "Can we go there?" More laughter ensued.

"Nihla, now stop it! Enough!" said Mohammed. "First you explode our little cousin, now you want to leave her at a gate in the dust. What are you trying to do? Get Bush to bomb Lebanon too?"

At the mention of bombing, the group sobered.

Mohammed explained. "Little cousin, you can't visit that grove either. They won't let people in; it's just for animals."

"Hmm," said Angela, seeing her chance for a comeback, "I see the problem. That means they'll let you in, but not me!" She laughed.

"Ha-ha! She's got you there, Mohammed," said ImmMohammed. "Good one, Angela *habeebtee!*"

"Forget about it," said Mohammed, who never found jokes on him as funny as when they were on others. "There is a small grove at the end of our plantation. You can go there this afternoon."

Nihla felt guilty about teasing Angela before she knew her better. "It is quite beautiful. Please let me take you there. Let's go on a walk around the farm right after breakfast. I will show you everything, and we can end up down there. Please?"

Angela looked for signs of protest from Mohammed; she would have rather gone with him. But there were none.

"That's more like it, Nihla! We've got to show our little cousin how we love her!"

Nihla got up and pointed. "Look down where the valley meets the next hill. That's where the grove comes up to the orchard. You can see where the trees change color and height." Angela stood and followed the pointing finger with her eyes.

"I will enjoy the walk!" Angela affirmed, as if to herself as well as those seated at the tables.

"Good! Let's clean up here then *yala nemshee*, let's go!"

## Chapter 76

# CHOUF MOUNTAINS, LEBANON

## July 13, 2006

Mohammed's strong sense of hospitality was suffering. And pride of ownership made him want to show off his jewel to Angela. But his reasons for deferring were good ones: he had management issues to attend to, they were in a war zone, and he had killed a man. He needed time to plan what to do next. And yes, a little sleep would help.

"*Tfaddaly.* Here, try one," said Nihla, offering Angela an apple—a small variety that ripens in the summer. As they walked the orchards, Angela picked fresh figs, apricots, and grapes. She was lucky to find several varieties coming ripe at the same time.

Nihla was a good guide. Her studies in architecture and landscape had trained her to notice the features that made an estate interesting. Finally they reached the end of the back valley and its transition to the cedars. "Here they are," announced Nihla, "the secret grove of the famous 'Cedars of Lebanon'!" She entered the grove, throwing her arms wide open. The shade felt nice and cool in the summer afternoon. The crush of needles beneath their feet left a sweet smell.

Nihla continued her homage. "It's the traditional symbol of Lebanon, the insignia on its flag and money, the historic source of its wealth, and the stuff of Solomon's temple!" She lowered her arms and switched her tone of voice, as if telling a secret. "Did you know that Solomon covered the carved cedar walls of his temple with gold? Suffocating that lovely fragrance. What waste!" said the architecture student.

She leaned over and picked up a fallen branch. Breaking it with her hands, a cedar fragrance was released. "Hmmm," she said, inhaling, and then passed it to Angela who echoed her.

"If Solomon had left the walls like this, he could have saved two fortunes," Angela said appreciatively, "one in gold and another in incense!"

They walked, each carrying a twig of cedar.

"For my part," said Angela, "here is the temple!" She stretched out her arms as she walked deeper into the grove. "There is a sacred feeling about being with trees this ancient."

"Exactly! Look at this tree, for example. It is fifteen hundred years old, one of the oldest in the grove. It was a baby when our Prophet, peace be upon him, walked upon the earth."

"A baby?"

"In a manner of speaking. It can take saplings up to forty years to produce fertile seeds!"

"Oooooh! That makes me feel young!" said childless Angela with a smile. Nihla couldn't understand this statement. Angela didn't look much older than her, and she felt very young.

"We have trees this old in California. They're called redwoods, because that's the color of their wood. They can live up to three thousand years and are taller than these, but not so graceful. I love to go walking among them in Muir Woods. It gives me this same sort of unearthly feeling... like eternity," she said quietly.

"This grove is precious in more than one way," said Nihla somberly.

"How so?"

"Besides this special feeling it gives us, it is special because it is rare. In the Stone Age, most of Lebanon was covered with cedars. But as far back as the dynastic ages of Egypt, the trees were known. They were used to help construct the pyramids. Their resin even preserved mummies. Once they were discovered, it seems that everybody needed them. A few attempts were made to preserve the trees, but you know how conservation fares against profit and progress. Now there are only a few groves. In fact, this may be the only one of significant size that is in private hands. Being hidden in this valley preserved them."

"Thanks to generations of your family's tender care," Angela said appreciatively.

"What? No! Didn't you know Mohammed's only had this estate about five years?"

"Mohammed owns this estate?"

## Chapter 77

# CHOUF MOUNTAINS, LEBANON
## July 13, 2006

"Mohammed bought the estate after the accident. I thought you knew. But I'm not surprised he didn't tell you. That's like him. He's so humble."

"Humble? He's the proudest person I've ever met!"

"Well, that depends on how you judge it. You can't go by what he says; that's just talk. Many *shabaab* do that. Just for fun."

"In America, it's just for pride."

"Sounds boring there," inserted Nihla.

"In fact, the more you have to be proud of, the less you brag about it." Of the many things she could accuse John of, bragging was not one of them.

"That's it. You see. I told you, talk doesn't make you proud!"

It was not worth arguing. Angela changed the subject.

"You said the grove is precious in several ways. What's another?"

"To Mohammed. But I should let him explain that to you himself."

The conversation was subdued on the way back as they walked mostly uphill. At one point they stopped to take a short rest where there was a good view of the house. They could see the full back side—the windows, the portico covered with vines, the ruined arch to one side, and the solitary large cypress shading half of its bulk.

"The house looks just as beautiful from the back as from the front. You're knowledgeable about architecture. Tell me about it," asked Angela in Arabic, Nihla's preferred language.

"Well, you must know the house is nineteenth century. Not terribly historic. Except for the dilapidated section on the side. That is part of an old monastery that was later made into a small keep for Crusaders. It became ruined over the centuries following the Crusades, and the entire area was neglected—thus the preserved cedar grove. About a hundred and fifty years ago, they planted orchards and built the house. Most of the stones from the ruin were reused in making the house. Then, of course, it became a ruin again."

"What do you mean?"

"Oh, I guess you don't know that either. Sorry. This area is quite far south in Lebanon. Everywhere around here got bombed during the Civil War about thirty years ago. In fact, there still are enclaves of Hezbollah in these hills." She paused.

Both women looked around, as if spotting for snipers.

Nihla continued. "When Mohammed bought the property, he moved here and started rebuilding it himself."

"Himself?" Angela echoed.

"He was like a hermit for a while. Working alone. Carrying stones up and down ladders. He was obsessed, working day and night in all weather. Sometimes his hands were wrapped with rags to bind up the cuts, but he kept going. And *alhamdulillah*, he finally recruited others to help him. Otherwise, I'm not sure I would feel safe walking up the stairs!"

*So the scars on his hands are not from the accident.*

When they returned to the house, it was cool and quiet. The excitement had kept her going, but after a refreshing drink, Angela was ready for a siesta.

## Chapter 78

# CHOUF MOUNTAINS, LEBANON
## July 13, 2006

Mohammed crashed in his room but couldn't sleep. Too much had happened, and he had so many thoughts to sort through.

Theoretically Mohammed could claim the best room in the house for himself—he had rebuilt it stone by stone. There was a large upstairs suite wrapping around the south of the house, with windows to the east, south, and west. But that honor he gave to Nasir and Zahara. His room was simple and small, with an eastern view of the farm and the distant cedars.

He had looked out at the cedars before he lay down. In the distance he could see Nihla and Angela walking toward them, ambling as if they were safe, without a care in the world.

Mohammed lay with his right arm over his head and looked at the ceiling, tense and haunted by what he had just seen. Being located in Hezbollah territory meant that the estate could again be ravaged by Israeli bombs. Mohammed's years of work, perhaps even the cedars themselves, could be destroyed.

But more than one destructive force was at work in his life.

*Cedars, home, family, research, al-Hajji, the bombs*...

From sheer exhaustion Mohammed fell into an uneasy sleep.

He tossed. The old nightmare tried to push its way into his dreams again, but he couldn't let that happen. Not now. So he got up.

Nasir was reading an academic book on the patio in the shade.

"I'm glad you're here. I've been waiting," he said, looking worried.

"*Asif*, I'm sorry, but we have to make important decisions, and I wanted to clear my head a bit first. I'm fine now."

He didn't look fine.

"Do you think we are safe here?" asked Nasir.

"No. First, there's the risk with the war. Then there's the risk that the Mus-haf Brotherhood will find us. It wouldn't be that hard. But at least your coming up here delayed them a bit. Who could predict what would happen on the border two days ago?"

"There are those who always do," said Nasir.

"We could go to stay with Angela in Turkey for the summer. She says she has a large house there—a Turkish *yalı*. It would give us space to protect the *masahaf*," Mohammed said as pleasantly as if he had suggested a vacation.

"I'm not going to Turkey. The airport and the port have been closed, and it's too far to drive. Perhaps Palestine."

"What about going to Abdul's in Damascus? It's only a couple of hours drive from here," said Mohammed, with one of the serious looks that only those close to him knew.

Nasir lifted an eyebrow. "I know our options are limited, but do you think that wise? You know how Abdul feels about Americans...."

"You mean Angela would be unwelcome?"

"I mean any American." Nasir continued slowly as if weighing each word. "There are things about Abdul that even you don't know. I don't trust him at all if he finds out what we're doing."

"Do you mean about..."

"That and more... best left unsaid..."

"OK. But try this. We go to Damascus tomorrow in two cars. You, ImmMohammed, and Nihla can stay with Abdul. Angela and I drive on to Istanbul with the *masahaf*."

"That might work," Nasir said, shaking his head slowly and slightly, his eyes glazed over in thought. "How are things in Beirut?"

Mohammed paused. He needed to explain what had happened at al-Hajji's apartment, in order to be sure that Nasir clearly understood the need to leave. They agreed to keep it to themselves; there was enough stress on everyone with the bombings.

Angela arose a few hours later, much refreshed. She walked down the stairs and into the living room.

Nihla was already there, standing in profile. She was covertly and intently listening to the conversation her father and Mohammed were having on the back patio. From where she stood, they could not see her, but she could see them.

Angela overheard, "*Mit akid al ethnane matu?*" Nasir was confirming the worst.

"*Mit akid*," Mohammed replied, in a grave voice.

At this Nihla's face turned to Angela, as pale as its olive complexion would allow. Looking not at but past her, Nihla walked out.

Angela turned to follow her. "Are you all right?" she asked, but received no reply. Nihla went upstairs into her room and shut the door. Quietly Angela went up to the door. She could hear sobbing.

Who had died, she wondered? Some relative? Probably on Uncle Nasir's side of the family, since she hadn't heard of the death. At least she hoped it was on his side. She would wait to hear what Mohammed had to say about it.

Quickly she went back down the stairs again, but by the time she got there, the conversation had ceased, and Mohammed was inside, waiting for her.

## Chapter 79

# CHOUF MOUNTAINS, LEBANON
## July 13, 2006

"Let's go upstairs," Mohammed said to Angela with a smile, as if nothing were wrong. "I want to show you something." Impulsively he grabbed her hand and dragged her as he ran up the stairs.

Mohammed took her to the front balcony she had seen on their arrival. As soon as she stepped onto it she was struck with the view.

"Wow! Thank you for bringing me up here. Oh, and thank you for saving it until the sunset!" she raved. One by one, Mohammed proudly pointed out each visible feature of his domain, both large and small. From this view, they could see the vineyard, the olive, apricot, fig, and almond groves, and a few small stone buildings.

"What a large estate!" she exclaimed. "I'm amazed you can run it and still attend graduate school."

"You know me, sister, I'm never alone! I have lots of help. Everyone wants to work for the funny Palestinian!"

"I hear you were alone for quite a while when you first came here."

"Oh," he brushed her remark aside. "Just until I had time to drink coffee and play cards with the locals. Then, that was it! They wanted to be with me, so . . . I put them to work!"

"Sounds like a good payback on coffee to me!" Angela laughed.

"Hey, sister, look now!" Mohammed pointed. Just beyond his finger there was a silvery strip of ocean, shining in the sun.

She strained to see it, and the sight refreshed her mind, freeing her from any worrying thoughts. "Oh, how lovely! I can almost smell the sea air."

Angela closed her eyes and put her head back, shaking her hair in the gentle breeze and trying to catch the fresh sea scent. She looked ecstatic, like a living Maxfield Parrish "girl on a rock." Chin lifted, eyes closed, and lips smiling, she was entirely gilded in the setting sun.

The word *rapturous* wasn't in Mohammed's vocabulary, but that's how he saw Angela.

"It's my moveable feast!" she said, turning her body in a circle, smooth as a dance, all but oblivious to Mohammed. She was simply enjoying the moment. As she turned, she held her hands palms up. One finger gently brushed against Mohammed without her noticing, and a single shining hair cascaded onto his sleeve.

An invisible shiver crossed Mohammed.

*She's not trying to be seductive; that's partly why she is.*

He had been attracted to Angela from his first glimpse of her across the crowded room in Ramallah, but he closed himself to her right then and there. She was married. His appetite for women had waned since his new quest started, and he certainly wasn't going to get into that sort of trouble—especially not with family. He knew how to walk away from women and cool his "hot Arab blood." He would simply push the door shut again.

Mohammed looked away from her and down to the trees.

*The harvest.*

Yes, he must think about the harvest.

## Chapter 80

# CHOUF MOUNTAINS, LEBANON
## July 13, 2006

Angela again leaned over on the railing. Still smiling, she opened her eyes and looked off at the small remaining glimmer of ocean.

Mohammed was not the only one to be struck by Angela in amber light.

John Hall first saw Angela one afternoon in mid-October. That Friday, the media had announced to Atlanta that the "peak weekend" of fall colors had arrived. Rallying to the call, traffic flowed out of the city—maybe for a local drive to Newnan or a more ambitious one into the mountain towns of Helen or Ashville. Emory University students enjoyed it differently, usually with a walk or a jog in Lullwater.

Lullwater was the estate of the university's president. Its grounds were open to students—for stretching the legs and relaxing the mind. And nothing surpassed it for autumn atmosphere.

Angela had been jogging. Having circled a few times around the pond and Tudor-style mansion, she sat down in the trees opposite the pond and pulled out a pocket book of poetry. Lullwater's trees were mostly deciduous, sporting yellow, orange, and gold in fall. The afternoon was beautiful. She wanted to think lovely thoughts, watch the pond sparkle in the angled light, and unwind.

After an hour she rose to leave, and instead of walking around the bend on the drive, she cut through the trees to enjoy the crunch of fallen leaves and the earthy autumn smells. She bent to pick up a perfectly preserved leaf, its waxy surface still intact. When she arose, the light coming through the trees flashed on her hair, which flew up in the breeze, just for a second. She smiled at the leaf in a simple act of appreciation.

John was sitting with Griselda, his Irish setter, across the path from her. He hadn't noticed her at first: her brown and green clothes camouflaged her in the trees. But with that flash, he was transfixed. It seemed to him as if the forest had come to life and a wood elf had sprung out of a tree. He was overcome by an aggression unusual for him.

"Go, girl!" he whispered to Griselda.

Griselda was true to her pure breeding and training. She ran up to Angela with just the right amount of speed, then sat up to shake hands in the friendliest puppylike way.

It was not the most original introduction, but it was effective. John ran after the dog, was apologetic, and did what every Emory undergraduate would do in such a situation: he asked her to Everybody's. Pizza that is. Sooner or later, everybody ends up at Everybody's Pizza. It's where half the relationships at Emory begin or end.

A moment can create a lasting effect. On an unhappy day, years later, Angela asked him, "If you feel that way about me, why do you stay with me?" He answered uncomfortably, "I imprinted on you."

"Sister, what is that 'fast moving' thing you said?" Mohammed asked.

"Oh, a '*moveable feast*.' Hmm," she tensed her lips, "how can I explain it to you?" She turned to him with an everyday teaching expression and tone. "Do you know Ernest Hemingway?"

"No, sister. You know I am not so educated in some things because of the Intifada, remember? Who is he?"

"He was a famous American author. He wrote a charming autobiography about his life in Paris as a young man called *A Moveable Feast*. Once he told his friend:

> *If you are lucky enough to have lived in Paris as a young man,*
> *then wherever you go for the rest of your life it stays with you,*
> *for Paris is a moveable feast.*

"This reminds you of Paris?" he questioned, pointing at the view.

"No, silly," she said gently, "a moveable feast is some beautiful thought that you can always remember to cheer you, to feed your soul when you feel weak."

"Wow," he said, "that's great."

"And that's what I say about a good book. It should contain a moment that you would want to slip yourself into and stay. If my life were a book, today would be it! I had been feeling sad, but once we drove up into the hills, and they were so beautiful, and your family so warm and welcoming, and the fresh food, and, oh—your house is gorgeous—and the cedars and the fragrance, and now the capstone—the pink and orange sunset into the distant sea! Today is my moveable feast! I will never forget it. Thank you so much."

Angela smiled at Mohammed, looking at him as if he had gone out of his way for her. Which he hadn't.

But in that moment he felt what it was like to bless someone, and it was nice. A nice, warm, and safe feeling. And that's where he wanted to keep it. *Safe.*

Mohammed smiled and answered, "Sister, that is beautiful. I'm glad you enjoyed the bombing. Do you know what is beautiful to me?"

"What?" she asked, prepared for whatever.

"The smell of the lamb on the barbecue. The breeze is blowing it right at us. It's driving me craazy *majnoon* up here! Let's run down!" At this he slapped his thigh, jumped off the railing, and ran down the stairs.

## Chapter 81

# CHOUF MOUNTAINS, LEBANON
## July 13, 2006

Nihla didn't show up for dinner. Aunt Zahara had made Mohammed's favorite—Middle Eastern–style barbecue. That meant they had a lot of meat—a lamb shank, a chicken, and a beef cut somewhere between a steak and a roast. It was too much food for the four of them. Under usual circumstances, they would have had several other families over to meet Angela, as they had in Palestine, but today was not usual.

Aunt Zahara seemed anxious that Angela forgive this insulting lack of hospitality, which was due to the remote location and the impending war, but Angela was not offended at all. In fact, she was glad of the chance to have her aunt and uncle to herself. This way she might find out a little more about her mother. And even if she didn't, it felt good to be with people who loved her, especially when one reminded her so much of her mother.

"Tell me about my mother," she asked at the first appropriate moment. "Some stories from when you were children. What did you do?"

Several homey stories of family life followed, a few funny, and a few sad. Nothing surprising. As she had previously understood, her mother was beautiful, and quiet in comparison to the other children, which probably meant "normal" by American standards. Mohammed listened and laughed appropriately but had nothing to contribute. It was the longest Angela had seen him surrender the floor.

"What do you know about her deciding to join Aunt Mona in America? That seems like an unusually brave move for a quiet Arab girl of only fifteen."

Blank looks drew over the faces of Aunt Zahara and Uncle Nasir, and there was just enough light on the patio to detect the furtive glances they passed. Mohammed saw it too.

Then Aunt Zahara, ever quick with the comeback, answered, "Remember, your mother was the intelligent one of the family, just like her daughter," she said in flattery, "so she went to America to continue her education."

Angela was about to say, "But she didn't continue her education, did she? Not until long after she was married, and she married young," but she could see that would sound argumentative.

Instead she asked, "What did the other people in her life think about her leaving. Her parents? The uncles? Uncle Ayman?"

Since uncles traditionally play a very important role in determining the future of Arab girls, acting as the mother's representatives, this should have been a safe question.

But asking about Uncle Ayman seemed to have touched a raw nerve. Aunt Zahara and Uncle Nasir clearly looked at each other this time, and their expressions were quite different: a peculiar combination of shame and indignation that could not be smoothed even by such an experienced charmer as Aunt Zahara.

Uncle Nasir didn't even try. He preserved a rather sour look on his face.

Aunt Zahara answered, "The uncles were fine with it, dear," she said in a rather stilted manner, reaching across the table to stack some dishes. "Otherwise she wouldn't have gone, of course."

She abruptly changed the subject. "Oh, my, look at the time! I must go and see how Nihla is doing." At this she got up and, carrying an armload of dishes, went into the house.

"I want to see what she's up to, too," Mohammed said, and excused himself to join the other two upstairs. He did not sound so much as if he was worried about her as he was worried about what she might be doing.

Angela was overcome with negative emotions.

She wanted to kick herself. Their response made her feel rejected where she had been loved. It was obvious that the secret Aunt Mona had confided about her mother's emigration to America was true, and the situation renewed her sorrow of its discovery.

But worse than that was the damage her question had done to the living.

*How stupid can I be?*

Angela had never even considered that others might be victims too. Uncle Ayman's sexual relationship with her mother was predatory, the kind of thing that would be repeated until forcibly stopped. And obviously that didn't happen soon enough.

Questions flooded Angela's mind. Did Aunt Zahara ever tell anyone that she had been raped by the deviant wolf? Had she learned from her older sister's experience that it would be better just to keep her mouth shut? Did she end up pregnant like Mother did? Was there a child? An abortion?

*Whatever it was, it was hurtful. And Uncle Nasir knew about it too.*

Nasir was protecting his wife, as he had protected her for nearly three decades.

Then it hit Angela like a bomb falling on Beirut. She trembled in her seat.

*Is it possible that my father—the angry drinker, the hater of all things Arab—was also a protector at heart?*

Could it be that he was angry because he knew what had happened to her mother? Was it possible he was angry with all Arab men because of what one Arab man had done to his wife? Now that she thought of it, she had never heard him say a bad word specifically against Arab women.

Angela gulped, and the entire appearance of her expression changed. She struggled not to cry. It was as though her father, her real father, had died afresh, an unsung hero that she could not kiss good-bye.

*If it hadn't been for the alcohol, I would have seen it, I'm sure. . . .*

Angela now felt that she, too, had suffered at the hand of Uncle Ayman. She would love to find out what happened to him. But she couldn't ask here. Did he suffer for his evil deeds? Not only for the lives of the women he had despoiled but for their husbands and children as well?

Angela's angry mind envisioned a mutilated leper, an outcast from society. Or maybe he died with neurosyphilis, crippled and crazy from advanced sexually transmitted diseases. An evil smile passed her lips. Whatever it was, it could not be enough suffering for a pedophilic sex offender like him: ruining other people's lives for his perverse momentary pleasure.

Vengeful thoughts kept her eyes dry. She looked at Uncle Nasir, hoping he would not know what she had been thinking. She tried to act as if nothing had happened. She could do it: there had been no overt confrontations, and Angela was skilled at acting cheerful when there was nothing to cheer.

"Aunt Zahara was right! It's nearly midnight! I love these late Mediterranean suppers. Thanks so much, Uncle Nasir. I won't need to eat for a week!"

"It is a pleasure to have you as our guest." His smile was genuine.

At this Angela got up. "Let me get these dishes started."

Alone inside the kitchen she could no longer contain the tears. For the second time today she had unexpectedly cried for a lost parent.

Angela heard a noise coming from upstairs. The sound of screaming came through the window. It wasn't very clear, but it sounded threatening, something like "Infidel, you will burn in hell!"

And the voice was Nihla's.

*Nihla didn't come downstairs after she overheard Mohammed and Uncle Nasir.*

There was nothing to do but wash dishes.

## Chapter 82

# CHOUF MOUNTAINS, LEBANON
## July 14, 2006

Upstairs, Mohammed spoke sharply. "That's it! I'm keeping the cell phone."

A scuffle was heard, and Mohammed came downstairs, dragging Nihla by the arm, with Zahara following sadly behind.

"We have to leave tonight," he told Nasir as they walked into the living room. "Apparently Nihla knew Ahmed better than the rest of us did, and she's put all of us at risk by calling him."

Nasir jumped up and started yelling at Nihla. Then he slapped her.

Nihla burst into tears and said, "You are all infidels. How could I be part of a family like this? You will all burn in hell if you don't repent!"

Angela thought they would have to restrain her, but finally she sat down, crying. The thought of them burning in hell seemed more to sadden than to anger her.

Mohammed barked orders. "Start packing, but keep her in sight. Angela, dress conservatively, we're going to Syria. I'm going to the foreman's house to make arrangements for the farm."

When Mohammed returned, everyone was packing food and clothing. They loaded up Mohammed's Isuzu and Nasir's Renault and left in the darkness of the early morning; Angela and Nihla in the Isuzu with Mohammed, Nasir and Zahara in the Renault.

Hostilities were high between family members. Only Angela was exempt.

*I guess I'm supposed to be the "calming influence" on Nihla. . . .*

Mohammed's plantation was near a main road, only about ten miles south of the Beirut-Damascus Highway. The route to Damascus would be easy—as easy as it could be in the darkness, with sleepy drivers navigating hairpin turns through the mountains on a two-lane road.

Ordinarily, the Beirut-Damascus Highway can take travelers from Beirut to the Syrian border in an hour and a half, and to Damascus in another hour. This, Lebanon's number two highway, has three sections: from Beirut into the mountains, over the mountains of the Mudayrij, and through the Beqaa Valley. The first and last sections have alternate routes, but there is only one main route over the mountainous middle section: the long and high bridge at Mudayrij.

The Renault led the way. The Isuzu was silent inside because Nihla was pouting, Mohammed was anxious and tired, and the only things Angela could think of saying would be unwelcome—like comments on Mohammed's risky driving and questions about who Ahmed was.

As they approached the bridge at Mudayrij, they heard a faint sound approaching, and getting louder. It sent a chill up Angela's spine.

*No, it couldn't be. Not again. Not here.*

Chapter 83

# BEIRUT-DAMASCUS HIGHWAY
## Early Morning
## Friday, July 14, 2006

*Why would planes be zooming here at this time?*

There was a whirling, swishing sound.

"Allah have mercy!" Nihla grabbed her head and screamed.

Everyone sensed what was coming in the following split second.

The passengers of both cars screamed in unison as the entire highway rocked.

"It's the bridge!" Mohammed yelled, and then let out a barrage of curses in Arabic. "Those damned bastard Israelis are after the bridge! May they burn forever in hell with all their airplanes and camels!" He knew if the bridge were destroyed, that was the end of the Beirut-Damascus Highway.

There was a screeching sound ahead. Mohammed slammed on his brakes.

The Renault started swerving. It had been closer to the bomb blast and experienced fierce reverberations.

"Your parents!" Angela yelled in shock as they watched the Renault spin a full circle and veer to the right.

"Holy angels, not to the right!"

"What is it?" asked Nihla, sobbing and peeking through her hands.

"Oh, my God. They're going off the edge," cried Angela. "Do something!"

Mohammed and Angela bolted out of the car. Nihla followed closely behind. The Renault had veered onto the exit ramp above where the bomb hit. The supports underneath were unstable.

Inside the Renault Nasir was slightly dazed from the power of the blast and the 360-degree spin, but in a second he perceived the situation.

Nasir started backing up the car, tires squealing. Zahara grabbed onto the handles and tightened her muscles. She groaned.

The three runners arrived at the exit ramp in time to see their fears fulfilled: the ramp was cracking perpendicular to the road and was about to break off like a chocolate bar.

"Oh, Momma, oh, Daddy, I'm so sorry," said Nihla over and over, biting the tails of her scarf.

Mohammed and Angela were scared but desperately thinking of what could be done.

The ramp angle was increasing. The Renault was having a difficult time backing up.

The crack was growing. It was becoming obvious that the Renault would not make it back to the bridge. Nasir gave the gas another strong thrust, and the car zipped backward. This time the car did not fall forward. It could not. The ramp had totally disengaged from the bridge. The Renault's rear wheels had caught over the top edge.

The now-separated fragment of ramp was wavering under the combination of instability and the momentum from the car's dashing.

The gap between the bridge and the ramp increased.

Angela and Nihla started yelling for Zahara and Nasir to get out.

Angela turned to Mohammed and said, "I don't think they can climb up. Do we have rope or anything we could throw down to them?"

Mohammed was looking straight ahead and didn't answer. Instead he did a surprising thing—he jumped onto the disengaged section of ramp.

"Oh, no!" Angela said, seeing the situation grow worse. Now she would have to rescue the three of them.

Mohammed grabbed Zahara and put her on his shoulders. With a little stretching she could reach the bridge road, where the two women helped pull her up.

They could hear muffled arguing between Nasir and Mohammed. Then they saw Mohammed shake his head and roughly grab Nasir.

Nasir was making things worse by not cooperating. He had felt he could do it himself. He tried to get out of Mohammed's grip, which made them more unstable.

"Stop it, Daddy!" Nihla yelled.

"Nasir, cooperate!" Zahara demanded.

Nasir looked up. Mohammed was trying to stabilize the position in which he was holding Nasir. The disengaged section of the ramp separated more, jiggling the setup Mohammed was trying to achieve.

As in an earthquake where the top of a building swerves more than the base, Nasir was swinging on Mohammed's shoulders.

"Daddy, Daddy!" Nihla screamed hysterically. She lay on the road and reached over, trying to grab at Nasir.

"Nihla, don't!" Angela said, bending down and trying to stop her. But it was too late. Nihla flew, arms out, over the edge of the bridge onto the exit ramp.

A muffled bomb was heard in the distance.

Zahara screamed. Angela ran back to Mohammed's car to get the flashlight she had seen when they packed.

Mohammed pushed with all his might, straining himself to get Nasir raised onto the bridge as fast as possible. Then he turned around.

Angela shone the flashlight on the ramp.

Nihla had rolled when she hit the ramp fragment and was sliding off the other edge. She disappeared out of sight.

Mohammed bolted to the far edge and peered down.

Nasir had trouble restraining Zahara, who wanted to jump back onto the ramp and die with her daughter.

Below the ramp, Nihla was standing on the bridge support crossbar that she had slipped onto. She was out of Mohammed's reach. There was no room for him on the crossbar, and he could think of no way to get down there and push her up.

"Angela!" Mohammed turned his head and yelled, "Throw down your abaya!"

Angela was confused but anxious to do anything that might help. She peeled off the abaya she had bought in Palestine and tossed it down to Mohammed.

Mohammed tied two knots into the garment, then looked back over the edge of the disengaged ramp.

The ramp jerked unstably. It was not helping to have his weight on the downhill side.

"Nihla," he yelled, "I can't reach you, honey, but here is what you do. It will be *sahil*, so eeeasy! I'm throwing over this rope thing. I know it's dark, but can you feel it?"

"Yes," she whimpered. "I'm scared."

"It's OK, *habeebtee*. Now feel for the knot. Did you find it?"

"Yes."

"Put your hands above it and hold on tight. Don't let go until you see my hand. Try to climb up the pole if you can."

The three people on the bridge were silent with tension. Angela held the flashlight tightly.

*If she lets go . . .*

The bridge's forty-million-dollar price tag was matched by the tremendous height it spanned. It was a long way down.

In a few seconds they saw Mohammed's body jerk. Then Nihla's arm appeared. When her upper half appeared they all cheered.

Mohammed then easily lifted her up and into the arms of her waiting father.

"Oh, Daddy, I'm so sorry, I'm so sorry!" she sobbed in his arms, as if the whole Arab-Israeli conflict were her personal fault.

There was no one to lift up Mohammed.

"Mohammed," Angela whispered, touching her hand to her mouth.

*I can't reach. They will grab for me and someone will fall to their death.*

What he did next may not have been more risky than anything else he had done since the bomb hit, but it seemed horrifying to the family.

Mohammed started climbing the Renault.

He stepped on the tire and lifted his long leg onto the trunk. The car jiggled. He stood up on the trunk.

The disengaged ramp fragment disengaged more.

"Move away!" he yelled.

It was no time to argue. Everyone obeyed.

Mohammed bent his knees and took a dramatic lunge forward. His upper body hit the top of the bridge, but he began slipping off.

The family all jumped on him and started pulling him up.

The Renault went careening below.

Mohammed scrambled with his legs and got a knee onto the bridge. The family reeled him in.

The five huddled together like quintuplets in a group hug, crying and kissing in relief.

The bridge underneath them started vibrating. They heard a loud crackling sound as the ramp fragment detached entirely from its supports.

The family stood and watched as it started to fall.

"Into the Isuzu!" Mohammed yelled. Everyone obeyed. They were all wondering, *Is that it? Are we safe yet?*

## Chapter 84

# BEIRUT-DAMASCUS HIGHWAY

## Early Morning
## Friday, July 14, 2006

The occupants of Mohammed's vehicle were cramped and quiet as they drove the remaining forty-four miles to Damascus, but they were lucky. Seventy-three bridges and four hundred miles of road would be destroyed before the conflict was over. Not only did they survive the bombing but they got over the bridge and continued their journey before the police arrived to detour the area. This would get them to the border ahead of most of the sixty thousand people who would be crossing it by August 16.

It was late, and they were tired and distressed.

Mohammed's mind was traveling on several tracks at once. First, he had to decide what to do about getting the group settled in Damascus. He never had intentions of staying there. With two cars, he and Angela would have simply parted company from the rest in Damascus. Now that wasn't an option.

How would he get Nasir, Zahara, and Nihla to Abdul's house without being obligated to stay? Middle Eastern hospitality codes were very rigid. The hosts must offer; the guests must stay. What if Angela didn't want to return to Turkey right away? What would he tell her?

Angela was feeling a mixture of trauma and admiration.

Aunt Zahara blotted her eyes intermittently. Their car and possessions were gone. Just like that. Now they really were refugees.

As they approached the border of Lebanon with Syria at Masnaa, they joined other refugees making their way into Syria. They were one family among roughly a quarter of Lebanon's population that would become displaced during the conflict.

"Sister," said Mohammed, very matter-of-fact.

"Which sister do you mean?" asked Angela. "You could try names, unless you aren't sure who you want; in which case you could try using your brain."

"It makes no difference. There are so many of you!"

"What he means," Nihla interrupted sarcastically, "is that he can't remember names."

"Hey, sister! You. The American one. I'm serious. This is important. Put your leeetle lips together and leeesten."

Angela said, "That wasn't 'the American one' who just put you down. But give me a few seconds and I will!"

His mind had moved on. "Getting out of Lebanon will be a breeze. I don't expect a close inspection getting into Syria, due to the flood of refugees we've become part of. Nevertheless, they're none too fond of Americans in Syria. So cover up well, Angela, and look uncharacteristically modest."

"Thanks."

"And keep that terrrible American passport out of sight. We'll try to slip you through as one of the family."

"Which she is!" said Zahara indignantly, patting Angela's arm.

Angela covered her hair thoroughly with the scarf she had brought, but her abaya was gone.

"Whoa, whoa, whoa!" said Angela in surprise. "Who would expect to find Dunkin' Donuts in this mountainous no-man's-land between two Arab nations? I hope they use halal oil for frying!" Angela started laughing and pointing in an anything but demure way.

"American donuts, American donuts!" Nihla squealed in delight. "Let's go! We *really* need a break."

"I'll treat everyone!" said Angela.

"Sister, are you crazy? How can I convince them you are Lebanese if you go running after American donuts and don't have papers?"

"I thought you were a good liar—'the best, the best!'"

"Sister, I am a good liar, but I have my limits."

"Oh, please!" Nihla begged.

"I know," said Angela, "You think up some lies, and we'll go shopping!" She and Nihla nudged each other then bolted out of the car. Mohammed shook his head. They were all a little crazy tonight.

The donuts were good.

A few minutes later at the Syrian border, the immigration officer asked for their papers. Through the window Mohammed passed four Lebanese passports.

The officer asked the routine question, "Where are you going?"

"To our cousin in Damascus," answered Mohammed.

The officer looked into the car and counted five heads. "We seem to be missing documents on one of you."

Mohammed was prepared. "That would be my wife's, Aneesa," he motioned toward Angela and continued. "We just got married. She is from a small village and did not have papers when I married her. We were in the process of getting her papers, but they haven't arrived. We weren't expecting to become refugees."

When the officer opened Mohammed's passport he could see a few Syrian lira notes of *baksheesh* in it.

Angela sat with her eyes downcast so that nearly nothing of her face was visible.

The officer spoke to her in Arabic, which, not for the first time this trip, she was glad her mother had taught her.

"*Isma Aneesa?*" the official said, asking if Aneesa was her name.

"*Awa,*" Angela answered, with a superb acting job of just the right attitude a village girl would have—looking up slowly, with sidelong rather than direct eye contact.

"*Hada zowjick?*"

"*Na'am hada zowji,*" she answered respectfully, in her best, soft Lebanese accent.

The official pocketed the note and let them into Syria.

In Damascus, they stayed together in the Hejaz Railway station until Abdul, Nasir's sister's husband, was nearly due to arrive. Then Mohammed slipped what looked like a large wad of bills into Nasir's hand, and he and Angela left them.

## Chapter 85

# DAMASCUS, SYRIA
## July 14, 2006

"'I am in Damascus. It is a wonderful fact—but really I am.' That's what Freya Stark wrote the first time she came to Damascus. I feel just like her right now!" Angela said.

"Of course! Another beautiful Arab city."

"I don't want to appear insensitive, what with Lebanon being bombed and all, but between here and Istanbul there are many sights I have wanted to see. Could we visit a few?" ventured Angela.

"That's one thing I don't understand. You are rich, you have been many places. You wrote a book on them, so why haven't you seen them before? Seems craazy to me."

"Well, if Palestinian brroootherr had ears as big as his nose, he would have heard when I said that my husband doesn't like to travel. Especially not here. But I like to travel! When Honey Jean was alive, she liked to travel too. She was a lot of fun. My husband would travel with his family, so we went to Europe and tropical places, but never anyplace dangerous."

"If honey's jeans liked to travel, why didn't they come here? It's not dangerous!"

"'Not dangerous, not dangerous' he says, as the bombs fly by!"

"I'm not talking about today. I mean, look, sister, the Middle East makes a lot of money from tourism. It's 'the Holy Land'!"

"Honey Jean was my mother-in-law. She died recently."

"I'm so sorry, sister." His apology sounded genuine.

"Honey Jean was religious. She had been to the Holy Land before I met John; before the First Intifada, when the natives weren't so restless."

"And John?" Mohammed asked.

"Not John. He's neither a traveler nor religious."

"What else is he not?"

Mohammed was prodding somewhere Angela wouldn't go.

"What else are *you* not? You're not answering my question, that's what!" she said, reversing the attack. "Can we peek around at places like Palmyra or not? I hear it's a miraculous Roman city out in the middle of nowhere, which makes it not far out of our way."

"No!"

"What do you mean 'no'? Why not? I'm not in a hurry to get back to Istanbul. Are you?"

"Yes, sister, it is as you said." His smile belied his words. "I am sensitive about the bombings."

She said, "Then I guess every time we pass a road sign for some sight I've been yearning to see, I'll just have to pull out my book and read what women said about it hundreds of years ago." She flipped through *Skirts on Camels*, "This being the Middle East, things don't change very quickly anyway." She whispered under her breath, "Except for the worse."

There passed a few moments of pouty silence.

*Well, the morning light looks beautiful on the hillside homes*, Angela thought, looking around. *And the green dome of that mosque looks like a water balloon Re-Pete might have thrown at me when we were kids.*

Finding an appropriate page, she read what Gertrude Bell said of Damascus when she was there in 1905.

> The view from Nakshibendi's balcony is immortal. The great and splendid city of Damascus, with its gardens and domes and its minarets, lies spread out below, and beyond it is the desert, the desert reaching almost to its gates.

Gertrude Bell was one of Angela's favorite writers. Also known as the "Female Lawrence of Arabia," she overcame the barriers of class and gender to attain influence in the Middle East under the British, and become the first and only woman Oriental Secretary to the British Imperial Service.

Angela lifted her head and prodded Mohammed. "You know, I shouldn't have to read about the oldest continuously inhabited city in the world while I am actually in it, should I? Doesn't that seem unnatural somehow?"

"No, sister, it's not unnatural at all. I'm sure that book is more accurate than your observations could be. You just read it. Besides, I am sorry to tell you, but Damascus is not the oldest continuously inhabited city in the world—Jericho is, everyone knows that!"

"The guidebook," she held up a Syria and Lebanon travel guide, "says that Damascus is. And I'm sure this book is more accurate than you are!"

*Touché!*

Angela thought Mohammed took for granted as mundane what to her was exotic and fascinating. She sought a way to annoy him.

"Since my zookeeper won't allow me to see Damascus, this oasis on the edge of the desert," she said dryly, "this prosperous starting point for pilgrimage to Mecca; the souks, the fountains, the minarets... I will continue reading what Gertrude Bell had to say about it." She read out loud at high volume with exaggerated inflection and English accent: "'My last day in Damascus was a Friday. Now Damascus on a fine Friday is a sight worth traveling far to see.'"

"Did you hear that, *Moe*? Damascus is worth traveling to see, and here we are. Think of all the money we could save by seeing it now!"

"Quit calling me 'Moe'!"

"Be quiet and listen!"

"'All the male population dressed in their best walk the streets. The sweetmeat sellers and the secondhand clothes sellers drive a roaring trade, the eating shops steam with dressed meats of the most tempting kind.'"

"Doesn't that sound tempting, Moe?" she asked. "Meat..." she dangled the word, knowing his weakness for it.

Mohammed's lips parted, but he said nothing.

Angela closed the book and picked up the map. They were both tired. Maybe that was why they quit arguing or even talking. But as Angela looked at the map, a devious smile crept onto her mouth.

# Chapter 86

# M1 MOTORWAY, SYRIA
## July 14, 2006

Driving north on the M1 Motorway, Mohammed noticed they were low on *al benzene*, as he called gasoline, about the time they reached the town of An Nabk.

Angela was glad he pulled over. She had noticed his eyes blinking for the last hour and was justifiably concerned that he was falling asleep —especially since he had been up all night driving. She had an idea.

"*Ya*, Mohammed, I'm bored just sitting here. I'd like to drive for a while. What do you say we switch off? There's no one around here but goats, and they won't tell."

"Ooooh, sister, I don't know. They might tell the sheep, and then think of the trouble we'd have!"

Angela looked so guileless, and Mohammed was so tired, that he gave in to her request. If he had been more awake, he would have suspected something.

Mohammed sat in the passenger seat. He disrespectfully threw *Skirts on Camels* into the backseat, knowing that Angela saw him, and picked up the guidebook she had also brought. "What has my leetle cousin been reading while I drive?" he asked. Then he started reading in slow English: "'In Syria, animals often get themselves into the middle of the road. Some say this is a government plot to assure tourists don't drive too quickly through the countryside. Those with less imagination point out the nearby farms.'"

Before the car pulled back on the highway, they did encounter livestock.

"Hey, sister," Mohammed said in Arabic, "now I know why you want to drive! You want a chance to hit those dozens *sheeps* blocking the way and that family of *sevens roosters* on the side of the road."

"Are you pointing out the local customs or giving me an Arabic test? I see a mother hen and six chicks on the side, and ten sheep in the road: either you are getting your gender and numbers all mixed up, or I need more help with basic Arabic grammar."

"Yes, you need help! Learn this good Arabic talk stuff: Look at sura 7, verse 160 in the Koran. You will see it talks that way."

"Sorry, I can't. I'm driving."

"Crazy grammar! The Koran says, *Waqataznahum ethnatai ashrat asbarta*—'We divided them into twelves tribe.'"

Not sure of the point, she said, "Thanks. I suppose if it says it that way, it was the correct way of saying it back then."

"No, sister, no! That's not correct. Ask any teacher of Arabic; only don't tell him you are quoting the Koran. See what he says. . . ."

"*Entrapment* is the English word we use for that sort of trick. It still wouldn't prove that Arabs didn't speak that way in the Middle Ages. For example, Shakespeare sounds funny to those of us who speak modern English, and he lived only four hundred years ago."

"You mean he couldn't count and didn't know boys from girls either? Ha-ha!"

Mohammed laughed loudly, then reached over and beeped the horn, while Angela drove cautiously through the sheep, wondering.

In about fifteen minutes, Mohammed put his seat back without a word, closed his eyes, and, just as Angela had hoped, began snoring. She smiled and her eyes flashed.

About half an hour later, near Hims, the car ever so gently made a transition east, onto Highway 3, toward Palmyra. Within about an hour, they would be there. But fate intervened.

"Drat!" exclaimed Angela. There was no way to avoid braking—and hard—as a flock of goats suddenly emerged from a gully onto the road. Mohammed opened his eyes into a squint, saying nothing. Angela started driving again, but a sense of unease replaced her former pleasure. Mohammed was quiet, but awake.

Suddenly he bolted upright. "Seesterr! Let's have some music. He put on the radio, looking for something he could turn up loud to drown out his ghastly singing voice. But the channels all seemed to be reporting the sad news from Lebanon. For a few hours they had forgotten the bombs.

Mohammed turned off the radio. Angela was preparing herself for another political lecture—and, in truth, Mohammed was starting to formulate one—when he stopped, mouth open. They had just passed a road sign that read "3."

Grabbing for the map, he said, "Angela! Where in Syria have you gotten us?"

Angela's heart started beating faster. Mohammed was not going to like this. She stayed silent, gripping the wheel.

"Ha-ha, sister!" He threw up the map and threw back his head. "You're driving to Palmyra! Now I learn it! The Americans are better tricksters than the Arabs. Now I can lie, cheat, trick—anything—and you can't say one word! Ha-ha! Not one word!"

This was not the response Angela had expected. She laughed, relieved. "As we say in America, 'You ain't seen nothin' yet'!"

"I feel *much* better, sister. Thanks for letting me rest a little. OK, now I'm ready to drive again."

"Oh, no problem, I've been driving less than an hour. I'm good for several more. Just lie back and relax!"

As if he were doing her a favor, he said, "No, rrreally, I insist. I drive!"

"I don't think Americans can be trickier than Arabs. I am starting to suspect that if you drive, I won't see Palmyra," she said evenly.

"Sister, like you said, 'You ain't seen nothing yet...'" He struggled with an American accent, "...of Palmyra, and you ain't going to." He became serious but not angry. "OK, liar angel, pull over."

"I am not a liar! A trickster, maybe, but not a liar, and not a 'sucker.' I'm not pulling over."

"Big brother's turn." He reached over and pulled on the wheel, toying with it—grabbing and then letting go—like a cat with a mouse, all the while laughing.

Angela gripped the wheel harder and clenched her teeth. "Yes, take your turn! Be a *gentleman.* You had your way last time, and I missed the UNESCO world heritage city of Damascus. Now we will see Palmyra! They say," she said in a strained voice that got progressively louder, alternating from slow to fast in relationship to the effort required to counter Mohammed's tugs on the wheel, "it has perfect Eastern Roman architecture: columns Greek in style and Egyptian in height. It's where Queen Zenobia was from—she created an Arab empire and held off the Romans for years... until, of course, she got captured and taken to Rome...."

"Ha," Mohammed inserted.

"Simply all the travel writers love it, including Byron and my *Skirts on Camels* ladies: Hester Stanhope, Rose Macaulay. Also," Angela assumed a cheerful tone, "Vita Sackville-West said, 'Palmyra is a Bedouin girl laughing because she is dressed up as a Roman lady.'"

She gestured whimsically with her left hand for a second, when Mohammed was off the wheel.

"OK, that's it! When you quote English literature, I can't handle it." Mohammed was trying to make a joke but was determined underneath. "I'm serious. Pull over now!"

Angela scratched his hand; he withdrew and rubbed it like a baby. "Hey!" he said, looking at it.

"Certainly I will pull over," she said, "if you can give me one good reason. I am in no hurry to get to Turkey; why are you?"

"Because I killed a man in Beirut."

Angela snapped her head to the right and looked sternly at him. She returned her gaze to the road. Did Honey Jean have a rule for a situation like this? The best she could think of was "Whatever happens, poise and self-control will see you through."

"I think . . . I'll just keep driving right on in to Palmyra," she smiled. "I can see the ruins while you wait for the police."

Chapter 87

# M1 MOTORWAY, SYRIA
## July 14, 2006

*Does he really expect me to be satisfied with that explanation?*

Angela had agreed to a compromise with Mohammed: she could continue driving as long as she turned back toward M1 and Aleppo. He would explain. If she was not satisfied with why they needed to keep moving, she would take them back to Palmyra.

He told a story about how, when he visited his friend's house in Beirut, a burglar was trying to break in. In valiant defense of his friend, he hit the man, who then flew over the balcony, plunging to his death several stories below. It was an accident, but Mohammed did not want to meet the police. A neighbor had seen him and might report him.

*Sounds lame.*

The explanation left many unanswered questions: What happened to the friend who was being robbed? Would he get the blame? With all the bombing going on, and South Beirut bombed to pieces, why would the police care about one more body on a patio? And most important, who was the other dead man?

Earlier, Angela had distinctly overheard Nasir ask Mohammed if they were "both dead." That means there were *two* dead men.

She was still confused, and she didn't totally trust her personable cousin. But Uncle Nasir didn't seem angry with Mohammed over the dead men. That would seem to indicate things were OK. If not, then Uncle Nasir would be evil, and him she trusted.

Angela remembered what Freya Stark wrote: "The great and almost only comfort about being a woman is that one can always pretend to be more stupid than one is and no one is surprised."

So she pretended to accept his explanation, while also keeping vigilant for clues to the truth.

About the time Mohammed finished his story they passed through Hama, a four-thousand-year-old garden city on the banks of the Orontes River.

"Ten thousand people died here in 1982," Mohammed said. "There was an uprising of the Muslim Brotherhood, a terrorist organization. Much of the old city was destroyed."

Mohammed didn't share details about the uprising—or how he knew them. The family in Damascus was always taking risks. He was worried about leaving Nasir and the others with them, but what else could he do? He thought about this until he fell asleep, just outside of Aleppo.

Considering all the distractions, they made good time and arrived at about one p.m. The citadel was basked in midday sun, dominating the skyline as it had since the neo-Hittite temple was built there twelve thousand years ago. It was hot.

"Look, sister, I will be good to you. Drive into town and we will have a niiiice lunch!"

"You mean, brrooootherr is hungry."

As part of Aleppo's restoration plan, several old houses had been converted into charming restaurants. They parked and walked to one of these, passing a souk, or Arab market, then a hammam, a public bath in the Turkish style.

"Do you feel like having a bath?" Angela asked hopefully. "It would be so refreshing! I would love having my sweat scraped off!"

"You are sick!" Mohammed said, looking at her. He hated thinking about germs.

"Oh, I remember. You are hungry. How about after lunch? Then we can relax and hit the road when the heat dies down."

"We need to keep driving. More than the heat could die," he said to her, then added to himself but so she could hear, "Woman was created from a rib. If you try to straighten her she will break; if you don't, she will remain crooked."

"Brother, that is wrong! Being from man's rib means that woman is near his heart and works at his side."

"Sister, you are wrong. I am quoting respected hadith. Our Prophet said it! Now bow in reverence to your master," he teased.

"Are you forgetting I'm not your wife? *Alhamdulillah!* That was just a story for immigration. And I'm not bowing to any man, especially not a *womanizer* like you," she said, using the English word.

"What is 'womanizer'?" He guessed, "I am *not* homosexual!"

"So I hear!" She laughed and changed the subject. "Oh, look in there!"

At that moment they passed the Khan al-Wazir, built in 1682 by the governor as a caravanserai, or khan—a traditional inn for caravan drivers and their animals. The ornate entrance portal was open, and they could see inside.

"Oh," she said. "That's fascinating—a khan!"

"What? It's just a warehouse of crates stored in an old building. No food at all!"

"Over the gate, look at the windows, one has a minaret, and the other a cross. What a beautiful idea. Do you see inside?" she asked, pointing to a structure in the center of the tree-studded courtyard. "That must be the mosque for the travelers."

Angela could see in her mind the way it would have looked a hundred years ago: animals in the large courtyard with its soaring vaulted ceiling, the central kiosk, and up above, the cells bustling with travelers.

To Mohammed it was just an old building.

"Oh, thank you for bringing me here!" She beamed at Mohammed.

## Chapter 88

# ALEPPO, SYRIA
## July 14, 2006

As the khan excelled in grandeur, the restaurant excelled in decorative detail. Through a bland exterior one entered a cool courtyard with a fountain and trees, surrounded by an *iwan*—an open, overhung shaded area. In the adjacent *madafah*, or reception hall, every surface was decorated: striped stone archways, carved wooden doors and ceilings painted with floral motifs, and inlaid colored marble on the walls creating geometric patterns.

Angela was thrilled with the restaurant. She started telling Mohammed how the style was similar yet different to Morocco, but she saw his eyes glaze over and changed the subject.

"How long do you think it will take us to get to Turkey from here?"

"About an hour, maybe."

After ordering drinks, Angela excused herself to freshen up. The drinks arrived. Angela didn't.

After ten minutes Mohammed got nervous. He couldn't see where Angela had gone from where he was sitting. He asked the maître d' if he had seen Angela and got a negative reply.

*Angela wouldn't just leave. Who would leave* before *lunch?*

He waited another five minutes. Finding no trace of her in the restaurant, he left money on the table and went into the street.

Angela had put on her scarf, but without her abaya, which she had lost in the rescue, her tight jeans showed too much of her figure. Mohammed had noticed all the men watching her as they walked to the restaurant. That didn't narrow the field much.

*What would ImmMohammed say if anything happened to Angela?*

Usually Mohammed was so cool. Why should he lose it now?

But he found himself wandering up and down the streets, asking everyone if they had seen an American in—what color was her scarf? He even asked women, especially women. They would have nothing to hide.

One told him yes, she had seen an American woman. She remembered because a man was scolding her and holding her wrist tightly.

They were going in the direction of the Great Mosque, away from the citadel.

Mohammed started running that way. He pushed past people and knocked over a stall of Aleppo copperware. He only paused a moment when he bumped a small child. He patted her head, and since no parent was around to scold him, kept running.

Who could it be? One of Ahmed's associates? What would they want with her? Surely it wouldn't be the police. Could it be just the usual—abduction and rape? He couldn't think about that. Best to just keep looking.

At last he saw a couple who fit the description he'd been given. The woman was being brutally held by the wrist and forced along against her will. He couldn't see her—she was covered from head to toe, and she was facing the other way. Could they have veiled Angela that quickly?

"Let me go!" she said in English, but the voice wasn't Angela's. "I won't stay here any longer!"

Mohammed had stumbled into one of the thousands of marriages that take place each year between American women and Muslim men. This unhappy wife was trying to escape and get back to America, but without success.

Mohammed fought an urge to rescue her, but it would only make it worse for her if a strange man came to her defense. And he would lose time looking for Angela.

He went back to the restaurant, but Angela had not returned. Mohammed was at a loss. He went outside again and started asking the same questions, this time heading to where they had parked the car.

From a distance he saw something on the windshield. A ransom note?

He ran up and got it. "A crooked . . ." he whispered to himself.

When Angela made her appearance, Mohammed was leaning on the car smiling and purposely looking nonchalant, as if he had not a care in the world—in total contrast to his behavior the last hour.

Angela strode bold as brass in broad daylight. When she caught sight of him, she literally started strutting. Her head was uncovered, and her glossy hair was shining and bouncing in the midday light. The pants she was wearing showed her curves in a way best seen only indoors in a country like Syria.

The strut was out of character for her, but she enjoyed feeling she had the upper hand. In spite of his appearance, she knew Mohammed had been looking for her and was worried.

*He deserves everything he got. He's not only a killer, he's proud and bossy.*

When she got close to Mohammed, she reached into her bag and pulled out a robe with a dramatic gesture, saying, "I needed another abaya!"

He wanted to say, "Then wear it!" But he hid his feelings of mixed anger and admiration under humor. "Could we eat the flowers on your abaya? I didn't order, and now I'm staaarrrving!"

"Oh, that's too bad. I had some falafel!"

Mohammed was writhing with frustration at her and at the thought of missing lunch.

"I'm glad you found the note," she said, then added, trying to sound as superficial as possible, "I would have asked you to come, *habeebee*, but I know how you feel about shopping in Syria. So I found this precious hand-decorated abaya all on my own!"

"Get in the car," he commanded in Arabic, "before I strangle you with that precious hand-decorated abaya!"

"What does 'strangle' mean? I don't know that word in Arabic. Does it mean 'to buy another'?" Angela asked. She truly did not know the word, but she guessed at its meaning.

"In the car, seesterr!"

"I did so much in an hour, I amaze myself. Ha-ha!" Angela laughed sincerely, imitating Mohammed's laugh. She even slapped her leg. "I got to see the oldest continually inhabited city in the world after all. Did you know that it's Aleppo? What a surprise. When I was in Damascus, *that* was the oldest city; now Aleppo is. Amazing how Syria can have the two oldest cities at once! Name me one other country that can do that! Palestine only has one...."

She was far too cheerful, like a child who tries to get out of trouble by pretending nothing is wrong.

Mohammed was reminded of something. That was good because it spared him scolding her. "Like the Uthman's personal Koran, the one with his death blood on it. It's located in *both* Tashkent and Topkapi." This made about as much sense to Angela as her English literature did to him.

"What?"

"Forget about it! It's like I told you, sister," said Mohammed, wanting to change the subject, "Jericho is the oldest city in the world. The Syrians are liars!"

"Oh, that's what your cousins in Damascus told you?"

"Of course not. My cousins, they are the best, the best! It is the people who write the travel books that are liars."

"I hope you are not including Angela O'Connor Hall, author of *Skirts on Camels*."

"Who knows what kind of book that is! It's just some fool thing to keep rich women busy between parties. Ha-ha!"

Angela said nothing. She knew him well enough by this time not to be hurt by his rudeness; but rudeness it was nonetheless, and it deserved to be treated as such.

Mohammed had expected a witty, or at least angry, reply. When none came he said, "Sister! That's good." He looked over at her, then back. "You agree with me about skirt books."

"Not at all," Angela responded pleasantly. "It is just that some comments are beneath my notice."

Angela continued, "I am so glad for *this* rich woman's guidebook on Syria!" she flashed the Syria and Lebanon travel guide. "I bought some recommended Aleppan olive oil soap, and look." Angela raised a bag so Mohammed could see it as he drove. "Famous Aleppan pistachios. I wouldn't even have thought of them without the book."

"Give me some!" Mohammed said. With his characteristic impulsiveness for food, he started grabbing. "Let Palestinian taste and see if they are good." He opened his mouth and threw in a handful. "Yes, sister, good. Verrry, verrry, good."

"I'm glad you agree about the guidebooks."

Chapter 89

# SYRIA TO TURKEY
## July 14, 2006

A series of mistrustful circumstances can cool relations between nations as well as people. So it is between Syria and Turkey, but in less than an hour Mohammed and Angela passed through the border and were nearly to Gaziantep, Turkey. From there they would continue to Cappadocia, Ankara, and their destination of Istanbul.

Gaziantep is another town crowned by a citadel—this one a fortress originally started by Emperor Justinian; the current thirty-six crumbling towers came mostly from the time of the Seljuk Turks. Just below the citadel is a bazaar, a happy sight for Angela, who was more interested in seeing new things and people than simply shopping.

Angela had eaten, but Mohammed was starved. After the episodes at Palmyra and Aleppo, he was disinclined to let her out of his sight, so they agreed she would stay by the entrance of the bazaar looking at what the *usta*, or craftsmen, had to offer, while he got some food to go—stew and seasoned bread, or *güveç* and *gözleme* as the Turks call it.

When Mohamed returned to the bazaar, Angela was gone. Knowing Angela a little better, and having grown up giving and receiving practical jokes, he was not immediately alarmed. But he was annoyed.

*That "crooked rib" has a lot to learn. She is taking this too far.*

He walked over to where Angela had been looking at some of the inlaid mother-of-pearl work the town is famous for, when an old woman grabbed his sleeve. She muttered something in agitated Turkish and pointed toward the Isuzu.

*Déjà vu* all over again.

He walked up the street, but without panic this time, trying to balance his food. Again, he saw a man and woman, her wrist apparently being twisted. The couple was moving fast and headed toward the car.

It was Angela! Mohammed started running.

The man pulled out a tool and started to pry open the door to get into the back of the extended cab. Angela was struggling hard, and the man had to choose between the door or her. He chose the door. Angela ran free down a side street, not seeing Mohammed.

Mohammed came up behind the man and said, "*Ya, akhuy!*" As soon as the thief turned around, Mohammed threw the hot stew into his face. Taking advantage of the resulting discomposure, he socked him in the gut and on top of the head. It wasn't a fair fight. The man was a foot shorter than Mohammed.

"*Ya, Angela, akhty! Yala ibinet!*"

Angela, who had turned around when at a safe distance, saw what happened and heard Mohammed call her. She ran back to the car as Mohammed was starting it. Opening the door, she jumped in.

They felt a bump and heard a scream as he quickly backed out of the parking spot and suspected they had run over their assailant. But there was no time to check.

"That was wonderful. I'm so glad we stopped!" said Angela cheerfully, as they got back on the main road. Mohammed looked at her as if she were crazy and saw her pulling a small box out of her purse.

"Fortunately I had a chance to buy this before your fellow-killer grabbed me!"

"But I lost my lunch!" Mohammed shook his head. "Something tells me this is going to be a looooong trip."

Chapter 90

# CAPPADOCIA, TURKEY

## July 14, 2006

As the sun started to set Angela said, "Let's face it, Mohammed, we need a break. I wonder if there are any five-star hotels in central Turkey? Let me check the guidebook."

"Forget about hotels. We're being chased, remember?"

"Ooooh. Mohammed, listen to this."

Angela read the guide in English: "Two of the tectonic plates that make up the earth's crust collide in central Turkey, pushing up mountain ranges and forming a series of extinct volcanoes. One of these snow-covered peaks was worshipped by the ancient Hittites, who called it Harkassos, or 'White Mountain.' The volcanic activity in the prehistoric past accounts for two additional remarkable geologic features of this region: fairy chimneys and caves."

"Fairies? What are they?" Mohammed asked.

"It doesn't matter." She continued. "Volcanic rock was responsible for both phenomena. 'Fairy chimneys' were created when the earth and the weather wrestled with two types of volcanic rock: soft volcanic ash called 'tuff' on the bottom, and hard volcanic rock on top. Erosion affected the softer bottom layer more than the top layer, leaving 'hats' of harder rock perched, sometimes precariously, on top of thinner spires of the softer rock. These structures are called 'fairy chimneys.'"

"Seesterr, why are you giving me geology lesson?" Mohammed interrupted.

"Just listen, mouthy!"

> The soft tuff also produces natural caves, and was discovered by the ancients to be amenable to carving. There are thousands of caves in Cappadocia. Some are visible from the road, becoming famous landmarks: Göreme Valley looks like a Flintstone village, and Uçhisar's complex looks like a mountain-sized lump of Swiss cheese.
>
> Other caves are remote, accessed by grassy trails that curve through small river valleys. In these valleys herds would eat below, and people would sleep in caves above them. Tiny spaces would be carved to house doves, for eggs.

Entire underground cities were created, like at Derinkuyu, where people could hide for months in case of siege. Early Christians hid here from persecution under the Romans, especially Diocletian. Later, they hid here from the Muslim Seljuk Turks. Some caves are churches, vaulted and painted with Byzantine frescoes of saints and Bible scenes.

"Do you get that, Moe? Cappadocia is the hideout capital of the Middle East, and we are almost there!"

It was night by the time they got to Cappadocia. They began scouring the countryside around Göreme for a secret resting place. They drove past fairy chimneys without noticing them.

"Let's stop here," Mohammed said.

Mohammed and Angela had stumbled into just the situation they were looking for: a cave in a crevice off the tourist beat, with a place to park the Isuzu in the bushes and a screened space in front of the cave where they could light a fire.

Mohammed hid the essentials in a cave and came out. It wasn't very cold, but it was dark, and a fire would provide light and let them heat water. Hidden as they were on three sides, there was little chance that a small fire would be seen from the road.

"Home sweet cave!" Angela said as she carried an armload of blankets for them to sit on.

"I am so crazy—I am going to call this little tiny thing a fire!" said Mohammed. "What do you think, sister, is it the best fire you have ever seen?"

"Well, now, I can't insult my dad and Re-Pete by admitting that, but I am quite certain it is the grandest fire in Turkey!"

"Ah, America. Your father shouldn't have died before he took me hunting with him. What about Re-Pete? Do you think he would take me?"

"Oh, I'm certain he would. He'd let you carry everything while he complained. But you don't suppose he'd give a Palestinian a gun, do you?"

"Hey, but he's my little Palestinian brother! No problem. When he sees me, he will give me gun and watch me kill many, many, leettle birds!"

"Elk."

"Many, many, leettle elk!" he affirmed, not knowing what an elk was.

They ate some of what Mohammed, in his foresight, had packed—the kind of Mediterranean food that kept well: cheese, dried fruit, nuts, and some dry *khubis* bread. They couldn't get the water to boil, but the tea was very warm, and it felt good to wrap their hands around their cups.

Mohammed sat with his back to the cave, looking out over the fire, Angela to his side. When Mohammed stood, the firelight threw his shadow into the cave. Noticing this, Angela said, "I've never seen that before."

"What?"

"Shadows in a cave," she answered, with a slight dipping intonation on the final word.

"Really! That is sooo amazing, sister! You see," he demonstrated in jest to an invisible audience, "I brought the American Princess to Turkey so she could see famous 'shadows in a cave.'"

"I gather you haven't heard of Plato's 'shadows in a cave' philosophy?"

"Plato, who's he? The potter that makes that majolly stuff you like?"

"Majolica. No, silly. I'm not sure if you are teasing me, so I am going to punish you and tell you about him!"

"No, sister!" He hid his face with his arms in mock recoil. "Not scary story!"

"There, there, little camper," she said in the gentle way she used with the young ones at drama camp. "It is nothing to be afraid of. The big philosopher man Plato just shared this funny idea that our lives are not real. Although they seem to be, they are simply reflections, like shadows on a cave wall. Is that really so very scary?" To complete the effect, she ventured to pat Mohammed's head.

His guard was slipping. The fire was a foolish idea. Better by far just to go to sleep. The firelight on her hair created that unearthly glow again, and combined with her soft tone and touch, it was too damn much.

If she hadn't been married he knew exactly what he would do. Now he did the only safe thing: switch from physical to mental. He pushed her away and said, "What seems to be real." He paused. "Angela, I'm going to share something with you."

## Chapter 91

# CAPPADOCIA, TURKEY

## July 14, 2006

"It's about that box of CDs isn't it?"

He recovered his smile. "You are sooo smart! But you will never guess what's in it!"

Mohammed rose and went for something in the cave. Returning with it, he sat back beside the fire.

"What's that?" asked Angela. "It doesn't look like a CD."

"Heaven forgive you, sister! What kind of Muslim are you? It's the Koran."

"Am I in for a sermon now, Sheik Mohammed, perhaps on how life on earth isn't real, just preparation for paradise, and what a crooked rib I am?"

"Seriously, sister," he spoke plainly, holding up the Koran so she could see the cover in the firelight, "what do you know about the Koran?"

"It is the Holy Book from Allah, sent down from heaven to the Prophet Mohammed by the Angel Gabriel."

"Has it ever been changed?"

"Of course not! Every Muslim knows it is an exact copy of the sacred text existing on a table in the presence of Allah himself. This is the first, or maybe second, thing we are taught in the faith."

"How do you know that, sister? Explain to me."

"Imams and sheiks and doctors in Islamic Studies have thoroughly studied the resources and assure us that it is the same as it was at the time of Mohammed—without change or corruption. It is the final revelation, preserved by the power of Allah."

"What are the 'resources' you are speaking of?"

"Oh, I've seen them, lots of them. In the mosques and Islamic bookstores there are encyclopedia-like volumes of books that go way back to the early days of Islam."

Angela paused. "Why are you asking me these questions? If you are trying to show that you know more than me, I surrender! I told you I am an average American Muslim, not a scholar." She paused and looked at him quizzically. "Are you?"

"You just tell me what you know, and I will tell you what I know. It will be fun!"

Angela looked doubtful. But she wasn't sleepy, and there was nothing else to do. "OK, why not," she shrugged.

"That's it! Tell me about the early days of Islam," Mohammed said.

Angela looked off, beyond the campfire. "It must have been a little like this, don't you think? Refugees huddled around the campfire in a desolate location. Oh, and the cave!" She looked into the one at her right. "Wow! How like Mohammed's retreat, except for the crosses painted on the walls," she smiled.

"Sooo, you know about the cave."

"Of courrse, silly brrooootherr!" She rolled her *r*'s and eyes in imitation of his accent and condescension. "The Prophet would often fast and pray in a cave near Mecca."

"Here is subject you will know better than me. America. When was your war to separate from England?"

"You mean the Revolutionary War? It was in the 1770s, about two hundred and thirty years ago."

"And if you want to learn about it, you ask your American grandfather, right?"

"No. He's not that old! Besides, his ancestors were in Ireland at the time."

"So how do you know anything about it? It was a very long time ago."

"As you might guess, oh, Grand Master Inquisitor, I can read!"

"So you read about it in books, but how do the authors know what happened so long ago?"

"Oh, I see what you are getting at. You mean how we investigate history! History isn't exactly my field, but I do some historical research from time to time, like for my PhD and now in Istanbul. For that I read as much of the original material as I can find. The Revolutionary War historians would do the same sort of thing—records from the Continental Congress, battlefield reports, newspapers from the time, old letters. I would look at a wealth of information like that."

"Wealth of information. That's it, sister! You are certain of what happened in the Revolutionary War, even though it was two hundred and thirty years ago because 'wealth of information' survives from that time. You do not depend on the memory of old people, even nice old people like your grandfather."

"He isn't nice..." Angela said, remembering her recent visit.

"When it comes to the early days of Islam, and the life of the Prophet, it is very different. Those books with all the gold on the covers you saw, they are collections of hadith, thousands of stories collected by scholars over two hundred years *after* Mohammed died."

"You mean, it was as if I started now to try to write the first history of the Revolutionary War and nothing remained from that time. Only stories passed down by word of mouth from generation to generation? That would be impossible!"

"Well, maybe not impossible, but highly imperfect. The Arabs of those days, like many nomadic peoples, had a strong oral tradition, meaning they memorized and recited a lot."

"Sure," agreed Angela. "There wasn't much more to do on a long dark night besides sit around telling stories and..." she stopped mid-sentence, but she could sense that Mohammed knew what she had been going to say. She continued, "That's what we're doing now. Sitting around the fire. It's almost like we are living history!"

"We are, sister, in more ways than you know." He gave a wry smile and then rose for a moment to put a few more branches on the waning fire. Angela went into the cave and came out with two blankets. One she put around herself and the other over Mohammed's shoulders as he bent forward to put the kettle back onto the rock at the fire's edge.

"Let's have some more tea!" he said with loud and rising intonation, stretching out both arms as if performing some joyous deed of hospitality. In doing so, he let the blanket slip off his shoulders. Angela watched, puzzled.

*He did that on purpose!*

"Now, sister, you can relax. I will tell some of what I know."

"This shouldn't take too long."

"Oh, but the best, the best," he waved his finger. "And you will tell me what you think."

"I will enjoy doing that!"

## Chapter 92

# CAPPADOCIA, TURKEY
## July 14, 2006

She could almost smell the camels. Angela felt as if she were a traveler of long ago, sheltered for the night in a khan, or a child sitting in the *halaka* circle around a fire, listening to an itinerant storyteller.

"Now, sister," the storyteller said. He looked into the fire.

Mohammed was not in a trance exactly, but his entire demeanor underwent a remarkable transformation. Angela had seen him in several moods before, but this was not a mood. His voice acquired a different tone. Gone were the rapid speech and the Palestinian accent he had in both Arabic and English. Instead, he spoke slowly in clear, classical Arabic, with crisp articulation seldom heard in this century and rich with rhythm and rhyme.

It seemed to Angela as if a mask had slipped and the man peeked out from behind the boy: a man who knew and cared about something. She listened, mesmerized.

Here is the story he told:

*Bismallah Ir-Rahman Ir-Raheem,*
*In the name of Allah the merciful and compassionate:*
*This is the story of the transmission of the Holy Koran.*

*What can be known of the past?*
*It is not given to man to know all things.*
*Allah is the knower and the keeper of secrets.*
*Fourteen centuries have passed since the words of the Holy Koran were revealed.*
*Who is now alive who was there to see and hear?*
*How can we, the living, know those who traveled the path before us and have gone?*
*Their footprints have faded in the desert sand.*
*How can we learn their message?*
*The word brings the message;*
*Spoken or printed or lived with us,*
*The Word of Allah reveals the mind of Allah.*

*For over two hundred years after the Prophet, there was no written history of Islam. Of the story of the Koran. Was the word then silent?*

*Ah! There were tales, told by the faithful, passed from generation to generation. Through the medium of the tongue and the power of the memory, "hadiths" were kept until they could be written. Most say hadiths are true and revere them next to the Koran itself. Some say, "Nay, they are but legends." Indeed legends some must be, for not every telling is the same.*

*Which then shall I repeat to you?*

*My lips shall speak and you shall hear only revered hadiths of the most regarded collection: the* Sahih al-Bukhari. *This is what they say:*

*The days of Ancient Arabia were a time of darkness. Then was a simple life of camels and tents, when one was close to nature, and felt closer to Allah, because death lurked around every corner. The land was full of idolatry. Clan battled clan. At birth, girls were buried in the sand.*

*Above this distress arose a man of integrity. An illiterate man, yet known for honesty and compassion. At the time of his calling, the Prophet Mohammed, may the peace and blessings of Allah be upon him, was praying in a cave during the month of Ramadan; when lo, an angel appeared, bringing revelation. For over twenty years the revelations continued. Only after they ceased were they assembled into the* Holy Koran. *Profound in meaning, eloquent in style; these revelations were received by the Prophet, but sent for all mankind:*

*As a call to worship,*<br>
*Allah in his oneness.*<br>
*To show the true path,*<br>
*And warn us not to leave it;*<br>
*To call us to war,*<br>
*To call us to peace.*<br>
*And to call us to paradise;*<br>
*For this life is but a test.*

*The Prophet would recite unto his followers, and those literate would record it. In the desert and dust, paper was rare. Whatever was at hand was recruited to hold the holy words—"palm branches, leather, the shoulder blades of animals, and the hearts of men"—became the receptacles of the Scripture.*

*Ah, but we must speak of the prophet himself: what said he about preserving the revelations? The very words of which contain power?*

*Much occupied was he with calling Arabs away from idolatry to the one true God. Much occupied was he with leadership in times of peace and times of battle. On earth, he was the spoken word and the living example to the people. What need then was there for written words? He neither compiled himself, nor requested compilation of the Koran. Some hadiths tell us he never wanted a compilation, even after his death. His revelations were both of the moment, yet confirmed "the books" that had been revealed before.*

*However, the Prophet knew the memories of men, and made provision for the preservation of the revelation. While alive, he designated four trustworthy men to be expert references. Their names were: Ibn Mas'ud, Ibn Ka'b, Ali, and Ibn Abbas.*

*In the year 632 of the Western calendar, Allah took his Messenger from the earth. The Prophet's death came rapidly. There was no provision for succession. The hearts and resolve of his followers were severely tried in the next decade. He had no son, had appointed no heir. He had established no definite code of law or religion, nor policies of empire. When he was alive, he was the law and the religion; and there was no empire. But things changed.*

*Four of his close companions followed him in succession, leading the people and carrying forth his vision. They became known as "Rightly Guided Caliphs," leaders both military and spiritual. Their names were:*

| | |
|---|---|
| ***Abu Bakr*** | *one of the first converts to Islam,*<br>*the first caliph,*<br>*and father of the Prophet's favorite wife, Ayesha* |
| ***Umar*** | *the second caliph*<br>*and the father of the Prophet's wife Hafsah* |
| ***Uthman*** | *the third caliph,*<br>*the father of the Prophet's wife ImmSalma,*<br>*and the husband of two of his daughters* |
| ***Ali*** | *the cousin of the Prophet,*<br>*the fourth caliph,*<br>*literary genius,*<br>*husband of his daughter Fatima,*<br>*the enemy of his wife Ayesha,*<br>*and the father of the Shiites* |

Sahih el-Bukhari *tells us that after the Prophet's death came the Battle Yamama. The fighting was fierce, a massacre in fact. So many of the faithful died that day that Caliph Abu Bakr feared soon all who knew the revelations might disappear from the face of the earth. He summoned a scribe of the Prophet, Zaid ibn Thabit. He told him, "You are a wise young man, and no one can say a word against you. You were entrusted with writing down the messages of the Prophet. Make a collection of the revelations and assemble them into the* Holy Koran*."*

*At first, Zaid had grave misgivings. He said, "By Allah, what I was asked to do could not have been more difficult if they had ordered me to pick up a mountain and move it." So he said to them, "How can you order me to do this, when even the Prophet did not order it?"*

*But in time, Caliph Abu Bakr, and the future Caliph Umar, persuaded Zaid. He then diligently sought and collected all the written and memorized portions of the Koran. This Koran was written on* suhufs, *or "rolls," which were kept in the custody of Caliph Abu Bakr himself. Upon his death the* suhufs *passed to his successor Caliph Umar, who in turn passed them to his daughter Hafsah.*

*Ah, you may say, so our Koran was collected two years after the death of the Prophet. But some say Abu Bakr made no such collection. He was just one of many followers who had kept notes of the Prophet's revelations. And this book was never copied or distributed. It remained the property of the caliph.*

*Soon the empire exploded in size. Of necessity, the believers of Medina developed forms of government to impose order as far away as Syria and Iraq. And the faith and its way of life must be taught in the newly converted regions. Who was to do this?*

*A new class of men arose: the* Qurra', *or "reciters" of the Koran. Now, it was not the companions of the Prophet alone who knew the messages but hundreds, even thousands, were trained in them. Many* Qurra' *were sincere and devout. But with the ability to recite came prestige. Some sought the office for power.* Qurra' *who had learned only a portion of the revelations by memory were ensured honor for what they knew. And whether noble or not, reciters did not have perfect memories.*

*Over the decades, scholars made their own written collections of the Koran. These became known by the major religious centers that spawned and followed them: Medina, Mecca, Damascus, Kufa, and Basra. Some centers had versions by more than one scholar, and so fifteen or more such Koranic versions emerged.*

*In the days of the third caliph, Uthman, one of his warlords came to him with a shocking discovery. He had been fighting in Syria and Iraq, yet what terrified him was not the blood of the battlefield but the variations he heard in the recital of the Koran. Fear came to the heart of Medina, for there was no uniformity in the sacred text, and the* Qurra' *considered themselves above the governing authorities.*

*Uthman became bold. He requested that Zaid make another collection of all the revelations but to remain true to the Medina Codex—the version of the capital. Uthman then officially canonized the new Koran and proclaimed it the final authority of Islam.*

*Copies were made and sent to the four other religious centers of the empire, with the original kept in Medina. Legends persist that one or more may survive to this day, but no one knows for certain. And what of the rival codices of the Koran? Well, my friend, by order of Caliph Uthman … no matter how respected, all manuscripts besides his … even those of the four men Mohammed called the experts, were to be collected …*

Mohammed paused for a moment and looked directly into Angela's eyes to be certain he had her undivided attention. He raised the Koran. The golden letters on its green cover gleamed in the firelight. "… *and thrown into the fire.*"

To her utter amazement, on this last word Mohammed took the holy book and threw it into the flames.

## Chapter 93

# CAPPADOCIA, TURKEY
## July 14, 2006

Jumping up, Angela cried, nearly hysterical, "*Haram, haram!* What desecration!" She waved her arms up and down, at the same time looking for something with which to pull the holy book out of the fire, but she found nothing.

"*Haram, haram!* Nihla's right, you are an infidel, a disbeliever! And a blasphemer! You will burn in hell like you just burned the Koran!" She was even tempted to reach in and pull it out herself, but discretion being the better part of valor where fire is concerned, she did not.

She stood transfixed in shock, staring at the fire. She watched the pages turn black and wither. As the green cover melted, it glowed a purplish color. She sat down, holding her head in her hands. A few quiet tears flowed down her face: tears of shock and futility and disillusion.

*What am I to do? What kind of man is this cousin?*

Before this, she had admired him in several ways, but now he was bizarre and ominous. Surely he must know what it is to desecrate the Koran. Was he completely unaware of the problems America had for lesser offenses when trying to shock its terrorist prisoners in Guantanamo?

The Koran had turned to ashes, but Angela could not raise her eyes to look Mohammed in the face. Her tongue could not formulate one word to say to him.

She started to shiver. Maybe only ten percent of it was due to the cold, but it was a good excuse to escape his pestilent presence and retire to her alcove in the cave.

*I won't say a word. He can just watch me go and assume whatever he wants.*

She made herself as cozy as possible with the pillows and blankets, and stuffed some warm clothes around her. She knew she was too wound up to sleep, but she could fake it and get some privacy. She hoped that he had violated enough rules of convention for one night and that he would leave her alone.

Angela's mind kept racing. *How did he think I would feel? Does he just get a kick out of shocking people? He seems impulsive at times, but I thought he had some limits! What could possibly be his motive? How could anyone enjoy such an act, knowing the penalty it would bring? He's like a child who laughs while throwing rocks at a bear, not thinking of the consequence.*

Mohammed had brandished a smile as he threw the book into the fire. It was not a planned move; it just seemed to come as a natural flourish to the end of the story. Well, it turned out to be the premature end of the story. He counted on Angela being shocked, but not the raving hysterics. Mohammed had been going to explain more, but Angela couldn't absorb it. Smile gone, his eyes followed her into the cave.

He sat back down. He wasn't shivering. The blanket Angela had brought was behind him, on the ground. At first, he was warm from the adrenalin. Then the breeze did start to cool him. He went from refreshed to cold in about thirty seconds flat. But he didn't fight it enough to shiver or pull up the blanket. He just let it reduce the temperature of his skin and move below it.

Mohammed was drained. This was not the way he had expected it to end. He had misjudged Angela. But it was better to find out now than later, when it could cause real trouble.

Then he smiled and laughed to himself. Well, he had done one thing right tonight: he certainly succeeded in dissipating any sexual tension between them.

Just then he heard two pops in the distance. Or was it in the fire?

*Are we found already?*

Even if it was not their pursuers, any Muslim who overheard might take even greater offense than Angela did.

That settled it. He would not sleep tonight. He had upset Angela; the least he could do was keep watch and protect her. If they were on better terms, he would ask her to share watch with him. She would even insist on it, he was certain, so that the drive in the morning would be safer. Now, if he so much as spoke to her, he feared he might get a pan to the head. But anyway, it was better not to worry her. She was not accustomed to living with danger, as he had been in Palestine since he was a boy.

He arose to make a circuit around the camp, not walking too far afield, but keeping the cave in sight. He also collected a few twigs for later in the night. Then he returned to the fireside and stoked it up. After a few nights without sleep, he was truly getting tired. He would need a little something to keep himself going. He pulled on the blanket and put the kettle on the fire.

## Chapter 94

# CAPPADOCIA, TURKEY
# July 14, 2006

Angela had a most fitful sleep. She had known hurt and grief and sorrow in her life, but she had not experienced atrocities. Outside of the evening news, seeing a holy book burnt was about as bad a thing as she had witnessed. How could she just set this aside and dream peacefully? Especially with an admitted killer nearby?

The stone bench she slept on was cold and hard. She kept shifting. Eventually she did fall asleep but with questions and indignation still racing in her head. So she dreamed. Images floated by. They seemed to be tied to her movements so that every time she shifted a new image came into view; each charged with meaning, whether she understood it or not.

The most frequent image was that of the Koran glowing and burning in the fire. The image would pass, replaced by another, but then it would return. She dreamed of the landscape of Cappadocia with the historical figures of early Islam. She saw people huddled around the fire and heard a voice reciting Koranic verses. Was it Mohammed's own voice or one of the Qurra'? Then people acted out what the verses commanded.

Then men on horses, brandishing swords, galloped past the fire, and their dust extinguished it. She saw Nihla's crying face, which melted into Fatima's face; and she heard Fatima whispering her last words over and over.

A red-painted cross like one she had seen in the cave chapels flashed by. A voice shouted, "The Koran has never been changed!" She saw hundreds of students of all races and faiths gathered on Sproul Plaza at UC Berkeley. A man or an angel dressed in glowing white emerged and stood in front of the Koran, saying, "The flower falls, but the Word of the Lord lasts forever."

Then she saw home and her husband's stern expression as he chided, "Well, you won!" Then Cousin Mohammed's face replaced John's. His arms were folded, and the corners of his eyes curled up impishly. "Seesterr!" he said in mock sternness. "You are sooo silly!"

But his face immediately melted into a demonic expression and became surrounded with fire. Hell fire. She saw again the image of the Koran emerge in the fire. But it was burned, and only ashes were left.

## Chapter 95

# CAPPADOCIA, TURKEY
## July 15, 2006

Angela awoke before dawn, and at the first hint of light she emerged from the cave. She looked like, well, like she had spent the night in a cave. No pristine socialite today. Without adequate washing facilities, she neither saw nor cared that her eye makeup had smeared. Her hair was tangled, and the blanket she had wrapped around herself against the chill morning air was chalky white, covered with decomposing "tuff" from the walls of the cave.

She found Mohammed asleep, curled up in an awkward position beside the fire. Good intentions had not been enough to counter three sleepless nights. If anyone had found them, they'd be dead by now.

She thought he looked rather innocent, as people often do when sleeping. But then she remembered what a blasphemer he was. So she gave him what he deserved—she kicked him.

"Get up, reprobate!" she said, which felt good, even though he wouldn't know what it meant.

Mohammed ached. His head felt stuffy. From his cramped position he squinted one eye open at this rude awakening. He wasn't at his sharpest either, but seeing Angela in her current state triggered his wit.

"Hey, dusty old Bedouin hag," he coughed out some dust and blinked, "have you seen my beautiful cousin Angela?"

The dusty hag kicked him again. "Hag or no hag," she said, "I am not staying any longer with a blaspheming murderer! At least until I know why he blasphemes and murders," she softened a little, then said, "So sit up, you've got some explaining to do."

Mohammed looked worse than Angela, which served to add credence to his claim: "I can't talk. My mouth is full of dust and all my joints are stiff." He sat up, legs crossed askew, rubbing his jaw. "Even my jaw." He said coaxingly, "Please make me some tea, to open my throat, and then some coffee to open my eyes, and I will talk to you."

"The hell I will!" she said in English, using uncharacteristic profanity. But she was mistrustful and angry at his deceptions. It wouldn't pay to be sympathetic to criminals.

"You just get yourself together enough to tell me what the hell is going on before the first tourist bus shows up, or I'm out with it. And I will be sure to let the police know where you are. They couldn't give a damn about me, but I suspect someone would be glad to know where you are."

"Wow!" said Mohammed, speaking calmly but lifting his eyebrows. "The old hag is a grumpy one. Go find my cousin, and don't come back without her. Tell her cute Palestinian cousin is making coffee for her."

"Humph," said Angela, turning around, chin raised, and clutching the blanket around her. She went off to see if she could find running water, which she couldn't. She snuck back and grabbed some water from their jug, as unobtrusively as possible, and cleaned up using her hand mirror. She shook out the blanket but kept it around her.

Mohammed had to wake up fast. He was thrust into the position of needing to make a major decision, the kind you don't like to make running on only two cylinders. Well, he would just have to find a way to make the two cylinders communicate with each other and come up with a full-power solution.

Should he tell Angela more? If so, what? His own personal story, how he got to where he is, and why he is there? Or should he go more into the theoretical? Considering how she came unglued when he tested her last night, he was not eager to put more fuel onto that fire.

But if Angela did not have some kind of explanation for why he was running, why he lied, why he killed a man, and why he threw the Koran into the fire, she would go on assuming he was a "reprobate," or whatever that word was, and would refuse to stay with him. Of this he was certain.

Mohammed knew Angela's personality enough to believe she would take a bus or train to Ankara, and fly to Istanbul from there. And what she would say of their experiences was anyone's guess. It wasn't just the past he was worried about: what about his plans for Istanbul? Would he be able to pull it off without her aid?

Meanwhile Angela was thinking much what Mohammed was imagining she was thinking, and more. She was more awake and thinking faster. She was about ninety percent sure that in a few hours she would be bussing her way to civilization.

*Was it possible to be so warm and have the hidden stone cold heart of a blaspheming murderer?* She thought of a beautiful castle covered with pink climbing roses reflecting peacefully in a moat but with a dark dungeon of bats, spiders, and skeletons in its core.

Aunt Rana was right: Mohammed Atareek was the most amazing person she had ever met. She found his *fahalawy* personality fun. He was devilishly cute and sweet in a way that could melt a hardened heart—just as water had eroded Cappadocia into a land of fairy chimneys.

Mohammed seemed so considerate. He would look straight at a person and say, "How are you doing?" with a big smile that went right to his eyes, and then in a minute ask the same question, "How are you doing?" as if he felt you hadn't quite leveled with him the first time, and he really wanted to know.

She liked his quick wit and unhindered laughter. His jokes were sometimes funny, and often not, but they fed his joy until it exploded into full, infectious laughter. He could be complimentary without harassing. And, perhaps best of all, she liked how his manner would make you feel when you were with him, that you were the most important person in the world, rather like Uncle Mohammed.

Not many people had such character traits and people skills. She sighed.

*That one may smile, and smile, and be a villain.*

She hoped this line from Shakespeare's *Richard III* would not be true of her dear cousin, and yet what hope was there? Very little.

Well, perhaps it was for the best. Not, of course for the man he had killed, but for her—and just in time.

*I think I was falling in love with my own first cousin.*

That may be acceptable in the Middle East, but she was American. They lived in separate worlds and cultures. To marry first cousins was both illegal and illogical. Also, she was older than him by what? Several years? He certainly didn't mind letting her know that she was "old." The idea of divorce was not hers, but she had relished her new freedom. Now was not the time to disable it with entanglement of the heart. Besides Moe was hardly a person who could truly love and remain faithful to one woman.

*Let him be a murdering blasphemer and let him go.*

The sooner the better, and the less lasting damage to her already limping heart.

# Chapter 96

# CAPPADOCIA, TURKEY
## July 15, 2006

Mohammed had come to a conclusion. This wasn't a setting he would choose, but *shwayy, shwayy,* little by little, he would have to tell her at least some of the truth.

He would drop the dramatic routine, speak naturally, and see how she responded. If she stayed reasonable, he would tell her everything that would not put the operation in jeopardy. If she reacted badly, then he would stop. Simple. It couldn't be worse than it was now....

After all, Angela was exactly the sort of person they hoped could be convinced by their discoveries—an intelligent Arab Muslim who was neither extreme nor irrational. He was sure she would be capable of independent thought in spite of what he saw last night. Last night they were both exhausted, and he did give a powerful performance. It engendered the kind of defensive response he wanted—only it was too intense. If he could get Angela to direct that intensity in the right direction, he might have the ally he so needed in this challenging battle.

When Angela returned fifteen minutes later, she found the fire relit, Arabic coffee brewing, and bread, cheese, and apricots set out.

"Ahhh, there's my beeeuuuutiful cousin," said Mohammed as if nothing had happened last night or this morning. He switched to Arabic and spoke into the coffee. "Now she will bring a good price at the slave market!"

"Oh?" Angela dipped her chin and popped open her eyes. "And what about you? I hear the ugly men bring the highest prices. They're safe in the harems."

Mohammed squinted, nodded, and said, "Hmmm. Sounds worth being ugly for!"

"But first they were... uh... made eunuchs," Angela said the word in English, making a slicing motion at the groin to secure its meaning.

"Oouu," Mohammed flinched. "Can't you find another way to get me in?"

They both laughed, which helped ease the tension.

"Sister, I will sell you a slave for a really good price."

"I'm not sure I want one...."

"Oh, but he's the best, the best."

"Let me guess, he's Palestinian. No thanks. They talk back!"

"Listen, here's the deal. Let's leave this dusty world. The sooner we get to your place in Istanbul, the safer we will be."

"It's not safe going anywhere with a murderer. Forget it."

"I'm not a murderer. What I'm asking is you ride with me. That is what you pay. I will explain to you eeeverrything!"

"We don't have that long. We're going to Istanbul, not Alaska!"

"And I will cook eggs for you every day until you go home to California...."

Mohammed said if she were not satisfied with his explanation, she could drive wherever she wanted—police, bus, wilderness. True, he could easily overpower her, but for some reason she accepted. Maybe she doubted he would kill a cousin.

Mohammed sat slouched down with his leg crossed, casually popping nuts into his mouth.

"So why did you kill a man?" Angela asked plainly.

## Chapter 97

# CAPPADOCIA, TURKEY
## July 15, 2006

"I killed him in self-defense, after he had killed my friend Jamal."

"Vendetta! Sounds like a gang war. Was it the Palestinian Shabaab versus the Lebanese Locals?"

Mohammed did not laugh. He started speaking Arabic so he could be very clear. "No, sister, don't joke about it. Jamal was over eighty years old. He was a friend and a coworker on our research project."

"What research project."

"Oh," Mohammed paused. "It's supposed to be a secret."

"It's too late for all that. You burned a Koran in my presence, killed a man, and did who knows what other crimes. You may have no secrets from Cousin Angela."

"OK. But you asked for it. Don't fall asleep at the wheel."

"Oh, murder stories seldom put me to sleep."

Mohammed began. "I told you that I was not well educated between the First and Second Intifadas."

"You've been killing since back then?"

Mohammed ignored this. "I worked hard, but I got involved in many bad things for fun. I stole cars and stuff; I drank, smoked, took some drugs, and chased women. What happened with me is... you heard about the accident?"

Angela shook her head. "Sort of."

"I should have died."

"Allah didn't want you."

Mohammed looked out at the unearthly Cappadocian landscape. The stubby vines and crops seemed unnatural, as if they were plopped into the powdery white soil for a scene of *Star Wars*. Not real. Like his life sometimes seemed.

Angela could see he was not in a mood for fun. She changed her tone. "OK, that's good. You're still here."

"Sister, when guilt comes hand in hand with grief, it changes your life. I..." he paused, "stopped smoking the next day and tried to become a good Muslim. I wanted to make up for my sins. I met with the sheik. He told me to practice the five pillars of Islam, and I would feel better. So I said the *shahadah*, I prayed five times a day, I gave alms, and when Ramadan came, I fasted. But instead of feeling better, I felt emptier.

He continued, "I thought it was because of all the distractions. You know how it is in Palestine—no one leaves you alone?"

"Not when there are people to feed!"

"Exactly," Mohammed agreed.

Then they said in unison by accident, "And there are always people to feed!"

Mohammed sat upright. "That's when I went to Lebanon. I bought the plantation. It wasn't habitable at first, so I thought people would stay away. I could be alone to practice pure Islam and recover from my grief. "

Angela remembered what Nihla had said about the plantation's restoration. "Did it work out that way?"

"Yes. I had more time alone. I could practice Islam purely. I did *wudoo* ritual ablution before every prayer. While I restored the house, I slept in a tent. I would arise before dawn to do the first prayer outside on the stone terrace, shivering in the cold, hoping to please Allah and be forgiven. I prayed regularly at the appointed times. I expected to feel better, but I didn't. I began asking myself many questions. "

"Such as?"

"First, about the rituals. In the mosque, the direction of Mecca is marked, so we know which way to face when praying. But what if I didn't know exact direction up there in the hills? Would Allah still accept my prayers? Why did I have to face Mecca when I prayed anyway? If God is everywhere, why does it matter which direction I face? And when I fasted for Ramadan I would look at the sunset over the ocean from my property—you remember the view, and how it seems almost as if you are at the top of the world?"

"Oh, yes..."

"I was looking out at the sunset, alone but feeling like fasting connected me to the *ummah*, to the family of Muslims all over the world. I thought about how fasting is specifically from sunrise to sunset. I started thinking about people in faraway places and realized some people live near the poles where it is dark for months in the winter and light for months in the summer. How do you survive if you fast for an entire season?"

"Whoa, that's a thought."

Mohammed continued, "Allah wants people all over the world to be under Islam, 'Dar al-Islam.' If Islam is for everyone, why does Allah require they learn and pray in Arabic? There are already more non-Arab Muslims than Muslims, like Pakistanis and Indonesians. Is it possible for a man to understand more languages than Allah?"

"I wonder that too. I would rather pray in English. God would seem closer that way."

"I went to Mecca on hajj. Maybe that would make me feel better. But it didn't. How could walking around a rock in the Kabaa seven times take away sin? The Koran tells us Allah has no partner. If I can take away my own sin, am I his partner in saving me? I needed answers, so I studied the Koran. But most of it didn't make sense to me. I thought it was my Arabic, so I studied Koranic Arabic. But the more I could appreciate the Arabic, the more problems I could see in the Koran."

"But it is perfect! The quintessential example of Arabic style."

"Why do you say that?"

"I've known it since I was little," said Angela.

"Obviously you weren't an Arabic expert then! The reason you 'know' it is because you were told it. If you started reading the Koran today, without preconceptions, you would see that although some passages are beautiful and powerful, there are many areas where the rhythm changes, or the rhyme drops, or the length of the lines abruptly changes. Not to mention the repetitions. Haven't you ever noticed that?"

"Well, I am not an expert on the Koran. When I run into something in the style that doesn't seem right, or content that confuses me, I put it down to my not being an expert in medieval Arabic."

"So you too have noticed that the Koran jumps from worship to curses to incomplete stories?"

"Well, yes, but as I said—"

"And some of it seems contradictory."

"I wouldn't say that. I'd just say it can be confusing to interpret. What contradictions are you talking about?"

"Here's a big one. You know how there are verses that say not to force people to believe Islam, like in sura 2, the one called *al-Baqara*, or 'of the Cow'? Verse 256 says, 'There is no compulsion in religion.'"

"Of course, that's what makes Islam a peaceful religion."

"But the Koran also has verses that incite violence, such as sura 2, verse 216, and sura 9, verses 5 and 29: 'Warfare is ordained for you.... Slay the idolaters wherever you find them, and take them captive, and besiege them, and prepare for them each ambush...' and 'Fight against those who have received the Scripture as believe not in Allah nor the last day, and forbid not that which Allah has forbidden by his messenger, and follow not the religion of truth,' and many others. So, on one hand we are told the Jews and Christians are our brothers, that they are also *People of the Book* from Allah. But on the other hand, because they don't accept Mohammed, we must kill them."

"But isn't there a special explanation for that. Like defensive war...."

"That's what I wondered too. So I bought collections of hadiths and commentaries—Sahih al-Bukhari, Sahih Muslim, al-Tabari, Ibn Kathir, al-Sayuti, and others. These books explain the situations under which the verses were revealed, which help me to understand their meaning."

"Did you learn anything?"

"I found the way experts explain the contradictions."

"What's that?"

"The Doctrine of Abrogation."

"Abrogation?"

"Yes, the idea that one revelation can cancel another. It is based on sura 2, verse 106: 'Such of Our revelations as we abrogate or cause to be forgotten, we bring in place one better or like thereof.' This doctrine explains that the peaceful verses revealed to Mohammed when he was in Mecca, and trying to gain favor with the Jews and Christians, are cancelled by revelations received after he moved to Medina, when he had the power to spread the faith by the sword."

"You mean the verses about war replace the ones about peace?"

"Exactly! For example, sura 9, verse 5 cancels 124 peaceful verses."

The implications of this soaked into Angela from the top of her head down, and she said slowly, "Oh, my God. Then Osama bin Laden has not 'hijacked the religion....'"

Mohammed finished the thought. "He is just practicing it strictly as revealed in the Koran through the Doctrine of Abrogation, and as assisted by the hadiths and commentaries."

"But most Muslims are peaceful!" She thought of her beloved Uncle Mohammed in Dearborn.

"Average Muslims don't know of or accept the Doctrine of Abrogation. If they don't, they either ignore or have a problem with the numerous contradictions. If they do accept it, as do many of the deeply religious Muslims, then—"

"Voila!" Angela interjected. "We have the kind of Islam that America is fighting. It almost makes me feel ashamed."

"That's the way I felt," Mohammed said.

"Al-Baqara is sura 2, right? Before, you quoted both peaceful and warlike verses from the same chapter; that doesn't make sense."

"An earlier verse can abrogate a later one, like verse 234 abrogates verse 240 in sura 2, because the suras are not necessarily in chronological order. A sura may contain both verses from Mecca and Medina."

"That makes me wonder: if some verses are abrogated, when I or any other ordinary Muslim is reading, how can we know which verses apply now and which are abrogated?"

"You are smart, sister! You can't. Either you have to study the commentaries or you can ask an expert. But even the commentaries and experts don't agree on how many verses are abrogated. They vary from five to five hundred verses!"

"Doesn't the Koran say that Allah protects his word?"

"Of course, sister, in sura 6 it says, 'Nothing can change His words.' But there must be at least some abrogation, because first the Koran says wine is from God, then it says don't go to prayers drunk, but later it says not to drink at all."

"Couldn't that just be that Allah was gradually increasing his standard as the people were able?"

"Oouu, do you hear what you just said? That Allah changes his standard? Isn't that like changing his word? Seesterr, you have so much to learn!"

Mohammed slouched back down in the passenger seat. "And I am too tired to teach you now. I think I will sleep for a while."

"Mohammed, you can't do that! You promised to tell me why you killed Jamal!"

"No, I didn't kill Jamal, Ahmed did. I killed Ahmed."

"OK, so tell me why!"

"Seesterr," he said in English, "if I talk now, you can have the good answer, or you can have the true answer, or you can have the understandable answer—but only one of the three. If you want all three, let me sleep. But please, wake me before Ankara, so I can keep you out of the museum."

Angela gritted her teeth and clenched the wheel. "Grrrr!"

## Chapter 98

# ANKARA, TURKEY
## July 15, 2006

"Mohammed, wake up, we're almost at Ankara, and I feel a tourist attack coming on." At this point, Angela didn't care about sightseeing. She wanted to hear the rest of Mohammed's story.

Mohammed kept sleeping.

*Ankara is Turkey's capital. Selim used to come here on business. I wonder how he is?*

She drove into a gas station and whispered to the still sleeping Mohammed, "We need gas." She got out of the car.

When Mohammed awoke, Angela was nowhere in sight.

"Where is that crooked rib now?" he thought. "There is nothing of interest in this spot—no museums, or souks or ruins. She must be in the bathroom." He opened the door, got out, and stretched. He walked around the pickup and sat back down.

*This time I will sit here and be cool.*

He felt a bump on the back of the pickup, but when he turned around, he saw nothing.

*It sounds like someone is searching the pickup.*

Mohammed jumped out of the car and around to the open back, only to find Angela bent over a suitcase.

"I found it!" she exclaimed. "My Koran. I want to look up those references you were throwing around. I'm not willing to take the word of a criminal—or anyone about something that serious. Let's go to lunch over there, by the lake, and you can show me."

"Where were you?"

"Oh, before, you mean? I was making a call to, uh . . . Selim."

"Heaven forgive you, seesterr! Who's Selim? What, I never heard of this guy and you sneak off to talk to him while I'm sleeping?" He folded his arms and looked petulant. "You may have *no* secrets from your brrooootherr!"

"Selim's my . . . sponsor in Turkey. I wanted him to know I'm OK and coming home."

"Home?"

"My place in Istanbul, of course."

Angela felt guilty, and Mohammed peeved; but neither knew why. There was one sure way to change the mood. "Do you want to eat?" she said.

Mohammed kept a close eye on the Isuzu while he and Angela ate lunch at a café overlooking the lake and fountain at Ankara's Youth Park.

"First I want to understand the good and true reason that you killed Ahmed," Angela demanded.

Mohammed looked around. He was glad no one was within earshot.

"That is sooo simple! The night we were out on the Corniche with my friends, do you remember I got a phone call?"

"Of course. I may be American, but I can remember things that happened in Lebanon."

He stood up and pointed at Angela, exclaiming loudly in Arabic, "My American cousin is sooo smart!" Everyone looked at her. She hid her face with a napkin, laughing.

When he sat down, Angela asked, "So who was on the phone?"

"Jamal. He said he had been suspecting his assistant, Ahmed, for some time, and was afraid that Ahmed was going to kill him that night."

"And he was right?"

Angela had to wait for hungry Mohammed to finish two mouthfuls of lamb *bamya bastısı* stew.

"Hmm. Tasty. I think it was insulin. When I walked in, Jamal was dead. I saw a syringe and diabetic stuff by the nightstand."

Mohammed recounted the details of the adventure to the intent ears of Angela. He left out Ahmed's gruesome death gasps.

"And now you see how lucky you are. You are eating those cute little *fırında mantı* with the braaaavest man in all Lebanon! Don't you feel safe?"

"Totally! Except that we're in Turkey, and my bodyguard has narcolepsy," Angela answered sarcastically.

"Seesterr, I am not on narcotics. My strength is natural." He posed, showing off his biceps.

*He thinks I'm accusing him of using androgens!*

"OK, strong man; that explains *how.* Now explain *why.* I can understand people wanting to kill you, for any number of reasons. But why Jamal?"

Mohammed became serious. He leaned forward and said, "Stay calm."

Angela's eyes flashed in anxiety.

Mohammed reached across the table and took her hand in his. He lowered his voice. "Excuse me for this, but if we look like lovers, no one will think it unusual that I am leaning over, talking to you softly. You said you do acting...."

Angela swallowed hard and said, "Yes."

*Poise will see you through, Angela.*

"Jamal al-Hajji was killed because he was a Koranic manuscript researcher, like me. He was part of our secret group studying ancient Korans found in the Great Mosque of Sana'a in Yemen. Have you heard of Farag Foda, Naguib Mahfouz, Theo Van Gogh, or Salman Rushdie?"

"I've heard of Rushdie," Angela answered, still very uncomfortable. "How does that relate?"

"All these are men spoke against the traditional interpretation of the Koran. They were either killed or live under threat."

Angela looked worried.

"Sister, your radiant love act is sick. Smile!" Mohammed said with a wave of one hand.

Angela looked around and flashed a less than convincing smile.

"Sheesh! And you're still married?"

A jolt of indignation loosened Angela. "You don't look loving either. You look like..."

Mohammed squinted his eyes at her as if in adoration, but he went overboard. He looked silly and insincere.

"...like a comedian!" She laughed.

Mohammed let her hands go. "This is not funny! Will you laugh at my funeral too?"

"Are you saying your work could get you killed?"

"Yes."

"Oh." Angela put down her fork. She looked out at the pedal boats on the artificial lake. It was Saturday afternoon and people were enjoying the sunshine.

*How strange the world is. Dar al-Islam and Dar al-Harb: the House of Peace and the House of War.*

"How did you get yourself into that mess?" she asked.

"Like I said, after the accident I tried to practice Islam better. First

I had questions about the rituals. Then I read the Koran and had many more questions. I went up to Beirut and shared these with your Uncle Nasir. He pointed me to reference books. But they couldn't answer much. The Koran was still far from *mubeen*, or 'clear,' as it claims itself to be. For example: *Sijill*, *abaabeel*, *sijjeen*, and *kalaala* are words in the Koran that no expert has ever understood. And the word *khafaa* has two *opposite* meanings—'to be hid' and 'to reveal.' So when Allah told Moses 'the hour' was coming, we don't know if he was going to 'keep it hidden' or 'make it manifest,' because you can read it either way."

"That's confusing," Angela agreed.

"Some suras start with a chain of initial letters, and no one knows what they mean either. I shared these concerns with your uncle. That's when he told me."

"Told you what?"

"That he had lost his professorship at al-Azhar for asking these same questions. And for the last few years he had been helping Lord Fenburton with..." Mohammed looked at the tables around them. No one looked suspicious or attentive to them, but...

He leaned in closer, as if he were going to kiss her. He paused, and Angela felt him exhale. Was it tension or...

"*Yala nemshee*, let's go," he said.

Chapter 99

# WESTERN ANATOLIA, TURKEY
## July 15, 2006

Recharged by rest and food, Mohammed drove.

Angela could tell Mohammed was in a mood to talk, so she decided to frustrate him.

"Ah," she said, "it's nice to have a chance to rest. I'm full and sleepy. Thanks for driving." She rolled onto her side and turned her head to the window.

"Hey, hey, seesterr!" he answered in English. "What are you doing? Brave Palestinian cousin wants to tell you more story. You know, the one you are craaazy to hear! Why I kill people and why they like killing me."

She yawned. "Oh, that's everyday stuff for Palestinians. It's just in our blood. I don't need to hear about it. Good-night."

Mohammed said nothing. He pulled out a bag of sunflower seeds and poured some into his mouth. "Mmm. *Hada latheed!*" he said, as if to himself. Then he started spitting the shells onto Angela. She batted a few, as if in her sleep.

Mohammed started spitting them faster, and they were getting stuck in her hair. Angela sat up.

"Hey! Who's stoning me?" She sat up and grabbed the bag away from him.

"Ha-ha! Sister, you should see yourself! You look like a Christmas tree for hungry birds."

"Yeah, and we know where the bird poop is coming from. Here," she started stuffing the shells back into his mouth, "let me put it back where it belongs!"

They both started laughing, and a car sped past, beeping its horn.

"Hey! If you don't want to crash us—"

"Me, crash us? May . . ." She almost called him a "maniac" again but stopped just as she opened her mouth. She didn't want to push that button.

"—sit there quietly and let big Palestinian brother talk."

"I didn't say you couldn't talk; I just said I wasn't listening."

Ignoring her, Mohammed went on. "This is the thing, sister. There is a big lie out there, and some of us want to expose it."

"Which lie is that? That you are a good guide or that you are brave?"

"I will punish you for that later. For now, try to control your ADD and be serious. You just aren't serious enough!"

"Ha! Me?" Angela let it drop. "OK, so you found a lie. Should I suspect it is something to do with the Koran?"

"Yes. It is one of the biggest lies ever told, and it is told and retold every day—that the Koran has never been changed. For it has been changed many times."

"You expect me to accept that? You are speaking against what billions of Muslims hold true. You need big proof before making a claim like that."

"There is proof, so much proof that you have to close your eyes tight not to see it."

"Such as?"

"Whoa, where to begin? Why do most of the Arabic Korans we have now look alike? Is it because that's how Mohammed wrote it? No! The Arabic Koran we use was established in 1924 in Cairo. How many people know that?"

"I never heard it before," said Angela, puzzled.

"I can prove that our Koran is not the same as Mohammed's from Muslim sources, Western research, and existing old Korans."

"Start with the story you told last night," Angela commanded.

"It wasn't just a story. That's the way Muslim history explains the origin of the Koran. The Koran was collected *after* Mohammed's death. Several people had personal collections of his revelations. In defiance of Mohammed's instructions, the third caliph, Uthman, canonized his own version and burned all the others he could get his hands on. So right away, most of the early source material was destroyed. However, variant versions persisted and were used here and there for hundreds of years. It is some of those old Korans that our research group is studying now."

"How could there be variants?"

"Many, many ways! There were bound to be. Mohammed's followers had different memories and organizational skills. The passages they wrote or memorized were not identical. When people remembered a passage almost, but not exactly the same, sometimes both accounts were put in the Koran, which explains some of its repetitions. Add to that the fact that abrogation had been occurring over time. It may be that some people knew a passage was abrogated and excluded it from their collection, whereas others retained it, unaware that it was abrogated."

"I thought abrogation just meant a verse didn't count anymore but it was still in the Koran."

"That's only one type of abrogation—where the words remain but the application is removed. There is also abrogation where the words and the application are both removed. And then there is the abrogation where the words are removed but the application remains."

"How does that work? Remove the words but keep the application? How can you apply what there are no words for?"

"*Taba'an.* Here's an example. If people commit adultery, the punishment in Islamic law is stoning, but the Koran only specifies flogging. The passage with the stoning rule was kept by Mohammed's wife Ayesha. But it got destroyed."

"What happened? A war?"

"Ha-ha! No. I will tell you, sister, but you will never believe it." Mohammed started laughing. "A goat ate it! Some people said it was a chicken, but the point is that an animal abrogated the word of Allah. Yet Islamic law still follows it."

"Oh, my God!" Angela grabbed her face, laughing, "Mohammed, are you serious?"

"Of course, sister! I don't lie about my work. I don't need to—it's crazy enough on its own."

"It's terrible, terrible! Can it be true? No wonder they don't divulge this."

"Ibn Ka'b, one of the ones Mohammed authorized, says this passage was in the Sura of the Parties, which used to be almost the same length as the Sura of the Cow, but it lost over two hundred verses!"

"Did the cow eat them?"

"Seesterr, you are so sacrilegious! How can an animal eat the word of God?"

"But you just said..."

"Ha-ha!" Mohammed slapped his thigh. "OK. Maybe Uthman had a cow, because the Shiites claim that there were verses in the Koran supporting Ali as the successor to Mohammed, but they disappeared too. You remember *Ashoura*, right?"

"The bloody parades? Sure."

"As I see it, Uthman's assassination and the war that divided Islam into Sunni and Shiite were at least partly over changes in the Koran. In fact, one source says that while assassins were stabbing Uthman they yelled," Mohammed raised his hand and voice for effect, "*You changed Allah's Koran!*"

"Wow! Seriously? If it's that major a factor in Muslim history, why isn't it well known?"

"It's the same with all these unflattering facts. By the time a student of Islam is deep enough to discover them, he is usually too devoted to be bothered by them. Bias has distorted his vision. Even if he is bothered, he has a vested interest in keeping them hidden. By then, *the cause* has become *the truth*, and the facts are irrelevant."

"Except to a few researchers like you and…" Angela paused at a fearful thought, "Are there others with you? Others who were… unlucky?"

Mohammed was silent for a moment. Then he continued as if she hadn't asked a question. "And also, some material appears to have been added to the Koran that was not original."

Angela gave up on her question. She would rather not face the answer anyway. "For example?"

"Consider Ibn Mas'ud. He was one of the four men Mohammed authorized as a reliable source for the Koran. And by the way, none of those four included Uthman. After Uthman standardized his version, Ibn Mas'ud would not surrender his version to the fire. It had many differences from Uthman's, had additional suras, and left out three suras we have today."

"Could they have gotten lost over time, or become included in the other suras?"

"Good thinking, but those are not the reasons. Get out your Koran."

"OK."

"What words do the suras begin with?"

Angela answered in Arabic, "'*Bismallah Ir-Rahman Ir-Raheem*, in the name of God, the Compassionate, the Merciful.'"

"Flip through a few suras: see how they begin and who is doing the talking."

Angela did. "Except for sura 1, they seem to be Allah talking to Mohammed or to people in general."

"Exactly! *God talking to man.* That's what the Koran is supposed to be. But you found the problem."

"Some places sound like man talking to God?"

"Yes. This used to confuse me too. Notice that suras 113 and 114 also sound like man talking to God. And brace yourself: Because of that, Ibn Mas'ud left them out of his Koran. And he left out the *Fatiha* as well."

"Are you sure? The *Fatiha* is not just the first sura; it's probably the most important one in the Koran. Millions of devout Muslims pray it several times every day, in belief that it is a prayer to God from the Koran."

"That is precisely why Ibn Mas'ud said it was *not* part of the Koran. He believed it was a man-made liturgical prayer for devotional use. Some early commentaries agreed, and it is absent from some old Korans. And remember, Mohammed had said that Ibn Mas'ud was..."

"... a reliable source for the Koran," Angela finished. She looked out at fields of sunflowers basking in the sun, and thought wistfully: *They are smiling, carefree. Like the paddleboats gliding on Youth Lake.*

"So even the *Fatiha* is in dispute?" she said quietly. "I would never have guessed it in a million years. I want to see the references."

"The references are not hard to find, at least in Arabic. The hard part is getting people to look at them!"

"You mean, the reason we don't see that the Koran has been changed is because our leaders tell us that it hasn't, and we believe them without checking."

"That's it!"

"Wow. Like the emperor's new clothes.... But, now that I think of it, these are Sunni sources you are using, aren't they? Maybe the Shiites tell a different story."

"Shiites are more open about the changes because they feel the cuts cheated them. They claim the Koran said that Ali's family should have been hereditary monarchs."

"I never knew..."

"Anyway, that's my story," Mohammed concluded. "That's why I have done what I have done and why I will keep on doing it. So turn me in if you want. But I don't think the police will be much interested in one more body in Beirut. And the manuscripts? Who knows which way the Turkish authorities would go when they hear of them. I think they're just as likely to be on my side as that of those that want to kill us—the Mus-haf Brotherhood."

"The Mus-haf Brotherhood?"

Chapter 100

# WESTERN ANATOLIA, TURKEY
## July 15, 2006

"Sister, I want to see if the professor is good student!" Mohammed said a few hours later. "I have question for you: Why did Caliph Uthman burn the rival Korans?"

"Presumably because there were variations from his preferred text."

"I am going to be like Muslim apologist and challenge you. OK?"

"OK," Angela agreed, a little uncertainly.

"They will say, 'The variations in the Koran are simply a few different vowel markings that reflect dialects.' Professor Hall, how would you answer that?"

"Uh, whoa ... uh, give me more time, please?"

"Ha-ha! This is sooo simple. Uthman burnt all the rival Korans centuries before the vowel marks were added, which shows they were significant differences, not dialect variations."

Angela asked, "After Uthman standardized the Koran, how could there be variants?"

"Because of the way ancient Arabic was written."

"I'm not sure I understand."

"Do you have paper?" Mohammed asked.

"Yes."

"Then write the word for *girl* in Arabic, but without any dots or dashes."

Angela wrote the three main letters that were the backbone of the Arabic word. It looked something like:

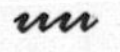

"Done. Oh, I see what you mean," Angela said, "If we don't have the dots and dashes, it looks like three letter *u*'s attached together. It could say either *bint* بنت for girl, or *bayt* بين for house. That's a big difference."

"You are sooo right! When I want one, don't give me the other!"

"I'm not even going to ask what that means."

"Uthman's version only standardized the backbone consonants of the writing. It's what we call a 'consonantal text.' But without the dots you still couldn't tell letters ن from ب and ت, and س from ش, and ف from ق."

"And ص from ض," Angela said. "I get it. Some consonants, long and short vowels, you couldn't tell apart because they are represented by dots and dashes, right?" Angela stated more than asked.

"Right. So you see, even with Uthman's Koran being standard, there was huge opportunity for variant readings. And they did develop—in Mecca, Medina, Damascus, Basra, and Kufa. For example, without the marks, in sura 30, we don't know if the Romans *were conquered* and then *would conquer*, or the other way around, so both variants arose. We don't know if the people were worshipping *females* or *idols*, and we don't know if people were *shown* or *caused to inherit*. And in many places we don't know the pronoun, for example, if the action refers to *you* or *they*. This usually doesn't make much difference, but in places like in sura 3, where we can't tell who saw the Miracle of Badr, it does," Mohammed explained.

"Sounds confusing."

"And at times it could be embarrassing! There's a funny story about a guy who became a famous scholar. He was publicly reading the opening of sura 2, where it refers to the guidance of the Koran, and instead of saying it was 'without doubt,' he said it had 'no oil in it'!"

"Oh, my! But in an obscure way, that has meaning in English. It's like saying it isn't 'unctuous.' *Unctuous* means 'oily,' as in insincere. Do you think that is what he meant? That the Koran is not insincere?"

"Seesterr. Be serious. His nicky-name was not 'the sincere,' but 'the oil dealer!"

"Did they ever standardize the markings?" Angela asked.

"About three hundred years after Mohammed's death, a scholar named Ibn Mujahid got the authority to do that, but he was forced to accept the variant readings of several Islamic centers. That's how the seven variants got considered 'canonized.' Did you ever hear that the words of the Koran are a copy of something?"

"Of... what is on the Preserved Table in paradise? But with all the variations in the Korans—both before and after Uthman—which Koran is on the Preserved Table?"

"Good questions. *Which Koran*? I have asked myself that a hundred times. Sometimes defenders say 'the Koran came down to us in seven forms.' But this is delusion."

"Because?"

"Because each of the seven centers had two variants, and there were three other centers with variants almost as respected as the seven, so you end up with seventeen different versions of the Koran all arising from Uthman's standard!"

Angela said, "You are saying that each of these centers had their own idea of the words of the Koran, so they added dots and dashes to fit them. In this way, they could have the same consonantal script but entirely different words."

"Right again. In a way the earliest Korans were more or less prompters for the reciters, or Qurras'. And they based a lot on memory. The fully marked standard, the *scripta plena*, which included vowels and consonants, was not established until the late ninth century."

"What a mess! And it's embarrassing that Arabic was so poorly developed at that time in comparison to, say, Greek or Latin."

"Rather amazing, isn't it?"

"So why would Allah reveal his word in a primitive and confusing language?"

"I asked myself that too. Wouldn't Allah want his word to be clear? Does he want us confused so he can trap us?"

"That's not the way I think of Him," Angela said quietly. "I guess it's impossible to say we can understand anything as unfathomable as a god."

"Here's another big, big problem. Did you ever hear that each 'letter' in the Koran is worth many good deeds—ten to forty, depending on how you pronounce them?"

"I did hear that, but it never meant much to me. Just that the Koran is holy."

"But think of what it means. That means there is power in the very *words* themselves, not just in the message."

"Like a magic spell or . . . a *mantra*!"

"A what?"

"Words that people say over and over for meditation and religious power, like Hindus or Krishnas use. If the Koran is a type of mantra, and each letter has the power of good deeds, it's extremely important to know *exactly* what letters are on that Preserved Table in heaven . . . but we don't!"

"Seesterr! Now you are starting to think like your cousin and uncle. That means you are smart! How would you like to research with us?"

"I'm not sure it's a job I would survive."

"Have you ever thought, Angela," Mohammed surprised her by using her real name, "that if something's not worth dying for it's not worth living for?"

Angela repeated slowly, "*If something's not worth dying for, it's not worth living for.* That's powerful. And we could rework it several ways: *If it's not worth living for, it's not worth dying for.* Yes, that makes sense. Or in the positive: *If it's worth living for, it's worth dying for.* Or, *If it's worth dying for, it's worth living for.* Oh, that last one has punch."

"The point is," he paused, searching for the right words and tone, "I grew up surrounded by killing. Body parts in the streets. I want to live for something worth dying for—but not like a terrorist who kills for a vague reward in paradise. I want to live for something that will make the world better now. Something that's true."

"Ahhh." Angela spoke quietly, looking down. "And now you have found that 'something worth dying for that is worth living for.'"

"You could say it that way."

"And what do you put your chances at. I mean, dying versus living."

"Ha-ha!" Mohammed laughed loudly. "Sister, you are so funny! My chance of dying is the same as yours—one hundred percent. The only thing uncertain is *when*."

# PART THREE

# Chapter 101

# ISTANBUL, TURKEY
## July 16, 2006

"How can I possibly keep you a secret from Selim? Even if you are my cousin, it won't seem proper." Angela didn't add that Selim would be jealous. "Hiding you in his own house will be like hiding an elephant in the living room."

"Seesterr, you worry too much!" Mohammed responded while munching grapes. "There is no problem. Haven't you heard of the Big Lie?"

"What's that?"

"The louder and longer you say something, the more people believe it."

"Right! All I have to do is keep announcing to Selim, 'Mohammed's not hiding in your townhouse. I left all my crazy cousins back in Palestine, where they belong.' Mohammed, don't you know that's not my style? *Methinks the Lady doth protest too much.* It will sound unbelievable."

"Don't be silly, of course it will work. *Yani*, for fourteen hundred years they say the Koran has never been changed, and the whole world believes it."

"The whole world except for one *craazy* person!"

"Only one? Mohammed asked, throwing a grape at Angela.

Caught unprepared, Angela grunted and struggled to catch it as it rolled down her shirt. Then she put up her chin and defiantly popped it into her mouth as if it had been her idea.

In Istanbul, life got more complicated. The best idea seemed to be for Mohammed to stay at the townhouse. There he could study the manuscripts, check the Internet for clues about the Mus-haf Brotherhood, and scheme to get the Topkapi Codex.

Angela's first challenge was dealing with Selim. Things were getting too close for comfort before she left. While she was gone, she had hardly thought of Selim, which went a long way toward convincing her that she was not his "Roxelana."

As much as she had promised herself she would not go back to the *yalı* Angela could think of no way out. Without Mohammed, she could have made any number of excuses for staying in the townhouse, because she would have had nothing to hide. But she did have something to hide. She couldn't afford to draw attention.

The day after her return she dined with Selim. As casually as possible she said, "It's sad that we won't be having our daily meetings. Now I'm studying the modern era, and I know that's not your field, so I'll have to spend more time at the libraries. And I'm getting anxious about all the work I have left. What with the war delaying my return, I'm going to have to whip myself day and night. Ah, me." Angela rested her head on her hand in an imitation of dismay. It not only looked convincing but the pose flattered her face in the candlelight.

Angela solicited good behavior from Selim by telling him that after the bombings in Lebanon, her nerves were jittery. She would be up late studying but couldn't take any surprise late-night visits.

"Far be it from me," he said. "I will only come when called."

The fact that Angela's excuses were at least partly true made them believable. Selim kept calling Angela, but when he did, she told him she was researching until late at the university. This was often true. Sometimes she would meet with Selim briefly in a public place. But she spent many hours at the townhouse with Mohammed, which she did not confess.

The second challenge was keeping Mohammed hidden. He liked being with people, and by his own admission he had ADD. Keeping him indoors 24/7 was like caging a large animal that needed to be exercised. Fortunately, almost no one in Istanbul knew Mohammed—and few knew Angela—so it seemed safe to let him out for a walk now and then. But the two rarely went together.

The next challenge was in coordinating their time. Mohammed was under pressure with three projects, each so pressing it seemed impossible to prioritize them. Angela needed to finish her research paper. She quickly discovered that work with Mohammed was not a quiet affair. It was difficult to concentrate around him unless she was working on what he was. He assumed that she wanted to know everything he was doing. She was interested in Mohammed's work, but it was not the driving force in her life.

Their first day in the townhouse Mohammed announced, "Seesterr, open your kitchen! How could you sail off with your lover on the Bosporus last night and leave your poor brother here, unable to sleep?

I need coffee! Tell me, what should I do? Destroy the Mus-haf Brotherhood, expose the differences in the Sana'a manuscripts, or discover the Topkapi Secret?"

"The Topkapi Secret?" Angela asked, amazed. "What could that possibly be?"

## Chapter 102

# ISTANBUL, TURKEY
## July 16, 2006

"I've explored every cranny of Topkapi Palace with Selim—even all the places the public is not allowed. And I didn't know it had a secret—unless maybe you mean the passage between the sultan's rooms and the pool."

"Ah, could it be that I have not told you of the greatest secret of the greatest secrets?" Mohammed asked, knowing full well that he had never before mentioned this object of his obsession.

"No, you haven't. But I'm a little nervous. The last time you got that faraway look in your eye, you started out telling a story and ended up burning the Koran."

"Oh, you are so craazy again, seesterr. Why are you worried? There is no fire here!" He laughed and slapped his leg.

"You're very creative. I'm sure you'll think of some outrage."

"No need. Topkapi Secret *is* the outrage."

"What scandal could be worse than what we already know—orgies, wars, stolen relics?"

"Aha!" Mohammed jumped a little in his chair and scratched the floor. He pointed his finger and waved his arm. "Now you're getting somewhere! The relics. Sister, have you seen the Topkapi Codex?"

"Uh, I'm not sure. Is it on display? I've seen everything that's on display."

Mohammed took a deep breath and shook his head. "You too? *Haram!* I was hoping the American Angel was more observant."

"So what did I miss?"

"In the Sacred Relics Chamber, at the foot of the swords, is the Topkapi Codex, possibly the holiest Koran in the world."

"And that's a secret? How can you hide a secret in plain sight?"

"That's the best way. You can see it sitting there, but its contents are secret. Topkapi will let no one study it. Both the Topkapi Codex and the Samarkand Codex claim to be the personal copy of Caliph Uthman."

"Why does it matter?" Angela asked.

Mohammed began a diatribe that sounded much like a rebuke. "Caliph Uthman's murder is part of what split the Muslim world into Shiite and Sunni factions. Is that significant to rich American Muslim lady?"

"No. Rich American lady is busy looking for chocolates." She lifted up papers, pretending to search for them. "Do you have any?"

Mohammed knew what she was up to. He grabbed her head and forced his finger into her mouth saying, "Here's one."

Angela wrestled to get his hand off of her face. "Let go! You're killing me!"

"Ooooh. That's what Uthman said?"

"Yick! Your dirty finger is salty tasting!"

"I don't think he said that." Mohammed let go of Angela.

"OK. I take it back." She knew one way to make him stop. "Tell me more."

"The Turks claim the Topkapi Codex is the one Uthman was reading while he was killed, and the Uzbekis claim it was the Samarkand Codex, which is in Tashkent."

"How did it get there?"

"Uh-uh. That's another long story. Don't get me started. The point is, they can't both have his death blood. And if one is lying, maybe both are. Some scholars think Uthman's Koran was destroyed with him—which makes sense considering what his assassins yelled as they slaughtered him." Mohammed stood as if poised above her with a knife.

Angela was cool. "Either way, he's dead," she said, looking at her fingernails. She would not repeat her antics at Cappadocia, even if he did.

When Mohammed saw her response, he said, "Have another chocolate."

"No, thank you." Angela yawned, covering her mouth. "Anything else?"

Mohammed took a moment to think, and then said flatly, "The other claim is that the codices were two of the five official copies made by Uthman and sent to major religious centers of the Muslim world, so they could have their own copy of the canonized text. I have studied the Samarkand Codex on microfilm. I don't think the Topkapi Codex could have been made by the same scribes that made it.

"Only two pages of the Topkapi Codex are visible on display. From this I can tell that it has the same script, or writing style, as the

Samarkand Codex. But it has eighteen lines to a page and is very formally laid out, whereas the Samarkand Codex is way more irregular and has between eight to twelve lines to a page. The Topkapi Codex is one of the earliest Korans. Whether or not it was Uthman's, we need to know what's in it."

"And that's the secret? The Topkapi Codex?" Angela asked, still looking bored. Then she jumped up in a surprising mood shift. "*Yala!* Let's go see it now!" she said, and ran out of the townhouse.

It was exactly the kind of trick Mohammed would pull, but he did not expect it from her. This meant he had to be the responsible one and lock up the townhouse—he couldn't risk the manuscripts.

Angela did want to see the Topkapi Codex. Really see it this time.

She quickly bought a ticket in the first courtyard of the palace. Mohammed nearly caught up with Angela by the time she reached the Gate of Salutations. She turned around. Mohammed was closing in behind her. She ran faster. People were watching, but she didn't care.

The second courtyard was more congested. They moved as rapidly as possible through the crowd, darting this way and that. While descending the stairs from the audience pavilion into the third courtyard, Angela felt a large hand grip her shoulder.

"I'm glad to see my guide has finally made it," she said to Mohammed. "I thought being so old and heavy, you might have tripped along the way."

"If you were a man..." Mohammed replied.

"If I were a man... I would have killed you in Cappadocia!"

They stood in front of the glass door in the Sacred Relics Chamber. There were a few details about the codex Mohammed wanted to share with her, but he did not want to announce to the entire room, so he whispered into her ear.

Now she *saw* the codex. Now that her eyes could see a little of what her companion saw, now that her mind could process the shape of its letters and the document's importance in history—now she saw it.

They did not linger. They retraced their steps through the terraced third courtyard and the sunny second courtyard.

"And that's the secret," Mohammed said as they walked through the leafy first courtyard. "If we can expose what is in the codex, manuscript experts around the world could discover the truth. I want to know: Is that stain really blood? How complete is the codex? What is the sura order? Is the writing the same throughout? What is missing or added? Is it as old as it claims to be? How does it differ from the modern Korans, which came after it, and the Sana'a manuscripts, which came before it? There must be much important information locked up between its pages or Topkapi wouldn't keep it a secret. It's a secret I'm wagering my life and fortune against."

"Fortune?" Angela asked. She stopped in front of the guard station and the egregious tropical-looking office Mohammed had visited before.

"Since I was here last spring, I have been seeking a way to get access to the codex. I sold a piece of property to use as a bribe."

"It would have to be a large bribe. How much have you got?"

"Three million dollars."

Angela whistled. She started walking again. "Not bad! And I thought Palestinians were poor!"

"We are poor, sister, but the Israelis are rich, verrry, verrry rich, and they will pay anything to get a piece of Palestinian land legally."

When they returned to the townhouse Angela asked, "Is selling to the Israelis acceptable?"

"No, of course not! It's a secret," he playfully cupped his hand over her mouth. "There are some, even in my own family, I suspect, who would kill me over it. It took me a long time to decide, but if this project isn't—"

Angela pulled his hand off her lips and joined him saying, "worth dying for, it isn't worth living for."

They looked at each other and smiled. They didn't laugh. Laughter is sacrilegious when a smile connects the corners of the mouth to the corners of the heart.

## Chapter 103

# ISTANBUL, TURKEY
## July 16, 2006

It was simple to soak red lentils. When they got back from the palace, Angela sautéed onion and garlic in olive oil, and threw carrots and potatoes in with the lentils to make *mercimek çorbası*, the Turkish soup recipe she had learned from Selim's cook. Angela and Mohammed ate it together early that evening before Angela returned to the *yalı*.

"Seesterr, you are cute, but I am sooo glad I am not married to you!" Mohammed commented at the end of the meal.

Angela was surprised. "I'm glad too, but out of curiosity, may I ask what I did that brought you such joy?"

"Thees food. Yes, OK, it tastes good, but it has two problems."

"Oh?"

"First, there is not enough. Look, this girly thing," he said holding up the bowl upside down. And second, where is the meat?"

"Thank you," Angela said, cleaning up the bowls.

"For which compliment? You are welcome for both." He crossed his arms and sat back.

"Thank you for convincing me that I don't have to cook for you again. Next time, you cook or we eat out! Unless you suggest that we hire Selim's cook a few days a week. But of course, it was his soup recipe. . . ."

Mohammed got up and went back to where his work was laid out. "Forget about Selim! Come here and we will see if you are better at orthography than cooking," he said.

"What's orthography?" Angela was not excited about another chance to earn criticism, however well-humored. But she complied.

"You will learn by doing." It was technical, so he switched into Arabic. "Look at these two manuscripts from Sana'a in Yemen. Compare them. Are they the same?"

"I can see they are different."

"Now tell me which is in the Kufic script, the same as the Topkapi Codex."

Angela looked at the two. She closed her eyes and visualized the

Topkapi Codex in her mind. Then she opened them and pointed out the correct manuscript.

"This one is more like the Topkapi Codex."

"Hey!" Mohammed clapped for her. "Very good, student! Explain why."

"It is smaller, of course, but it also has letters that are stretched out horizontally, and the layout of the book is broad and short—landscape format."

"Now, describe how the script differs from the Ma'il script of the other Koran."

"This Koran," she demonstrated, "has letters that are compressed, more vertical. And they are curly-looking, and... slanted."

"Exactly!" he said, pleased.

"I'm going to ask a question. I expect an insulting reply, but I'll tough it out—so don't expect to have too much fun. What do the different styles mean?"

"Actually, that's a very good question. Different styles of writing originated in different places at different times. They either spread or died out and were replaced by a different script. If a manuscript in a certain style is dated, we can link that style with a time. We then know other manuscripts with a similar style have some relationship to it in time and location. For example, the Kufic script is named for Kufa, in Iraq, where it was prominent and may have originated. Kufic became a standard Koranic style for about three hundred years, and much longer in North Africa."

"Where is Ma'il?"

"It's in California. Right next to San Francisco." Mohammed started laughing. "I knew it would be fun teaching you. You are so naive! Ma'il is not a place. *Ma'il* means the *slanted* script. Like you noticed."

Angela was not laughing. Mohammed sobered.

"It originated in the area of Mecca and Medina, in Saudi Arabia," he explained. "This area is known as the Hijaz, so it's also called Hijazi script. It is probably the earliest script of the Koran. Here is another quiz for you, sister: you have seen the oldest surviving Koranic scriptures. Tell me where."

"Uh. All I can think of is the Topkapi Codex. I think that's the only old one I have seen... that I remember."

"Were you listening, sister, or did the soup make you sick? What script is the Topkapi Codex in? Remember? I just told you that the Ma'il script is older." Mohammed held up a Koran.

"Oh, yes. The Topkapi Codex is in the Kufic script. Then I don't know where the oldest Koran is. I don't think I saw any others."

"Hint: the inscriptions are not in a Koran, but they are *from* the Koran."

"I have no idea."

"Heaven forgive you, sister! You were with the best, the best guide in the Holy Land. The Dome of the Rock!"

Angela shook her head. "Oh, so that's what you were doing! I mean, why you were acting so strange on the Temple Mount. You were reading the inscriptions."

"Ha-ha!" Mohammed laughed. "It is so hard to hide things from my leetle red cousin! She may not know what it means, but she sees everything!"

"Did you find what you wanted?"

"Yes, I did. The verses on the Dome of the Rock are not the same as the ones in the Koran. They are more evidence that the Koran has been changed."

"That's harsh. Are you sure? The inscriptions must be difficult to read—so high and ornate."

"I was just confirming what I already knew. It is true. The mosque was built on the Temple Mount for political and religious reasons, so it has many Koranic inscriptions, and some of them vary from the standard wording."

"For example?" Angela asked.

"OK." He paused and rubbed his chin. "The word used for the 'oneness of Allah' is *waHdahu*, different from the Koran. And there is the phrase," he quoted in Arabic, "'incline toward your messenger, Jesus the son of Maryam,' which is not even in the modern Koran."

"Interesting."

"More than that. The date of the inscriptions on the Dome of the Rock is about 692, sixty years after Mohammed's death, at the beginning of the Umayyad period. That's also about thirty-five years after Uthman's death—which means *after* he canonized his version of the Koran."

"I get it!" Angela nodded and spoke slowly as she worked it out. "If the Ma'il script originated in the Hijazi area and was being used as far away as Jerusalem after Uthman's death, why would Uthman use the Kufic script from Iraq for his Korans?"

"Exactly! That's what the majority of scholars think, including Nasir and me. Both the Topkapi Codex and the Samarkand Codex are in Kufic script. People who want to believe the manuscripts date to Uthman don't care what script they are in. They just point to the blood. But think. Uthman had his authorized Koran and the copies made in Medina. His scribes would be using the local Hijazi style, which was Ma'il."

"That makes sense to me," Angela agreed.

"OK, then you pass. Let's go out and get some meat!"

# Chapter 104

# ISTANBUL, TURKEY
## July 19, 2006

Angela had given up the idea of accomplishing much at the townhouse, but she liked being there, so she made up for it by working in the *yalı* at night.

In the mornings Mohammed would research the Mus-haf Brotherhood on the Internet while Angela did research at the university. She would come to the townhouse for a late lunch, and they would spend the afternoon together, each engaged in their respective research, with occasional breaks to talk and joke.

After a few days Mohammed's work frustration was starting to rise. He had discovered little about the brotherhood. And he had no good ideas on accessing the Topkapi Codex.

"What do you think, sister?" Mohammed asked out of the blue, popping his head up from the Sana'a manuscript. "Do they make janitor uniforms big enough to fit me?" He displayed the biceps of his right arm. "I could disguise myself and go in to clean."

"Forget it. They probably don't have janitors. Didn't you see how dusty their displays are? What about approaching the director of the manuscripts and relics again and offering him a bribe as an 'access fee.'"

"It's not that I am trying to save the money; I know the director. Ergun Türbe would never allow it."

"Oh," she said, "you mean you want 'creative access' to the codex, something not entirely legal."

"Do you think a bribe is legal?"

"Maybe not legal, but perhaps... routine?"

Mohammed's frustration only increased as evening came and Angela left. With her gone, he had no one to bounce ideas off. No one to talk to. No one to look at.

It was hot. By seven o'clock he couldn't handle it anymore. He had eye strain, no strategy for the codex, and was stressed out worrying about the brotherhood.

*I need some fresh air.*

Mohammed walked down to the water. The air outside felt better.

Almost without consciously realizing it he boarded a dinner cruise. He ate alone while the sun set and lights came on, shining on the water. The last part of the cruise went partway up the Bosporus.

Yes, it was the place. Angela had pointed it out to him when they went up the Bosporus together: three conjoined *yalıs* on the European side of the Bosporus. And there, on the second-floor balcony, silhouetted by lights from inside, were two people. A man and a woman. They were standing at the railing looking out at the lights. He could not see them clearly, but he was sure the woman was Angela.

*I thought she didn't like Selim. Why is she standing so close?*

## Chapter 105

# ISTANBUL, TURKEY
## July 21, 2006

*I don't need to steal it, just be alone with it long enough to photograph it.*

If he released photos, even of mediocre quality, they would pressure Topkapi into opening access to scholars. Regardless, he would be the first to study the most famous Koran in the world.

Mohammed had checked the walls of Topkapi Palace for external defects he could exploit for entry, but found none. Also, the walls were floodlit; so although he could physically scale them, he would be like a fly on the wall to motorists and police on the road surrounding the palace. He might be able to find a hiding place in the garden, but he was not yet prepared to take that kind of a chance without someone on the inside to facilitate his entry.

So he developed a new plan. He would use the tried-and-true Arab method: relationship first, business later.

*A guard in the manuscript division.*

After a few visits, the guard would recognize him and Mohammed would make himself known as a student. Mohammed would become more and more friendly, until he was liked. Of course, the guard would think himself totally above a bribe, but Mohammed would find out about his life and what specific ways money might benefit it. A few weeks later he would make an offer—whatever it took.

If morality became an issue, the guard would be assured that nothing would be missing and no one would know. In a month or so, before the contents of the codex became published, the guard could find a good excuse to retire. The codex would be left intact, except for its secrets. Perfect.

This would take time, but it was the best plan he could think of and it was not too risky. The trick would be to maintain a low profile while making enough visits to become friends with the guard.

*The main thing is to avoid being seen by Ergun Türbe.*

## Chapter 106

# ISTANBUL, TURKEY
## July 22, 2006

Mohammed was making notations in a notebook. Angela had never seen him focused for so long. To see what could be so fascinating, she walked to where his research was laid out.

"What are you doing?" she asked.

Mohammed jumped up as she approached. Immediately she regretted her move—his concentration was broken.

"My tongue is as dry as a Turkish towel. I need some water!" he exclaimed.

"Why don't you keep a glass beside you?"

"I can't believe this rich American lady. She says she collects antiques, but she hangs her paintings in the handball court."

"I don't have a handball court anymore, and I never hung paintings there."

"Ha-ha! I mean if you knew anything, you wouldn't put water next to manuscripts."

"OK. Good point. But what were you doing?"

"I'm comparing this Ma'il manuscript from Sana'a to the Koran we use now and recording the variations."

"What are you finding?"

"In the manuscripts using Ma'il script, the ways the suras are divided up is different, kind of like how Ibn Mas'ud did. And, there are thousands of variants. Look, this is what most of them are like. They have to do with the letter *alif.* A lot of words leave it out, and as you know, it is the long *a* vowel, but it is usually part of the consonantal script."

Angela looked at the words Mohammed was pointing out, first in Angela's own Koran, then in the Sana'a manuscript.

"You see," Mohammed said, "without the *alif* this word looks like *qul*, for 'say' instead of *qaala* for 'he said.'"

"Amazing what a single vertical stroke can do."

"That's great, sister. I'm glad you like orthography. Most people don't get so excited over it."

"Oh, it's not the orthography. It's that people kill over something as small as an *alif.* Even if you published it, how many people would care, really? Like you said, variants have been recognized for over a thousand years, and almost no one *knows.* They just hide it or ignore it. So what does it matter that a few *alifs* are found to be missing?"

Mohammed was quiet.

"First, it's not so small. There are thousands of variants in the Sana'a manuscripts. They prove more and more that we don't know the original Koran. But there's something else...."

Mohammed paused, chewed on his lower lip, and thrust out his chin as if he were weighing something in his mind.

"What is it?" Angela asked, curious.

*Why not? I've already told her so much... and she has risked her life...*

"In England I met DW, the son of Lord Fenburton, who headed this project before he was killed. DW told me about an even bigger project Fenburton had in mind. Lord Fenburton, he thinks like Angela."

"DW told you that? You mean Fenburton was going to do something you didn't like. Did you kill him too?"

"Ooooh, sister, you are twice wrong! Of course I didn't kill Fenburton. You know that."

"Do I really know that? You were in England. And I overheard you talking to Nihla and Aunt Zahara, the day you admitted to Uncle Nasir that there were *two* dead men."

"Crazy bent rib! You can't count. I told you the two were Jamal and Ahmed. Fenburton would make three. I was in Lebanon when he had the accident and didn't even know about it for months! When I heard that he was in a coma I went to England to find out what happened and who might have done it. He died just before I left England."

"How does that clear you?" Angela asked.

Mohammed realized this sounded suspicious, and a defensive tone slipped into his voice. "But it wasn't me—he was in the hospital... I mean, seriously, sister, why would I kill people on both sides—those who want to hide the truth, and those who want to reveal it? Seesterr, you are such a crazy!" He tried to cover his defensiveness with humor, but he was lacking his usual offhand delivery.

"I'm still listening. Talk on."

"Fenburton left a letter for me, but it didn't explain everything. That's why I chased DW to his hiding place. As it turns out, Lord Fenburton was not just a world-class scholar; he was a visionary."

"Aha! Scholarly and visionary. Now I see how he is like me." Angela blew on her nails and buffed them on her shirt.

"You are so proud, sister! You are not like Lord Fenburton, except that he agreed with you that our research should not be buried for another thousand years."

"We Westerners are so practical."

"He wanted world peace. I'm not sure how practical that is, but I think it is good."

"Make the world a better place, or y'all just takin' up space," Angela quoted reflectively.

"Fenburton believed that exposing the Koran would stop the jihad and the terrorism," Mohammed said, then paused for a split second.

"It hasn't worked so far...."

"Hey, his goal isn't reached yet! Not only was he working on a complete commentary of the Koran—one that would contain all the thousands of known variants—but he was just about to begin a television series. It was going to be called *The Origin of the Koran.* You know, sister, much of the Muslim world is illiterate. Fenburton wanted the series translated into every major Muslim language and shown all over the world by satellite. He was ready to sink his entire fortune into it if necessary."

Angela whistled and nodded. "Now I can see the problem. If all this were revealed on TV before the world, instead of teetering old academics—"

"Hey, sister, watch who you call 'old teetering'!" Mohammed interrupted. "Fenburton was going to narrate the English version. *I* had been chosen to narrate the Arabic." Mohammed imitated her, blowing on his fingernails and buffing them on his shirt.

"Oh, aren't you lucky. Chosen as the target for every Islamic terrorist between here and Indonesia! And such a nice, big target you make."

Mohammed and Angela looked seriously into each other's eyes, as if to say words they dared not speak—

*Our lives are in danger, maybe even this minute....*

Just then, a knock came at the door. Their hearts jumped.

The look between the two changed to panic, and without a word they jumped into the plan they had agreed upon for such an occasion.

"I hope it's Selim."

Angela helped Mohammed pack up his research as quickly as possible. They were certain courtesy would prevent Selim from going upstairs.

Mohammed's protective side emerged. "But sister, if it's not Selim..."

At that, Mohammed dropped a pencil on the stairs, and it made the hollow clank of wood on wood as it rolled down the stairs. Mohammed stifled a laugh. He reached to pick it up but succeeded only in dropping a few papers, which gently floated downward.

"It's Selim!" Angela said with a smile as she opened the door, waving Mohammed up with a hand behind her back. The two pages were left within view on the stairs.

Upstairs Mohammed spread out his work and tried to resume his research. But it was impossible to concentrate. He had that "invaded" feeling you get when uninvited guests show up before the invited guests, and you can't think how to send them away.

Mohammed sat at the computer, flitting aimlessly, and Googling nonproductive subjects. He wasn't concentrating. He kept finding himself wondering what Angela and Selim could be doing downstairs.

*Why can't she get rid of him?*

Every now and then he heard Angela's bright laughter. It didn't seem right. Somehow he had never imagined that she laughed with Selim.

## Chapter 107

# ISTANBUL, TURKEY
## August 6, 2006

On the outside, Mohammed and Angela were always happy, even when arguing. But inside, each struggled with old and current issues. Laughter helped. And for Mohammad—food.

It was afternoon, and Angela and Mohammed were at the town-house. Mohammed was depressed. The guard he had developed a relationship with for two weeks had been transferred for mandatory military duty. Now he was out of ideas for getting at the codex. He shifted his attention to the Sana'a manuscripts, but his subconscious worked on the codex.

*Delicious.*

Angela had brought some Turkish food, and they ate too much. Late nights studying and the heavy meal were making Angela somnolent. She tried reading.

*"Atatürk believed that men and women should have equal rights before the law. He brought in coeducation of women with men, the vote, and abolished polygamy. Some thought this significant progress was enough. But in time it became evident that legal rights were not entirely equal. . . ."*

Angela's eyes started to blink slowly as she read the material she had collected at the university this morning.

*"In 1990, the* Bapbakanlyk Kadynyn Statüsü *became an official national women's organization, established to encourage laws that assured equal . . ."*

Relaxed among the cushions of the banquette, she loosened her grip on the papers. Mohammed heard the quiet shuffle and looked over from his table. There were two ways to deal with seeing Angela this way, and he chose the safer.

"*Ya*, Angela," he yelled loudly, "come over here. I want to show you something."

Angela moved her head but didn't open her eyes. Mohammed got up and went over to her.

"Are you asleep? You little rat skull." He nudged her roughly with his knee and laughed. "What have you been doing at night, that are you so sleepy during the day?"

Angela half rolled off and half got up, saying, "I'm not asleep."

Mohammed pulled her over to the table.

"Seesterr, what word does this look like to you?"

He pointed at a Sana'a manuscript. There was water damage and slight disruption of the velum where it had stuck to an adjacent page.

Half awake, she looked down. Her rumpled hair hung forward.

"They should cover up..." Angela said, making no sense.

As she spoke the words, she became more alert and realized what she had said. Angela turned her head to the right and blinked. Mohammed met her in the eye. Angela blushed and looked away.

Mohammed looked at the manuscript again. Then he saw what Angela meant. The blurred characters looked like figures in an erotic position. Her somnolent state had allowed Angela to see and say something her frontal lobe would otherwise have forbidden.

Another time she might have been able to laugh it off, but right now she couldn't. Even Mohammed was silent.

Angela went back over to the banquette and quickly gathered her papers. "I have to go," she said.

"Where?" Mohammed asked. "It's still early." His mind was jumping. *Selim.*

"I..." she stuffed papers and books into her tote, while she thought up an excuse. "I... need a bath."

*No, you don't.*

"I mean, a Turkish bath." Angela spoke quickly and breathlessly. "Umm. It's part of my research. How the bath affected women's rights in Turkey. It's fascinating, really. I'll tell you about it sometime. I meant to go earlier, but I went to Palestine, and it got delayed. I'm at a point now where I really need to go."

"So you'll be back in what, a few hours?" Mohammed asked.

"No, I don't think I'll be back today. I... ah... also want to visit the Basilica Cistern. I hear it's fabulous. It's right across the street from the baths."

Angela stood up. As she brushed her hair out of her eyes she again caught Mohammed's glance.

"Angela," he said.

## Chapter 108

# ISTANBUL, TURKEY
## August 6, 2006

"Forget about it!" Mohammed told himself after Angela left.

He was not going back to the Sana'a manuscripts again and let those figures taunt him. Whatever they had done to Angela, they had done at least as much to him.

*I will get online and find some Mus-haf brother to smash!*

Mohammed sat at his computer and vigorously retraced every lead he had ever had about the Mus-haf Brotherhood.

And he found something that amazed him.

*That's it, I'm going.*

And he meant immediately.

But he had to say good-bye to Angela. She would be going to the *yalı* directly after her outing without coming back to the townhouse. If he didn't see her today, he may never see her again.

*The Orientalists were right. It's like a different world in here.*

The steam wasn't as thick as billowing clouds, as Angela had read, but sitting in a marble room behind the closed doors of a three-hundred-year-old Turkish bath, there was still the inescapable feeling that the outside world was cut off.

Angela took the full bath option, but it did not prove to be the mind-washing experience she had hoped for. She looked up at the fenestrated dome of the colonnaded steam room and tried to remember what she had read several weeks ago about baths improving women's rights.

But thinking seemed at cross purposes to the stifling sensuality she was experiencing. Thoughts of a different kind kept reintroducing themselves. She learned a lesson.

*Never take a Turkish bath when a cold shower would serve better.*

Neither Angela's stated purpose of improving her research nor the hidden purpose of dispelling her thoughts about Mohammed were accomplished when she left, but her body was relaxed, and that dampened her anxiety about the other two.

"*Hayır!* No, sir, you certainly cannot speak to Mrs. Hall, if she is here. The privacy of our clients is protected." The stern Turkish matron with a mustache waved a finger at Mohammed and said indignantly in Turkish, "In the Ottoman days a man would be killed if he were found in the women's bath."

At the last, a tall thin man with slick black hair walked up behind her and examined the appointment book. "It appears she has already left."

# Chapter 109

## ISTANBUL, TURKEY
## August 6, 2006

*It's like the waiting room between heaven and hell.*

The Basilica Cistern. Angela had thought the bath was a different world. She was in for a greater surprise.

As she had exited the bath, Angela turned left and walked toward Hagia Sophia along the street called Yerebatan Caddesi. On the right, a few blocks and several tourist shops later, Angela came to the inconspicuous entrance to the Basilica Cistern. She paid the fee and descended the stairway.

*This place is ethereal, unreal.*

She read the visitor's folder: "Built by Justinian in AD 532, by the time of the Ottomans the Basilica Cistern had become forgotten. It was rediscovered when people began pulling buckets of water out of their basements, some including even fish, and found this underground building of 336 columns, 26 feet in height."

Angela looked up from the folder. The room was indeed filled with evenly spaced columns. They grew out of clear water, four to five feet deep, which seemingly doubled the column length by reflection. At the top of the columns sat capitals in Byzantine variations of Corinthian and Ionic styles, with a few in simple Doric. Reddish illumination of the arches at the ceiling and floodlights at the base of each column enhanced the mood and gave the dark room a peachy glow.

Classical music was playing and she could hear occasional dripping sounds, but otherwise the room was quiet.

She stepped onto the stuccolike surface of the boardwalk trail, which allowed visitors to walk over the water of the cistern. It was wet due to dripping, and muddy from the shoes of tourists. She trod carefully so as not to slip.

*Am I in level seven of a computer game? I almost expect someone to jump out from behind a column and shoot!*

The time was 5:20 p.m., near closing time. A maintenance man, who spent most of the day mopping down the boardwalk, was on the dead-end branch to the right. He was coming back toward the closed snack shop and restrooms, which clung to the wall below the stairs. Besides him, the occupants were a few tourists, climbing to exit.

Angela walked straight to the far left end. Time was short and she wanted to see the Medusa heads before she left.

A man descended the stairs. Angela did not see his tall, shadowy form. It was Mohammed.

He recognized Angela in the distance by her silhouette and the orange glow on her hair. Mohammed was feeling tense, probably due to his impending departure and what he would say to Angela, but there was more.

Yes, it was true; there were snake-headed maidens at the bases of these columns, which were lit with underwater lights. Angela read that the columns were formerly part of a temple to the water nymphs and were reused by the Byzantines.

*Building up, tearing down. Death and life come together in a place like this.*

Another man, shorter, descended the stairs. He moved both quickly and quietly.

At the opposite end, Angela descended another stairway to a lower platform that surrounded the Medusa head for better viewing. The color of the Medusa heads was more greenish than the rest of the columns. Above the head was classical detailing that reminded her of egg-and-dart molding. She leaned over the rail to look closer.

Just then a shot rang out.

Instinct served well. Angela gasped and squatted, unsure why she was doing this and half thinking that what she heard was simply a sound effect, befitting this eerie place.

Mohammed dove into the water and swam behind the closest column. He took off his shoes. Now he knew why he had felt uneasy: it wasn't just distress at saying good-bye to Angela and hello to danger far away. He had smelled danger here. He had been followed.

Another shot. It ricocheted off one column to another and then into the wall.

Surely this was a gunshot. Angela was afraid but also indignant at the vandalism.

*Who would do such a thing in this beautiful place?*

Mohammed had one immediate goal.

*I must draw fire away from Angela, let her escape.*

He started swimming from column to column away from the boardwalk Angela was on, toward the opposite one, which had just been mopped.

He hoped the assailant had not seen Angela. So far, her form was hidden from view because she was on the lower platform looking at the Medusas.

Angela stayed down, but she heard the splash.

*What the hell was going on?*

She commando-crawled closer to the edge where the splash came from.

Mohammed swam underwater to another column.

Angela recognized his form.

"It's Mohammed!" she exclaimed in a whisper, with her hand over her mouth.

Another shot went out, this time into the water.

*Someone's trying to kill him.*

With her heart racing, Angela lay paralyzed, trying to think of what to do.

The gunman was heading down the boardwalk toward Angela, closing in the gap between him and Mohammed.

Mohammed's head came above water behind a column.

He darted through the water to another column, then another. Each time a shot rang out.

In the background, the rapid counterpoint of Bach music could be heard on the speakers, accentuating Mohammed's movements and the shots.

Angela stayed put: afraid but quiet, looking for some chance to help Mohammed.

Mohammed had gotten to the walkway on the right side of the cistern. He was currently out of view, in the shadows next to the wall and behind one of the wooden posts of the boardwalk. He could have kept going along the edge and tried to slip out of the cistern unnoticed, but he didn't.

Mohammed started climbing up the slippery wooden post. His hands gripped at nothing but slimy water on top of the boardwalk.

The gunman was getting angry, pacing back and forth, looking into the water.

Angela looked cautiously at the gunman. She did not recognize him.

*Where's the management? Why don't they do something?*

Mohammed pulled himself on top of the boardwalk. He was now almost directly opposite the gunman. What he did next seemed crazy. He shook his finger fiercely and let out a barrage of taunting Arabic.

"*Ya majnoon mujahid!*" He continued in Arabic, "You are on the wrong path, and you will die on the wrong path. Over here, I am on the right path. If you don't give up fighting and join me, you will die like a dog protecting a rotting bone!"

Surprisingly to Angela, the gunman stopped and listened.

Then he shot again. This shot ricocheted off several columns with resounding "pings" followed by empty echoes. One of the bullets broke the glass covering a floodlight, and the column went black.

Mohammed dove back into the water, shirtless, on the close side of the boardwalk. He was putting on a remarkable display of the kind Angela had not known Mohammed was capable of.

*He told me he could swim, but I never...*

With the speed and technique of a competitive swimmer, he was propelling himself literally from pillar to post so rapidly that the gunman could not track him.

At times Mohammed would catapult himself out of the water like a large dolphin. As he did this, he carried such a huge spume of water with him that his form was obscured by the reflectance.

The display accomplished its purpose. The gunman ran out of bullets, and as he struggled to reload on his knees in the artificial twilight, he slipped. The gun jumped out of his hand and slid into the water. He flattened himself on the walkway and reached down hopelessly after it.

From behind he felt a shove. Angela had crept toward him during the confusion and pushed him into the water. And she noticed something.

*That gunman's wearing a suit!*

Mohammed heard the splash of the gunman's fall.

Now he and Mohammed would be on an equal playing field, but they would not be equal. Without a gun, Mohammed had the upper hand in size, strength, and swimming ability. This is what he had hoped for.

"Angela, get out of here!" he yelled.

Mohammed wanted to join Angela and escape. Escape from here and escape to wherever they could be safe—and together. Mohammed could have escaped, but he knew he must deal with the attacker now. He sensed, rather than thought, that it would give Angela time to escape. And he wanted to disable this man before he caught them again—or worse, attacked Angela while he was gone.

But Angela was not one to do exactly what Mohammed asked.

Mohammed swam over to the man. As the assailant was lifting himself out of the shoulder-height water, Mohammed grabbed him by the knees and pulled him under.

In what looked like a crocodile fight, the two rolled and thrashed back and forth.

Angela was anxious and felt helpless.

*What can I do?*

She remembered something she had seen on the lower platform built around the Medusa heads. Was it still there?

She ran back while the thrashing went on, hoping Mohammed's lungs held enough breath to sustain his life.

*There it is!*

Angela grabbed the mop that the maintenance man had left standing in the corner of the railing, and dragged it behind her, running back to the scene of the struggle.

But the wood was slippery. She fell onto her hands and knees. Her nose came close enough to the wood to smell the musty scent of cistern water and mud. The mop fell on top of her, its handle accidentally hitting her head as she fell. Her nose touched the mud. She heard a splash in the distance and scurried up again, dragging the mop behind her.

When she returned to the underwater battle, Angela saw a glint of metal.

*The gunman has a knife!*

The men came near the edge of the boardwalk. Mohammed was pushed against the glass of the broken floodlight and started bleeding. Angela gasped.

Angry now, when the gunman came near, Angela slammed the mop onto his head and shoved as hard as she could. The second time she did this it unsettled him enough that Mohammed managed to knock the knife out of his hand. It fell to the bottom.

Angela kept hitting the gunman as Mohammed dove for the knife. She shoved hard on the back of his head and neck, and unknowingly thrust him onto the knife as Mohammed emerged holding it.

Mohammed held the man with his left arm as his right hand thrust upward on the knife.

The man gagged in a moribund mix of drowning and stabbing. His lung was punctured. His head fell backward and his face was exposed.

"Ergun Türbe!" Mohammed said in shock.

Mohammed recoiled. Angela kept pushing downward on Türbe's head. She was taking no chance that he would rise again.

"Mohammed, *ya kaslan!* Get up here and help me!" she yelled.

Mohammed climbed up one of the slippery posts that suspended the wooden walkway.

"*Shokran!*" he said as he took the pole from Angela.

But Mohammed was no more inclined to do what Angela asked than she was to obey him.

Türbe's head was again coming out of the water. The small knife had not been effective. Mohammed decided to put a finish to this final interview with Türbe.

Rather than hit Türbe with the mop head, he inverted the mop, gripping it just below the head. Then he thrust it with all his might into the water and onto the shattered floodlight, submerging its exposed electrical components.

Sparks flew.

At first, they flew from the broken fixture. Mohammed and Angela saw something truly shocking: Ergun Türbe standing, shaking back and forth under the power of electrocution.

Then shorts seemed to spread from the broken fixture all through the dated and insecure wiring of the cistern. Sparks flew up everywhere. It was a spectacular display as they shot into the air, illuminating the columns in places before unseen. Their reflection in the water doubled the light show that made Angela feel as if someone had dropped a match into the Fourth of July fireworks stand at San Francisco's Crissy Field, and she was in the middle of it. It was enormously loud and ominous, but it was beautiful.

"Mohammed!" she yelled.

Mohammed said nothing. He jumped on top of her, sheltering her under his bulk, which was nearly twice hers.

When the sparks quit flying, it was quiet and very dark.

## Chapter 110

# ISTANBUL, TURKEY
## August 6, 2006

In the darkness of the cistern, with their near-death experience time and reality had slipped sideways. Mohammed and Angela knew that they should not be together, that they should not touch each other. They had embraced for protective reasons—to escape the sparks. Yet the sparks seemed to pass from outside the skin to the inside, where they ricocheted, unable to find a path of escape.

Angela's lips brushed Mohammed's shoulder, but she held back and did not kiss him. She simply let her lips touch his skin.

Mohammed's hands were above Angela's head in a protective position, but his fingers were tangled in her hair, and he could smell its scent.

The closeness was something comforting to cling to, and they were reluctant to let it go. They stayed together, with Mohammed covering Angela for a moment, then two. Time that was nothing and yet…

When it was more than obvious that there were no external sparks, Mohammed rolled to the side and kneeled.

"Seesterr! Your hair smells like smoke. Go home now and wash it!" he said.

"Sure, wizard, just show me the yellow brick road."

"I can't see the lizard in this darkness. Just hold onto me, and we'll crawl out of this tank together."

They tentatively made their way down the walkway on all fours.

"Follow the yellow brick road, follow the yellow brick road," Angela sang weakly.

"Whoa! Hold it, not this way!" Mohammed called as they almost went off the side. They redirected and made it back to the rest area, stumbling on the transition from the boardwalk to the floor.

Then Angela remembered that she had a small keylight in her purse. The beam was weak, but it was enough to show them the layout of the break area and where the stairway was. The door at the top was locked only from the outside. They pushed the handle and received an incredibly welcome sight—daylight!

A body was crumpled in the corner of the ticket booth. They decided not to investigate, but looking down at it Mohammed said, "I will never understand Turkish hospitality."

After Angela wiped the blood off Mohammed, they moved on, as nonchalantly as a mud-splotched couple can. A policeman passed, taking note of shirtless and shoeless Mohammed in wet pants.

Quickly, Angela said loudly in English, as if to Mohammed, "The guides were right! That must be the best Turkish bath in the world!"

# Chapter 111

# ISTANBUL, TURKEY
## August 6, 2006

Back at the townhouse, feeling much like a Spartan woman in a Greek play, Angela said, "I know it's dangerous, but you are right. You must go to Yemen."

Mohammed was as pleased with her as if she were his own blood sister. Angela was not the whining sort he usually associated with womanhood: someone who can't see beyond her own front door. She was worried about what might happen to Mohammed in Yemen but accepted that the manuscripts were important to him. And he was right—the brotherhood must be stopped. Until that was done, the manuscripts were not safe—and neither was he.

"Mohammed," Angela said, "if I'm going to keep looking for a way to get the Topkapi Codex while you are gone, it will mean I have really joined this quest."

"Ha-ha! Finally, sister wants to help!" Mohammed said emphatically. "That is good!"

"I need to be *more* convinced that it's good, so I have a few questions."

"Ah. Don't you know the Koran says not to ask questions about things that would make you doubt? But no problem. You can sin. I will answer eeeverrything!"

"That sounds like you. First let's review the basics. You want to see what's in the Topkapi Codex because you think it will prove that the Koran has been changed. Since it's a famous book it would get a lot of attention."

Mohammed shook his head. "Yes."

"And you want to check if there is human blood on it to see if it possibly *could* be Caliph Uthman's."

"Yes." He shook his head again, then crossed his arms and leg.

"And if it is identical to other Korans, that will prove that the Koran is unchanged, and we can go back to being contented Muslims."

"No." Mohammed shook his head negatively.

"Why not?" Angela looked disappointed. In spite of their discussions, she was hoping there was an easy way out.

"Because the Topkapi Codex is not the only evidence that the Koran has been changed. Seesterr! You are smart. Doctor even. Don't you remember all I have taught you?" He scratched his chin with a mischievous look. "I think I have to give you exam before I leave."

"Couldn't we have a review lesson first? You know, just lay out all the evidence for me in an organized manner... well..." Angela also got a mischievous look, "... as organized as a crazy ADD Palestinian can make it."

"Ooooh, if you want organized, sister, you had better make me some coffee so I can focus!"

After a few sips of strong coffee, Mohammed turned to a blank page in a notebook and wrote down key words as he spoke.

"No one knows what Mohammed's Koran was like. Look here at what Umar, the second caliph said." He pointed to an ancient quotation in his notebook and read in Arabic: "Let no one of you say that he has acquired the entire Koran, for how does he know that is all? Much of the Koran has been lost, thus let him say, 'I have acquired of it what is available.'"

"I'm thinking," Mohammed continued as he tapped his pencil, "how can I explain to slow American woman?"

"Follow the yellow brick road," Angela sang quietly as Mohammed thought.

"Brilliant! Yellow brick road! Lizard! Seesterr, you live in America. There are many museums in America, right?"

"Right," said Angela, wondering where this was going.

"And when you were a cute leetle girl with buck teeth and carrot orange hair—"

"It was never carrot orange...."

"—ever did you see big, big lizard there? *Shismo*... very old kind, big as house."

"Oh, a dinosaur. Yes, I saw dinosaurs."

"And did you see it with skin or without?"

"Both. Some museums have bones wired together into a skeleton, and others have reconstructed dinosaurs."

"Tell me about reconstructed dinosaur, what he is like."

"Well, it is the kind where they make a life-size model out of plaster or concrete of what they think the dinosaur looked like."

"Tell me how they make a bone dinosaur."

"Uh. Well, first they find bones in the ground. I think they make drawings or take pictures so they know the relationship of the bones. Then they carefully dig them out and preserve them somehow, I don't know. Then they fill in the broken spots and wire the bones together."

"Aha! Exactly. That is what the Koran is like. Made from pieces the followers of Mohammed found and put together like old bones. The Koran is a reconstructed dinosaur!"

"You make bold statements, you know."

"Ah, watch how bold this is...."

Mohammed took a pencil and paper and started drawing an elaborate stick figure that resembled a dinosaur skeleton. "This," he narrated, "represents the basic consonantal script. It really *is* the backbone of the Koran. Originally, the Koran didn't even have spaces between words; the letters just flowed together and people had to figure it out. So we'll connect the bones like that."

"Mohammed, maybe you can swim and hunt, but you can't sing or draw." Angela pointed at the sketch of what was vaguely a triceratops. "Your dinosaur is all crooked. His head looks funny and this leg is shorter than this one."

"That's on purpose! Even the letters in the consonantal scripts differ—like the Sana'a manuscripts I've been studying differ from the Samarkand Codex, and probably the Topkapi Codex."

Mohammed started encasing the dinosaur in skin. "This is the surface," he said.

"Hey, the skin here is bumpier than it is there."

"That's because the dots and dashes were added in different ways in the literally thousands of variants."

"You have seven zigzags coming down his back and tail. I suppose they mean the 'canonized seven'?"

"Yes! Those are the most accepted ways of adding the dots and dashes; although as we said there are others. And these two cute spikes on his tail are for the two most popular versions today: the *Hafs*, used in most of the Muslim world, and the *Warsh*, which is used primarily in North Africa. *Ya*, Angela. I know what you can get me for a present next Eid al-Fitr."

"What's that?"

"The Koran edition that has ten of the most popular variant readings marked on each page."

"Sounds like happy holiday reading."

"Hey! You're a woman. Just be glad you can read!"

"And I can write!" she said, taking a pencil and cutting off a leg of the dinosaur.

"Thank you, seesterr! That was brilliant. I was going to do it, but you beat me."

Angela looked at him, puzzled.

"That's for the missing passages."

"Oh." Angela watched Mohammed draw another stick figure. "What's that?"

"Thees cute leetle man is Mohammed. Mohammed Atareek! I am going dinosaur hunting! My attacks will summarize the problems with the Koran. Here is my bow. Now watch my arrows!"

## Chapter 112

# TOWNHOUSE
## Istanbul, Turkey
## August 6, 2006

Mohammed used his pencil and sound effects to imitate an arrow flying from his sketched bow. "Here comes the first hit," he said as he drew it landing in the dinosaur's flesh. He wrote two words in Arabic on the shaft and explained the meaning:

*LATE RECORDS*

"The records of early Islam were written two hundred years or more after Mohammed's death."

With more sound effects, Mohammed sent a rain of arrows and wrote words on their shafts as well:

*QUESTIONABLE SOURCES*

"The revelations were collected after Mohammed's death, from scattered records on plant and animal materials, and memories."

*INADEQUATE MEMORY*

"Apologists make great claims for oral traditions, but faulty memory is the cause of many variants. Here's an easy example, Angela. Some versions of sura 1, the *Fatiha*, say, '*King* of the Day of Judgment' instead of '*Owner* of the Day of Judgment.' The meaning is pretty much the same, so the difference was probably memory, not intention."

*DUPLICATED PASSAGES*

"If we took out the repeated passages, the size of the Koran would shrink by about two-thirds. Many passages are just dissimilar enough to be variations due to memory."

*TAFSIR*

"*Tafsir* are the Muslim commentaries. These explain the meaning of some of the variants. Abu Hayyan, a scholar who had one of the best collections of variants, admitted he doesn't even mention Koranic variants that are too far different from Uthman's text. Because of this, scholars think that the most divergent variants were lost."

*MULTIPLE TRANSIMSSIONS ADMITTED*

"The hadith and commentaries do not hide that Ibn Mas'ud, Ali, Abu Bakr, Ibn Ka'b, and several others had made their own Korans directly from Mohammed. They admit that variations arose in Uthman's Koran and try to explain them by calling them 'the canonized seven.' But there were even more than seven."

*RIVAL KORANS BURNT*

"This is what I demonstrated in Cappadocia, the night sister got hysterical. Caliph Uthman knew about the variants in the consonantal script of the Koran. He canonized his own version and burnt everyone else's."

*EXISTING VARIANTS*

"There was a huge stash of variant Korans that Professor Arthur Jeffery of Columbia University had collected for a commentary, but it is claimed they were destroyed during World War II. Still, there are many variants around. Look at the Sana'a manuscripts. Even simpler—compare your Koran—which is *Hafs*, to the *Warsh* version. Or the *Hafs* to the Samarkand Codex."

*EARLY INSCRIPTIONS*

"The Dome of the Rock and dated old coins don't correctly quote the Koran. They must either be quotations from variant texts or verses from before the Koran was formally assembled."

*QUESTIONABLE SPEAKER*

"Some places in the Koran we don't know if it is God or Mohammed talking, like in the *Fatiha.* Or sura 19:64. The Koran is supposed to be God speaking to man. Ibn Mas'ud wouldn't accept suras that sounded like man speaking to God."

*MISSING PASSAGES*

"The goat ate the verses about stoning the adulterers. He also ate some about women suckling grown men to make them relatives. And there are the ones Uthman took out favoring Ali, and the parable of the valleys of gold and others that were accidentally left out."

*DIFFERENT SURAS*

"Ibn Mas'ud and Ibn Ka'b had different numbers of suras and different orders. Possibly some suras got merged into others. And Ibn Mas'ud's Koran had the 'Sura of the Succession,' which favored Ali."

*APOSTATE SCRIBE*

"Mohammed's scribe, Abdullah Sarh, was one of the first apostates, because Mohammed accepted his corrections to the Koran. He questioned, 'How can I, a man, correct the Word of God?'"

*PERSECUTED POSSESSORS*

"Ibn Shanabudh, an eminent Bagdad scholar, was one of those persecuted for having old Korans. He was caned until he could endure no more pain. Only then would he recant for using the noncanonical Koran."

*PRIMATIVE WRITTEN LANGUAGE*

"Why would Allah choose such a primitive language as medieval Arabic to hold his unchangeable word? If he cares that people understand, why didn't he use a more developed language that had letters for all vowels and consonants?"

*UNCLEAR MEANING*

"Many passages are unclear, even with the commentaries' help. The Koran claims to be clear, but is not. About a fifth of it is incomprehensible."

*UNEVEN FLOW*

"Some passages have great grammar and poetical form, but others are choppy and poorly composed. Many times the speaker jumps from first person to third person in the same sentence, and the subject changes nearly as much."

*CONTRADICTIONS*

"In one place, the Koran says God made the world in six days, and in another, eight days. Which was it? Sura 2 says Jews and Christians are saved. Sura 3 says only Muslims are. Is there no compulsion in religion, or are unbelievers to be subjugated or killed?"

*SCIENTIFIC MISTAKES*

"There's a popular book by a French Muslim who says the Koran is scientific. But it's been refuted. In America do they teach that babies start from a clot?"

"No," Angela answered, "from their parents' cells joining together."

"Excuse the question, but in America do they teach that a man's seed comes from the back, near the kidneys?"

"No."

"Ha! And they should know!"

Angela decided not to ask why.

"Does the sun set in a muddy pool, like the Koran says, or because the earth moves around it? And do the mountains *prevent* the earth from moving, like the Koran says, or do they *result* from the earth's plates moving? Like you said in Cappadocia?"

"These ideas aren't so bad if you consider them in the light of science at the time of Mohammed," Angela responded.

"Ooooh, sister! Do you hear what you said? True, Mohammed wouldn't know science—but God would. So whose words are we reading?"

## *PERSONAL NATURE OF REVELATION*

"How can the Koran be eternal and holy, yet so much of it be given in response to Mohammed's personal whims—to settle his family squabbles and excuse his behavior? Would God really prefer Mohammed so that only he can have more than four wives, that he should not be annoyed, and that his adopted son must divorce his wife so that Mohammed can have her to fulfill his lust? Or cover for Mohammed's mistakes, like the 'Satanic Verses'?"

## *THE SATANIC VERSES*

"I've heard of the 'Satanic Verses' because of Rushdie's book. Remind me what they are?"

Mohammed explained, "They refer to sura 53:19. Some experts think they used to say that three goddesses worshipped by Mohammed's tribe were intercessors to Allah. Afterward, when Mohammed realized this was against monotheism, he abrogated it. He received a revelation that told him not to worry—Satan always mixes his words with the ones Allah gives the prophets."

Incredulous, Angela asked, "Seriously? If that's the case, the cure is as bad as the disease. How do we know which words are God's and which are Satan's?"

"Exactly. But that's what the Koran says. Check out sura 22."

Angela picked up her Koran and read it.

"So you see how the dinosaur is reconstructed," Mohammed said, pointing at his sketch, which now resembled a pin cushion, "and how easily it is shot down."

"I will show you a dinosaur San Francisco–style!" Angela boasted.

## Chapter 113

# TOWNHOUSE
## Istanbul, Turkey
## August 6, 2006

Angela reached for paper and a pencil and drew the outline of a Tyrannosaurus rex. "This outline with its bumpy skin represents the Koran in the script we have today." She picked up the highlighters she used for study and started decorating it.

"Why are you putting all those girly pink and purple dots on him?"

"Those are the variations in vowel and consonant markings."

"Couldn't you make them brown and black?"

"Hey, you said we don't know what the Koran was like, so why can't my dinosaur be yellow with pink and purple dots?"

"If we don't know what he looked like, why do you give him huge teeth?"

"Because he is a fighter! He lost parts in battle. Look, I will erase this arm and this foot and the end of his tail. They represent the lost verses of the Koran. Now, underneath I will draw the skeleton. This represents the basic, unmarked script that Uthman assembled."

"What's that thing on his head?"

"A red hat! It's a flashy addition, like the *Fatiha.* And the red boots are the two other suras Ibn Mas'ud didn't recognize. Now, you see how fashionable mine is? Yours looks like a voodoo doll," Angela said.

"What's *wudoo* doll? One that washes and prays? Sick, you Americans."

She picked up an orange highlighter. "And this represents the flames of Uthman that burned the rival Korans." Angela vigorously rubbed the marker up and down the page to make flames.

"But why complicate it? Let's stick with the big three." Angela put the marker down and counted on her fingers. "First, Uthman's bonfires. Second, missing and added pieces. And third, the different dots and dashes. In America we say 'three strikes, you're out!'" Angela picked up the paper, crumpled it, and threw it across the room like a baseball. It hit the outside of a large copper pot and made a dull sound.

"Maybe you can draw, sister, but you can't throw or cook!"

Angela sneered.

"But I have way for you to remake honor," he said in English. "One more question. Final exam."

"Why do I need a final exam? My drawing was perfect!"

"OK, if you know so much," Mohammed squinted and nodded, "who is deceived: the one who follows a deceiver or the one who doesn't?"

"That's so obvious I'm suspicious."

Mohammed feigned indignation. "Suspicious of what, sister?"

"Of a trap. But OK, I'll walk into it. It can't be more dangerous than the Basilica Cistern. The deceived is the one who follows the deceiver."

"No trap. This is open-book test. Get out your Arabic Koran and read sura 3:54."

"'Allah is the best deceiver.' Oh," Angela said. "I never saw that before."

"Now read sura 14:4."

"It says, 'Allah leads astray whomever he will.'"

"Which Koran have you been reading? Aha. I know. Have you been reading in English?"

Angela felt a little sheepish. "I've been reading Arabic since Turkey. In California I had a bilingual edition with English on one side and Arabic on the other. I confess, I mostly read the English."

"That's the problem. Western translations won't be accurate. They wouldn't use a word as strong as the Arabic for 'deceived.' People wouldn't convert! Would Americans willingly follow a deceiver?"

Angela sat quietly, but she was equally as shaken as when she had screamed at the campfire in Cappadocia. On that night the Koran had been blasphemed. Tonight she heard blasphemy against Allah himself.

*Calling him a deceiver!*

And yet, how could it be blasphemy if it was in the Koran?

She picked up Mohammed's drawing. "The evidence you present is powerful. But I can't just accept your research without studying it myself. If what you say is true, how can we believe in the Koran, or Mohammed? And how can we believe what they say about God? We're talking life and death here. Heaven and hell." She paused. The two looked from the paper to each other in dead earnest. "This is not a subject any of us should take lightly," she concluded.

"I don't take it lightly. I'm giving it my life," Mohammed replied. "Do you see why the Koran says not to ask questions?"

Angela took a black marker and drew a very irregular line under Mohammed's dinosaur.

"What's that?" he asked. "You'd better have a good reason for marking on my beautiful picture, sister!"

"This rough ground represents all the suffering of the world." She looked Mohammed in the eye. "How can we believe in a god like that in a world like this?"

"Seesterr, you convinced me: from now on, I'm atheist!"

Chapter 114

# DAR AL-MAKHTUTAT

## Sana'a, Yemen
## August 9, 2006

Mohammed had already spent a day at Dar al-Makhtutat. *Dar* means "house" in Arabic. Founded in 1984, Dar al-Makhtutat in Sana'a, Yemen, housed one of the largest collections of early Korans.

The Great Mosque of Sana'a and its manuscripts date back to the early days of Islam. Famous for Arabica coffee, frankincense, and the Queen of Sheba, Yemen is an ancient country hugging the southern edge of the Arabian peninsula—across the desert from Saudi Arabia and across the Red Sea from Africa. It was also one of the first countries converted to Islam.

When Korans became old, they were respectfully buried within the ceiling of the mosque. Totally forgotten, a stash of aged Korans lay hidden in the ceiling of Yemen's Great Mosque in the city of Sana'a for over a thousand years. As if under a spell, the manuscripts slept while the city grew, its brown basalt buildings edged with lacy white stucco looking like giant gingerbread wedding cakes. Then, in 1972, during repairs for rain damage at the Great Mosque, the cache of Korans was found.

Whether from ignorance or inability, once found, the Korans were stashed in potato sacks and stored in the basement of the National Museum. When the existence and situation of the Korans became known, the Germans pressured the Yemeni government and provided funding for their preservation and study. Thus Dar al-Makhtutat was founded. Since then, UNESCO and Italy have also supported the project.

Mohammed Atareek had no idea of how difficult it would be to get into Dar al-Makhtutat. It wasn't open to the public. As a sort of admission ticket, Mohammed had brought the two fragmented manuscripts he and Nasir had been studying before they left Beirut. These would validate his claim to be one of Fenburton's researchers. He would say he wanted to return the manuscripts in person, now that Fenburton was dead.

But the ruse wasn't necessary. All he had to do was present his credentials to the conservator and submit himself and his briefcase to a search by the guard. It was a risk to admit who he was, but he was already known by the man who wanted him dead. And the conservator looked benign.

Mohammed knew the institution was in danger. He needed to spend time there so he could discover *how.* He wanted to absorb the *regularities*—how things looked and operated, so that he could spot the *irregularities.* But he didn't want to raise suspicions regarding his presence. He decided to ask to "finish studying" his two manuscripts onsite. He would compare their "signatures" to others in the stacks and on microfilm to see if he could collate them with any other Koranic fragments at Dar al-Makhtutat.

This made sense to the curators. They needed help.

A manuscript's "signature" consists of a series of numbers that describe its attributes. For example, how many lines per page and the length of each line. Signatures help simplify the overwhelming task of collating the fifteen thousand leaves from about a thousand jumbled Korans in the collection.

Mohammed also needed to know the institution's layout to determine its vulnerabilities. He said he wanted to tour the facility—to have the thrill of being surrounded by the objects of his devotion for the last few years. What he said was true.

Pilar Arena, an expert in manuscript conservation on loan from Spain, accepted it and welcomed him. She showed Mohammed that Dar al-Makhtutat is divided into display, storage, photography, and microfilm-reading areas.

The first day, he was there alone except for Pilar. Mohammed knew the attack would not occur until the following day. It was in the stars. Or, more precisely, in the moon.

The Islamic calendar is lunar: it depends on the cycle of the moon. Moon sightings are necessary to determine the beginning of the holy month of Ramadan. The moon is a banner symbol of Islam. Some say that Allah was a moon god in ancient Arabia, before he became the one true God. The sacred rock in the Kabaa in Mecca is probably a meteor—a piece of space that fell from the sky in token of God.

And the predicted destruction of the Dar al-Makhtutat would follow the course of the moon. The message Mohammed had heard on Paltalk had bragged about it in advance: *"Alhamdulillah! As the sun sets on the full moon, a joyous deliverance will occur, as Yemen is purified from the dirty touch of infidels."*

Yemen is an Islamic state. After the civil war in 1994 there were ongoing charges of governmental repression and corruption, but there was no question of it being under foreign domination. Political deliverance was not the issue.

What would be purified? Where he had heard the message was a clue: a radical chat room dedicated to preserving the honor of the Koran. According to sura 56, the Koran was a book "... which none may touch except the pure...."

Mohammed knew the "dirty hands" had to be those of the researchers—European infidels who had contaminated the "Word of God" merely by touching it. Dar al-Makhtutat would be purified by destruction of the building, its contents, and all those who had touched them. It would be a literary form of "honor killing."

Now it was the afternoon of the second day. The moon would rise in a few hours. Only one other man had been there today, arriving just a few hours ago. Mohammed didn't know who he was, so he called him و, the Arabic letter called "wow," which makes a *w* sound and looks a little like a person.

Wow and Mohammed worked on their separate studies without speaking. When they were not checking boxes in the storage stacks, they were most often in the microfilm room. Neither spent much time in the ground-floor room, which displayed selections of leaves for the few authorized visitors. The room was kept dark, and the display cases were covered with cardboard to keep out light. And there was no call for them to be in the photography lab.

During the entire time that Mohammed was comparing the signature of his manuscripts to others in the stacks, or sitting at a microfilm-reading booth, he was watching the activity of Wow.

*For once ADD pays off.*

He was worried that Wow might try to get into the locked photography lab.

*Where's Wow?*

Wow had disappeared. Mohammed walked by the restroom to see if he was there. Mohammed didn't hear anything, so he opened the door.

There was Wow, text-messaging on his cell phone. "So sorry," Mohammed said, and walked out.

Wow seemed to be doing much the same thing as Mohammed, but in a different sequence.

Both spent time with the previously sorted manuscripts. These were stored in drop-open boxes, like the ones in which Mohammed, Maarten Hoog, and the others had been receiving their manuscripts. Inside each box were folders of Koranic leaves, bound together under pressure from boards and linen tape. This was for the protection of the friable pages and to reduce warping—especially of parchment, which tries to crawl back into the shape of the animal it came from. On the top of each folder was a window that would allow for an easy style check. The boxes were in a storage room, horizontally stacked behind the glass doors of wooden cabinets donated by UNESCO.

The procedure for collating Korans was as follows:

1. Designate a signature code for the Koranic fragment you are working with.
2. Compare that signature with those printed on the outside of boxes of previously sorted materials.
3. When you find a matching signature, open the box and check the style of the pages inside.
4. If the signature numbers and appearance inside the box match, the pages are very likely from the same decomposing Koran.
5. If not, try another box.

Mohammed changed activities frequently so he could walk by Wow. Wow did not seem interested in Mohammed at all.

Everything Wow did looked appropriate. This frustrated Mohammed. And he grew more and more frustrated as closing time approached. He had no lead to go on.

Mohammed had no idea what was going to happen, but he was certain something would.

*I've got to take action.*

He'd have to use direct confrontation again.

Wow was in the stacks. Mohammed walked into the stacks from the microfilm room. But he was being followed.

## Chapter 115

# DAR AL-MAKHTUTAT

## Sana'a, Yemen
## August 9, 2006

"Gentlemen," Pilar said in Arabic with a Spanish accent, "it's time to close for the day. But we very much appreciate having experts from Europe and the Levant here to help us."

"Ooooh, you must be the one from Europe," Mohammed grabbed the chance to speak to Wow. "Where are you from?"

"I am Dr. Ali Ibn Fakkar from the University of Leiden, Middle Eastern Studies division, specializing in ancient manuscripts," he said, flashing a cordial smile with a gold tooth on the right.

*Liar.*

"*Tasharrafnaa*, honored to meet you. I am Mohammed Atareek. I work with Dr. Nasir Atareek, perhaps you have heard of him?"

"Oh, yes, indeed."

"Shall we walk to the door?" asked Spain's contribution to the project. "We do hope you will come back tomorrow."

"I'm afraid that won't be possible," Fakkar answered.

*I don't like the way that sounds.*

"Oh, that's too bad," Mohammed said. Obviously Fakkar didn't know that Mohammed had been to Leiden. Mohammed had seen the list of all the professors in the Department of Middle Eastern Studies, and there was no Fakkar on it. That also meant Fakkar didn't know that it was Mohammed who had killed Mehmet Kasap.

Mohammed continued, "I would love to meet with you and talk about Leiden. I am thinking about going there for my postdoctorate studies and would like to visit."

Fakkar looked nervous. Mohammed noticed.

*I'm right.*

"Excellent idea," Fakkar lied. "I'm out of cards, but if you give me your phone number I'll put it into my cell phone and give you a call when I get back to Holland. Then we can talk."

*He called my bluff!*

Mohammed did not want to give a phone number. He wanted to keep his private conversations private.

"On second thought, I didn't bring my cell phone. Please write it on this paper for me."

Mohammed obliged. He wrote his name and country code, followed by Jamal al-Hajji's number. He was certain Fakkar did know who killed al-Hajji but wouldn't recognize his number.

"Gentlemen, the time," Pilar said as they reached the door.

At these words a flash of panic crossed Fakkar's face. It was just a flash, and he recovered, but Mohammed noticed. Fakkar was worried about the time.

"You are right," Fakkar said. "We have imposed long enough. My thanks to you, Ms. Arena. Mohammed, I am sure we will meet again."

"I am sure we will."

Mohammed stood still inside the entrance, dumbstruck. He watched Fakkar leave. What should he do? Follow him?

*I have a feeling I shouldn't leave Dar al-Makhtutat.*

"Mr. Atareek?" Pilar tried to get his attention.

Mohammed had no idea what Fakkar had been up to. He had seen nothing suspicious. But there must have been something. All Fakkar had done was look at microfilm, go through boxes, and send a text message.

*That's it!*

"Mr. Atareek, are you OK?"

*Now what should I do?*

Mohammed stood riveted.

*If I don't follow Fakkar he will get away. If I do, and don't catch him, Dar al-Makhtutat will be destroyed. And even if I do catch him, Dar al-Makhtutat may be destroyed anyway.*

For no apparent reason, Mohammed punched the guard on the jaw. Caught by surprise, the guard hit his head on the wall and slouched in the corner, unconscious.

"*Ave Maria santissima! Qué pasa? Qué hace este loco? Aqui no tenemos ningun dinero tampoco!*" Pilar railed on in Spanish as she ran over to the guard.

Mohammed made no explanation. He ran back into the stacks. By the time Pilar looked in, he had already made a shambles of the room that was formerly her pride.

"*Ay! Este hombre va a destruir todo!*" she screamed, then ran out to call the police and an ambulance.

Mohammed had opened the doors of the storage stacks and was emptying them as if his life depended on it. Which it did.

The floor was haphazardly covered with boxes, most closed, some open. Several folders were free on the floor. But there was little actual damage.

Mohammed picked up one of the largest drop-open boxes and detected a faint odor.

*I found it!*

He opened the lid. Inside was a wad of thick, ruffled paper, soaked in some fluid. And under the paper was a cell phone.

Gently, Mohammed took out the cell phone—the phone he had seen Fakkar with in the restroom but that he later denied having. Mohammed dropped the box onto the floor. Ordinarily he treated manuscripts as if they were truly holy, but now was not the time for fussing.

The cell phone was a detonator. He had to handle it carefully.

He didn't know much about bombs, but this cell phone was clearly jury-rigged. Two wires came out of the ringer, and along the wires were two nodules, like detonating caps. A telephone call at sunset was all it would take to set it off.

Fakkar didn't need to smuggle in twenty-two pounds of TNT or a great deal of shrapnel like the cell phone–triggered bombs in Madrid and Bali. The goal of those detonators was explosion. The goal of this detonator was fire.

*Like Uthman!*

As with Uthman of old, fire would again be used to preserve the canonized version of the Koran from competition and embarrassment. All Fakkar needed to do was get enough spark to light the flammable paper. He could easily smuggle in such small quantities. Then he could wire the cell phone in the restroom and set it up in the drop-open box while he was "working in the stacks." There was no fire prevention or detection system in the building. Mohammed didn't know that, but Fakkar did. The fire in the stack would spread rapidly from manuscript to manuscript until the entire building was burned.

Mohammed knew he had to get rid of the detonator. He started walking quickly but carefully toward the front exit. He held both hands out in front of him, cradling the phone. His deliberate and peculiar steps made him look like an Olympic speed walker.

In the entryway, Pilar and the guard were huddled in the corner. They looked up as Mohammed passed.

"It's a bomb," was all he said.

Dar al-Makhtutat was located next to the Great Mosque. It was near sunset, and people were arriving for prayer. Later, the moon would rise. He had to get the device out of the medina and away from the crowd before sunset.

He could easily have gotten lost in a strange medina, but the Great Mosque was near the edge. All that lay between him and the Bab al-Yamin exit of the medina was the salt market. Know in Arabic as the *Suq al-Milh*, it now sold everything and was the most crowded part of the medina.

He was uncertain how to navigate in this crowded spot. If he weren't given berth, he could easily be bumped and drop the device, and he didn't know what that would do. If he yelled, or started kicking people out of the way, he would likely get in a dangerous confrontation or gain other attention that would delay his progress.

*I have an idea.*

He pulled the tourist map of Yemen out of his pocket and covered the phone with it. He did it in such a way that it ended up looking like a wrapped purchase. He carried the package in front of him as if he were trying to prevent damage to something inside.

*With any luck they will think I am bringing home pastry.*

He moved quickly past the unique buildings of the old city. Just a few more streets and he would be at the gate.

He thought of Wow and lifted his eyes long enough to take a furtive look around. Instantly he was sorry because he stumbled on a bump in the pavement. The phone jiggled and he dropped the map.

*Damn it. I nearly lost it!*

Shaking a little, he replaced the map. Finally, he saw the Bab al-Yamin gate. His memory had been right. Just beyond the gate he could see an open area used for parking and overflow merchants.

He walked under the gate and into the square. It was less crowded, but there were still many cars around.

*Where to throw this thing?*

Mohammed was willing to throw it into a car and let come what may. A car would insulate people on the square from the explosion due to happen any second.

There were no open car windows, and he didn't have the skill or time to hold the phone and try doors.

There was one option. It wasn't perfect, but it would have to do.

One car away was a pickup truck loaded with vegetables for the market. Mohammed tossed the cell phone package into the back just as the sun set.

"Get out of here!" he yelled.

Some people ran in panic. Others looked at him as if he were crazy, thinking, "What for?"

Then came the explosion. Vegetable fragments went flying into the air.

The children screamed. One deaf child jumped up and down, chasing food flecks.

The sunset call to prayer started from the loudspeakers of the two white minarets of the Great Mosque, barely visible behind the wall.

Mohammed breathed a deep sigh of relief. But it was short-lived.

"Freeze!" he heard from bchind.

*The police!*

# Chapter 116

# ISTANBUL, TURKEY

## August 10, 2006

Mohammed spent the remainder of the night in a Sana'a police station. Fakkar flew out under another name. There was no one to stop him.

When Mohammed returned from Yemen, he learned that Angela had found a way to get at the Topkapi Codex. It would not require the money Mohammed had gotten for selling his land, nor Angela's fortune either. She had used a trick, not a bribe.

They did not need to steal the codex. All they needed was time to photograph it. And time in the seraglio alone was the brilliance of Angela's scheme.

Dr. Ergun Türbe was general director as well as in charge of the relics division of Topkapi Palace. His death left a hole in the authority structure that, as minister of culture, Dr. Selim Soglu was temporarily filling until he could appoint a replacement.

"Selim," Angela had said to him on the balcony of his *yalı* one night while Mohammed was in Yemen, "do you remember that you once said you could give me a night in Topkapi Palace if I wanted?"

"I can't say that I do, but I could. Is that something you would like?" he asked.

"I enjoyed having a Turkish bath, but I have been thinking that it would greatly benefit my research if I could spend a night alone in Topkapi Palace. I have no experience with what it must have been like to be a concubine. I'd like to be there without tourists, take a bath, sleep, and absorb the atmosphere, that sort of thing. Could you please arrange it? I would make a nice fat donation to the museum fund. . . ."

"Are you sure you mean 'alone'?" Selim asked, lowering his chin and raising his eyes in a way that spoke more than words.

"Yes," said Angela, looking guilty, but not for the reasons he hoped.

*Chapter 117*

# A NIGHT IN TOPKAPI PALACE

## Istanbul, Turkey
## August 11, 2006

The moon was almost full. It aided Mohammed as he entered after dark through an unlocked gate, one of several penetrating the wall surrounding Topkapi Palace. These gates were created to allow its inhabitants access to the sea for recreation—and to dispose of the remains of court members who had fallen from favor.

Angela had found one gate that was shielded from view of the perimeter road by vegetation. And it could be easily opened from the inside with the skeleton key Selim had given her. Earlier tonight she had unlocked it and returned up the hill before dark.

Mohammed made his way by moonlight up the planted hill and through the garden, emerging from the stairway beside the Revan Pavilion. In front of him was Süleyman the Magnificent's pool. The fountain in the center was running, and its droplets were shining in the moonlight.

Behind the pool, two torches were burning under the colonnade between the Revan Pavilion and the former Sultan's Chamber. The torchlight illuminated colors and forms.

As he walked around the pool it became clear that carpets, tapestries, a chaise longue, pillows—even a palm tree—were set up by the torches in a manner so sensually opulent that he half expected to see a fat sultan luxuriating there. There was someone, but it wasn't a sultan.

Angela had worked out a plan for the evening that would include enough verifiable research to explain her presence at Topkapi Palace, yet allow time for their work with the Topkapi Codex. She would "get a feel for what it would have been like to be a royal concubine" by first preparing herself according to the tradition for presentation of virgins to the sultan. This would mean a Turkish bath with "physical purification," dressing in a magnificent Ottoman costume, then resting in a royal setting. She would supposedly absorb the feel of the palace at night and imagine herself to be a concubine. When she was finished, she could change into her work clothes before Mohammed arrived at dark.

Selim had agreed to assist her "research" night in Topkapi Palace. Most of the preparations were made in the late afternoon, after the museum had closed, but the work in the Sultan's Bath had gone on all day. Ostensibly for maintenance, its marble walls, floors, and basins had been cleaned and polished, with fresh water run through the pipes and the boilers stoked with wood.

Angela was tired from the preparations for this evening, and with the relaxing power of the steam bath she had fallen asleep unexpectedly, still dressed in her concubine's costume. This was not part of the plan.

The costume was so fabulous that even a fashion philistine like Mohammed was awed—especially with Angela in it. It was a detailed replica, with multiple pieces, including the loose brocaded *şalvar* harem pants and the button-front top, called an *entary*, which was tight like a waistcoat and had long open sleeves and a split skirt. Jewels glittered on her sash, around her neck, and on the small *fortaza* headpiece. She indeed looked regal.

And there was one unexpected detail that came into view as he neared the chaise. In fact, it stunned him. The costume was authentic even to the original style of the *entary*: it was cut beneath the breasts to expose them, with only a transparent silk covering.

Mohammed, like most men, was visually wired. His flesh had been aroused every time Angela lay reading in the pillows at the townhouse, but those urges were nothing compared with what he felt now.

*Angela is the most wonderful, gorgeous, sexy creature in the universe, and I'm jealous as hell of John Hall.*

The fountain's spray flew high above the pool. Originally intended to hide the sultans' private conversations, tonight it muffled the sound of Mohammed's footsteps so that Angela did not hear him until he was next to her.

"*Ya*, Angela!" he called, keeping himself a safe arm's distance away.

Angela opened her eyes. Her heart jumped. Quickly for modesty's sake, she pulled a silk *kuşac*, or shawl, over her.

There stood Mohammed dressed all in black. Black—the best color for nefarious action but also the best suited to his hair and complexion. She didn't pause to study him, but she knew he looked good.

"Mohammed, you're here already!" she said, getting up to change inside the Revan Pavilion.

Mohammed knew she was embarrassed.

*I will make her laugh, and everything will be better.*

"Seesterr, what is this tablecloth you are wearing? How can you do spy work when you are flapping and tripping all over the palace?"

"Oh," Angela answered, "I know it looks silly, but it is part of my research. An Ottoman *kadin* costume, which is like a sultan's wife. I'll go change my clothes and we can get to work."

"Sure, seesterr, but I feel sorry for the sultan if his 'kitten' wore that! He would think of going tenting, not making love!"

Angela pulled at the shawl on her shoulders and said, "This is just a shawl I'm wearing to, uh … keep me warm."

"Could I see the costume?"

"Really, I don't think so. I'm not a very good *kadin*."

"Hmm," he said, pulling up his lower lip as he did when he was thinking something pleasant. "If you weren't married to John Hall," he said, trying to sound light, "you would make a wonderful 'kitten' for the sultan, the queeeen of aaaall the empire!"

Angela paused. "Actually, John divorced me," Angela said solemnly, "but I couldn't bring myself to tell that to the aunties."

Mohammed understood what she meant.

*The shame.*

But then it struck him. "He did? That's awesome, that's wonderful! I never liked that guy," Mohammed replied, suddenly animated and with a big smile.

Angela put a hand on her waist. "How can that be? You don't even know him."

"But he had you, and I didn't like that! I'm sure he can't be worthy of my dear little angel cousin."

"If you weren't angel's cousin, that might make a difference." Angela regretted the words the moment they passed her lips.

Mohammed turned around to the fountain, his back to her, and covered his face. Angela was ready to die of embarrassment when she was met with surprising laughter.

*Is he laughing at me? Does he think I was forward?*

"Ha-ha!" Mohammed laughed loudly and slapped his thigh.

Angela waited in suspense for him to calm down and tell her what he was laughing at.

Mohammed grew quiet and slowly turned to face Angela. With his dark eyes wide open he asked, "Angela, little angel, you don't understand?"

"No."

Mohammed walked up to her and reached for her fingertips, holding them gently with his own.

"Let your big brother explain. All this time I have been thinking you were happily married to a rich American, and you're not. And you have been thinking I am your blood cousin, and I am not. . . ."

"You're not?" Now Angela's eyes were wide, incredulous. "But you're my little Cousin Mohammed, the son of Aunt Zahara and Uncle Nasir."

"Ah, little sister, this is what happens to girls who do not pay attention to their Arab culture lessons. What is the name of the firstborn son in a good Muslim family?"

"Mohammed."

"Right, and I am a firstborn son. But I am not the Mohammed Atareek who is the firstborn son of Nasir and Zahara Atareek; I am the Mohammed Atareek who is the firstborn son of Nasir's firstborn brother, Mohammed Atareek. Heaven forgive you for not recognizing me!"

"You mean you're the cousin of my cousin? That wild boy my age, not the little one playing on the floor when I visited Palestine with my mother?"

Mohammed beamed.

Angela's mouth dropped open, and she pulled her fingers back. "*Haram!*" she said sharply. "You mean I have been traveling all over the Middle East with a man who's not even a blood relative?"

"And loving every minute of it!" Mohammed replied boldly.

## Chapter 118

# A NIGHT IN TOPKAPI PALACE
## Istanbul, Turkey
## August 11, 2006

*I loved you, so I drew these tides of men into my hands*
*and wrote my will across the sky in stars.*

—T. E. Lawrence ("Lawrence of Arabia"),
*The Seven Pillars of Wisdom*

Mohammed and Angela stood looking at each other, with nothing to say. Poised between the fountain and the chaise, half bathed in cool moonlight, half in warm torchlight, they stood. It was as if two opposing forces, equal in strength, tugged on them and held them upright. Any movement would upset the delicate equilibrium and trigger who knew what consequences.

A gentle breeze. It ruffled Angela's hair and blew her fragrance into Mohammed's nostrils.

Mohammed lifted Angela's fingers to his lips and kissed them tenderly. This time she did not pull them back. As he drew them forward, Angela's body came closer to his. He could feel her breasts touching his chest. The sensation of what was now so close to his skin aroused Mohammed fully.

Angela's head naturally went backward for breath, and her eyes closed. When she opened them Mohammed had stopped kissing her fingers and was looking so deeply into her eyes that she knew he wanted to kiss more of her. She parted her lips only a millimeter, but it was enough. His lips were welcome.

Mohammed bent down and kissed Angela with more gentleness and sincerity than he had ever kissed a woman in his life.

It was the night of the annual Persied meteor shower, and shooting stars began streaking through the sky overhead. The two did not notice.

The sensation they experienced was not merely that of lip on lip, of two pieces of skin touching each other—that was something that could be reproduced any day anywhere by anyone, and always was. The meeting of their lips was only a token of what they experienced on a deeper level: the superficial sign of something already united. Like the signature on a treaty. And it was the fulfillment of two forbidden dreams that had magically become unforbidden; unclean fantasy washed into a clean and beautiful reality.

An embrace followed. Kisses continued. Angela's shawl fell to the ground.

Their hands loved each other with all the tenderness their hearts had been cherishing. When their bodies united the movement was not contrived but flowed as naturally as the passion fate had unstoppered in this fairy-tale setting.

Before his quest, Mohammed had slept with many women, but only for fun. He had never experienced physical union with someone who was part of him, as Angela was and, he knew, always would be. When he shook with physical release, it was part of his soul he sent into Angela, something he could not take back.

Angela had never felt like this. To her, sex had been a way to appease an angry husband, a man who consumed her like a drug for his depression. Sex with Mohammed was entirely different. She felt adored by the one she most adored, and it lifted her above anything she could have imagined.

In her moment of greatest passion, Angela raised her right arm over Mohammed's head. She opened her eyes and saw the warm torchlight shining on his hair and her arm. Then she drew her arm back down and held Mohammed tight and close.

They embraced as if they would never let go, and between gentle kisses said the things all lovers have said since the Bosporus was first crossed.

Later, Angela slid out from Mohammed's embrace and said, "I'm hot!"

"That is so true!" Mohammed responded.

"I need to rinse off perspiration and . . . other things," she said coyly, removing the jewels from her hair.

Taking the shawl with her, she partly covered her body as she walked around the balustrade to where the Marble Terrace directly merged with the pool. She dropped the shawl and sent an inviting smile to Mohammed before diving into the water, as graceful as a water nymph.

Mohammed stood on the balustrade and dove in. When Angela surfaced, she found Mohammed beside her.

"Seesterr, you are crazy. You know what a good swimmer I am. You can never escape me!"

"Am I trying to?" she asked, but she swam away quickly.

Mohammed watched her for a moment, then swam after her. He quickly caught her, bringing her up with his arms around her waist, inside the fountain's spray. He started kissing Angela's belly. Angela laughed loudly, tickled by both his lips and the fountain water raining down on her. She kicked hard and splashed so much water in Mohammed's face that he had to loosen his grip so he could wipe his eyes. She gracefully swam away.

Swimming naked in Süleyman the Magnificent's pool by moonlight was delightful to both of them. Mohammed was struck by the beauty of Angela's fair body as she glided through the silvery waters. It made him feel strangely proud to watch her—she was something of heavenly grace, and now she was his.

Finally Angela drew herself out of the pool and sat on the marble pavement, holding her legs like a cold, wet nymph. Mohammed pulled himself out with an intentional display of strength and sat beside her.

"Now I'm cold," she said, shivering a little.

Mohammed considerately wrapped the shawl around her. "Me too," he said. "Do you have any more shawls?"

Angela stood and pulled up Mohammed by his hands. "I know something even better!" she said excitedly.

She led him down the passageway that connected them to the Sultan's Bath. There she turned on a golden tap.

"The water's still hot and steamy!"

She let the water run until the room was filled with glorious steam. It filled their noses and covered their skin and warmed them into pink.

The marble tub and basins overflowed, and, just as in the days when paladins kept bathers from slipping, the floor became warm and soapy and covered with bubbles. It was a soft and slippery, cozy world.

What happened in the Sultan's Bath that night had never happened before—at least as far as history admits—for men's and women's baths were strictly separate under the Ottomans.

But Mohammed and Angela joyously shared together in all the rituals of the bath, which rewrapped them in a fabric of tender love.

The massage was not just a massage but an act of adoration, almost worship. The rinsing, the shaving, the hair washing were all new ways in which they expressed their affection and silently pledged their devotion to each other. It warmed their hearts as well as their bodies.

And when their warm flesh was again aroused, they fulfilled their desires anew.

Relaxed, Mohammed gently touched Angela's ear and whispered into it, "You are a moveable feast."

Angela laughed and said, "You're not, you're too big to move!"

When they were no longer breathing hard, they washed themselves clean again.

A few hours in the bath had heated them so much that they lusted for another swim. And so the night progressed. Between the cushions of the chaise, the waters of the pool, and the suds of the bath, the hours evaporated like steam into the predawn morning.

## Chapter 119

# AN HOUR BEFORE DAWN

## Topkapi Palace
## Istanbul, Turkey
## August 12, 2006

Mohammed awoke, pleasantly surprised to find himself lying among the cushions with Angela inside the shelter of the Revan Pavilion. A second later the same sight startled him. He remembered why he was here and grabbed his watch. He swore.

"Angela, darling, wake up. We're craazy lovers. We forgot what we were here to do." He rolled out from her and pulled on his pants. "Get up! Forget about love—I mean we'll have forever together, but now we've got to get moving."

Mohammed knew they would not have time to photograph the entire manuscript before the morning guards opened up the palace, but they could get some of it.

The Revan Pavilion was on Süleyman the Magnificent's Porch and was conveniently close to the Sacred Relics Chamber. Since it had formerly been the sultan's private apartments, he had an easy passage out to the pool. They simply had to unlock the door to this passage and they were inside the chamber. Only one more barrier—the glass door protecting the holiest of Islam's relics.

They dressed rapidly. As they were getting out the tools, Mohammed turned and gave Angela an embrace and kiss. Then he released her so quickly it seemed he was pushing her away.

"Whew!" he said, "No time for that now!"

The passage was dark and a little dank smelling. Angela held the flashlight for Mohammed. With the skeleton key, they easily opened the door into the chamber.

It was dark inside, but the chamber was small and they easily found the glass door. Mohammed plied the skills for breaking and entering that had become natural to him during his younger days. There was an electric alarm cord extending from the ceiling. He had seen it before and had brought just the right kind of depolarizer to inactivate the sensor but keep the circuit open so it sent a continuous signal back to the monitor. No alarm would sound when they opened the door.

The lock to this door was elaborate and difficult to break but still relatively primitive, considering the value of what it protected.

Mohammed had been quiet long enough. Sometimes it helped him to concentrate if he babbled a little while he was working.

"Seesterr!" he said. "Do you realize if you hadn't worn that darn kitten costume, we'd be locking this door now instead of unlocking it?"

"*Kadin*," Angela corrected, "not 'kitten.' And if you want to play the blame game, I can play too! It's not my fault, it's Selim's. He's the one who bought me the costume."

"Selim bought it for you? Why?"

"Well, actually, it was part of the deal for tonight."

"You paid for tonight? I don't understand. I thought you said it didn't cost us anything."

Angela took a deep breath. This was neither the time nor the place to tell Mohammed. In fact, if she had known how tonight would turn out, she would never have made the deal.

"In order to get in here, I agreed to *muta'a*, temporary marriage with Selim."

There was a click as the lock released.

Mohammed turned and looked at Angela. "You what? You have *muta'a*?" he asked with a twisted expression of pain she would never forget.

Then he stood up and walked out, pushing her carelessly aside with his broad shoulders.

As dawn arose over Topkapi Palace, Angela found herself in a situation she could never have imagined—seated under the bronze Iftar Canopy, watching the sunrise over the Golden Horn, crying over what she had gained and lost in the course of a single night.

Mohammed's attempt to get the codex was a failure, but Angela's research was a success beyond her dreams. She truly felt like a discarded concubine.

## Chapter 120

# ISTANBUL, TURKEY
## August 12, 2006

Daylight came brightly through the window of the Ottoman townhouse, finding Angela still asleep. She stirred and stretching her arms over her head. Her half-opened, half-focused eyes fell on her right wrist.

*It's my scarlet letter!*

The light bathing the room this morning had floodlit the small red birthmark on her wrist—the same spot the torchlight had flashed upon last night at a moment of ecstasy in Mohammed's arms.

She groaned and pulled the pillow close to her, drawing herself into a fetal position. She didn't know she was fully awake until she found herself crying again.

Red-eyed, she dragged herself to the sink under the illusion that she could go through with the day's plans. But it was impossible.

*My birthmark.*

The birthmark was like a strobe light that flashed at her every time she moved her wrist.

*How could I have lived with it all my life and never really noticed it until now?*

As she splashed water to rinse her face, the mark seemed to leap into her eyes.

It taunted her: *Angela, you're a fake, Mohammed exposed you and rejected you, John threw you out, no one loves you, and you're shamed beyond redemption. There's no hope for you!*

Mohammed was gone.

She had dragged herself back to the townhouse an hour or two after dawn, and, as she suspected, he had left. His passport, small suitcase, and the manuscripts were gone.

Seeing this made Angela feel like an adulteress. In fact, she knew she was. Legally, she was still married to John until the waiting period was over, a few more months from now. She had explained this clearly to Selim, but not to Mohammed. Selim had asked the cleric who gave them *muta'a*, and since only a three-month separation period is required by Islamic law, he said she was legally divorced and suitable for *muta'a.*

When Angela had asked Selim for a night in the palace, he had offered himself to stand in as the sultan, but Angela said she couldn't possibly agree to that. It would disturb her imagination, and besides, they weren't married and she was an honest woman. That was when Selim proposed *muta'a*.

The situation was a godsend for Selim, who was still looking for a way into Angela's bed. With *muta'a* he could have her with no guilt and let her go at the end of the summer so they could pursue their separate careers in different countries.

The idea was not so welcome to Angela. "Give me a few days to think about it," she had said, "I've never slept with anyone except my husband."

Selim belonged to the Turkish Shiite sect known as Alivi. Both Sunnis and Shiites agree that the Prophet Mohammed had originally approved temporary marriage for his military campaigns: a man could have a "marriage of enjoyment" (the literal meaning of *muta'a*) for an agreed period and price.

The Sunnis point to hadiths in Sahih al-Bukhari that show that Mohammed canceled the practice; but the Shiites deny this and say it is still in effect, since the Koran refers to it. In some airports frequented by Muslims, one can find a form of prostitution that legally marries a man and woman, according to Shiite Islamic law, for however long the man has between flights. However, some Sunnis, especially Saudis, have a similar practice of temporary marriage, called *misyar*.

Angela knew Selim would do anything to sexually fulfill his Roxelana fantasy. And she had promised Mohammed to keep looking for a way to get into the palace while he was in Yemen. It seemed she had found a solution.

But she was still legally married in America. In addition, her heart was married to a third man. A man she had believed she would always love but never have. This frustration empowered her to agree to a bigamous temporary marriage with a man she didn't love, to fulfill the dream of the man she did. It would be the best gift she could give him.

So she was a double adulteress. Unfaithful to two husbands at the same time.

*Hester.*

The name sounded nothing like her own, and yet she had a newfound feeling of kinship with it. As with all the nameless concubines of Topkapi Palace and every harem.

*Who was this Hester? Hester Stanhope? The crazy English lady of Lebanon? Hester Bateman, the eighteenth-century silversmith? No, no! Hester Prynne—the adulteress in Nathaniel Hawthorne's novel* The Scarlet Letter.

Hester had worn the scarlet "A" for "adultery" so long it became part of her. She wore it with dignity and came to peace with it. The letter made her grow. Angela wished she could reduce all her pain and shame to this one scarlet spot on her wrist. A small visible token of the huge invisible pain. A badge of courage, like Hester's.

But Hester Prynne the adulteress had worn her scarlet letter openly forever. Could Angela do the same?

*No! I will scrape it off.*

She started frantically scratching at her birthmark. It bled red on red.

*Or burn it.*

If she could do that, and deliver herself from the pain of rejection by the person she most loved—and the guilt of what she had lost for the sake of him— the cost wouldn't matter, even if it scarred her.

*I have to find a match.*

If she could cauterize all her wounds, if she no longer needed anything from anyone . . . if she could go back to just being Angela, then she would be OK. She would be happy in not needing anything to be happy.

*Detachment. Self-acceptance. Content.*

She rummaged in the kitchen and found a pack of matches. She lit one over the sink. With her left hand she brought the flaming match to her right wrist. She felt the heat, but at the first feel of burn she dropped the match into the sink.

*If I burn the birthmark, the scar will flash at me.*

There was no escape. A scar on the wrist would be a more powerful reminder of the scars she held inside. And people would ask her about it. At least a birthmark brought no questions.

Where was the remedy? Why couldn't she burn this scarlet letter off her heart?

She went over to the banquette to cry—but one look at the Turkish cushions reminded her of last night on the terrace.

*I can't go through with it. Not tonight.*

This was to have been the night that Angela and Selim would consummate their marriage. Selim regarded her night in the palace as Roxelana's preparation for her wedding night. Tonight he would have her in his golden bed in the *yalı.*

At five o'clock she called him with the news. Since she could barely speak, her voice sounded convincing as she explained that last night's exposure had left her ill. She would let him know as soon as she felt better.

Angela climbed up the stairs to the one bed in the townhouse. It was Mohammed's bed. She grabbed the pillow and buried her head in it, breathing deeply. It smelled of him. She cast it across the room as she herself felt cast off.

Angela had lost her lover, her parents, her mentor, her friend, her marriage, her lifestyle, her image, her safety, her religion, and her self-respect. What was left? What was her purpose for existence? And if there were none for her, was there any purpose for anything? Was the entire sphere of all existence a mere mockery?

*I should die.*

Shakespeare's Hamlet, one of her favorite heroes, had contemplated suicide. His words played in her head:

> *O, that this too, too solid flesh would melt, thaw, and resolve itself into a dew...*
> *To die, to sleep. To sleep, perchance to dream,*
> *But in that sleep of death what dreams may come*
> *Must give us pause. Who would bear the whips and scorns of time,*
> *But that the dread of something after death makes us rather bear*
> *Those ills we have, than fly to others that we know not of?*

Tonight the words sounded sacred and were as true as scripture should be: indeed they practically were scripture to one who loved English literature as she did.

How did she know she would go to a better place if she died? Would she be with those she loved—her mother and Honey Jean? Or would she simply cease to exist? Or, alas, face even greater suffering than she felt now?

Grief and guilt are a powerful combination, synergistic.

She reached down and picked up the pillow from the floor.

*Oh, Mohammed, why did you leave me? Where are you?*

Without realizing it, Angela was experiencing emotional anguish similar to Mohammed's of several years earlier. The sense of profound loss coupled with guilt set him on the quest that had absorbed him ever since.

*Oh, Honey Jean! I miss you. I need you. But what would you think of me? Your "Princess Angela"? So fallen. So wounded.*

Deep inside, Angela could sense Honey Jean's presence. It wasn't a mystical channeling experience. She just knew what Honey Jean would say. She would still love her. Perhaps there was a love that never died. It was only a tiny sense, but when you are falling down a dark hole into the center of the earth, even the faintest glimmer of hope is a lighthouse beacon.

## Chapter 121

# TURKEY TO THE HEBRIDES ISLANDS, SCOTLAND
## August 12, 2006

*The injustice of it!*

Mohammed was angry. All the passion he had felt for Angela had reverted to the intense anger he had felt as a young man at the injustices that surrounded him in Palestine. His country wasn't his country. Their land was taken. Opportunities for standard education and a normal life were stolen.

Now he loved a woman who wasn't his woman. Someone had had her before, and someone else had her now. And the fact that others had her meant that she wasn't the woman he thought she was in the first place.

And so he left her.

He didn't know where he would go; he just wanted to get out of Turkey as soon as possible. He grabbed his passport and laptop, threw some clothes into a bag, and started walking toward the airport until he caught a taxi.

In the terminal, Mohammed saw that one of the earliest international flights was to London. This was perfect. He had promised to see DW again after his father's funeral. Now would be the time. He would return to the island retreat in the North Sea, where Pots had first directed him to find DW.

Mohammed caught himself snapping at the reservation clerk. Clearly he needed to dissipate some anger before he met DW again.

# Chapter 122

# ISTANBUL, TURKEY
## August 13, 2006

*Now I can write poetry.*

Such was her consolation on the second day without Mohammed.

The price was far too high in her mind, but at last Angela was able to write poetry as she had always wanted. Everywhere she looked she found an analogy to how she was feeling. She inhaled air and exhaled poetry. She wrote about a Discarded Concubine, life inside and outside a box, Jupiter's moons, all kinds of classical themes, and numerous other subjects.

This wasn't a cheerful pastime, and because it was mostly blank verse Angela didn't feel it was great poetry, but it was therapeutic. Seeing how words on paper could capture human feelings encouraged her.

Angela's body ached from lying around so much. She couldn't eat at all and felt nauseated as a result. She scarcely drank. She didn't sleep much or well. Days and nights drifted together as if they were merely the pages holding her poems.

The third day, and still no news from Mohammed. There was no call. No e-mail. She didn't expect any, but still she hoped.

She needed to get outside, to see some of the world beyond that which she and Mohammed had shared together. She walked down the street encased in a sense of unreality that insulated her like a wooly blanket from everything going on around her.

She passed a tree that had recently been pruned and seemed to be wilting.

*Loving Mohammed was like finding my roots, only to have my branches hacked off.*

She walked by two men arguing in the street. Through the window of a travel agency she saw someone on the phone, angrily waving her arm. She wondered why people were so upset about everyday life, since everyday life was not real after all. People should be told that.

She had already mourned not only for her own suffering but for everything that suffered. For what were her losses compared to those of the AIDS orphans, the starving, those living a daily death of pain to cancer, or those in Lebanon at risk of being bombed out of this world while she sobbed over her life in it?

*The best way to get over your suffering is to help someone else get over theirs.*

Angela remembered Honey Jean saying this.

But who could she help here in Istanbul? She didn't know the language or the people. Was there a way she could help someone or make the world a better place?

She stopped in her tracks in front of the fountain of Ahmet III, outside Topkapi Palace. She had an answer.

*I will do it.*

She would pay her debt. She would buck up and fulfill her commitment to Selim. Then she would find a way to get back into the palace at night. She would take photographs of the Topkapi Codex and send them to Mohammed. And never speak to him again. It would be one final unselfish sacrifice she could make for him, even if he was unworthy. And it would prove that although she was an adulteress, at least she was a faithful one.

Besides, it was something she could do for the Truth. She needed to be certain for herself in this world of uncertainties. Was the Koran of God, or was it a man-made forgery by followers of a medieval, megalomaniacal tribal chieftain?

## Chapter 123

# RAMALLAH, PALESTINE
## January 2001

Where do you go when you are walking a narrow corridor and bullets rain down from the open sky? Where do you hide when there is nothing but solid pavement and walls? How does it feel when blood and bodies hit you?

What did they do?

They screamed—but no one rescued. They ducked—but there was no place to hide. They grabbed at their loved ones in a last futile gesture of connection: the touch of humanity in an inhuman world. They cowered in defensive postures, much like those who were suffocated by the ash of Vesuvius. But it was no volcano. It was the eruption of pent-up human anger.

This time they knew. One doesn't always know what starts the shooting. At the checkpoint outside Ramallah a man had behaved suspiciously.

Things can happen quickly. When you are a sniper in a tower, or opposite it on a roof, you look for anything out of the ordinary. You can't always wait for your compatriots in the checkpoint below to send word to you. Lives are in your hand.

This day, the news reported that the Israeli soldiers were right. A young Palestinian man did have explosives strapped to his body; the size and positioning of which made it clear that the checkpoint was not his intended target. He had hoped to get farther afield—probably to Jerusalem. There he could hit a bigger crowd with more Jews.

The two ground soldiers saw him reaching into his vest. The Israeli snipers started shooting. The bomber panicked. Tanzeem militia, hidden until now, began to crossfire. The Israelis struggled to get the bomber's hands away from the detonator, but they did not succeed. An explosion went off like the grand finale of a war film.

Then the shooting stopped. You could see the casualties and blood. Innocent blood. Seven were dead at the scene: four from the explosion—the bomber, the two soldiers, and a Palestinian man—and three from the bullets. Four more were injured and taken to Ramallah Hospital, where two subsequently died of their injuries. But there was an amazing grace—a small child in the center of the conflict miraculously survived.

## HEBRIDES ISLANDS, SCOTLAND
## August 14, 2006

Day three since he had left Istanbul, and Mohammed had slept only a few hours. His mind kept bouncing between what had happened in the seraglio with Angela and what must have happened to his family when they were bombed at the border crossing.

*Guilt.*

He should have been there with his parents. They had asked him to come. They needed him. But his cousin, the good Mohammed, joined them in his place.

He was Mohammed the playboy. Living for fun. Smoking and drinking, joking and having sex. Instead of going with his family, he had stayed at his friend's house. He was playing cards when his father and cousin died. The ravaged body of his mother lingered in the hospital a few days longer before joining them wherever people go when they die.

*Why did I run out on Angela?*

He felt like a cad for how he had treated her. Like whores he had known in his youth. Using them for pleasure and going on with life as if nothing had happened.

But it had not been that way with Angela. He had never chased her for fun. He had found her spiritually, like the missing part of himself, before he united with her physically. Yet he walked out just the same.

*Did I leave her because of what she did with Selim or because of what she did in me?*

Not only had he walked out on her; he placed her life in greater danger. He didn't think anyone knew where he was, but quite possibly the Mus-haf Brotherhood still thought he was in Istanbul and now might be suspicious of Angela as well.

Mohammed thought DW Fenburton was a great kid, and a sharp one. They had started studying Lord Fenburton's two manuscripts, plus the two that Jamal al-Hajji had sent back. But Mohammed couldn't give the work his full attention. Compared with what was going on in his life, orthography was dull.

*That's it, I've had enough!*

Mohammed changed gears. He apologized to DW, but he would do nothing more until he discovered who was the head of the Mus-haf Brotherhood. By throwing himself into it, maybe he could save the manuscripts and themselves, and somehow atone for what he did to Angela.

DW was pleased with Mohammed's suggestion. He felt Scotland Yard had done nothing to identify the driver who had essentially killed his father. If he could help Mohammed, it would be a legal form of revenge.

Mohammed reasoned with DW. "Leetle brother, let's think. Only twelve manuscripts at a time they were released from Sana'a for your Lord Dad's study group. We know your Lord Dad he kept two, Uncle Nasir and I, we got two, Ibrahim he got two, Maarten he got two, Jamal he got two. That makes ten manuscripts. That means there is only one researcher left. That man, I'm sure, he's the chief of the Mus-haf Brotherhood. He's the terrorist.

"And a murderer," DW added.

Dr. Ergun Türbe had held a position of authority, but Mohammed was sure he was not the leader of the Mus-haf Brotherhood. He had neither the experience nor the personality for it. He was more likely of the ilk of Mehmet Kasap, Ahmed, and whomever they had run over in Gaziantep—simply a Paltalk recruit who made himself available to do whatever was needed to be done to protect the "honor" of the Koran. And Mohammed was certain of something else. He told DW, "Only an Arab he would be respected enough to lead Mus-haf Brotherhood."

"But many countries speak Arabic," said DW. "That doesn't narrow the field much."

"Brother, do you have a map?"

DW opened a world map.

"*Shoofa.* Look at this," Mohammed said. "The researchers, we know they lived in these countries." He put *X*s on the map. "Lebanon, France, Holland, and England. If we include where they were trained, we can check Algeria for Ibrahim, and Yemen for Ahmed, Jamal's assistant—the traitor."

"I see," said DW.

"And if we include where they went to school, we add Egypt and Saudi Arabia."

"Yes, I see. That quite broadens the picture. Interesting. Collectively Father made his study group representative of the scholarship from the great Islamic centers of the world. But there must be something missing."

"Exactly," said Mohammed.

Mohammed started a nonstop, day-and-night investigation of the terror chat rooms on Paltalk and blogs until he had some clue as to the leader's identity.

"Leetle brother, let your big brother teach you the best, the best game on the Internet. This time you will play for real!"

DW was quick with anything on the computer. Mohammed trained him how to pick up clues from the English terror chat rooms, while he himself screened the Arabic rooms. This way, they would find the killer, and Mohammed would get him before he got Angela.

## *Chapter 124*

# ISTANBUL, TURKEY
## August 14, 2006

The third night, Angela took a boat to the *yalıs*. She would fulfill her end of the bargain with Selim tonight. As the breeze blew in from the Bosporus, she would play Roxelana in Selim's bedroom.

The boat docked. Angela looked up to see a shocking sight: there was a woman on Selim's balcony.

Angela braced herself.

*Oh, well, Selim proved he wasn't faithful in Berkeley. He's not my love. I'm just carrying out my part of a deal. I'm used to loveless sex.*

He provided a delicious meal, but it was hardly the sort of wedding feast Angela had expected. Throughout the evening, Selim had been courteous, but the conversation was stilted.

*Is it because he has another woman now, or is he angry over my stalling?*

As they finished mint tea, Selim said, "I understand you had a man with you in Topkapi Palace."

Angela nearly panicked. She groped for words and hoped it wasn't obvious that her jaw was sitting on her sternum. There was no way out. She had to tell the truth.

"It was my cousin. He was visiting from Palestine and wanted to see the inside of a harem, so he came with me to take a few photos. He's gone now," Angela said in a totally truthful lie she hoped would suffice.

"Don't worry. It doesn't surprise me that you wanted a man there to help you act out your fantasies."

Angela didn't like the way Selim had put it, but at least he didn't sound angry. In fact, he was entirely too cool about her indiscretion.

*What is going on here?*

"Angela, I wonder if you could do me a favor." He got up and opened the door to his bedroom. This was definitely not the way Angela had pictured him seducing his Roxelana.

"Come out, please, Mayda." An attractive woman with auburn hair walked out of the bedroom. "Angela, meet my ex-wife. She has just been released from a year in prison, and I think you will enjoy knowing why.

She wrote about the Armenian genocide in a way the court felt 'insulted the Turkish identity' in violation of Revised Penal Code Article 301."

"Oh," said Angela, surprised and forcing an uneasy smile.

*That explains his jokes.*

"I want to remarry her, but according to Islamic law I can't until she marries another man first. Angela, do you think you could get your 'cousin' to perform *al mohalil* by sleeping with my wife?"

## Chapter 125

# ISTANBUL, TURKEY
## Day Four since Mohammed Left
## August 15, 2006

Even if she asked him, Mohammed wouldn't have sex with Selim's wife, Angela was sure of that. But the mere suggestion caused Angela's emotional progress to regress. Mohammed couldn't be hers, but she hated to think of his being with someone else.

The good news was that Selim was releasing her of her *muta'a* demands, now that his wife was back.

*I'm sick of Istanbul.*

The people here weren't friendly. Her relationships had gone sour. She was weary of living in two houses at once. She was bored with harems and superficial sensuality. She wanted to go back to her cozy Arts and Crafts home in the hills of Berkeley. Back to where she had felt Honey Jean's love. She could finish writing her research paper there.

But before she could leave, she had to finish her onsite research—and she needed to photograph the Topkapi Codex.

Having a goal gave her direction and cleared her head remarkably. Today she would go one last time to the Women's Library in Istanbul and visit a small museum in the house of a wealthy Jewish woman who had served as a business agent, or *kira*, for harem-bound Ottoman women. Tonight she would go back to Topkapi Palace.

As soon as I get what I need, I'm out of here!

# HEBRIDES ISLANDS, SCOTLAND
## August 15, 2006
## Day four since leaving Istanbul

Mohammed exclaimed, "Woo-hoo! Leetle brother, this is the guy. He's the big one, I'm sure. Mr. Wow, you are not smart enough to escape Mohammed Atareek!"

"Show me," said DW. He wore a Scottish fisherman's knit and a punk earring, but he spoke with upper-class British elocution, "I want to learn how my splendid friend found him out."

"Leesten, Dee. I am going. I will show you, and then I am going. But you are doing something great. Keep it up, OK, man?"

## TOPKAPI PALACE
## Istanbul, Turkey
## August 15, 2006

It was surprisingly simple and almost anticlimactic, but Angela was pleased.

After visiting the Kira Museum, Angela went to Topkapi Palace an hour before it closed. She walked back to the fourth courtyard and hid among the bushes, but with a different game in mind than that the sultans used to play.

After closing and the security check, she came out of hiding. She was already dressed in black.

Emotional pain was unavoidable when walking across the Marble Terrace, but she looked straight ahead, avoiding the pool, and kept her head clear. The door in the royal passageway was locked, but she still had the skeleton key.

The Sacred Relics Chamber was just as they had left it, with the circuit feedback still working. Angela easily entered the room that held the Topkapi Codex.

Something hit her that she was not expecting: As Angela stood alone in the chamber, she was struck motionless by the sense that this room was holy, at least to many people. It seemed a violation to enter.

She reminded herself that she was not going to steal or do anything immoral—for the entire world deserved to know what was in the Topkapi Codex. But the objects here were venerated and had seldom been touched. It was the breaking of this continuity of respect that disturbed her—like removing the custody band from forensic evidence or breaking a chain letter started by God.

Her photographs were not professional, but they were good. She had brought Mohammed's collapsible photographic platform to hold the macro-lens camera and battery-run lighting to augment the flash.

Once the assembly was set, the work progressed smoothly—she simply turned the pages, repositioned the Lucite sheet that compressed the pages flat, and snapped.

She worked all night. If someone were watching this time, Angela didn't sense it.

## Chapter 126

# ISTANBUL, TURKEY

## August 16, 2006

By early morning Angela had finished the photos, replaced the codex on its stand, removed the circuit depolarizer, and relocked the two doors that kept the codex "safe" from the outside world.

This time, since her presence in the palace was a secret, she had to hide again. It was still cold outside, so she used the skeleton key to enter the harem, which she knew so well. Selim had shown her rooms not open to the public, and upstairs was one with wood paneling. It would be warmer than the marble and tile of the more public rooms, and it was one of the rooms Angela adored. Valide Sultan Mihrişih, mother of Selim III, had decorated it in the French taste, with green Louis XV style carved and gilt paneling.

Her second sunrise in Topkapi Palace found her curled up, looking at a different view—an idealized landscape painted on the boiserie panels. It depicted a sunny and beautiful day. Angela wished she could step into it, and walk down its path into a new life. There was a song about a day like that, if she could only remember....

Angela heard a noise. She lay disoriented for a second, thinking she was in her French room at home. She awoke. Voices. People were downstairs.

*Can I get out unnoticed?*

When the voices stopped, Angela crept down the stairs and carefully emerged from hiding, leaving the harem for the last time.

Walking the short distance to the townhouse, she felt elated, like a SWAT mission had been accomplished. But she couldn't sustain the feeling. All it took to bring her down was the fountainlike sound of water splashing in her shower.

She finally ate—a little lentil soup—and fell asleep again. When she awoke in the early afternoon, she felt like a servant carrying the crown jewels—the sooner they got back where they belonged, the better. She decided to download as many photos as she could to the computer, then get online and forward them to Mohammed before she left for California.

But there was an instant message alert when her Internet page flashed up.

*It's Mohammed!*

Her heart jumped and she felt like a schoolgirl. The message on the screen read:

> *Angela—I tried to call tonight, but couldn't get you. I've been on island with DW doing research.*
>
> *I know who's leader of MB. I'm idiot for not knowing before. Also I'm idiot for how I treated you. When I think of your sacrifice, its amaze me. I am not worthy.*
>
> *Look, sister, this guy he's evil. I have to find him soon before he finds us. In e-mail I can't say who's this guy or where he is, but it's someplace you've been where they do what you do longer than anywhere. When I come back I'll tell sister aaaall about it. And if I don't come back—you know how to publish research. Please just don't call it* Manuscripts on Camels.
>
> *You are the best! I have loved you like myself since Palestine.*
>
> *Mohammed*

Angela read the letter again and again. The first time she was desperate to know where he was and what he was doing. The second time she read it to be sure that Mohammed had actually said that he loved her and wanted to see her. The third time she read it, realizing what he must face before she could see him again.

*Mohammed's life is in danger.*

Angela didn't know how she could help, but she knew she had to join him.

*Even if there is nothing I can do but hat a mop, I'm going!*

Angela was mostly packed and anxious to leave Istanbul.

*But where* is *Mohammed?*

She read the message a fourth time, scouring it for clues of where he could be. It said he was going somewhere she had been before. She wrote on a scrap of paper the places she and Mohammed had been together:

PALESTINE, JORDAN, LEBANON, SYRIA, TURKEY... *oh, yes, and* ISRAEL.

It should be one of those six countries.

*That doesn't narrow the field much.*

In addition to the places in those countries she and Mohammed had visited, there were numerous other cities. She knew Mohammed wasn't trying to give her clues, but there must be another one in his message.

*OK, there are some initials. What do they mean? The MB I think is fairly obvious. It must be the Mus-haf Brotherhood he talks about all the time. He has found out that its leader is in one of those six countries.*

*And someplace where they have been doing what I do the longest. What do I do? Or, more important, what does Mohammed think I do? God, I hope he's not talking about "the world's oldest profession"! No, he wouldn't insult me at the same time he says he loves me. Mohammed knows I—spend money, do charity, dance, research, write, teach....*

*Hmm, and "longer than anywhere." We know many cities claim to be the oldest....*

Chapter 127

# FEZ, MOROCCO

## August 17, 2006

Al-Maghreb.

That's the Arabic name for the country of Morocco. It means "the Sunset," and it is so called because Morocco is the western extent of the of the Arab/Muslim world. Thousands of miles remote from the Middle East, who would expect that the oldest Islamic university—in fact the oldest continuously operating institution of higher learning on planet Earth—is located at the heart of its medina?

Mohammed mentally kicked himself for overlooking this. His Middle Eastern mind-set had discounted Morocco. Being unique in its position as an Arab country just a few miles across the Straits of Gibraltar from Europe, it had acquired a flavor that Muslim purists considered contaminated.

Yet Morocco, conquered in AD 705, was an early center of Islam. The Karaouiyine University was founded in AD 859, in Fez, the dynasty's first capital. And over the thousand years that followed, the university's mosque was expanded until it could hold twenty thousand worshippers.

Scholars from the Karaouiyine University excelled in science as well as Islamic Studies. World cartographer al-Idrisi; the father of sociology, Ibn Khaldun; Leo Africanus, who wrote the first geography of Africa; and the Jewish philosopher Maimonides are among the medieval greats who studied there. During the middle ages, the Karaouiyine University served as a center of intellectual exchange between Muslims and Europeans. Its library still contains many rare books, including volumes written on gazelle parchment.

To this day Fez is a very religious city that proudly guards its Islamic past. Mohammed should have known the final researcher was from Fez.

Professor Hamzeh Kareem looked the same as he had in Yemen, when Mohammed called him "Wow." His office was buried in Fez's World Heritage Site—the largest medina in North Africa. Mohammed would never have found it, except that it was next to the Karaouiyine University in a renovated *riad*—a traditional home built around a central courtyard.

Ostensibly Mohammed was there to request permission to view the famous Koran donated to the university by Sultan Ahmed al-Mansur al-Dhahabi. Although the manuscript did interest him, he was actually there to confront Hamzeh with the bombing in Sana'a, and to accuse him of masterminding the deaths of researchers. If Hamzeh agreed to turn himself in to the international police, Mohammed would accompany him there. If not, he would... become resourceful.

Hamzeh had made mistakes. He counted his chickens before they hatched. His bin Laden–like boast about the explosion in Sana'a before it had happened had made it easy for Mohammed to track him.

Claiming to be from Leiden was foolish. Mohammed knew all the Islamic scholars of Leiden. In fact, thanks to Nasir's list, there were very few locations Hamzeh could have safely claimed to be from.

But how did Mohammed know he was from Fez?

Dialect. Modern standard Arabic is related to the classical Arabic of the Koran and is understood by all educated Arabs. But every country has its particular dialect, which is a combination of Arabic and other regional languages as they evolved over more than a millennium. The Arabic of Morocco is one of the most exotic dialects, being heavily influenced by French and the Berber languages of the native inhabitants.

Mohammed knew this. Through television Arabs become exposed to a variety of dialects. Hamzeh came from the educated elite of Morocco, whose first language was French. He also spoke Moroccan dialect and excellent modern standard Arabic. This is the language he used in his chat room on the Internet; the language he used to incite young Muslim men to rise up and defend the faith and its manuscripts from falling into infidel hands.

His Arabic had the slightest French accent. Very little, noticeable in just a few words now and then. But Mohammed had been studying his diction every day and had been composing a mental lexicon of his vocabulary, searching for anything that would betray him. And he found it.

About a month ago it dawned on Mohammed that the Mus-haf Brotherhood's leader spoke French. That meant he probably came from

France, Lebanon, parts of Asia, or North Africa; but he might not be living there now.

Then a few days ago it happened. Hamzeh made another slip. It probably would not mean much to most listeners, but Mohammed was a man whose life depended on finding a clue, no matter how small.

Hamzeh Kareem was frustrated at being thwarted in Sana'a. Mohammed could detect it by the increased anger and rapidity with which he spoke. He was more candid in his invective against the West and secular Muslims. In the midst of a tirade against *kufara*, or "infidels," he made a slip. He raved that "*in attempting to gain converts, Muslim organizations in the West even invite infidels into mosques for events and give them free Korans. OK, they must be converted, but they should not be allowed to touch the uncorrupted word of Allah in Arabic until they are. Their hands are the filthy hooves of pigs and paws of monkeys.*"

So went his hate speech. It was not all that different from what Mohammed had heard every week in Palestine, except for one word. The word used for "OK" was not "*kwayyes*" or "*na'am*" or one of the other common expressions.

It was "*wakha.*" A unique word, not from standard Arabic.

"What was *that*?" Mohammed had asked himself out loud.

In a guttural language like Arabic, such a word blended in. It might simply have been a random sound, but Mohammed wasn't convinced. He memorized the word and researched until he found its country of origin.

It was Moroccan. Then he remembered Fez. The hate-mongering murderer must be from the oldest Islamic university in the world.

And so, here he was sitting across from the international terrorist, Hamzeh Kareem.

Chapter 128

# HAMZEH KAREEM'S OFFICE

## Fez, Morocco

## August 17, 2006

"*Ya*, Hamzeh, we meet again! Amazing how we scholars frequent the same places," Mohammed Atareek said to Hamzeh Kareem. His speech was casual, but his eyes cautiously searched the room.

Hamzeh had a second-story corner office in a converted *riad.* On the outside, like most Fez buildings, the *riad* was plain white decomposing plaster, but inside, it was opulent with the handwork Fez was famous for.

It was early in the day and not yet hot. The intricately carved wooden shutters lay open. To the left, Hamzeh sat at his desk across from the window looking out onto the street; another window looked onto the courtyard. Mohammed sat to the right, facing Hamzeh.

Mohammed couldn't believe his eyes. He would not have to press Hamzeh to admit he was part of the Sana'a study group, since on a table to his right stood two drop-open manuscript boxes with the words "Dar al-Makhtutat," followed by its signature.

*Now if he only confesses to the murders and bombing attempt, this will be sooo easy!*

"You should learn not to tamper with other people's cell phones," was Hamzeh's response. He continued, "You have done other things not to my liking, Mr. Atareek."

As if paying no attention, Mohammed slowly lifted his foot, bent his knee, and looked at the sole of his shoe. "Did I dirty your Berber carpets with my old shoes?" he asked. "That's what I get for not buying a pair of Fez leather slippers!"

Mohammed kept his leg crossed with the sole of his shoe directly in Hamzeh's face, a blatant insult in Arab culture. But that was the least he felt for the man who had made Maarten Hoog's wife a widow and his three young children orphans.

"Your shoes do not trouble me at all. What I cannot understand, however, is how you, a Muslim, and a caretaker of the Holy Koran, can kill your brother Muslims."

"Simple," Mohammed said with a big smile and an upturned palm. "They had nasty habits." Mohammed leaned forward, looked left and right in a confidential manner, and whispered, "They were murderers."

"That's not the way I see it," Hamzeh said, sounding much more reasonable than he had the last time Mohammed heard him on the Web. "They were *shaheeds*. Holy warriors. Those they killed were infidels. Under Islamic law, no one is to be killed for killing an infidel." Hamzeh stood up, still speaking calmly.

"I could argue very effectively that most of them were *not* infidels...."

"Only as defined by those who *are* infidels. And Mr. Atareek, do you remember the penalty for one who opposes Allah's warriors?"

"Are you talking about the cutting off of the hands and feet followed by crucifixion? Sura 5:33 is not a verse I care to apply," Mohammed said. He shrugged and waved his hand. "Let's abrogate it!"

Kareem was not amused. He stood. Mohammed didn't like that. It seemed to signal an end to the interview, and he had not yet had a chance to present his proposal. The power play was going the wrong way. Mohammed started looking around for options.

"Have you noticed the excellent *zellij* tile work in this *riad*?" Hamzeh asked, pulling out a gun. "And the carved plaster on the posts and arches? It would be a shame to damage it, don't you agree? So I will have to ask you to come with me to another place where we won't need to worry about your blood on the carpets."

## Chapter 129

# HAMZEH KAREEM'S OFFICE
## Medina of Fez, Morocco
## August 17, 2006

*Should I jump?*

Mohammed was closer to the window than the door. From his seat, he knew the courtyard was below. If he jumped, he would have a head start, but he had no idea of what lay directly beneath the window. And he was betting that Hamzeh would not want to use a gun in the *riad* and draw attention to his true plan and nature.

*I'll do it!*

Mohammed was surprised at his self-control: he left Hamzeh's manuscripts on the table. He would make better time carrying nothing and increase his chance of escaping. If he got out alive, he could get the police and come back for Hamzeh and the manuscripts. It was a "winner takes it all" situation. If Hamzeh caught him first, he hoped that no one would think of looking for Angela when he was dead.

Mohammed quickly jumped onto the table next to the boxed Koranic manuscripts and out to the window ledge. He latched his fingers through a latticed shutter, hoping it would hold into the wall long enough to lower him gently to the floor of the courtyard fifteen feet below.

The shutter not only held, but it let him swing around to aim his descent before breaking off. Mohammed jumped onto a potted palm tree, grabbing its branches as he roughly slid to the ground. A few splinters from the shattering shutter grazed him as it fell, creating a racket. Then the brass planter with the palm fell over, clanging loudly as it hit the tile floor.

Hamzeh wanted to cut Mohammed off at the pass, if possible. He ran out of his office, through the low corridor with the carved plaster ceiling, and down the stairs.

Several of the workers' bicycles were parked inside near the entrance of the courtyard. Hearing the noise, a worker emerged into the courtyard, looking shocked.

Mohammed smiled at him and said, "*Areed a-shay, mu al-an, ba'dayn, min fudlak*," as if the man were a waiter in one of the hotels of Fez. Then he picked a large bicycle and rode into one of the thousand alleyways of the Fez medina.

Instinctively, he turned right. The crowd was thick. Unbeknownst to him, just as he pulled ahead, Angela came from the left, the direction of the mosque, to the gate of the *riad*. She recognized Mohammed's back on the bike, although he did not see her.

*Mohammed!*

Hamzeh followed him, also on a bicycle.

*And Hamzeh!*

"Oh, my God, it's Fatima's brother!" Angela said aloud. She grabbed a bike and turned down the road, following what she hoped was their trail.

After getting Mohammed's e-mail, Angela had checked the Internet for the oldest university in the world, and found it in Fez. Then she vaguely remembered having heard about it from Fatima when she told Angela about her family. At the time it didn't seem to matter that her brother was a professor at the oldest university in the world.

Angela had left Istanbul later than Mohammed had left Scotland; but he had a longer trip, needing to take a boat and a train before he could get to an airport. Angela was close to a major airport. So they had arrived in Fez nearly simultaneously.

Walking the medina of Fez is one of the most amazing experiences in the world. Trying to escape through it pushes the limit of imagination. The network of these passages is so complex that they were not mapped until recently—and then by satellite. But escape is what Mohammed had to do. To get out alive and to get help.

Biking is the fastest way to get through the medina, but you can't count on the "fastest" part. To call it an obstacle course is an understatement. It's a donkey's world. Anything that is delivered or otherwise needs transportation must be moved on donkey back or human back. The ways are narrow, only twenty inches wide at some places. They are filled with and frequently blocked by people—residents, shoppers, tourists—and merchandise.

From the Karaouiyine Mosque the medina is laid out with related craft stalls clustered together. The shops that line the paths are open to view and are little deeper than a closet. Mohammed hit them all—literally. The fallout from this trailblazing fell into Hamzeh's path and helped keep him behind.

Outside the mosque a group of men in *jelabas* was coming to prayer. Pushed aside by the bicycles, these men were the first casualties. A few fell. The men would have to be more vigorous in their *wudoo* cleaning ritual that day.

Seeing what happened to the worshippers, other people started scuffling out of the way, screaming. From the commotion created, one would think they were racing motorcycles, but in the ancient and cramped world of the medina, bicycles were modern speed machines. And the three were pedaling for their very lives.

Mohammed turned a corner into the spice market. Stall after stall had domes of artfully displayed spices on top of barrels, intense with color and the odors of sumac, cumin, and saffron. Every morning the spices were remolded into their characteristic shape, which resembled the conical lid of a traditional *tagine* cooking dish.

The shop workers, standing near their wares, looked nervous as they saw the bikers approach. Two small children were throwing a ball in the street. They dashed inside a spice stall. As they ran, their ball escaped and bounced into a spice heap, sending a cloud of spices into the air. Some of it blew onto Mohammed.

A bowl of spice slid into the street where Hamzeh could not avoid it. He ran through the clay dish, breaking it and scattering spice through the street. It blew a cloud of red smoke onto his face, which set him coughing and blinking.

Angela rode around the spice disaster to the left but got a trim of red on the hem of her khaki skirt.

The shopkeeper held one of the children in his arm, and waved a fist after the bikers, cursing in Arabic. As people scuffled out of the way, some slipped in the spices. Other incidents of spice mixing occurred as the three made their way past other shops. As a result, the trail through the spice market was decorated with blotches of orange, yellow, and red. Colored footprints led away in every direction.

Mohammed turned left into the metalwork alley. An old man was sharpening knives and scissors on a huge whetstone in the doorway of his miniscule shop. Hamzeh reached out and pushed a woman into the sharpening shop to clear his path. The newly sharpened knife was grabbed out of the way just in time as the woman stumbled into the shop and fell against the whetstone, abrading her hand.

Several shops were selling metalwork of different varieties. There were lamps and water pipes in a shop to the left. The copperware shops had their wares hung along the walls, between the open doorways of shops and the closed doors of living quarters. Stacked on the street were large copper and brass planters, stewpots, and water jugs.

There was a small expansion of the street in this zone that served as a square. In the overpopulated medina, this relatively spacious spot tempted children of all ages to come kick a ball.

Mohammed entered the makeshift square and swerved to the right to get around a donkey on his left. In so doing, he bumped against one of the metal pots along the wall, causing it to bang against the next vessel. Subsequently each vessel in turn clanged against its neighbor. Two of the top pots fell off and brought down more on the underlying level, starting an avalanche. Numerous vessels of varied shape found their way to the cobblestone pavement of the medina. Loud resounding sounds were heard as cauldrons fell, followed by higher-pitched clanging from small pots.

There was a slight grade in the trail that sent the pots rolling down toward Hamzeh and Angela. Robed old men were sitting catty-corner from the shop, drinking coffee and fingering worry beads. The flashing and clanging that erupted were of the likes they had never seen or heard before.

Brightly polished pans and jugs flashed as they rolled around. Delighted, the children abandoned kicking the ball in favor of the pots. When Hamzeh entered the square, the children were squealing with enjoyment, running all over, chasing pots and making riotous sounds with their new game. The shop owner played defense, darting back and forth, collecting his merchandise and batting at the children. One child, too small to play, sat beside an inverted pot and drummed it with a spoon, loudly trying to sing and pleasing himself immensely.

Hamzeh, attempting to avoid the children and the pots, looked like a character in a pinball machine. He tried weaving around the commotion, but it slowed him remarkably. Then the shop owner struck a child. The child fell into Hamzeh's bike, knocking it over. Hamzeh roughly pushed the child off and got up. He tried to walk his way through the remainder of square.

A group of children scuffled for a pot by Hamzeh's feet. In the confusion Hamzeh stepped into the pot and couldn't shake it off. He was so frustrated at the delay that he remounted the bike and rode ahead with the pot on his foot. The shop owner, encumbered by a variety of pots with their handles over his arms and one on his head, chased him, yelling and clanging. The children laughed hysterically, as if they had suddenly become part of a staged comedy.

When Angela rode up, she saw Hamzeh trying to walk away with a pot on his foot, while being laughed at and chased. One of the brass pots that an older boy kicked hit a large copper platter of about three feet in diameter. The platter started rolling down the street directly toward Angela.

Angela would have been knocked over by it, but she stopped, turned her bike perpendicular to it, and waited as it rolled toward her. With a maneuver worthy of a soccer star, Angela stopped the platter with the bottom of her shoe, then pushed and reset it in motion. It rolled a short way up the hill, finishing with a circular spin, like a huge copper penny.

The crowd of children watched and went wild. Angela laughed with them, then took a bow and jumped back on her bicycle, now significantly behind the men.

Mohammed was pleased by the activity behind him, knowing that Hamzeh was waylaid at "street soccer" but not realizing Angela was there too.

His lead was short-lived.

Mohammed turned left onto a street of carpet makers. He cut the corner close and ended up to the left of center on the road. On the left, a display of carpets hung perpendicular to the front of a shop. He couldn't pull back into the center of the road because it was filled by a tour group that had just exited a different carpet shop. So he ducked and tried to focus straight ahead. The effect was like a kaleidoscope, as beautiful hand-knotted carpets hit Mohammed's head one after another—blue, red, brown, yellow, green, and burgundy.

At the end of the string of carpets, the crowd totally blocked the street. Mohammed had to get off of his bicycle.

On this street, carpets were both sold and produced. Out of the corner of his eye he caught sight of looms with girls attending them.

Mohammed started pushing through the crowd, insistently but smiling and trying to look casual.

Slap!

*What the hell?*

Mohammed had accidentally groped a veiled local woman who was mixed in with the tourists. Looking back he apologized and hopped back on the bike.

He didn't look straight ahead.

Mohammed faced an obstacle as unique as it was unexpected: a father and son team performing an unusual form of weaving. The father sat inside his closet-sized workroom, which was too small to hold a traditional loom. He had found a solution. His son became one end of the loom. Standing out in the street, he held about six cords and moved them in tandem with his father, who leaned over a textile on his lap. Whenever anyone came by, the boy would step out of the way, essentially moving the entire loom with him. Usually, he had time to give his father notice that he would have to move, but when Mohammed burst out from the crowed, he and his father were deep in a technical maneuver. The boy could not move fast enough, and it spelled disaster for their project.

Mohammed screamed, "Get out of the way!" in Arabic as he rode unavoidably right into the cords.

He was tangled like a fly in a spider's web. It's nearly impossible to stand still at a time like that; so rather than trust the nimble fingers of the boy to release him, he did more harm than good by struggling to get out.

As he was pulled free, Mohammed smiled broadly and exclaimed in relief, "You are the best, the best spider I know!"

It only took a minute to free him, but it was enough time for Hamzeh to catch up. The tourists had moved into another shop, so the road was clear. Mohammed's moments were numbered.

Chapter 130

# MEDINA OF FEZ, MOROCCO
## August 17, 2006

Mohammed knew he could not escape. He thought fast and reached into his pocket.

*Yes, I have change!*

He threw it into the air, loudly calling in Arabic, "For the beautiful children of Fez!"

It's amazing how children appear when money is thrown. Hamzeh's progress was not only impeded by the children's presence but now by their purpose as well. Mohammed had wagered on the power of generosity to affirm goodness, and it worked. Children aged five to fifteen determined that Mohammed was the good guy being chased by a bad guy. Bored, they were excited to have an adversary.

They did everything from throw rotten food at Hamzeh to bite his ankles above the pedal. The largest boy grabbed the handle bars of Hamzeh's bike and demanded equal money to what Mohammed had paid, as tribute to allow him to pass.

Mohammed quickly mounted his bike. He passed through a quiet alley where nothing seemed to be going on. At the end he turned right and entered the butcher's street. There was a small private dwelling immediately to the right. As he turned, an old woman opened her front door and shook out a carpet. The action, dust, and distraction made him swerve left into the first butcher shop. Cuts of lamb and chicken were laid out on the open-air counter facing the street, which served as the front wall. A man was hanging a large piece of meat above the counter in the manner that meat was hung in all the shops. Mohammed ran over his foot. The worker screamed and turned, grabbing his foot and dropping the meat.

Two surprises hit Mohammed. First—the meat fell into the basket of his bike. Second—the meat was a camel head, intact with eyes, fur, and teeth. The insipid smile on the camel's face took Mohammed aback. He hadn't known dead camels could look so happy.

*Those lips!*

Mohammed pushed himself to drive on, camel or no camel.

This did not please the meat vendor. He ran after Mohammed. Hamzeh passed the vendor on his bicycle. The vendor yelled at Hamzeh in Arabic, "*Waqif hada al-jamal!*" Behind him ran the pot man.

Other meat shops flew past Mohammed as he rode, each with exposed cuts of meat attracting flies.

Then the street merged into a grocer's street. The first shop sold dates. Rich shades of gold and brown in a wide variety of oval sizes were stacked up neatly in display. Mohammed passed without incident.

The shopkeeper, however, was standing on the street to be sure passersby did not sample his wares. He was amazed by the sight of a camel head casually situated in a bike basket. He stepped out of his shop to take a look. His timing was off, because at that moment, Hamzeh came racing down the street and shamelessly sideswiped him. The worker lost his balance. His knees collapsed, and he fell down and backward. In an attempt to right himself, he reached out with both hands and placed his elbows on two display tables.

Date display tables are not built for leaning on or for catching people who duck from camel heads on bicycles. The tables fell forward, spilling dates and rolling them onto the floor and into the street.

The shop owner chased Hamzeh yelling, "Hey, come back and pay for these dates."

By the time Angela rode up to and over the dates, quite an entourage was forming: the camel head, then Mohammed, Hamzeh, the three workers, and Angela in the rear followed by children.

The street was narrow.

There were three donkeys parked ahead for loading and unloading.

The first donkey on the left had baskets on both sides: oranges on the street side and prickly pears on the other.

Mohammed swerved to the right around the first donkey, then to the left to get around the donkey on the right. This second donkey was parked in front of a bread closet-shop, and had round loaves of fresh *khubis* bread stacked in baskets on his sides, ready for delivery. His owner had ambitiously stacked more loaves than wise in a basket on his back as well.

The third donkey, on the left, had old blankets on its back, on which he was balancing flour sacks. Mohammed easily cleared it with a fast swerve to the right.

Hamzeh was not so lucky. The master of the fruit-laden donkey came out to take off the orange basket, and when he unhitched it, he accidentally dumped the fruit onto the ground. Avoiding the oranges was impossible for Hamzeh. He collided with a few, one of which redirected his wheel so that he hit the donkey with the bread. Loaves fell into his basket.

Angela could tell which way the men had gone by the train of disorder in their wake.

*Yes, this is the way.*

Mohammed hung a very hard right onto a street with handicraft workshops. An old man was sitting cross-legged, wearing a white jelaba and tight hat. He was stitching a gold cartouche trim onto a boy's blue velvet jacket.

To the right was a clothing store that sold the hand-crafted caftans Morocco makes for tourists. Angela was catching up. As she drove by this store, a salesman held up a beautiful caftan with gold trim and matching hooded cape. He tried his favorite line on her, "*Voulez vous ça pour votre mariage?*"

Angela disappointed him by riding right past.

Another tiny shop had a woodworker making intricate cutwork designs with colored wood and mother-of-pearl inlay. He stopped and looked up from his work in wonder at the parade zooming past.

Mohammed had unwittingly found the narrowest section of the medina. At the end of the next street were the pottery and tile shops.

*Oh, no! Oh, no! Not that!*

Straight ahead of him Mohammed saw exactly what he had been most dreading. A single donkey in front of the pottery shop, packed with one box on each side, so that he totally blocked the way.

Mohammed yelled, "Move the donkey!" but no one came out of the shop. He drove his bike up to the animal's tail and stopped. He called again for help, but none came.

The meat vendor had finally caught up with Mohammed.

Between cries for help, Mohammed casually picked up the camel head and deposited it into the waiting arms of the screaming meat vendor.

The vendor immediately changed. He showed not the slightest anger or resentment. He simply walked off, embracing the camel head and wearing a contented smile, as if he were promenading his wife.

Close behind the meat vendor was Hamzeh. Mohammed could wait no longer. He had to take action.

He pulled the donkey's tail. No motion.

He was sure Hamzeh's gun was in his pocket. Mohammed did what he had to.

Since the donkey didn't kick when he pulled its tail the first time, he used it as a fulcrum to leap atop the animal.

He spoke to it. "Little donkey, if a Dutch bull couldn't stop Mohammed, you have nooo chance!"

He quickly scrambled over the boxes on top of the donkey to get beyond and over. The donkey groaned under the increased weight and shook reflexively.

Then it happened. The ropes loosened. First the left box, followed by the right box, dropped off the donkey. Their fall to the stone pavement was accompanied by loud crashing sounds.

Now the shopkeeper noticed. He ran out hollering just as Hamzeh was trying to climb the donkey.

So Hamzeh got the blame. The owner pulled him down, and an argument started.

Angela rode up. She quietly set her bike against a building to the left. While Hamzeh was arguing to the right, she started to climb over the crate of broken pottery to pass.

Seeing action in the corner of his eye, Hamzeh turned around. "*La! Ya!* No, you don't!" he yelled in Arabic as he threw her roughly to the ground and passed in her place. His eye rested on her only a split second, enough to recognize her as someone he knew, but he couldn't place her.

Angela sat on the ground with a much bruised bottom and dusty hands. The pottery shopkeeper then laid into her in French, hoping to get some remuneration. She surprised him by responding in indignant Arabic.

"*Mit akid*, certainly you know I have nothing whatever to do with this mess," she said, brushing herself off. "I have to go now." She started to leave, but, hating to be rude, she added, "I'll come back to look at your nice majolica."

Angela ran off. She had lost track of which way the men went. She ran up the alleylike road and frantically looked up each branch. There was no trace of them.

## Chapter 131

# MEDINA OF FEZ, MOROCCO
## August 17, 2006

Something did not smell wholesome. It was a sour, rancid smell that Mohammed couldn't register.

Mohammed was nauseated, and on top of that he was lost. He wasn't frightened or claustrophobic, like a Westerner might be, but he was anxious from the chase—and from not knowing which way to go.

*What's the point of running to nowhere?*

He heard footsteps behind him. A shot ran out.

*That's the point!*

Mohammed turned left up a very narrow passage with a few irregular stairs at the end, leading to he knew not what. It was not the kind of passage he liked being in when he was being shot at, but at least it wasn't a dead end—in more ways than one.

He ran up the stairs and was overcome with the sight and pungent smell that hit him like a wall.

*A tannery.*

So that was it. The sour smell. One of the *chouaras*, the tanneries of Fez. Here its world-famous leather is made by hand and foot in the time-honored way.

Fez's tanneries are open-air assemblies of round vats the size of Jacuzzi tubs, fused back-to-back like a giant slice of honeycomb. As intense as the smell are the colors in the brick and tile vats: deep opaque shades of blue, green, yellow, and red. Men in caps stand in the vats, bent over leather in various stages of curing. Then the hides are hung on the walls and roofs of the surrounding buildings to dry.

Here Mohammed faced tactical problems. The tannery was a large open space with little area to hide. There were about a hundred and fifty vats in this complex, which gave Hamzeh an open space to track him. To get through the tannery, Mohammed would have to walk on the narrow brick ledges between the vats, the upper rims of which seemed to be made of little more than crumbling mud.

But along the left edge he saw something else. There was a donkey path between the vats and the buildings. If he ran around to the left, he could get away faster.

Maybe if he knocked, someone would open one of the doors along the trail. Still, there was no cover to speak of if Hamzeh chose to use his gun—the vats were only about three feet above the ground, which wouldn't shield the donkey path. He was rather sure that Hamzeh's family honor in Fez would keep him from shooting when so many innocent workers were present.

Hamzeh's reconnoitering only took a few seconds, but it was enough for him to see Mohammed's head from the top of the steps. Hamzeh was so close to him that Mohammed decided his best way out was through the vats. He trusted that his skills—and shoes—were more dexterous than Hamzeh's.

Mohammed climbed onto the vat complex. His first bet was right. Hamzeh did not pull out a gun. Mohammed started walking like an uneasy tightrope walker, foot in front of foot, until he got the feel for it.

Angela was still checking the alleyways. She wanted to see what was above the stairs leading to the tannery. When she got to the top, Mohammed was just getting his footing sure, and Hamzeh had made it to the vats.

"Mohammed!" she yelled out, instantly sorry because both Hamzeh and Mohammed turned to look at her. In the case of Hamzeh, this was good. It delayed his entry into the vat field until Mohammed was secure. But in the case of Mohammed, it was a disaster.

*My God, it's Angela!*

Mohammed lost his footing.

*Oh, no! He fell.*

Mohammed slipped into a vat of cobalt blue dye.

Hamzeh was angry with Angela for no reason, since her presence would obviously make it easier for him. He wanted to turn on her and grab her as a hostage.

*That's Angela! Fatima's friend. The one who was with her when she died.*

Angela did not like the fact that Hamzeh was chasing Mohammed, nor the look on his face as he turned to her. Rather than run away and become an easy hostage, as Hamzeh had hoped, she startled him by running toward him and pushing him into a vat of saffron yellow dye.

Men from all over the vat yard noticed the action. Glad for distraction, and sensing a fight coming on, they came from both ends toward this central section. A few enterprising fellows started taking bets

Angela ran to another trail, to the right, not seeing that it terminated quickly. Hamzeh pulled himself out of the vat. He still thought catching Angela would be the fastest way to force Mohammed to go with him to a remote place. So he ran after her.

Mohammed had been balance-walking toward Hamzeh's vat when Hamzeh got out and followed Angela. Mohammed then adjusted his course to intercept Hamzeh before he got to Angela.

Going through the vat yard was more direct than taking the path, but it was a lot more precarious. Several times Mohammed's foot slipped, and he wavered. So he lifted out his arms like a soaring bird to help him keep balanced.

But he didn't get to Angela first. Hamzeh did.

Angela decided not to wait around for Hamzeh's embrace. She climbed up onto the vat yard. Hamzeh climbed up right behind her. He got his arms around her and started to pull backward, toward the donkey trail. Angela dug her heels into the friable surface of the thin ledge under her feet.

*I'm not going away with Hamzeh!*

Keeping her heels down meant her bottom began to sag. Hamzeh's grip slipped. He dropped Angela into the vat of orange dye.

Hamzeh left Angela and ran off, hoping he'd come up with another idea of how to get Mohammed.

But he didn't have time to think. Mohammed caught up with him as he was just about to jump off the vat field. He grabbed the back of Hamzeh's shirt and unsettled him enough that he once again fell, this time into a vat of green dye.

Hamzeh reached out from his vat and pulled on Mohammed's ankles. The ledge under Mohammed's feet was slippery, and he also lost his grip and fell into another vat of blue dye.

By now Mohammed and Hamzeh were color saturated; even their heads were colored. Angela stood up in her vat. Her clothes were stained orange and clung closely to her body—a sight not lost on the workers, who cheered for it as much as the fight.

Angela didn't notice. She was looking around for something like a mop handle.

As if they were participants in a newly invented form of box-wrestling, the two men stood in their respective vats.

Hamzeh hit Mohammed—one punch on his right arm and one that

grazed his belly. Mohammed hit Hamzeh on the chin. Hamzeh grabbed Mohammed around the waist, but because Mohammed was taller, he was unable to bring him down.

Angela found something. There had to be a use for the stack of leather pelts passing by on the donkey's back. She climbed out of the vat, giving the workers more curves to cheer over, and jumped down onto the donkey trail. She grabbed several pelts and set them on the edge of the ledge.

The workers did nothing to stop her. They were curious to see what use she would make of them.

Mohammed and Hamzeh were rocking back and forth, occasionally socking each other.

Angela took a pelt over to Hamzeh and threw it at him. He reflexively reached back, but she avoided his punch. For her second attack Angela kept a safe distance from his arm as she threw the pelt.

That was the moment Hamzeh bent his head down. The pelt whacked Mohammed in the face.

"Hey! Whose side are you on, woman?"

"Sorry!"

Hamzeh took advantage of their momentary loss of focus to flail his arm backward again. This time he knocked Angela into a vat of poppy-red dye. As she slid down, she dragged the hides in with her. Then she stood up, dripping coral pink.

Angela reached back into the vat, fishing for hides, and came up even more pink, colored up to her neck and hair. She flicked Hamzeh's head with the dripping red hide as someone might flick a wet towel.

The smacking sound was audible even to the watching workers. The ones who bet on Mohammed cheered. They hadn't a clue of what the fight was about or who was right or wrong. But this was entertainment!

Angela had an idea. If she could get a hide big enough and throw it just right, she and Mohammed might be able to tie it over Hamzeh's head and disable him.

Angela hunted on the bottom of the red dye vat. She slipped on the muddy bottom and fell, covering what was left of her head in pink. She pulled up hides until she found a large one. Then she climbed out of the vat to get height advantage and slapped the hide onto Hamzeh's head.

This gave Mohammed the free arm he needed to punch Hamzeh solidly on the chin. Hamzeh's head went back. He hit his neck on the back of the vat. His mouth fell open and his gold tooth flashed from the right.

Hamzeh wasn't unconscious, but he was dazed enough that Angela and Mohammed could tie up his head in leather. They worked together as if it had been planned, crossing the leg portions of the hide from front to back, and vice versa, so that his neck was surrounded. They pulled the hide down over his face so that he couldn't see but left a flap for breathing. Angela got another hide, which they used to tie Hamzeh's hands behind his back.

Hamzeh was safely immobilized.

Then Angela picked up another hide and intentionally hit Mohammed with it. Caught unawares, he fell back into his blue vat.

"That's for leaving me in Istanbul!" she said in English, not wanting the onlookers to understand.

Mohammed stood up, dragging the hide with him. He looped it around Angela's ankle and pulled. Angela fell back into an adjacent vat of red dye.

"And that's because pink's my favorite flavor," he said.

Angela thought he was confused in his English again. "I thought blue was your favorite color?"

They stood looking at each other from their respective vats—Mohammed totally stained blue and Angela totally pink. It was another moment when life seemed to stand on the edge, about to color itself one way or the other.

Mohammed gave a smile and reached out.

"Ooooh, that's my smart seesterr! She remembers blue is my favorite color." He put both his arms around her and said, "But I said pink is my favorite flavor."

Mohammed pulled Angela close to him and gave her a kiss worthy of all the colors of the rainbow.

The onlookers, who now included the children of the medina, went wild with applause and catcalls. From one of the neighboring doorways, a small group of musicians emerged, a banquet appeared as if out of nowhere, and before long this tanning neighborhood of Fez was singing and dancing. Even the caftan merchant was there, holding up his gold brocade set and saying, "You wear this for your wedding!"

# Epilogue

# ATLANTIC COAST OF MOROCCO
## August 19, 2006

Somewhere along the deserted beach between Essaouira and Agadir, two figures walked in the surf at sunset. One wore a *haik*, the sheetlike wrap of the women of Essaouira. The other threw his arms wide apart and said, "Now we can be happy, sister. We have nooo problems!"

Life again was good. The Topkapi Codex was photographed and would soon be published; the Mus-haf Brotherhood was exposed, its leader arrested, the murders stopped, Dar al-Makhtutat saved, and Angela's research completed. To top it off, after hours of soaking, the dye even washed off. The lovers were together on the beach.

"Hmm. You make it sound like we're dead."

"Not today. Let's have fun first!"

"You mean like, uncover Koranic variants lost in the Agadir earthquake of 1960?"

Mohammed looked serious and rubbed his chin. "Sounds interesting.... But there's something better to uncover," he said, purposely pulling on the edge of her *haik*. The twisting motion unwound Angela and tumbled her onto the sand, exposing her white bathing suit with gold Moroccan braid.

Spray flew into the air as the tide cast a wave against a nearby rock. Mist sprinkled down. Angela batted it, laughing. Her hair glowed in the fading sunlight, and the droplets on her skin sparkled like diamonds.

Mohammed stood, hands on his hips, looking at Angela with the smile that climbed to his eyes. "Sister, you are covered with ocean spray," he said.

"Whose fault is that, I wonder!"

There was a subtle crunching sound as Mohammed fell on his knees in the sand beside Angela. Lowering his head, he spoke softly, saying, "I wonder... if sea salt tastes as good as dye."

Mohammed gently moved his lips up her glistening skin. When he reached Angela's mouth, he hovered over it a breathless second while his hand pulled the *haik* to cover them both. Sea breeze billowed into the *haik*, making it their private tent.

As the sun melded with the ocean in the west, the sky blushed from orange to pink. A minute horse silhouette was seen on the sand in the distant north. From the east a voice called the faithful to sunset prayer. Its mournful sound was like the cry of a dying tyrant, who would soon release his captives to the dawn of a better day.

THE END

*POSTSCRIPT: In 2007, Topkapi Palace finally published the Topkapi Codex of the Koran. It is currently under academic study, but preliminary findings show significant variations from other ancient texts of the Koran, as well as the 1924 Cairo edition used by most Muslims in the world today.*

Appendix 1.

# GLOSSARY

## ENGLISH TERMS AND TERMS ADAPTED INTO ENGLISH

**Boiserie.** French-style paneling.

**Coup de grâce.** French term referring to a decisive event.

**Déjà vu.** French term meaning "already seen"; describes the feeling that one has been in a certain place or situation before.

**Orthography.** The study of writing.

**Textual criticism.** The scientific study of old manuscripts. The purpose of textual criticism is to:

- record existing variants,
- discover how a document developed over time as a result of these changes, and
- reconstruct the most likely original wording of the document.

Some ancient manuscripts, such as the Bible, have been heavily subjected to textual criticism and have had their variants documented. The Koran, however, which upon preliminary criticism has much textual variation, has not been subjected to such examination. Access to old manuscripts has been denied to scholars. Of particular interest are the Topkapi Codex of Topkapi Palace in Istanbul and the pre-Uthmanic Korans from Sana'a. This author joins with academics in calling for open and objective examination of Koranic manuscripts by qualified researchers from around the world, including non-Muslim academics.

**Tuff.** Soft volcanic ash rock.

**Voila!** French exclamation meaning, literally, "See there!"

# ARABIC TERMS

Note: When Arabic words are converted into English, there can be a variety of different renderings of spellings. The variants are especially noticeable in those words that begin with *al/el* (meaning "the"), because of the interchangeable short vowels *a* and *e*, and words beginning with *o* and *u*, for similar reasons (for example: *Omar* and *Umar* are the same name). Other variants include the long *a* sound, which may be written as *ei* or *ay*, for example, in *beit* and *bayt*, both of which mean "house."

**Abaya.** Full-length robelike covering.

***Abd.*** Literally "slave"; the common Arabic term for people of the black race.

***Ahlan wa sahlan.*** "Welcome."

***Akhty.*** "My sister."

***Akhuy.*** "My brother."

***Al-bayt baytik.*** "Our house is your house."

***al-Bukhari.*** A collector and screener of hadiths, or traditions, of Islam.

***Alhamdulillah.*** "Praise God!" (an everyday expression)

**Al Jazeera.** Independent international Arabic news station, commonly viewed all over the world by Arabs.

***Allahu akbar.*** "God is great!" (used as an expression of religious zeal and as a call to worship)

***Al-mohalil.*** "The legalizer," a name given to the man who is designated to have sex with a divorced woman before she can remarry her former husband. This is still practiced today, based on sura 2:229, 230.

***Areed a-shay mu al-an, ba'dayn, min fudlak.*** "I would like tea, but later please."

***Ashoura.*** Shiite holiday commemorating the death of holy men in battle, who are considered martyrs. These martyrs are called upon to intercede for the faithful with acts of self-discipline and punishments of varying intensities.

***Asif/asfay.*** "I'm sorry." (male/female spellings)

***Awa.*** "Yes."

***Baksheesh.*** Tip or alms.

***Bismallah Ir-Rahman Ir-Raheem.*** "In the name of Allah the merciful and compassionate."

***Burj.*** Tower.

***Chouaras.*** Tanneries.

***Da'wa.*** Outreach. (literally "invitation")

***Enti.*** "You." (feminine)

***Fahalawy.*** A uniquely Arab type of personality characterized by a strong sense of humor, overconfidence, and a drive to please people.

***Fiqh.*** The term means "deep understanding" but refers to legal advisements in Islam made through jurisprudence on issues on which the Koran is silent or less clear than "Divine," or Sharia law.

***Habeebee.*** "Dear" or "beloved." (spoken to a male)

***Habeebtee.*** "Dear" or "beloved." (spoken to a female)

***Hada zowjick?*** "This is your husband?"

**Hadith.** A story or tradition from the early days of Islam. These were not written until about 220 years after the death of Mohammed.

***Haik.*** A woman's wrap made from a single piece of fabric, which is draped around the body.

***Halaka.*** Circle, especially one formed for storytelling.

**Halal.** Food prepared according to Islamic standards, especially meats (similar to kosher preparation).

***Hamam.*** "Bath" in both Arabic and Turkish.

***Haram!*** "Disgraceful!"

***Hezbollah.*** Also spelled *Hizbollah* or *Hezballah.* A Shiite political group in Lebanon, meaning "God's army," considered by some to be a terrorist group.

**Hijab.** Traditional head scarf.

***Illi faat maat.*** "Let bygones be bygones."

***ImmMohammed/UmmMohammed/OmmMohammed.*** "Mother of Mohammed." The characters in this novel use the word Immohammed rather than the more common Arabic UmmMohammed or OmmMohammed because they are Palestinian, and in that dialect the word is pronounced ImmMohammed.

***Isnad.*** A chain of those transmitting a hadith, an Islamic tradition, allegedly from the time written, extending back to the time of the Prophet Mohammed.

***Jumma'.*** "Friday"; also a way of referring to the weekly midday prayer service on that day.

***Kaslan/Kaslana.*** "Lazy." (male and female spellings)

***Kathir.*** "A lot," "much."

***Khalia.*** Meat preserved in rancid fat, a Moroccan specialty.

**Khan.** A caravanserai, or inn for caravans.

***Khubis.*** Flat bread.

***Khutbah.*** Sermon at a mosque.

***Kwayyes.*** "OK."

***La.*** "No."

***Lebany.*** Soft cheese made by hanging plain yogurt overnight in cheesecloth, so that the moisture drains out.

***Lesh La?*** "Why not?"

***Majnoon/majnoona.*** Crazy. (male/female spellings)

***Masahaf.*** Manuscripts.

***Ma tkuny.*** "Don't be." (said to a female)

***Minsaf.*** Palestinian casserole.

***Misyar.*** Temporary marriage in the Sunni sect. This arrangement usually involves the man paying a woman's parents for the right to have sexual visits with her for a designated time period, rather than the couple living together.

***Mit akid?*** "Is it certain?" "Are you sure?"

***Mit akid al-ethnane matu?*** "Are you certain they are both dead?"

***Mubeen.*** "Clear"; what the Koran claims to be, although even experts find it confusing.

***Mukhtar.*** An elder or leader whose counsel is valued.

***Mumtaz.*** "Wonderful."

***Mus-haf.*** Koran manuscript.

**Mus-haf Brotherhood.** A fictitious extremist organization, formed to defend the Koran and prevent exposure of its origin from those who would use it against Islam.

***Muta'a.*** "Marriage of pleasure." Temporary marriage for Shi'a Muslims. It is less popular with the Sunnis. Usually it involves living together for a set period, which results in a payment to the woman.

***Sah.*** "Right?"

***Sahih al-Bukhari.*** The investigated "truthful" hadiths of the chronicler al-Bukhari, which were assembled over two hundred years after Mohammed's death. Considered to be one of the most reliable sources on the Prophet Mohammed by Sunnis.

***Sahil.*** "Easy."

***Salat al-Janaza.*** Islamic funeral.

***Shabaab.*** Young single men.

***Shahadah. La ilaha illallah, Muhammad-ur-Rasul-Allah.*** "None has the right to be worshipped but Allah, and Muhammad is the Messenger of Allah." The Muslim statement of faith, first of the Five Pillars of Islam. To become Muslim, an accountable person must say and believe the *shahadah.* It requires not only recognition of God but also of Mohammed.

***Shaheed.*** Martyr in the cause of Allah.

***Shay*** or ***a-shay.*** Tea.

***Shismo.*** "What is its name?" "Whatchamacallit?"

***Shoofa hanak medina jamila.*** "Look at that pretty town."

***Shwayy.*** "A little."

***Shwayy, swayy.*** "Slowly."

***Taba'an.*** "OK."

***Tahina.*** Sesame seed paste.

***Tfaddal/tfaddaly.*** "Please." (male/female spellings)

***Ummah.*** The worldwide community of Islamic believers.

***Wakha.*** "OK" in Moroccan dialect.

***Waqif hada al-jamal!*** "Stop that camel!"

***Wudoo.*** Ceremonial washing prior to Muslim prayer.

***Ya.*** Common expression, like "Hey!"

***Ya Allah!*** "O Lord!"

***Yala*** or ***yala nemshee*** or ***yala ibinet.*** "Let's go!"

***Yani.*** "I mean…"

## TURKISH

***Alivi.*** A Shi'a sect of Islam that originated in southeast Turkey and includes about 10 to 30 percent of Turks and about 70 percent of the Shiites.

***Arkadaş.*** "My friend." *Arkadash* is the Americanized version.

***Bamya bastısı.*** Okra and tomato stew, with or without lamb.

***Fırında mantı.*** Small noodle packets stuffed with meat.

***Gözleme.*** Rolled-up bread-based snack.

***Güveç.*** Turkish stew made with okra and tomato, with or without lamb.

***Hamam.*** "Bath" in both Arabic and Turkish.

***Kira.*** A female agent, usually Jewish, for women of the royal harem who could enter the outside world and conduct business for them, since women were not allowed to leave the harem. Safiye's *kira*, named Esperanza Malchi, became so rich and powerful that she and her son were murdered by the palace guard.

***Kuaşac.*** Shawl.

***Mercimek çorbası.*** Turkish lentil soup.

***Merhaba.*** "Hello."

***Mevlevi.*** A sect of Sufi Islam that originated in Turkey in the thirteenth century around a poet named Rumi. His followers, the "whirling dervishes," believed in spiritual union with a loving God through chanting and dancing.

***Mezes.*** Appetizers.

***Orada.*** "Over there."

***Tamam.*** "OK."

***Tesekkur ederhim.*** "Thank you."

***Tugra.*** Royal monogram.

***Usta.*** Craftsmen.

***Yalıs.*** Eighteenth- and nineteenth-century villas, especially along the Bosporus.

Appendix 11.

# REFERENCES

## PRIMARY ISLAMIC REFERENCES

Abu Dawud. *Sunan, The Third Correct Tradition of the Prophetic Sunna.* Vol. 4, *Book of the Ways of Reciting Qu'ran* (24/29). Translated by Mohammad Mahdi al-Sharif. English-Arabic text, 3995–4008.

Al-Banna, Hasan. "Risalat al Jihad." http://faculty.smu.edu/jclam/western_religions/hasanalbanna.html (accessed February 8, 2008).

Al' Bukhari, Mohammed, and Al 'Bukhari's Sahih. *The Correct Traditions of Al 'Bukhari.* Translated by Mohammed Mahdi Al' Sharif. Beirut, Lebanon: Dar al-Kotob Al-Ilmiyah, 2003.

Al-Hilali, Muhammad Taqi-ud-Din, and Muhammad Muhsin Khan. *Interpretation of the Meaning of the Noble Qur-an in the English Language.* Riyadh, Saudi Arabia: Darussalam Publishers, 1996.

Ali, Ahmed. *Al-Qur'an: A Contemporary Translation.* Princeton, NJ: Princeton University Press, 1984.

Al-Imam, Ahmed Ali. *Variant Readings of the Quran, A Critical Study of Their Historical and Linguistic Origins.* Herndon, VA: International Institute of Islamic Thought, 1998.

Al-Misri, Ahmad ibn Naqub. *Reliance of the Traveler, A Classic Manual of Islamic Sacred Law.* Rev. ed. Edited and translated by Nuh Ha Mim Keller. Beltsville, MD: Amana Publications, 1994.

Al-Naysaburi, al-Imam Muslim Ben al-Hajaj. *Sahih Muslim: The Authentic Hadiths of Muslim with Full Arabic Text.* Translated by Muhammad Mahdi al-Sarif. Beirut, Lebanon: Dar al-Kotob al-Ilmiyah, 2005.

"Al-Qur'an at a Glance." Islamic Dawah Center International. Why Islam Project USA. http://www.whyislam.org.

Al-Wahidi An-Naisaburi. *Reasons & Occasions of Revelation of the Holy Quran.* Translated by Adnan Salloum. Beirut, Lebanon: Dar al-Kotob al-Ilmiyah.

Aydin, Hilami. *Pavilion of the Sacred Relics—The Sacred Trusts.* Istanbul, Topkapi Palace Museum: Light Publisher.

Bin Laden, Osama. "A Declaration against the Americans Occupying the Two Holy Places." Statement from Afghanistan. September 4, 1996. http://faculty.smuedu/jclam/western_religions/ubl-fatwa.html (accessed February 8, 2008).

Habib, Mohammed. *The Proof of the Changes in the Lord of Lord's Book.*
Ibn Asakir, Al-Hafez. *Biography of Uthman.* http://nosra.islammemo.cc/one new.aspx?newid=2245.
Ibn Majah, English. *Sunan Ibn Majah, Book of Nikah.* Karachi: Al-Islam.com. http://hadith.al-islam.com/Display/Dislpay.asp?Doc=5&Rec=2583.
*Ma'il Codex of the Koran.* British Library.
Malik, Mohammed Farooq-i-Azam. *English Translation of the Meaning of Al-Qur'an, The Guidance for Mankind.* Houston: Institute of Islamic Knowledge, 1997.
Pickthall, Mohammed Marmaduke. *The Glorious Qur'an Translation.* Elmhurst, NY: Tahrike Tarsile Qur'an, 2003.
Salamah, Ahman Abdullah Salamah. *Shia & Sunni Perspective on Islam.* Jeddah, Saudi Arabia: Abdul-Qasim Publication House, 1991.
Tayyar Altikulac, ed. *Al-Mushaf Al-Sharif Attributed to Uthman bin'Affan, The Copy at the Topkapi Palace Museum.* Translated by Semiramis Cavusoglu and Salih Sadawi. Istanbul: Research Centre for Islamic History, Art and Culture Publisher, 2007.
"Understanding Islam and the Muslims." Islamic Affairs Department. Washington, DC: Embassy of Saudi Arabia.
Von Denffer, Ahmed. "Early and Old Manuscripts of the Qur'an and the Printed Qur'an." In *Ulum al-Qur'an* (An Introduction to the Sciences of the Qur'an). http://quranicstudies.com/article126.html, 4/23/06.
"What They Say about the Qur'an?" Riyadh, Saudi Arabia: WAMY.
Why Islam Project, USA. "Al-Qur'an at a Glance." Islamic Dawah Centre International. http://www.idci.co.uk.
Yasin, Muhammad Naim. *Book of Emaan According to the Classical Works of Shaikul-Islam Ibn Taymiyah (d.728H rahimahullaah).* London: Al Firdous, 2003.
Yusuf Ali, Abdullah. *The Meaning of the Glorious Qur'an.* Asir Media, Istanbul, 2002.

Note: Several Arabic sources were used in the writing of this book, including the works of Ibn Majah and Mohammed Habib. Habib is one of the foremost Shiite sources for changes to the Koran.

## ACADEMIC STUDIES

Baker, Colin F. *Qur'an Manuscripts: Calligraphy, Illumination, Design.* London: British Library Publishers, 2007.
Caetani, Leone. "Uthman and the Recension of the Koran." Originally in the

*Muslim World* 5 (1915). In *The Origins of the Koran.* Amherst, NY: Prometheus Books, 1998, pp. 67–75.

Cook, Michael. *The Koran, A Very Short Introduction.* Oxford: Oxford University Press, 2000.

Dreibholz, Ursula. "Preserving a Treasure: The Sana'a Manuscripts." *Museum International* 51, no. 203 (1999). Malden, MA: Blackwell Publishers, 1999.

Ettinghausen, Richard, et al. *Islamic Art & Architecture* 650–1250. Yale University Press.

Grohmann, Adolf. "The Problem of Dating the Early Qur'ans." In *What the Koran Really Says*, pp. 713–38.

Jeffery, Arthur. "Abu 'Ubaid on the Verses Missing from the Koran." Originally in *The Muslim World* 28 (1938). In *The Origins of the Koran.* Amherst, NY: Prometheus Books, 1998, pp. 150–53.

———. "Materials for the History of the Text of the Koran" (1937). In *The Origins of the Koran.* Amherst, NY: Prometheus Books, 1998, pp. 114–44.

———. "A Variant Text of the Fatiha." Originally in *The Muslim World* 29 (1939). In *The Origins of the Koran.* Amherst, NY: Prometheus Books, 1998, pp. 145–49.

Kahle, Paul E. "The Arabic Readers of the Koran." In *What the Koran Really Says*, pp. 201–10.

Lester, Toby. "What Is the Koran?" *Atlantic Monthly*, January 1999. Also in *What the Koran Really Says*, pp. 107–28.

Margoliouth, David. "Textual Variations of the Koran." Originally in *The Muslim World* 15 (1925). In *The Origins of the Koran.* Amherst, NY: Prometheus Books, 1998, pp. 154–62.

Mingana, Alphonse. "Three Ancient Korans." Originally in *Leaves from Three Ancient Qurans Possibly Pre-Othmanic with a List of their Variants* (1914). In *The Origins of the Koran.* Amherst, NY: Prometheus Books, 1998, pp. 76–113.

Nevo, Yehuda D. "Towards a Prehistory of Islam." In *What the Koran Really Says*, pp. 131–68.

Nöldeke, Theodor. "The Koran." Originally in *Encyclopaedia Britannica*, 1891. In *The Origins of the Koran.* Amherst, NY: Prometheus Books, 1998, pp. 36–63.

Puin, Gerd-R. "Observations on Early Qur'an Manuscripts in Sana'a." In *What the Koran Really Says*, pp. 739–44.

Reeve, John, ed. *Sacred Books of the Three Faiths: Judaism, Christianity, Islam.* London: British Library Publishers, 2007.

Rosenthal, Franz. "Some Minor Problems in the Qur'an." In *What the Koran Really Says*, pp. 332–42.

Ruthven, Malize. *Islam, A Very Short Introduction.* Oxford: Oxford University Press, 2000.

Sharon, Moshe. "Islam on the Temple Mount." *Biblical Archaeology Review* (July/August 2006).

St. Clair-Tisdall, W. "The Sources of Islam." Originally in *SPCK*, London (1901). In *The Origins of the Koran.* Amherst, NY: Prometheus Books, 1998, pp. 227–92.

Warraq, Ibn, ed. *The Origins of the Koran.* Amherst, NY: Prometheus Books, 1998.

———, ed. *What the Koran Really Says.* Amherst, NY: Prometheus Books, 2002.

———. *Why I Am Not a Muslim.* Amherst, NY: Prometheus Books, 1995.

Yeğenoğlu, Meyda. *Colonial Fantasies: Towards a Feminist Reading of Orientalism.* Cambridge: Cambridge University Press, 1998.

## GENERAL, HISTORICAL, AND CULTURAL REFERENCES

Aksit, Ilhan. *The Topkapi Palace.* Istanbul: Aksit Kültür ve Turizm Yayıncılık, 2007.

Al Ghazoli, Mohammed. *Christ, Mohammed and I.* Arabic and English versions. Chicago, 2004.

Ali, Ayan Hirsi. *The Caged Virgin.* New York: Free Press, 2006.

Amari, Rafat. *Islam: In the Light of History.* Prospect Heights, IL: Religion Research Institute, 2004.

Bell, Gertrude. *The Desert and the Sown: The Syrian Adventures of the Female Lawrence of Arabia* (1907). Cooper Square Press, 2001.

Boutros, Zakaria. "The Abrogator and Abrogated in the Koran" and "Converses on Adult Suckling." http://www.FatherZakaria.net.

Can, Turhan. *Topkapi Palace.* Istanbul: Orient Publishing.

Caputi, Anthony. *Masterpieces of World Drama: Classical Greece.* Lexington, MA: D. C. Heath, 1968.

"The Caucasus and Turkey." In *Encyclopedia of Women and Islamic Cultures.* Brill Online. http://www.encislam.brill.no/public/womens-studies.html and http://www.encislam.brill.nl/public/womens-unions.html.

Croutier, Alev Lytle. *Harem: The World behind the Veil.* New York: Abbeville Press, 1989.

"Dar al Makhtutat Exhibition." *UNESCO Newsletter*, November 2, 2006. http://portal.unesco.org/culture/en/ev.php_URL_ID=33240&URL_DO=DO.

Dolinar, Lou. "Cell Phones Jury-Rigged to Detonate Bombs." GlobalSecurity.Org in the News, *Newsday*, March 15, 2004. http://globalsecurity.org/org/news/2004/040315-cellphones-bombs.html (accessed August 11, 2007).

Doughty, Charles M. *Travels in Arabia Deserta.* Cambridge University Press, 1888; New York: Dover Publications, 1979.

Emmanuel, Ali El-Shariff Abdallah. "Testimony of Ali El-Shariff Abdallah." Anaheim, CA: Arabic Christian Perspective.

Eraslan, Nüket. *The Topkapi Palace.* Net Turistik Yayinlar, 1989.

Faroqhi, Suraiya. *Subjects of the Sultan: Culture and Daily Life in the Ottoman Empire.* First published in German in 1995. New York: I. B. Tauris, 2005.

Freely, John. *Inside the Seraglio: Private Lives of the Sultans in Istanbul.* New York: Penguin Putnam, 1999.

Gabriel, Mark. *Islam and Terrorism.* Lake Mary, FL: Charisma House, 2002.

Genisse, Jane Fletcher. *Passionate Nomad: The Life of Freya Stark.* New York: Random House, 1999.

Goodwin, Godfrey. *Topkapi Palace: An Illustrated Guide to Its Life and Personalities.* London: Saqi Books, 1995.

Heath, Jennifer. *The Scimitar and the Veil, Extraordinary Women of Islam.* Mahwah, NJ: Hidden Spring, 2004.

Inman, Nick, ed. *Eyewitness Travel Guides: Istanbul.* New York Dorling Kindersley, 2004.

———, ed. *Eyewitness Travel Guides: Jerusalem & the Holy Land.* New York: Dorling Kindersley, 2002.

"Inventory and Restoration of the Manuscripts Collection of Dar Al-Makhtutat Italian Trust Fund at UNESCO." Embassy of Italy in Sana'a, 2005. http://www.ambsanaa.esteri.it/Ambasciata_Sanaa.

Kadushin, Raphael. "The Blooming Route: Holland's Bloemen Route Bursts with Vibrant Flowers and Several Dutch Diversions." *National Geographic Traveler*, 2007.

Keskin, Naci. *Ephesus.* Translated by Anita Gillett. Istanbul: Keskin Color, 2007.

Knauer, Kelly, ed. *TIME: The Middle East.* New York: Time Books, 2006.

*Lebanon: The Official Guide.* Beirut, Lebanon: Paravision.

Lewis, Bernard. *The Middle East, A Brief History of the Last 2,000 Years.* New York: Touchstone Publishers, 1997.

Loti, Pierre. *Disenchanted.* Translated by Clara Bell. New York: Macmillan, 1906.

Marquet, Catherine, ed. *Eyewitness Travel Guides Morocco.* New York: Dorling Kindersley, 2004.

Marshall, et al. *Islam at the Crossroads: Understanding Its Beliefs, History, and Conflicts.* Grand Rapids, MI: Baker House, 2002.

McWilliam, Ian. "Tashkent's Hidden Islamic Relic." BBC News. http://news.bbc.co.uk/go/pr/fr/-/2/hi/asia-pacific/4581684.stm (accessed May 14, 2007).

Othman, Omar. *Let's Speak Arabic: A Course in Colloquial Jerusalem Arabic for Beginners.* Jerusalem: Al-Quds University Center for Jerusalem Studies, 2004.

Patai, Raphael. *The Arab Mind.* Rev. ed. New York: Hatherleigh Press, 1976, 2002.

Penzer, N. M. *The Harem: Inside the Grand Seraglio of the Turkish Sultans.* Philadelphia: Lippincott, 1936; Mineola, NY: Dover, 2005.

Pierce, Leslie P. *The Imperial Harem, Women and Sovereignty in the Ottoman Empire.* New York: Oxford University Press, 1993.

Pryce-Jones, David. *The Closed Circle: An Interpretation of the Arabs.* Chicago: Ivan R. Dee, 2002.

Rockness, Miriam Huffman. *A Passion for the Impossible: The Life of Lilias Trotter.* Wheaton, IL: Harold Shaw, 1999.

Sabini, John. "It's Calligraphy." *Saudi Aramco World* 27, no. 3 (May/June 1976). http://www.saudiaramcoworld.com/issue197603/the.world.of.islam-its.calligraphy.htm.

"Sana'a Manuscripts: Uncovering a Treasure of Words." *Courrier de l'Unesco*, no. 5 (2007).

"Saudi Arabia—Earliest Islamic (Kufic) Inscription." Nomination submitted by Saudi Arabia in 2002 for inclusion in the Memory of the World International Register. http://portal.unesco.org/ci/en/ev.php_URL_DO=DO.

Shahr-Yazdi, Roya. "Verily God Is Beauty: Islamic Art at the Hermitage, Part 1." *Exhibition Review* (May 16, 2000).

Stannard, Dorothy. *Insight Guide Syria & Lebanon.* Maspeth, NY: Langenscheidt Publishers, 2000.

Swan, Suzanne. *Eyewitness Travel Guides Turkey.* New York: Dorling Kindersley, 2006.

Tidrick, Kathryn. *Heart Beguiling Araby: The English Romance with Arabia.* Cambridge University Press, 1981; London: I. B. Tauris & Co., 1989.

"Uzbekistan—Holy Koran Mushaf of Othman." Documentary heritage concerning Uzbekistan and recommended for inclusion in Memory of the World International Register. http://portal.unesco.org/ci/en/ev.php_URL_ID=3929&URL_DO=DO.

"Uzbekistan—Holy Koran Mushaf of Othman." Memory of the World International Register Nomination Form. http://portal.unesco.org/ci/en/ev.php-URL_ID=3929&URL_DO=DO_TOPIC&URL_SEC.

Vamosh, Miriam Feinberg. *Israel, Land of the Bible.* San Francisco, CA: Purple Pomegranate Productions.

Veith, Gene Edward. "Sex Appeal: How a Branch of Islam Wants to Convert the West." *World*, July 26 and August 2, 2009, p. 29.

Wortley Montagu, Lady Mary. *Letters from the Right Honorable Lady Mary Wortley Montagu 1709 to 1762.* Edited by Ernest Rhys. New York: E. F. Dutton & Co., 1763, 1914.

## ONLINE NEWS REPORTS

Al-Ghabiri, Ismail. "Old Sana'a Has Overwhelming Charm." *Yemen Times*, 2003. http://yementimes.com (accessed November 15, 2008).

Bendern, Paul, and Thomas Grove. "Turkish-Armenian Editor Shot Dead in İstanbul." Reuters, January 19, 2007. http://news.yahoo.com/s/nm/20070119/wl_nm/turkey_author_shot.

*Human Rights News*. http://www.hrw.org, November, 1, 2002 (regarding suicide bombings).

"Minarets in Sana'a: Unmatched in Architecture." *Yemen Times Online*, 2003. http://yementimes.com.

The following sources were consulted for updates on the Israeli-Lebanese War in 2006 and were used for ensuring that the times given for bombings and other wartime situations were accurate:

*Aljazeeranet*, August 10, 2006.

*CNN Online*, July, 12, 2006, and July 14, 2006.

*Fox News Online*, July 13, 2006.

"International News." Safety Institute, July 14, 2006.

*Jerusalem Post Online*, July 14, 2006.

Ladki, Nadim. "Lebanese Army Increases Forces in Tense Beirut." Reuters, December 4, 2006, http://news.yahoo.com/s/nm/20061204/ts_nm/lebanon_government.

*Middle East Perspective Online*, July 13, 2006.

*National Public Radio Online*, morning edition, July 13, 2006. http://www.npr.

"Traveling on the Beirut-Damascus Highway." *All Things Considered*, Michele Norris, host. August 4, 2006, *National Public Radio Online*. http://www.npr.orf/templates/transcript/transcript.php?storyId=5618378.

*Washington Post Online*, July 14, 2006.

## OTHER ONLINE ARTICLES

"About TIMA." Islamic Manuscript Association, 2007. http://www.islamicmanuscript.org/About.html.

"The Collection of the Quran." Message for Muslims online. http://www.message4muslims.org.uk/Quran/Quran/collectionof Quran.htm.

"The Early Surviving Qur'an Manuscripts." Message for Muslims online. http://www.message4muslims.org.uk/Quran/JamalQuran/08earliestsurvivingQuran.htm.

Green, Samuel. "The Different Arabic Versions of the Qur'an." http://www.answering-islam.org/Green/seven.htm (accessed November 19, 2007).

Karim. "Was There Something Wrong with the Early Qur'anic Fragments/Specimens Found in the Great Mosque of Sanaa in Yemen?" http://www.answering-christianity.com/karim/mosque_of_sanaa.htm.

"Rare Quranic Manuscripts Found in Yemeni Mosque." Iranian Quran News Agency, News No. 109596. http://www.iqna.ir/en/news_print.ph[?ProdID=109596.

## RELATED WEB SITES

http://www.arabnews.com/?page=9&section=0article=64891
http://www.bibleprobe.com/othmankoran.jpg
http://www.groupsrv.com/religion/about157212.html
http://www.islamicawareness.org/Quran/Text/Mss/samarqand.html
http://www.metimes.com/storyview.php?StoryIDDD=20060425-070226-4676r
http://www.middle-east-online.com/english?id=16308=16308&format=0
http://www.muslimheritage.com/topics/default.cfm?ArticleID=161
http://www.sacred-destinations.com/egypt/cairo-al-azhar-university.htm
http://www.understanding-islam.com/related/history.asp
http://www.whyislam.org/forum/forum_posts.asp?TID=1399&PN=1

The following subjects were researched on Wikipedia in 2007:

Al-Aqsa Intifada (Second Intifada), beginning 9/2000
Al-Azhar http://en.wikipedia.org/wiki/Al-Azhar_University
Gerd-R. Puin
"Israel/PA: Suicide Bombers Commit Crimes Against Humanity, http://en.wikipedia.org/wiki/al-Aqsa_intifaca
Lebanon Bombings, 2006
Misyar marriage http://en.wikipedia.org/wiki/Misyar-marriage
San'a'
University of Al-Karaouine
Uthman
Yemen

## SOURCES FOR DEBATES ON ISLAM

The Center for Religious Debate, including "Has the Qur'an Been Perfectly Preserved?" between Bassam Zawadi of Saudi Arabia and Nabeel Qureshi of the United States, London, July 18, 2009. http://www.youtube.com/watch?v=KWK1xv0Bt-A.

Licona: Ataie debate, which ends with comment on Topkapi Codex. http://elitezenith.com/videos/20061130/. http://www.youtube.com/watch/vzbfw N26p0Jj8.

Wood-Ataie debate: "Who Is Mohammed," April 2007 (available on DVD and online). http://www.youtube.com/watch?v+YiVKA21MtI.

## MISCELLANEOUS SOURCES

Onsite research in Middle East, North Africa, and Europe.

Personal interviews, classes, and consultants on Middle East and Islam.

San Francisco Decorator Showcase 1990.

University of California, Berkeley: publications and Web site

Center for Middle Eastern Studies Publications regarding:

Al-Falah Program, 2006

Center for Middle Eastern Studies

Lectures, Films, and Events series, Spring 2006

The Sultan Program: Arab Studies at Berkeley

Website Academic Calendar

University of Leiden, Netherlands, Web site information regarding:

Arabic Language and Culture, Persian, Middle Eastern Studies, and Turkish Studies

Islamic Studies, Islamic Theology